Huntress of the Sky

HUNTRESS OF THE SKY

To Meghan,

R. F. KEENAN

Richard Keenan

EILIN BOOKS

This is a work of fiction. Names, characters, places and incidents are the product of the author's imagination or are used fictitiously. Any resemblance to actual persons, living or dead, events, or locales is entirely coincidental.

Copyright © 2017 Richard Francis Keenan

Cover and interior art: © 2017 Richard Francis Keenan.

All rights reserved. Printed in the United States of America. No part of this book may be used or reproduced in any manner whatsoever without written permission except in the case of brief quotations embedded in critical articles and reviews. For information, contact the publisher through dbk-mari.com.

Eilin Books is an imprint of D.B.K./MARI. Eilin Books, its colophon and D.B.K./MARI are trademarks of the D.B.K./MARI Company.

Keenan, R. F., 1986 -
    Huntress of the Sky / R.F. Keenan - First Edition
    Chronicles of Dannan trilogy, Book 1
        pages ; cm

1. Adventure and adventurers – Fiction   2. Animals, Mythical
3. Fantasy – Fiction, American 4. Dragons – Fiction
5. Quests (Expeditions)   I Title.

Series: Chronicles of Dannan

Cover and interior art by Ryan Durney

ISBN 13: 978-1-886274-00-6
ISBN 10: 1-88627-400-2

To my muse,
my family, my friends,
and all those who helped me.

Chapter 1

The first time he saw her as a young boy, he was awestruck. Her scales reflected the sunlight like the surface of the water, and even at a distance, he could see her eyes were shimmering pools of the most innocent blue. Though he knew that they were worlds apart, as he watched her from the tree he was playing in, he felt so close. The woods surrounding them were silent but for the birdsong that echoed between the trees, making it feel even more private. He was certain she knew he was there, because every so often when she leisurely scanned the area, her eyes would meet his.

Although the stories the village elder told always painted dragons as monsters and villains, looking at the beautiful creature sunning on the huge rock before him, he felt his heart lift.

Time seemed frozen like this when he suddenly saw her head swing sharply to the left. Staring into the woods, she seemed absorbed by something. After a few moments the bird song cut abruptly, and he heard the crashing of a large group of people forcing their way through underbrush.

Standing up, she unfurled her wings, their length seeming to cover the sky over the clearing. He watched her leg muscles bunch up as she lowered her body, and gasped as she flung herself into the air, the whoosh of her wing strokes drowning out the sound of approaching people.

With each beat she lifted herself higher into the air, her head swaying as she sought a path towards safety. When finally she found it, he watched her tilt her wings and push forward, losing a little altitude as she lifted herself up and away.

He watched her rise slowly and majestically, far enough away that the grass, twigs, and other debris stirred up by her wings didn't hinder his view. He continued to follow her with his eyes until she was lost from sight.

The sound of cursing and tromping boots brought him back to his surroundings, and he turned towards the clearing. A group of rough looking men, who might have been bandits or bounty hunters, judging by their clothing, lumbered into view.

One of the men, who looked rougher than the others, approached the rock, casting his eyes over it. "She couldn't have been gone long." He said as he let his fingertips caress the stone where she had lay. "It's still cold."

"Guess that means we're on the right track, eh, Calkon?" Another man, slightly shorter and with fewer scars said as he sidled up.

The man named Calkon glared intensely. "Yes, Minod. This means we're on the right track. But we haven't found her yet."

Spinning suddenly, Calkon grabbed the shorter man by his throat, causing the other men in the group to back further away. "And every day we don't find her is one more day we don't get paid. The wizard might be lenient about any of us acting like a fool because he feels we're so far beneath him, but you know I never tolerate idiots. Clear enough for you?"

Minod nodded his bald head quickly, his already puffy cheeks starting to change color from the hand suffocating him. Calkon sneered at him for a moment, then released his grip, causing the other man to stumble away. "And that goes double for the rest of you! Minod may be a survivor from the last hunt, but you newcomers have to prove yourself. If you screw up on this mission, it won't be just the dragon who could kill you!"

The other men hollered an affirmative, and Calkon quickly checked something hidden in the chest pocket of the leather armor he was wearing. "She's moving fast, so you'd all better be running! After her!"

With that, Calkon took off back the way he came, his boots

pounding on the ground as they went. The last look Dannan had of the man's face terrified him. Calkon's eyes were like stone, a dead gray that contrasted harshly with the savage smile he wore.

Waiting a few minutes, Dannan held his breath. Once he was finally certain they were gone, he dropped down from the tree. As soon as he hit the ground, he took off running through the woods towards the village, the opposite way from the hunters, his heart set on what he now knew was his destiny.

Chapter 2

All the while the village elder scolded him, he could think of nothing but the dragoness. "And you know that you've been told before that The Forbidden Woods are just that. Forbidden! How many times do we have to tell you to stay away from that area?" The Elder finished. After a few seconds, the old man scowled. "Well, Dannan, what do you have to say for yourself?"

"I know what I want to do with my future now, Honored Elder."

The old man gave him a surprised look, then chuckled. "At eleven years of age, it's certainly taken you long enough to find an apprenticeship. So, what could possibly have caught your interest so, that you've got such a steady gaze now?"

Standing a little taller, the boy said firmly. "I want to study weapons training in Whitehaven, and become a Swordmaster." The elder's eyes narrowed, and his mouth curled into a small frown.

"What would make you want to enter intentionally into the services of war?"

Looking around, the boy found himself at a loss for words. After a few moments, he finally turned back to the village elder. "There are things that only the strongest can do and fight for, and I've realized that. The weak can't protect, or succeed, without help. For that reason, I want to be strong."

The village elder studied him intently; the resolve he was seeing now so unlike the playful young child who refused to concentrate on anything his elders told him to do. After a minute or two of silence, the elder nodded. "Alright, I'll give you permission to go with the next caravan to one of the sword schools of Whitehaven. However, if none of them will accept you as a student, then you will have to return to the village and find a respectable profession."

Nodding, Dannan kept his eyes steady, refusing to budge even an inch. Finally, the elder's frown fell away and he smiled. "I'm just glad to see that you finally have some resolve. I was worried you'd wind up like the village drunk, Falmon."

Dannan shook his head, and then met the elder's eyes again. "What should I do to prepare for going to Whitehaven? A sword school won't want a child without any idea how to fight."

The elder raised his eyebrows, and his smile deepened. "I'm glad to see you're starting to think ahead. Tomorrow, ask your father about sword training. He's the most skilled we have in the village. I'll speak to him tonight." Dannan nodded again, his mind reeling at the idea that his father, an absolutely average man, was the most skilled at anything. Ducking his head, he rushed out the door of the house, not noticing the wistful smile on the elder's face.

Dannan ran down the side of the main village street, making a beeline for his home at the edge of town. Stopping at the front door, he looked back the way he came.

For the first time in his life, he really saw the village. Each house, carefully built from the local oak trees, looked almost identical to the one next to it. Four round logs anchored the corner of each house, with smaller logs forming the sides. Long cut planks that were held slightly at an angle by interior beams made up the roof. One chimney rose above each house, located over the fireplace in the common room. Wisps of smoke rose from a small hole on the other side of the house, where the kitchen fire was located. A front door and a window allowed the entry of both people and light. A window on each side of the house located towards the back allowed light into the parent's room and the fourth room, which was usually a storage room or a child's room.

Thinking it over as he opened the door, he thought about how a person's skills and foundation defined them. He wondered if he had what it took to be as sturdy as these small homes that housed the loggers, hunters, and the close-knit community that surrounded them.

Walking into the living room, he looked over at his father, who was sitting in the corner chair, reading a book he had traded some furs for when the last caravan came through.

As Dannan shut the door behind him his father looked up, then went back to his reading when he saw who it was. Walking into the kitchen, Dannan saw his mother standing in front of the stone fireplace, where she was stirring a pot of soup. Glancing over, she smiled at him as he walked in. Stirring the pot a few more times, she turned and walked over to the kitchen table. She sat down, then looked up at him as he stood nearby.

Looking at her sitting there, a partially knit sweater for his father sitting on the table, suddenly he felt unsure of himself. Walking over to the chair at the end closest to him, he sat down quickly, and rested his hands on his knees.

After a few moments of sitting in silence like this, his mother finally cleared her throat softly. "What's bothering you, dear one?" Dannan flinched a little, unsure of how to tell his mother he would be leaving in a few short weeks.

A few more moments passed when she reached out her hand, gently laying it across the top of one of his. Looking up at her, Dannan relaxed, her smile always putting him at ease. "I have found where I want to be apprenticed, ma-mann."

She leaned across the table and gave him a hug, gently stroking his hair. "That's wonderful news. There's no reason to be anxious over that, dear one."

Pulling back slightly, Dannan shook his head. "No, ma-mann, you don't understand. My apprenticeship will be in Whitehaven."

Her smile saddened a little, but didn't disappear. "I always knew you'd leave one day. Your father wasn't content to settle in one place as a young man, either." Dannan opened his mouth, but she shook her head. "Don't speak. It's alright. I know you worry about leaving us here, but I know your father will also approve of the fact that you've found something that you know in your heart you want to pursue. Just promise that you will stay true to your heart, and what your father and I have taught you."

With a soft laugh, she added. "And when you find a wife, make sure you bring her home to meet us before getting married." Dannan flushed bright red, and muttered under his breath about girls. His mother laughed again, and he smiled. Her laughter always reminded him of a small brook cutting its way through the forest. Hugging her tight, he nodded, some of his anxiety having gone away with her approval. "We'll have to tell your father, of course."

Dannan pulled back suddenly, catching her by surprise. "The

village elder said he wanted to tell father tonight." She raised an eyebrow at him slightly, and he shook his head. "He said that I would start training some for my apprenticeship tomorrow, but that he wanted to be the one to tell father." She looked him in the eye again, and then nodded a moment later.

Rising from the chair, she walked over to the pot. Standing there silently, she began to stir again, her back towards him. After a minute or two, he stood up. "Is there anything around the house that I can help with today?" Her pale green eyes met his over her shoulder and she smiled, giving him a nod.

The rest of the time before lunch and after lunch was filled quickly. Dannan remained silent at both meals, and excused himself quickly after dinner to go to his room.

Laying in his bed, he thought about the day, the feeling of finality in his decision seeming to cast it's shadow over the rest of his life. Although he knew in his head that he was young, in his heart, he felt like he had grown immensely with this one decision.

Smiling ruefully, he wandered back to his mother's words. "And when you find a wife, make sure you bring her home to meet us before getting married." The whole idea of marriage was beyond him right now, and he was sure it would be for a long time. All he knew was that he wanted to find that dragoness again. He wasn't sure how he would, or what he would do after he found her, but to see a creature that magnificent, he was willing to do anything. Even saying it in his own head felt childish, but at the same time, he knew it was true.

He jumped slightly when he heard the front door slamming shut, and he heard the sound of footsteps stomping through the living room. A minute later he heard his father yelling, and he cringed, certain that his hopes would be dashed in the morning.

Though he couldn't hear them clearly from their bedroom, he could still hear his father's yelling for quite some time after his arrival. Finally, it grew quiet, and while he was sure his parents were still talking, he knew his father had probably calmed down. As his eyelids drifted closed, he remembered how the shadow of the dragoness had covered him as she flew overhead, and that same darkness carried him to sleep.

Chapter 3

Dawn's light streamed in through the small, one foot window on the opposite side of Dannan's room. Abuzz with energy as he woke up, he dressed quickly, walking out towards the living room. As he stepped out of his room, he stopped.

His father, already awake, was reading once again in the corner chair. When Dannan walked into the living room, his father looked up, and then set the leather bound book on a small, round table next to the chair. Standing up slowly, his father looked down at him, and Dannan suddenly had a feeling like he was standing before a giant. Just as suddenly, the feeling was gone.

Although he was about a foot and a half shorter than his father's fairly tall five and a half feet, he had never felt like his father towered over him so immensely before. Shaking his head slightly to dispel the feeling, he walked forward until he was just outside of arms reach of his father.

"The village elder told me what you're planning to apprentice in. It seems that you also told your mother." Dannan nodded, knowing better than to say anything in reply. "I'll tell you right now. I think you're an idiot for wanting to follow the path of the sword." Dannan's father shook his head.

"The amount of blood spilled in that path makes it idiotic for anyone to follow it. And for what? Most of the time, they only want 'to be the best'. They don't even have a real purpose to their actions, just to be the biggest bully in the area."

"I know why I want to learn how to be a Swordmaster. It has nothing to do with being the strongest." Dannan said defensively.

Dannan's father looked at him closely, and nodded. "Yes, the village elder told me about that. That you had something you want to protect. I won't ask you who she is, since your mother is already certain its a woman, but I will make sure that in the fortnight before the next caravan comes, you understand just how hard it will be. If at any point you can't handle it, then you're going to give up on this silly idea, and you'll find something in town that you're good at. Understood?"

Staying silent, Dannan bobbed his head. Then, before he could speak, his father walked past him towards the front door.

Grabbing two long bundles from next to the door, he also picked up his bow and quiver, which he slung over his shoulder in a single fluid motion. Tossing one of the bundles at Dannan, he opened the door. Dannan caught it with a grunt, and was surprised as he heard the sound of metal on wood from inside.

Moving to unwrap the bedroll, he stopped and looked up at his father's sharp whistle. "We're losing daylight hours. While it will only take an hour or so to get where we need to go, there's plenty to do once we get there. Just make sure you run to keep up." Dannan nodded, and with that, they both stepped outside.

It surprised Dannan to find that his father was familiar with the clearing he had been watching the dragoness at. He was also surprised to find that there was a quicker way to reach it than he had gone, and that it could be reached in a single hour of running.

None of that mattered to him as he collapsed on the grass at the edge of the clearing, totally out of breath.

His father, while seeming slightly winded, immediately walked towards the large stone at the middle of the clearing. Lifting himself up, Dannan forced himself to walk the hundred or so feet to the rock, which he leaned against, still breathing heavily.

Walking around the rock for a moment, his father finally got back to where Dannan was leaning, and nodded. "Good, nothing dangerous living right around the rock." Dannan looked at his father oddly, but said nothing. "Now, here is what's going to happen. I already discussed this with your mother, and while she wasn't happy with the idea, since this is my area of expertise, she agreed to let me train you. Until the caravan arrives, you are going to live in this clearing."

Dannan opened his mouth to say something, his shock obvious on his face. Cutting him off with a shake of his head, his father continued. "There is a small pool of clean water about three hundred feet through the woods to the north, so you will have water. You will hunt for your own food, you will practice the sword techniques I tell you to, and at the end of each day, I will spar with you, to tell you what you aren't doing correctly."

Trying to absorb the information, Dannan barely heard his father's next words through the tumult of his own thoughts. "If at any point you come home, I'll assume you are giving up. If I check on you and you either haven't been able to fend for yourself, or you haven't been practicing your sword work, I will assume that you are not up to the task." Dannan quickly met his eyes at this, and nodded, his resolution showing on his face.

"We'll see if you can make that face in a week. For now, I'm going to teach you a few sword techniques. I'm going to leave the bow and quiver with you, and we'll have our first sparring session an hour or two before sundown. Any questions?" Dannan shook his head and moved away from the rock, even though he was still winded. "Alright, now you can unroll the bedroll."

It took Dannan a moment or two to slowly kneel and unroll his bedroll while he continued catching his breath. When he had finished unrolling it, his breath caught in his throat.

Inside the bedroll were a wooden practice sword, a water skin, a small cloth sack, a sheathed sword, and a waterproofed leather hide. Although the sword had an unmistakable allure to him, he looked at the hide first.

Unrolling it, he saw it was just large enough to wear like a hooded cloak. He had known his father had bought several, but he had never been allowed to play with them, since they were too expensive to easily replace if he damaged one.

After carefully rolling it back up, he took hold of the sword's handle, and examined the unadorned hilt. "Just remember this, for the outside world. Never remove your sword from the sheath unless you plan to use it. Being careless as a Swordmaster will get you killed." Dannan nodded, running his hands up and down the sheath, feeling every bump and ridge in the wood.

"For now, I want you to pull it out and look it over. If you're attacked by wolves, a practice sword won't cut it for defending yourself."

Dannan looked up at his father in surprise, and then back at the sword. Slowly and reverently he pulled the sword free, admiring the sound as it slid from the sheath. He moved to run his fingers along the blade, and his father shook his head. "Although there is nothing special about these swords, and they have not been sharpened recently, they can still cut. Be careful with it." Dannan contented himself with simply studying it, looking it over from the tip down to the small, leather wrapped handle. After a few minutes, his father cleared his throat, and Dannan slid the sword back into the scabbard slowly.

Rolling everything back up into the bedroll except the wooden practice sword, Dannan set the bedroll by the rock. Standing up, he held the sword at his side.

"I'm going to teach you a few basic exercises, and these are what you'll practice for the next few weeks."

Dannan lifted the sword up in front of him, and held it in what he thought was the best manner. Shaking his head, his father made a few disapproving noises, before moving Dannan's hands to the right spot. "Whenever you hold a two-handed sword, you're going to hold it like that. A one-handed sword, it will really depend on how you're using it, but the standard way is like this."

His father gripped his own practice sword, which he had drawn without Dannan noticing, and held it out straight ahead of him. Looking at him, Dannan attempted to imitate it, with limited success. "You'll get used to it if you practice. For the next few hours, you're going to practice the swings I tell you to, alright?" His father didn't wait for any acknowledgment, and began to show him several of the basic swings, making sure that he could do them with each hand.

Several hours quickly passed in this way, and when the sun finally began to drop a little from the sky, Dannan's father stopped him. "You already know how to hunt, so I don't need to show you that. However, since this first day you'll have started later than you would have to in order to get dinner, I'm going to help you. But you still need to keep up." Lifting his bedroll, he looped it over his left shoulder, and took the bow from Dannan.

Motioning at Dannan to do the same, he waited while Dannan struggled to get the loop to stay together over his shoulder the same way.

When it finally held, they started into the woods, jogging

gently through the trees. After about half an hour of this, his father held up a hand, and Dannan quickly stopped.

Pulling an arrow out and stringing it slowly, his father drew back, aiming at a target that Dannan couldn't quite see. After a few seconds, he released, and Dannan heard the small squeak of a rabbit's life ending.

Jogging forward quickly, his father picked it up by the ears, and gently pulled the arrow free. "We'll skin this and cook it back at the rock. Most of it will be for you, since I've got a meal waiting at home after I get back from our sparring lessons." Dannan nodded, his stomach grumbling jealously.

It didn't take long to get back to the clearing. When they arrived, his father promptly skinned the rabbit and cooked it over a tiny fire he built on top of the rock. Dannan hungrily devoured most of the rabbit, while his father had a single leg, "to tide me over" as his father put it.

After a few minutes, his father took the scraps out into the trees and tossed them away, coming back with clean hands. "Just remember not to keep anything near where you sleep, whether you sleep in the clearing or a tree." Dannan nodded, and stood, the practice sword at his side again.

His father walked to the center of the grassy area, then looked back at him. "We're going to spar for a little bit, or until you can't keep going. Come at me whenever you're ready." Dannan walked forward, trying to appear confident as he gripped the practice sword with both hands. Approaching slowly, he looked at his father's relaxed stance, and wondered where would be best to attack from.

He quickly decided that since his father was right-handed, he would try for the left.

Dannan rushed forward, bringing his sword in as hard as he could. His father sidestepped easily, sliding Dannan's practice sword past with only one hand. Dannan stumbled past and tried to reverse direction, but only managed to make himself trip.

Hitting the grass with a small thump, he quickly jumped back up, determined to hit his father on the first try. He made numerous attempts like this, his father easily deflecting all of them.

After about fifteen minutes of this, his father shook his head. "Stop, stop. Do you understand what you're doing wrong, Dannan?"

Breathing heavily, he shook his head, holding the sword up in front of him. "You're obviously trying to decide where to hit with your head, and you're trying to make the swing as heavy as possible. The problem is, while you're deciding, your eyes are showing exactly where you plan to attack, and that makes your power even more useless to you. You need to attack with your body, not your head. Your mind is for coordinating a fight, not for the act of fighting."

Dannan looked at his father curiously. Diving forward, he thrust with the sword, the slight wobbling of the tip making it easy for his father to deflect it to the side.

Stepping forward past Dannan, he swiftly brought the sword down on the back of Dannan's left leg, leaving an immediate but light bruise on the thigh. "Unless you're trying to get yourself cut down, don't leave yourself so defenseless when you attack. I could have gutted you or slit your throat if I had a knife or shortsword in my other hand. You need to think about where your attack will leave you once you've made it." Dannan nodded, muttering and rubbing his left leg a little.

Looking up at the sky, his father made a small noise with his tongue. "Alright, you get one more attack, then it's time for me to start walking back to the village. Let's see if you've got any shot."

Dannan took a few deep breaths, and looked at his father in a new light, noticing for the first time that he wasn't even breathing heavily, much less winded. Inching forward, keeping his right foot ahead of his left, Dannan swung his sword at waist height from the right side, making the blow heavy enough to deal damage, but concentrating more on controlling where it landed.

As his father began to deflect it down and out, Dannan pushed forward with his body, trying to force his sword back up along his father's. His father moved out of the way so suddenly that he toppled forward, landing face first in the grass.

Letting out a little laugh, his father looked down at him. "That was a good choice, though it will only work on those slower than you, or weaker than you. But it proves that you're at least trying to think of what will happen after you swing your weapon."

Dannan lifted himself up on his elbows, and looked up at his father. "How long have you used a sword, father? Nobody ever comments about it, even though ma-mann obviously knows, and so does the village elder."

His father's smiling face immediately grew grim, and he

shook his head. "If you ever become a Swordmaster, I'll tell you."

Dannan grumbled and stood up, brushing the grass off of his pants and cotton shirt. His father began to walk past him, and then, remembering something, set a skinning knife, flint and tinder in Dannan's hands. "You'll need those for tomorrow. I'm going home to your mother for now. Remember, I expect you to practice at least fifty of each type of swing I showed you, or there's no point. And think about where the weight of the sword is when you're swinging it. That might help you." Dannan took the essentials his father had given him over to the bedroll and placed them in the small cloth bag with the bowstrings. He watched as his father left the clearing, and disappeared among the trees, leaving him completely alone in the woods.

Chapter 4

The first night was the hardest for Dannan. He had chosen one of the larger oaks to sleep in, and he had found a nice spot where he could lean against the tree trunk, cradled in between two branches while sitting on a third.

As he tried to sleep, he was kept awake by the sounds of owls, and the feeling of insects as they occasionally explored the newest addition to their home. Finally, about the time the moon reached its peak, he managed to fall into a fitful sleep, which lasted until the first rays of sunlight.

As soon as he woke up, Dannan felt the familiar stirrings of hunger in his belly.

Lifting up the bedroll from the branch below him where it had slipped to, he wrapped it around the practice sword and the real sword, placing the waterproofed poncho in between them so that they wouldn't rattle as he moved. Slinging the bedroll over his left shoulder, he pulled the bow and quiver over his right, and slowly made his way down the tree.

Although his sleeping spot was only about fifteen feet off of the ground, it was easily high enough that he could hurt an ankle if he fell the wrong way. When he finally climbed all the way to the ground, he jumped in surprise, as startled by a small family of squirrels as they were by him. They immediately rushed up the tree, chittering at him from branches near where he had slept.

Letting out a small sigh, he began to scout around the area slowly, setting up a few snares as he went. Although there weren't many small saplings that he could use to trap with, there were plenty of low-lying branches that were five to ten feet off the ground that worked perfectly. Although he had no bait at the moment, he was more than satisfied to hope for the best.

After a few hours of searching, he finally managed to catch a rabbit, though it was smaller than the one his father had caught yesterday. Taking it back to the clearing, he readied it for lunch.

It took much less time to cook it than it had to catch, and he thought about how he would have to thank his mother, and his good luck, that he did not have to eat like this every day.

Immediately after lunch, he began practicing his swings. Although his father had said he only needed to practice fifty of each, he decided to go with one hundred. After one hundred right-handed swings, his arm was tired. After one hundred with his left hand, his muscles ached. After one hundred swings with both hands, his arms were exhausted.

By the time he had finished with his three hundred sword swings, his stomach was grumbling again.

Muttering to himself about how horrible it must have been to live before kitchens, he went out to check his traps. The first five of the ten he had set were empty, and Dannan was quickly getting discouraged.

When he got to the sixth, he stopped, his eyes bulging from his head. Hanging upside down by one foot was what looked like a tiny purple person, clad in ivy green pants and an open vest. Dannan couldn't help but stare, unsure of what to do. He was too surprised to even realize he was being scowled at.

Finally, after a minute or two, the creature spoke. "Hey! What do you think you're doing in this part of the woods, placing traps and hunting? I don't care that you're a kid, you should know better!"

Dannan jumped in surprise when it spoke, and he stared at it even more incredulously. "What are you?!" He managed to gasp out, even as he continued to stare.

"What, you've never heard of a pixie before?"

He murmured something, unsure of how to respond, when he saw the tiny set of gossamer wings on the back of the tiny (what he assumed to be a male) pixie. "I've heard of pixies… but only as stories that the village elder tells us. But those are just stories. That's what most of the adults say."

The pixie sighed, and quickly slipped his foot out of the snare. "Gods, no wonder there are so many humans stamping through the woods these days. You all think we're fairy tales!"

Dannan tried unsuccessfully to resist the urge to snicker at the pixie's pun. The pixie gave him a cold glare, and he immediately stopped. A moment later, the pixie burst out laughing, a high pitched sound, similar to a bird's chirp. "Glad to see you have a sense of humor. That's something we fey tend to hate. People who can't take a joke."

His eyes went wide again. "There are more of you?"

The pixie looked at him as if he was stupid, then began to laugh. "You're really serious. That's the funniest thing I've heard all day. Of course there are more of us. There's a whole colony of us in what you call 'The Forbidden Wood'. There's a reason your village elder forbids it, and this edge of the woods near it, from hunters and loggers."

Opening his mouth to speak, Dannan shut it quickly, remembering how vehemently the village elder, as well as his own father, had spoken out against anyone going anywhere near that tract of woods. "So that's why they made sure that no one went near here. But then, why'd my father have me training here?"

Letting go of the snare trap the pixie landed gracefully, using his wings to slow his descent. "Who's your father?" Dannan looked down at him, then sat down in front of the pixie.

"My father's name is Andros Bellmen. Why?"

The pixie stared at him, then leaped into the air, flying in a small circle. "Oh, that's too rich! You're his son!"

Dannan scowled a little, before blurting out angrily. "Enough with that! My father is Andros Bellmen, son of a bell maker, and no one special."

"No one special? No one special?! You have no idea who your father is?!" The pixie pulled up from his cavorting suddenly, and he stared slack-jawed at Dannan. "You really don't know. Wow. Well, come with me then, I'll tell you while we walk towards The Wood."

Shaking his head, Dannan stood up. "There's only an hour or so until my father comes for sparring practice. I need to be back by then. I still have other traps to check."

The pixie held up a hand, palm out towards Dannan, a stern look on his face. "Do you solemnly swear that you are only hunting for food, and not at all for profit?"

Dannan looked down at him in surprise. "There's no point to hunting for fur you're not going to use. That's just wasteful."

Smiling slightly, the pixie nodded. "Spoken just like your

father. Alright, I'll help you hunt a little. And, depending on how bad you are at it, I might give you some tips, to."

Flying up to about head height on Dannan, he hovered there for a few seconds. "When I look at you, you definitely have aspects of your father. That chin, and certainly your hair, to. You have your mother's eyes, though. I imagine you'll probably look more like him when you grow up."

Gaping at the pixie, Dannan was caught off guard. "You know my mother to?!"

The pixie let out a laugh, and nodded. "Just because you don't know about them doesn't mean that they aren't special. It just means that you haven't taken the time to learn about them. Or, knowing you father, he hasn't talked a lot about it. He never was fond of that mercenary job of his."

Dannan followed the pixie as he floated forward, stopping as soon as he heard the word 'mercenary'. "He was a sellsword?"

"No, he wasn't a 'sellsword'. Those are the thugs who pass themselves off as mercenaries. No, your father was a real 'sword-for-hire'. He was one of the best. To my knowledge, and the knowledge of everyone I know, he's never fought for an unjust cause, either. And trust me, despite acting like airheads sometimes, we pixies pick up a lot of things. Helps to keep us alive and hidden."

Letting out a little laugh, he started off again, heading unerringly straight for Dannan's next trap. Dannan immediately moved to catch up until he was walking a few steps behind again.

He marveled at how the pixie looked from behind, and pinched himself lightly on the arm. He let out a small hiss when he did, but shook his head, certain now that this was really happening. "By the way, what's your name? You know mine, after all."

The pixie grinned back at him. "I can't believe it's been eleven years since Kayla gave birth. But yes, I did already know your name. Andros stopped by…. Five years ago maybe? That's when he told us about you. Time is a little different for us, so, we didn't know what age you were."

"As for my name? I'm Elvistir. Pronounced 'ell-vi-steer'. I don't think there's any fey in the area who doesn't know me. So if you run into trouble with another, or even just meet another one of us, feel free to drop my name. Probably safer than dropping your dad's, anyway."

Dannan nodded, grimacing as they passed his empty trap. Elvistir quickly tripped it, the branch whipping back up with a cracking sound. "There's nothing smart about leaving traps unattended. You never know who or what will get hurt."

"Ah."

He remained mostly silent, listening as Elvistir talked about the Forbidden Wood, and also the area around it. He was surprised to find out that Elvistir had been here one hundred and fifty years ago, when their particular village was first founded.

"How old are you, anyway?"

Elvistir burst out laughing, and shook his head. "You humans all ask that one eventually. Even the ones like your father, who don't really care about the answer. Some fey consider it an insult, asking that."

Dannan opened his mouth to apologize, and the pixie burst out laughing. "But I'm not that stiff-necked. I'm two hundred and forty five. Yes, that means I'm almost double the age of your village. It was a beautiful area, but thanks to your village elder and the two before him, it hasn't gotten much worse, even with human loggers coming in. As long as it stays like that, we'll be more than happy to deal with any bandits who try to move into the woods. Or worse."

He shook his head, trying to understand even as he heard it. "So you mean... all those stories we heard as little kids were true?"

Elvistir looked over his shoulder, and laughed. "You still have to ask?"

"I assumed what we heard from the caravans were simply tall tales. Even though orcs and goblins sound believable, without ever seeing one, it just sounds crazy. And elves, pixies, and dragons? They just don't exist to most people in small villages like mine."

Laughing again, Elvistir's eyes twinkled. "Dragons are definitely real. We had one recently visit us, though she had to take off quickly for some reason."

"I know,. I saw her."

Elvistir looked back at him, tripping the next empty trap they passed. "So you've seen a dragon first hand, but you didn't believe in me when you saw me?" Laughing harder, he shook his head. "While I know she doesn't eat children, why didn't she shoo you away, I wonder?"

Dannan grimaced angrily, the sudden change in expression

catching Elvistir off guard. "A bunch of filthy thugs were looking for her. Thinking about it, fifteen to twenty hunters couldn't have really scared her, but when she heard them coming, she took off. They searched the clearing I practice in now, but then went off again quickly."

Scowling at that, Elvistir muttered to himself. "I'll have to tell the other patrols to keep an eye out for them, then. If they pass through this area, I'll deal with them."

"I think they know exactly where she's going. She headed south when I saw her leave, but I don't know. If pixies and dragons exist, then magic must to. If it does, that's probably how she's being followed."

Elvistir nodded, tripping the third empty trap as they passed. "You really are bad at making traps, you know that?"

Dannan laughed, then shook his head. "Having no bait doesn't help, but yeah, I'm probably not all that good at making traps."

"A good trap is in the right place at the right time, it doesn't have to have the right bait. I'll help you with that. If you're practicing to be like your father, it will probably be useful to you."

When they tripped the fourth trap, Dannan shook his head, and sighed. "Well, guess that means no dinner tonight. Oh well, I'll find something in the morning then. But for now, I have to get back, before my father arrives."

Elvistir held up a hand, and pointed out a rabbit chewing on some flowers, not twenty feet from them. "No sudden movements. Let's see if you can hit him." Dannan nodded, surprised he hadn't seen the rabbit sooner, and slowly pulled the bow off of his shoulder.

At first, it seemed like the rabbit might bolt as he put an arrow with agonizing slowness to the string, but in the end it continued munching away. Pulling back, he sighted along the arrow, finally releasing it with a sharp twang.

The rabbit let out a small squeal, and Elvistir grimaced a little. Dannan noticed and opened his mouth, but Elvistir shook his head. "Eating meat isn't for everyone. Some, like me, who talk to the animals often enough, eventually foreswear it. For everyone else though, as long as they're fair and good about it, I won't stop them. After all, can you imagine how many rabbits there would be if you let them multiply unchecked by nature for a year? Ha ha!"

Dannan laughed a little at that and quickly retrieved the rabbit. "Thank you, for the help, and the conversation. It's been a pleasure to meet you, Elvistir."

Nodding, Elvistir smiled. "I'm on patrol for the next month in this area, so I'll see more of you, I'm sure. Here, I'll follow you back to the clearing, at least for now. Don't want your father thinking you're getting too much help. Not if he hasn't changed in the past five years." Dannan nodded, a wry smile on his face, and began the quick walk back towards camp.

"So what made you want to follow in your father's footsteps if you thought he was the son of a bell maker?"

"Well, I didn't actually know that he was a Swordmaster. But I met someone who I just had to meet again, and realized I wouldn't get the chance if I didn't leave this small village."

The pixie chuckled at that. "Ahh, young love. So, who exactly did you fall for? What's her name?"

Dannan blushed red at being needled so personally, and then shook his head. "I don't know her name, and I only met her briefly. I doubt she'll remember me."

Elvistir laughed a little longer, when finally he caught what Dannan just said.

All of a sudden he looked like he had been struck someplace sensitive, and he dropped towards the ground as his wings stopped. Flapping them rapidly, he came back up next to Dannan, surprise all over his face. "You don't mean you're trying to...?"

Dannan let the question hang in the air for a moment before nodding. After another moment, Elvistir started laughing so hard that he flew right into a tree. Dannan walked back a few feet to check on him, but then scowled when he saw that the pixie was rolling around in the grass and tree roots, holding his side as he practically howled with laughter. Trying to help himself back up, Elvistir fell to his knees, tears streaming down his face as laughter shook his body like a leaf in a gale.

He waited a few more minutes, looking everywhere but at the pixie, before stomping back towards the clearing.

After a minute or two more, the high laughter had mostly stopped, and he saw Elvistir fly up from the corner of his eye.

The pixie was wiping tears of mirth from his eyes, and occasionally let out a little chortle. When they were near to the clearing, he took a deep breath, letting out one last chuckle. "Oh, but I haven't laughed that way in at least fifty years. Not even when Mollister accidentally got eaten by a frog, and we had to get him out."

Seeing that Dannan's expression didn't change, he finally stopped chuckling. "I'll tell you something good though. I've got one of the dragon's scales that I can enchant to help you find her. It's a big world, and it gets even bigger once you go past the one you know. This way, you might actually meet her again. I'll bring it with me tomorrow, how about that?"

Dannan finally stopped scowling, and nodded. "I would appreciate that. I hadn't really considered how to find her. Maybe by following rumors I hear? I didn't really think about it too hard. Only that she was so amazing that I just had to see her again."

Elvistir chuckled again. "Next time, just don't assume because they're graceful that they're peaceful. Or that they're female. You'd have had a hell of a time if that was a male."

He blushed red again, eliciting another chuckle from Elvistir. "I'll see you tomorrow though, when you go hunting around lunch time. For now, good luck with the sparring!"

Giving the pixie a small wave goodbye, he watched his new found friend flit quickly through the trees. Stepping out into the clearing, he took a deep breath, hoping his father wasn't already there.

Chapter 5

He was in luck, his father still hadn't arrived. Dannan used that time to skin and cook his catch, though he grumbled to himself, accepting that without Elvistir's help he wouldn't be eating tonight.

Lifting up the rabbit from the small ring of stones he used for his fire, he let out a small yelp, dropping the still burning hot meat onto the rock.

Hearing a little chuckle, he looked over, surprised to see his father standing at the edge of the rock. "You can't let your guard down just because you're hungry, Dannan."

Dannan grumbled to himself, then lifted up the rabbit again, ignoring the almost painful heat as he bit into it. It only took him a minute or two before the whole rabbit was gone. Wrapping the bones inside the skin, he brought it all a few hundred feet away from both the clearing and where he slept, and tossed it in between the roots of a large oak.

Walking back into the clearing, he saw his father hadn't moved. Dropping the bedroll down next to the rock, Dannan pulled out the practice sword, and walked to the middle of the grassy area.

His father smiled and pulled the practice sword off of his back before walking over to join him.

As his father approached him, Dannan noticed that the only thing he had brought was the practice sword. Opening his mouth, he was about to comment on it, then decided it was better not to.

Holding the sword up in front of him, Dannan was uncomfortably aware of just how tired his arms were, even though his practice swings were hours ago. His father also seemed to notice, as he nodded approvingly before taking his stance as well.

After a few moments, his father gave him a small nod, and Dannan started moving forward slowly, waiting until he was just outside of sword range before lunging forward. He raised the practice sword over his head with both hands, but as he brought it down, he let it slide fully into his left.

Bringing it in suddenly from an angle, he heard the wooden swords crash together, and before he knew it, his practice sword was flying through the air to land a dozen feet away.

For a moment, he was unsure of what his father would do. The stony look on his face was enough to make Dannan scramble to his sword, lifting it in his right hand.

Spinning around once it was in his hand, he saw that his father stood there, unmoving, simply holding his stance. Dannan approached even more cautiously this time, aware that his father might finally be taking this seriously.

Several feet out of reach, he stopped, trying to decide what direction might be best to attack from. After a moment, he took two quick steps to the left, and swung upwards with the sword, hoping the right-handed angle would be disadvantageous for his father.

Sidestepping neatly, his father let the wooden blade pass right in front of him, and he quickly took another step, gently rapping his own blade against Dannan's ribs. Dannan let out a little grunt, then stepped forward again, gripping the blade in both hands as he swung it sideways. His father's blade stopped his, the harsh block jolting his arms. Cursing, Dannan stepped back, even as the practice sword dropped from his numb hands. Looking down at it in surprise, he stepped forward to pick it up again, and found that he had a hard time gripping it.

"That will be enough for tonight."

Looking up, Dannan opened his mouth to say something when his father cut him off. "You've obviously been practicing enough swings, so just make sure that you continue that. I'll be back tomorrow night to check on you again."

Dannan nodded, watching as his father turned to leave. "Father, wait. I have question for you." Looking back over his shoulder, Dannan's father raised an eyebrow at him, but waited. "What is a Swordmaster truly a master of?"

His father looked at him, a distinct lack of surprise in his face, and he let out a small sigh. "Most Swordmasters now are content to know the forms for one hand or two with the longsword, shortsword, the bastard sword, a two-hander, and how to use a shield with any of them."

He waited, hoping more would be forthcoming. Turning around, his father started walking away again, and Dannan closed his eyes, cursing inwardly.

    Although his father hadn't said anything, he still got the distinct feeling that he had to be better than that to earn his father's respect. Sighing, he gathered his things into the small bag and climbed into the tree, where he waited for the night, and sleep, to come.

Chapter 6

He opened his eyes at first and was surprised to find that it wasn't quite dawn yet.

The grayish light seemed to fill the air, and for a moment, all he could do was look around at the forest in wonder. The dewdrops made all of the leaves glisten, and soft bird songs wafted through the forest.

Taking a deep breath, he sucked in the clean air, loving how he could practically taste the scents filling the forest as he did. Taking a few more deep breaths, he enjoyed the sensation, wondering if this was how people felt when they lived as one with nature.

Shaking his head at himself, he decided he would have to see what it was like after his first storm, or his first snow, and he grinned, almost wishing it would rain so he could see how he fared.

"After all, I managed to catch at least a little food out here, so I wouldn't totally starve." Shaking his head again, he chuckled at himself softly, not wanting to wake up the rest of the inhabitants of his particular tree.

Climbing down quietly, he dropped the last few feet to the ground, the wet grass muffling his landing.

Looking around, he sniffed suddenly, wondering what the slightly stale smell was. After a few seconds, he realized it was the smell of his day old sweat. Grimacing, he realized if he could tell how bad his scent was, he was sure the animals would smell him coming.

Foraging around for a few minutes, he managed to find a berry bush a short distance from his tree. Crushing one of the berries between two fingers, he sniffed, taking in the slightly sweet scent. Lightly touching his tongue to the juice running over his fingers, he found it tasted like a sweet cake. The taste reminded him of the few times his father had purchased sugar from the merchant caravans as a treat for the family.

Smiling to himself, he gently rubbed the berry on the shoulder of his cotton shirt. Sniffing at it, he was glad to see that it still retained its smell, and he hoped it would for a little while longer. Taking about a dozen more, he gently crushed them against his shirt and pants, trying to evenly distribute their scent in order to mask his own.

Walking back to his tree, he climbed up as quietly as he could, slowing down slightly when a branch creaked. Sliding his bow over his shoulder, he stood on two branches while he wrapped everything up in his bedroll. When it was done, he strapped it across his back before climbing down again.

Although he had grown up in a community of hunters and loggers, he felt for the first time he was truly learning what the woods were like. For some reason, that thought made him smile. He felt the woods could be harsh if you weren't skilled, but he was also filled with a feeling of independence and happiness that he was finally getting to be himself. Whether he was hunting rabbits or fighting off a wolf, it would be he and he alone who decided just what he would do.

Striding through the woods slowly, he did his best to remain alert, searching for any potential prey. After about twenty minutes of this, he finally spotted a rabbit hiding at the base of a tree.

Lightly stringing his bow, he pulled an arrow from the quiver, setting his bedroll down as he did so. Nocking it, he stood patiently, making sure that the rabbit wasn't moving before finally releasing the string.

Following a twang that sounded so much louder to his ears than he thought it ever had, he heard the rabbit's small squeal break the silence of the forest. Wincing, he felt a small tinge of guilt at having to break the peaceful beauty around him. At the same time, he acknowledged that everything had to eat something, whether the rabbit ate the grass, or the wolf ate the rabbit.

Picking up his bedroll, he quickly retrieved the rabbit, withdrawing his arrow even as he hurried back to the clearing.

It took him less time to skin and clean the rabbit the third time around, and he was proud that while he wasn't as fast as his father, he was probably better than the other boys in the village. Shaking his head, he decided he probably wasn't better than the sons of some of the hunters, who had already been doing this for years. But better than the others, at least.

As soon as his meal was done and he had discarded the skin

and bones, he began his practice exercises. He noticed quickly that his arm muscles were still exhausted from yesterday. Forcing himself to ignore the sensation, he continued.

It still took him about an hour and a half to complete all of his swings, but he was pleased that he had succeeded at all. Just a few days ago, he'd never even contemplated working this hard. He chuckled, thinking how much his life had changed just by seeing that dragoness.

He did a small amount of physical exercise for the remaining few hours, until the sun was almost directly overhead.

Picking up his bedroll, he slung his bow back over his shoulder and set out into the woods, determined to find some food before Elvistir found him. After about fifteen minutes of hunting to the north near the water, he still hadn't found anything.

Looking around, he suddenly spotted Elvistir relaxing on a branch a few feet away from him. Dannan started, then gave him a small wave.

Elvistir chuckled and floated over to him, his wings beating softly in the air. "You really aren't that good at sneaking about, or paying attention, huh?"

Dannan turned crimson, then shook his head. "This is still only my second day of being out here. I've got time to learn."

"Well, looks like I'll have to help teach you. You never know how long you'll have to learn, or when you'll get embroiled in a fight you can't avoid."

Agreeing silently, Dannan watched Elvistir calmly while he waited. After a minute or so, Elvistir cocked his head to the side "Well? Aren't you going to start hunting again?"

"Did you bring what you mentioned?"

Elvistir looked at him, then sighed. "I'll give you the dragon scale after today's lesson. You're definitely not going to be able to concentrate on anything I tell you once you've got your hands on it."

Dannan grinned sheepishly. "Alright. I'll start hunting again, and you can show me later."

"That's the spirit." Elvistir said with a grin. "Now, let's go!"

Dannan took a deep breath, and slowly started to search again.

They spent the next three hours doing this, with Elvistir refusing to allow Dannan to catch anything less than a full-grown rabbit. Three times he had to pass up taking a shot at rabbits that Elvistir called "scrawny" or "underdeveloped".

Grumbling, taking every comment Elvistir made and trying to apply it, finally Dannan managed to find one that Elvistir was happy with. After collecting his kill, they immediately started heading back towards the clearing.

A few minutes away from the clearing, Elvistir stopped, making sure that they were fairly surrounded by trees. Dannan went a few steps further, before turning back to look at him.

"Now, I've enchanted the scale in two ways. You mustn't show it to anyone, though. You probably shouldn't even show your father, unless you want to explain everything to him. Now, I have no problem with that, but I know that he tends to be a pain in the rump about getting help. So just tell him what you feel comfy telling him." Elvistir chuckled at his own comment.

"But anyway, back to the scale. The first spell is the locator spell. As long as you wear it on a chain or thong around your neck, you will always feel a pull in the direction to the dragoness. The second function is much more visible, though."

Pulling out a small pouch that seemed too tiny to hold anything, Elvistir removed a perfectly smooth scale, the color of polished steel. A chain of solid silver seamlessly wrapped around it, yet never moved, despite not being attached to the scale in any way.

Staring at it, Dannan felt an inexplicable tug, and he thought of the dragoness' shimmering scales, so beautiful in the sunlight. Shaking his head to clear the image, he held his hand out slightly, and he waited as Elvistir dropped the scale onto his palm.

The actual size of the scale was about that of a large amulet, maybe three inches across, and four inches tall. Turning it over in his hand, he examined it closely, before finally looking back at Elvistir.

"This second spell requires attuning, so now that you have the scale, I'll attune it to you. Now, the thing about attunement is that once it's done, nobody but you will be able to use this spell. For this, I want you to close your eyes, and picture the scale inside your mind." Elvistir waited a few moments as Dannan closed his eyes, and finally Dannan nodded.

"Now, you just need to picture the scale, and think the word 'illuminate', and the scale will glow." Dannan bobbed his head, and concentrated on the scale.

After a few moments, it grew cooler, and he could see an oddly purple-tinged light through his eyelids. Opening his eyes, he let out a gasp, unable to believe what he saw.

The scale shimmered in his hand, emitting an eldritch purple glow. Although it didn't light up the area like daylight would, it showed everything within about twenty feet in stark detail.

"This second spell has several functions. First, as you can tell, it will provide you with light, no matter where you are. This will help you to never get lost. The second is that it will reveal things that are hidden by magic, whether by fey magic, or any other kind."

Stopping so Dannan could absorb what he said, Elvistir looked him in the eye. "The last thing isn't really a 'function', but anything unnatural inside this circle of light will feel extremely uncomfortable, and try to avoid you. A byproduct of how much fey magic is in it. Not that that's a bad thing." Elvistir grinned at this last bit, showing his immaculate teeth. "While I doubt you'll be likely to run into undead, considering your search, you never know. And there are worse things out there, to."

Dannan stared at Elvistir's face in the purple light, the direction of it casting strange shadows across his cheeks, and making his eyes seem whiter than before.

For a moment, Dannan couldn't help but shiver as he remembered that although Elvistir was supposedly a friend of his father's, he was also from a very different world. Concentrating on the scale again, he noticed the light winked out faster than it had come.

"You'll also be able to make the scale glow wherever it is, it doesn't have to be touching you. That was just for attuning it." Dannan nodded mutely, and looked around, blinking slightly as the normal colors of the grass and trees returned.

Looking back at Elvistir, he gave a little bow and smiled. "Thank you."

Elvistir laughed. "You're welcome. Just don't bow like that, alright? It looks just as strange when you do it as when your father did it. Besides, in the long run, who knows if you'll be thanking me for giving it to you? That could be the decision that ruins your life. We won't find out until further down the path, though."

Shrugging, Dannan refused to be disturbed by the comment. "I'm going to cook up my rabbit. Since I want to be done with dinner before my father gets here this time."

"I'll see you tomorrow. Take care of yourself until then."

Dannan smiled and started walking towards the clearing. Glancing back over his shoulder, he saw that the pixie was already gone, continuing his patrol of the area most likely. Shrugging, Dannan reserved himself to another rough sparring session.

This session went much better, or, as Dannan thought, his father might be going easier on him today than he was yesterday.

While they were sparring, Dannan asked his father about Elvistir, but his father, after a moment of surprise, only shrugged it off. "I've never met a pixie, and I doubt I ever will." Dannan nodded, holding back his resigned sigh, and continued with the spar.

After it was finally done, his father left again, saying that they weren't expecting the caravan until the beginning of the next fortnight. Dannan was surprised to find that he wasn't that upset about spending another twelve days out in the woods. "Tell ma-mann I miss her, alright?" His father nodded without saying anything, then began walking back towards the village.

That night after the sparring session, Dannan sat in his tree, staring at the scale, even as the moon took its place high in the sky. He put the chain around his neck briefly, and was startled when he felt a tugging in his chest.

Looking east, he had the unshakable sensation that was where the dragoness was right now. Shaking his head, he sighed. "I've got years before I see her again." He murmured softly to himself. Sighing again, he adjusted himself in between the two branches to get comfy, and drifted off to sleep.

Chapter 7

The next eight days passed like this, with the training getting a little easier as his body got used to the beating it was taking.

On the eleventh day, while he was tracking rabbits with Elvistir, Dannan decided there was more he should learn while in the woods. After about an hour of tracking had passed, Dannan interrupted one of the old stories Elvistir had been telling. "Do you mind teaching me something about how to forage, Elvistir?"

Giving him a sidelong glance, Elvistir let out a dry chuckle. "While I appreciate the effort to humor me, I doubt a diet of only vegetables will suit you."

"I mean it. If I'm lost in the woods and can't hunt, I'll need another way to survive. And if I'm going to do that, I need to not only know what to look for, but what to avoid. Consuming a poisonous mushroom could be the end of me, and I'd really rather not go in such a silly way as food poisoning."

Elvistir looked at him again, his face dead serious, and then he nodded. "Alright then. For the next four days, or until the caravan comes, I'll fill your head with every bit of knowledge I have about regular mushrooms, poisonous ones, edible ferns, and everything else you need to know about local and legendary flora. And even some unusual ones, like some things that you'll only find growing in caves, like lamplight moss."

Dannan chuckled at the last one, and then stopped when he saw that Elvistir was serious. "You mean there really is moss that glows?"

Smiling, Elvistir nodded. "The world is a vast place. Even after nearly two hundred fifty years, I've experienced only a fraction of it." Dannan remained silent, unable to keep the surprise from showing on his face, and yet, at the same time, he felt a little giddy. Thinking about it later, he realized it was all so very new and fascinating. It wasn't surprising he was so happy to learn about it.

The sparring that night went by like a blur, and his father

even commented that he seemed more distracted than usual by something. Dannan shook his head, knowing there was no point in talking to his father about Elvistir any more, and simply went through the spar as best he could. The night also flew by, and before he knew it, it was already morning.

He found it easier this morning to catch a full-grown rabbit, and even his sword exercises and physical training seemed to be easier while he had something on his mind.

When he finally went out hunting around lunch, he was so abuzz with energy that every little thing seemed to stand out. He paid extra close attention, trying to see if he could spot exactly when Elvistir snuck up on him. In the end, he didn't manage to notice, but Elvistir said that it took him less time today than it had before.

The whole time they hunted together, Elvistir pointed out plants, trees, and even a few insects that apparently were pretty tasty if cooked with the right spices. Dannan made a face, but decided if it were life or death, he'd rather eat bugs than die.

When it finally came time to spar that night, he caught his father off guard by trying the entire fight left-handed. Although it was no more successful than any of the other ways, he had the feeling that his father was pleased by his efforts.

For his trouble, Dannan was rewarded with a few more bruises. Although they stung for hours afterwards, Dannan was proud, because at least once he thought he had managed to avoid a worse bruise than his father might have given him.

Climbing into his tree later that night, he wedged himself between the branches as usual. Feeling his ribs, he let out a small hiss, and realized that some of the bruises were starting to pile on top of each other. Letting out a strained laugh, he relaxed against the tree, wondering if he might actually score a hit on his father before the caravan came.

The next day, while Elvistir was teaching him about several types of fungi he should avoid, including one that Elvistir said was actually able to move on its own, Dannan noticed that his pixie friend seemed somewhat distracted. It wasn't until later, when his father arrived, that he found out why.

Chapter 8

Looking up as his father entered the clearing, Dannan smiled. He was looking forward to trying to hit his father this time. Standing up, he picked his practice sword up from where it lay, and hopped off of the rock.

His father seemed unusually solemn as he walked up, and for a moment, Dannan worried something might have happened to his mother. "Why the grim face, father?"

After a few moments of silence, his father looked him up and down. "The outriders for the caravan arrived in the village today. The caravan will arrive tomorrow, and they'll stay for three days before leaving for Whitehaven again."

Dannan grew somber, realizing that soon his seemingly carefree time in the woods would be over, and he would have to deal with living in a real town. Thinking back, he never would have expected how attached he would grow to this life, or the freedom of it.

He smiled, thinking about meeting Elvistir out here, and realized that his leaving tomorrow was probably why Elvistir was so distracted. Sighing, he stepped back from his father, and readied his sword in front of him.

His father nodded at him, and for the first time, his father charged.

Momentarily caught off guard, it was all Dannan could do to deflect the intentionally poor swings his father was sending at him. As he continued blocking, he noticed his father was speeding up ever so slightly with each deflected swing and blocked blow. Finally he noticed his father stopped getting faster, and as soon as that happened, Dannan opened his guard to let one blow through.

His father stepped forward, accepting Dannan's challenge to strike, and the tip of the practice sword scratched along the outside of Dannan's ribs. Pulling his sword in quickly, his father made a move to step back, but not before the side of Dannan's sword managed to hit his arm.

Taking two more quick steps back, his father stopped and looked down at it, and Dannan was surprised that with his father's speed, he had managed to get a hit at all. Shaking his head, he realized that pulling someone into a particular rhythm could also be useful as a battle tactic.

Looking back up at him, Dannan's father nodded, and slung the practice sword across his back. "Alright. Since you can hit me, even if it is only when I'm being careless, I'll allow you to go. None of the other students at your level should even be able to give you that much trouble. Make sure you don't forget anything before we run back." Dannan shook his head, and his father gave him a look filled with curiosity.

"I want to spend one more night in the woods. I'll come back home before dinner tomorrow night." Dannan's father stared at him sternly, but Dannan simply shook his head again.

"Alright, that's fine then. If that is your decision."

"I'll be back before dusk tomorrow evening." Dannan said quickly. Nodding, Dannan's father turned to leave.

"Oh, and your mother will be happy to see you. She's missed you."

Dannan looked up in surprise, and his smile grew wider. "I'm looking forward to seeing her when I get home tomorrow." Dannan's father didn't say another word as he walked out of the clearing, and Dannan retreated back to his tree, wondering how he would adjust to leaving the little home he had made for himself here.

The next morning when Dannan woke up, he went straight to the clearing, to practice his sword swings all morning. After pushing himself nearly to exhaustion, he relaxed on the rock, the hunger of not eating breakfast gnawing at him.

Ignoring it, he started his sword exercises again an hour later, trying to lose himself in the motions of the swinging blade. He couldn't help but think about the sword in his bedroll, and wondered how long it would be before it drew blood. He shook those thoughts away, not wanting to worry about something as heavy as having to take someone's life before he was faced with that situation. It would be bad enough when it actually happened without him obsessing over it beforehand.

As the noonday sun passed overhead, Dannan let out a sigh,

sad that he wouldn't be able to see Elvistir one last time before he left for who knows how many years.

After another hour of sword exercises, he let his arms drop limply to his side. His exhaustion was almost more than he could take. Shaking his head, he went and grabbed his bedroll from beside the rock, and slung it over his shoulder. Grabbing his bow, he turned to leave when he heard a whistle from the edge of the trees.

Glancing in that direction, he saw Elvistir sitting on one of the branches nearest the edge. Trotting over, Dannan grinned at him. "Glad to see you one more time before I have to head off."

Elvistir smiled. "Some others wanted to meet you as well, so they're here to. Come into the trees. Although it's not exactly open out here, when you spend your life hiding, you tend to feel exposed anywhere without close access to a hiding spot."

Dannan nodded, and followed Elvistir into the shade of the trees. About twenty feet back, five other pixies sat in a semi-circle. More surprising to Dannan than all the pixies sitting there was how vastly different they were.

There were three women and two men other than Elvistir, and each had a different skin color and hair color. Their skin colors ranged from pale purple to a deep green, and their hair was just as diverse. "Since this is the last day you'll be in the area for probably a number of years, I brought some of my friends who wanted to meet you. They've all met Andros before, though I doubt he remembers most of us. He doesn't visit, after all. And you humans do tend to have such short memories. It's amazing you ever accomplish anything long term."

Shaking his head, Elvistir grinned and sat down at one end of the semi-circle. "The wonderful pixie to my right is Viveca. Next to her is her brother, Mollister. The fellow on the other side of him is Thimnel. Next to him is Hovlin, and finally, on the other end opposite me is Jeezelin."

Each pixie nodded to him at the sound of their name, and Dannan nodded back, amazed at how odd their names were. He gave himself a mental rebuke, remembering that, although odd to him, they were a totally different race, so normal for them should seem different to him.

Immediately after introductions, they all started trying to ask him different questions at once. Elvistir held up his hands, trying to get them all to stay silent long enough for Dannan to answer each question in turn. In the end, they wound up doing a round-robin style question session, with each one asking a different question before moving on to the next.

While he truly enjoyed the conversation, as well as getting to see how the pixies really were when they relaxed, he did get some very odd questions. Four hours seemed to pass in the blink of an eye, but after it, Dannan really had the feeling that he understood what each of their personalities was like. It was amazing to him just how childishly innocent the pixies were in some things, even though from Elvistir he knew just how dangerous they could be as enemies. It made him regret that he only had these few hours with them.

When the woods finally started to darken, he glanced up at the sky, and sighed. "I hate to leave, but I need to return for dinner. Otherwise, I'll have to explain to my parents why I stayed past dark, even though I said I'd be back before then. And, as you can see, after a fortnight in the woods, I need a bath. Badly."

The pixies all laughed at this, and Dannan shook his head, amazed at the variety of sounds. They were equally varied, from Elvistir's bird song laugh to Hovlin's, which sounded like the wind rushing through leaves. He couldn't help but smile to himself, and enjoy some of the same pleasure they took just from being alive.

Standing up, he gave them all a wave, and started back towards the clearing. Their goodbyes followed him to the edge of the clearing, and then were lost in the woods as he was walking back towards town. After he got about halfway towards town, he started jogging, the sun falling further as he did.

Chapter 9

In the end, he still arrived back at town after dark, and he nervously approached his house. Opening the door, he stepped inside, where his mother immediately swept him up in a hug. Hugging her back, he pushed her away gently after a few moments. "I still need a bath badly, ma-mann. They haven't closed the public bathhouse yet, have they?"

She shook her head, and then gave him a stern look. "You'll barely be ready for dinner in time if you don't hurry, though." Dannan smiled, then went to his room to quickly grab fresh garments.

"I'll be less than a quarter hour, then." She nodded and hurried back to the kitchen, the sound of soup starting to boil over coming through the doorway. Dannan hurried to the bathhouse, where he quickly rinsed at the back. As he watched how the water poured off his body, he set the bucket down, enjoying the feel of being clean.

Looking down at the dragon scale amulet, he gently lifted it in his hand, amazed at how clean it was, even though he had been wearing it since that first night Elvistir gave it to him.

Gripping it gently, he felt it pulse in his hand, and it gently tugged him in the direction the dragoness was. Concentrating on that feeling, he pictured her once again in his mind, and wondered just what it would be like to meet her again. Sighing, he let it fall back to his chest, its weight a reassuring presence at the back of his mind.

Scrubbing himself down with a piece of pumice that was on a long rope attached to the wall, he resolved himself to work harder to see her as soon as he became an official Swordmaster.

The night air was cool on his skin as he left the stall, stopping to quickly don his clothes. Walking out into the main bathing area, he was glad to see that no one else was around.

The street outside was equally empty, and he got home quickly without having to deal with anyone else on the way. Opening the door, he was immediately bombarded by the smell of hot bread and meat stew, the meat probably coming off of one of the cow shanks that were sitting in the salt storage chest behind the house.

Walking through the living room, he saw that the bow had been unstrung, and the bedroll had been put away somewhere. Stepping into the kitchen, he saw that his father was already seated at one end of the table, and his mother was holding some of the bread she had heated up inside the hotbox next to the fireplace. Dannan could feel his father's eyes on him as he sat down at the end of the table, and he stared straight at the tabletop.

He heard his father take one of the plates from his mother, the metal making a small clunk as it was set on the wood. Dannan did the same, accepting the plate with a bit of butter and some bread on it, and also eagerly taking a bowl of soup. It smelled delicious, and after having only had rabbit for the past fortnight, beef with carrots and lettuce was a treat.

Finally, his mother poured herself a bowl of the stew, sitting down in the chair on the side closest to the fireplace. They all sat quietly through the meal, the only sounds being from the wooden spoons dipping into the soup and the crunch of bread.

At the end of the meal, when Dannan's mother stood to take the dishes to the counter, Dannan helped her, taking his plates as well as one of hers. After all the plates were scraped out into the trash pit that lay underneath a small wooden hatch in the kitchen wall, Dannan's mother closed the foot wide door with a solid thunk. Dannan sat back down, trying not to look either of his parents in the eyes.

The oppressive silence lasted for a few minutes, and Dannan wondered if he should be the first one to say something. Finally, his mother cleared her throat, looking over at his father. Taking a deep breath, his father finally spoke. "Your mother and I both have reservations about you leaving the village at such a young age; however, at least you have a clear idea of what you want to do now."

His father's mouth twisted into a small scowl. "I don't necessarily agree with your choice, but it is your choice to make. Just make sure that you keep in touch through a letter every so often. We'll both worry with you gone, even if we know you're capable of handling yourself." His father paused, his scowl intensifying momentarily. "Make sure that the next time you come back to the village, you're an official Swordmaster."

Dannan nodded, and turned towards his mother as she began to speak. "We're both very proud of you for finding a path to follow, even if it's one that will take you far away from us. Just make sure that you come back to us unharmed. No matter what, you'll always be our child, and we love you and want to see you safe. Alright?" Dannan nodded, swallowing a little harder than he had anticipated.

All of a sudden, the events of the past fortnight seemed so very real, and he realized that he might never be back to the village if he didn't actively try to return when his training finished. Thinking about why he was going to become a Swordmaster, he wondered if he would ever get that chance, or if he would die on the journey. He shook that thought away quickly, refusing to give into despair before he had even tried.

"Now, you must be exhausted from sleeping on the hard ground every night. You should go enjoy your bed. You'll only have a few more nights in it before you leave, after all." Dannan nodded and wished them both good night. Although the tree hadn't been that bad with the bedroll, there was something comforting about being back in his bed. A fitful sleep quickly claimed him, and strange creatures with dead gray eyes haunted his dreams.

Dannan woke up before the sun had fully risen again, and he quickly went out back, taking his practice sword with him. Although he knew that he didn't necessarily have to practice his sword swings, he felt comforted by doing it. When he had finished, he noticed that it had taken less time than practice normally did, even though he had done the same number of swings as usual. Pleased with himself for getting faster, he left the practice sword inside the door before quickly heading to the bathhouse.

He was back in time to find his mother just starting to make breakfast, which today was hot bread with jam, and fried eggs. Sitting at the end of the table, he casually chatted with his mother about the time in the woods, leaving out anything that involved Elvistir or the dragoness.

His mother clucked her tongue at him a few times as he said he 'tried' various plants to see if they were edible, even though in reality Elvistir had been the one to tell him. By the time his father rose and came into the kitchen, breakfast was just about to be served. Grabbing several plates for his mother to put everything on, they were all quickly served and eating.

Partway through the meal, Dannan's mother looked over at his father. "Are you going to be taking some of the furs over to the merchant caravan just outside of town?" Nodding, Dannan's father took a bite of his toast, the strawberry jam getting caught in the edges of his auburn beard.

Wiping his beard off gently with a cloth napkin, he looked over at Dannan. "I'll also confirm with the caravan master that they've got the room to take Dannan along. They might need to buy another horse, but we'll see." She nodded, and silence once again took over the table.

Chapter 10

Shortly after breakfast finished, Dannan and his father went out to the caravan, which was camped less than half a mile from the last house at the end of the main road. Although Dannan had seen plenty of caravans and the merchants before, this time he was paying closer attention.

The wagons, although garish, were quite sturdy, appearing to be nothing so much as wooden boxes on wheels with a seat for the driver at the front. And although they might have looked like tempting targets to bandits, this particular caravan always had some of the stronger guards. Part of the benefit of having the money to pay for protection, Dannan mused. Noticing some of the merchant children playing with wooden swords, he chuckled to himself, wondering if anyone here would have reasons like his.

After a moment, he heard his father call his name, and Dannan walked over to where he was standing with the caravan master. "My son will also need to travel with you when you head back to Whitehaven."

The caravan master nodded, and opened a small book he had on a leather loop at his waist. "Right now, we're mostly full, so the cost will be two gold coins." Dannan's father grimaced, but reached for his belt pouch. "Or, of course, there is something else you could do."

The tone in which the caravan master said this immediately set Dannan on edge, and his father's eyes narrowed. "One of the guards in Whitehaven was talking about 'Andros Bellmen, the famous mercenary'. While I know several who go by the name 'Bellmen', there is only one Andros I know of. An expert in swordplay supposedly, and someone who has seen more campaigns than most people have seen years in their life."

Dannan's father remained silent, though his lips had tightened to a fine white line. "Now, I don't know if you're one and the same, after all, you live here, and why would a rich mercenary do that? But if you are, a display of swordplay might convince me to take him along for free. After all, the son of a famous mercenary would be great protection for the caravan by himself."

Dannan's father let out a harsh laugh, and shook his head. "No, I'm definitely no famous mercenary. The only one in my family who's got any interest in weapons is Dannan here. He's better than I am with a sword. He can prove it, to, if you want. Then you could just hire him directly." Dannan's father ended with another chuckle, and shook his head.

It was the caravan masters turn to look annoyed, but it quickly turned to a sickly sweet smile. "How about it, boy? Fancy trying one of my guards? With practice swords, of course. It wouldn't be good to injure a paying customer, or, if it should happen, have you injure one of my guards." The merchant let out a dry chuckle at the last bit.

Dannan looked at his father, who nodded, and then he turned back to the merchant. "I would like that very much, though I don't know how much of a challenge I'll be for one of your expertly trained guards."

The caravan master preened a little, and then made a strange whistling noise. One of the more fit guards trotted over, looking at the two of them, then back at the merchant. "What can I do for you, Merchant Salazar?"

"Samust, I need someone to be a sparring partner for the young sir here. He apparently wants to go to Whitehaven to be trained as a sword master, and was interested in testing out his skills."

Samust looked doubtfully at Dannan, and Dannan thought for a moment that he might refuse. After a moment though, he nodded. "Alright. I'll go grab two of the practice swords. Should we spar on the town side of the ring, or away from town?"

The merchant chuckled. "Away from town, of course. We wouldn't want to disrupt any of the other merchant's business."

The guard bobbed his head, trotting back out of sight, and came back fairly quickly with two wooden practice swords. Nodding to Dannan, he headed towards the edge of the caravan, with Dannan following close behind.

Although it was only a few hundred feet to the spot on the other side of the caravan, they had quickly attracted a crowd as people found out what was going on.

Looking worriedly back at his father, Dannan was unsure of what to do, when Samust thrust out one of the practice swords to him, hilt first. Taking it gingerly, Dannan looked at his father again. Meeting his gaze, his father gave him a small nod, and smiled.

Sighing to himself, Dannan took a readied stance, holding the sword with both hands. He wasn't sure how skilled the man across from him was, but he seemed to have enough scars to be a lifelong veteran.

"First one to surrender, or who is unable to continue, is the loser! Fighters, go!" The caravan master called.

Stepping forward cautiously, Samust's slow approach reminded Dannan of his father. Mirroring the older man, Dannan circled in just as slowly, until they were both just outside of sword reach. Samust made the first move, suddenly coming in from the left side. Although Dannan knew in his head the man was fast, it still felt like he was watching it in slow motion, when he considered it in comparison to his father.

Bringing his sword up, he slid past Samust's blade, using his own blade to hold the larger man's sword to his side. Samust quickly jumped back, not losing his balance, but certainly more wary of Dannan now.

While the crowd had started jeering at the beginning, this first move had silenced them all, and anticipation hung heavy in the air. Samust lunged next, obviously trying to use his larger size to overpower Dannan. Remembering what his father had taught him about using his smaller size to his advantage, he held his sword slanted backwards next to his head, and dove under the guard's blade.

Samust was obviously unprepared for this tactic from a child, and took a heavy strike to his upper right arm before Dannan jumped to the side.

Switching to a one-handed style, Samust held the blade in his right hand, moving so that his side was the only thing facing Dannan. Some of the people in the crowd muttered in surprise at this, but Dannan had no time to think, as immediately Samust's sword started to dart in, trying to find a hole in Dannan's two-handed defense.

Despite the fact Samust was going faster now, Dannan was proud of his ability to deflect swords after successfully defending against some of his father's quicker thrusts. Samust's were no exception; although to the crowd they must have seemed too fast to block. With Samust and himself standing still, Dannan found it almost easy to deflect them all.

Watching Samust's shoulder, he just barely caught Samust repositioning himself in time to duck the two-handed swing at his head. Moving low again, he was about to thrust forward, when something told him to jump aside.

Throwing himself sideways, he dodged the downward blow from the butt of Samust's wooden practice sword, and he quickly hopped back onto his feet, only to be forced to start deflecting Samust's one-handed thrusts again.

Sweat was beginning to pour down Dannan's forehead, but he felt relieved, because he could see all these attacks were beginning to take their toll on Samust as well. Although he assumed the larger man had more stamina than he did, Dannan was certain with a few well-placed hits he should be able to remove the difference.

He continued to deflect the thrusts until it seemed Samust was going to switch postures again. The moment Samust did, preparing to bring his sword in a diagonal slice towards Dannan's left leg, Dannan raised his own sword above his head, preparing for a full downward strike.

Dannan was prepared to take the strike from Samust's practice sword, but he wasn't prepared for Samust's sudden back step. His sword came down suddenly on empty air, and he struggled to get the sword back up to block the thrust he was sure was about to come. He stopped when he saw that Samust was standing a few feet back now, sword tip to the ground, breathing heavily.

Staring at him, eyes narrowed, Dannan held his sword up in a defensive position, his own breath coming in panting gasps.

Samust shook his head, and looked over at the caravan master. "I yield."

The crowd let out a gasp of surprise, and an angry look crossed the caravan master's face, though it was quickly replaced by an insincere smile. "Oh Samust, just because he's a child doesn't mean you should go easy on him."

Samust gave the caravan master an angry look, and the merchant took a small step back. "I'm not sure what you were trying to prove, but since you failed to notice, he left himself open to injury so that he could make the final blow on me. You'd either have been short a customer on this trip back, or short a guard. Possibly both."

Grimacing, the caravan master looked at Dannan with a new respect in his eyes. Although he obviously didn't think that a child was worth much as a fighter, he also didn't look like he was able to ignore the experience of his guard.

"Alright everyone shows over." The caravan master waved his hands at the crowd in a shooing motion, before walking over to Samust and Dannan.

Dannan looked over at his father, who nodded as he came to join them. Holding out two coins, Dannan's father stepped forward, but the merchant held up a hand to stop him.

"A deal's a deal, and what I asked for was a display of swordsmanship. The fact that he made Samust go all out is definitely proof of that. Besides, having him along with us on the road will save me money, especially since all the merchants know how good Samust is. No one will complain about having a child skilled enough to beat him along for the trip."

Nodding, Dannan's father dropped the coins back in his pouch. Samust gave Dannan a small bow, and Dannan gave him an awkward half-bow back, before holding out the practice sword. Chuckling, Samust took it, before walking back into the circle of caravans.

"Just make sure that you're totally ready in two days. We leave then, with or without you." Dannan bobbed his head, and the caravan master walked away, muttering both happily and angrily to himself.

As Dannan walked back through town with his father, he could hear people already talking. He hunched his shoulders every time he heard his name, and wished he could take back that stupid duel.

"Don't be afraid; whether of words, or blades. The moment you are afraid, you give them power over you. And if you plan to succeed as a Swordmaster, people will definitely know your name. The better you are, the further they'll come to fight you."

Dannan looked at his father in surprise, but his father didn't elaborate at all. When they arrived home, Dannan immediately rushed to his room, only coming out for lunch and dinner later on. When finally night came, it was a relief to let sleep take him.

Chapter 11

Dannan spent the next two days indoors, not leaving the house for fear of other villagers asking him about the duel, or when he learned how to use a sword. When finally his mother told him it was time to leave, he let out a sigh of relief.

As he met his mother and father in the living room, he was surprised to find a small bundle sitting on the end table next to the corner chair. Before he had a chance to ask what it was, his mother hugged him tightly, not letting go until he finally pried himself free.

Giving her a rueful smile, he chuckled. "I will be coming home you know, ma-mann. It's not like you could get rid of me that easily." She shushed him, and gave him a light tap on the nose like you would a puppy. Shaking her head at him, she smiled, then looked over at his father.

Stepping forward, his father handed him the sheathed sword that he had originally taken with him into the woods, now with a loop for it to hook onto his belt. "You'll need to learn how to draw it from that stance easily before you can even hope to start getting good at the basics."

Dannan nodded, keeping his face impassive, even as his mother hung the waterproofed hide over his shoulders. "This should keep you dry and somewhat warmer when the rain and winter months come. Make sure to keep it with you." Dannan smiled somberly at her sad tone.

His father picked up the bundle from the table, and held it out to him. "You won't need your bow in the city, but in case you get lost, you might want it and your traveling gear. If you'd go grab the bow please, Kayla." Dannan's mother nodded, and went into their bedroom, coming back in a moment with the bow, a quiver, and a small leather pouch.

"The pouch is waterproofed as well, and holds a few extra bow strings. That way, if you do get lost, you'll have extras if your string breaks. Because there will be no one in the woods to save you."

Packing the extra strings into the small bag containing the flint, tinder, and the sheathed skinning knife, Dannan tried to smile a little more enthusiastically. Slinging the bow and quiver over one shoulder, he quickly strapped the bedroll over the other.

Giving his mother a quick hug, he said softly. "Don't worry. I'll make sure to write." She nodded, obviously holding back tears as he stepped away. Looking over at his father, he bobbed his head, and then walked out the door.

The caravan wagons were all packed up when he got there. The merchants that were still walking about were doing a last inventory of sold goods and feed for the horses that were pulling the wagons.

As Dannan strode up, the caravan master nodded, before motioning to one of the wagons at the back. Hopping in, he found that there were a number of merchant children and wives in back. The children were completely enraptured by him, and couldn't stop asking about the duel, while the wives looked at him as if he were some strange beast that might turn on them at any moment.

After about a quarter hour, he felt the wagon lurch into motion and he sighed, waiting for the kids to grow bored of asking about sword fighting. Looking out one of the windows in the side, he hoped it was sooner rather than later.

As it turned out, it would be later. The children nagged him for details about how he fought, and why, and if he was doing it for a girl, and a million other details that he thought were insignificant.

Staying long enough to satisfy his urge to be polite, he finally climbed out the front to sit next to the driver, who, although taciturn, was not unfriendly. This suited Dannan much more, and he was quite happy to watch the forests to the north pass by as they traveled east. He had never been more than a day's travel from the village, but he didn't expect the land to change much.

By the time they had made camp that night, he learned that he was right. While waiting to find out where to get food from, he saw Samust, who nodded at him as he passed by.

Shrugging his shoulders, Dannan followed him, quickening his pace to catch up as the guard walked the perimeter. Samust glanced back at him, then returned to his patrol, obviously used to being the first line of defense against whatever brigands might appear. "Is it alright if I eat dinner with the caravan guards?"

Samust looked at him, a little surprise showing in his eyes, but he nodded anyway. "You're more like us than like them. Is it starting to bother you?" Samust said quietly.

Dannan looked out towards the darkened woods to the north, then the star-lit plains of the south. "It's not that it's bothering me if I might not be like them, or if I might be more like the experienced campaigners. But some of it seems so silly. I know I've never drawn blood yet, but at the same time, I don't... no, I can't regard it as a game, like the children do. At the same time, I look at the adults who know what I'm capable of, and they look at me like a wolf on a leash. They're not sure what I'll do, or if I'll bite them if nothing else is available."

Samust gave him a wistful smile, then nodded. "That's what it's like to be feared by people. Something you'll have to deal with if you're trying to become a Swordmaster like it seems."

Giving him an odd look, Dannan waited for him to continue. When it didn't seem like anymore was forthcoming, he spoke up. "Aren't Swordmasters supposed to heroes and natural leaders, though?" Samust chuckled, not bothering to turn.

"Swordmasters are just like swords; a tool. Whether a sword is used by the king or a bandit, a beggar or a blackguard, doesn't matter to the sword. For the Swordmasters, that's usually the same."

Dannan quietly absorbed that information, following Samust as he completed his patrol. Samust was on watch until well after midnight, but Dannan didn't slow down or stop at all, making it a point of pride to keep up and keep an eye wherever Samust wasn't looking.

By the time he sat down on a stool next to a small cooking pot full of meal, his feet were tired, but he was glad to be eating. Samust ladled them both a bowl full and they ate in silence. After dinner, while Samust went to get his bedroll, Dannan pulled out his sword and began his practice swings, getting used to the feel of the heavier metal sword in his hands.

A little while into his practice, he noticed that Samust had laid his bedroll down, but was sitting up, watching Dannan practice. "How many years have you been training?"

Glancing over, Dannan continued swinging. "I only started practicing in the past two fortnights. I learned a lot of how to be flexible and use my arms in the wild, but I've only been swinging a sword for a short time."

Samust muttered something unintelligible, the shadows from the tiny fire making his face unreadable. "Just make sure you get some sleep. Tomorrow night we'll arrive in Whitehaven. The guards always have the day after arrival off, so I'll show you around the town a little, and also the three Swordmaster schools. But for now, get some sleep."

Dannan looked over at him, ready to ask questions, but saw that Samust had already lay down and closed his eyes. Laying out his bedroll on the other side of the fire, he quickly dropped off, his sheathed sword still clutched in his hand.

Chapter 12

An hour before dawn, Dannan was awoken by a sudden noise. Opening his eyes, he looked around, though the mist that had formed in the area didn't seem to be hiding anything. Looking over, he saw Samust was still asleep in his bedroll on the other side of the now burned out fire. Sitting up, he slid out of his bedroll, and quietly drew his sword.

He heard another small noise, and he realized it was the sound of a twig snapping. Staring towards the woods, he could see dark shapes starting to move about, and he quietly crawled over to Samust, keeping his body low to the ground. He reached out lightly, and before he had even touched Samust's shoulder, he felt Samust grab his hand.

Looking him in the eye, Dannan put a finger over his mouth, and then pointed towards the woods. At this point, the shapes were obviously people, but no details could be made out. Samust quickly pulled himself from his bedroll, and motioned for Dannan to wake the caravan. Moving to the opposite side of the camp, Samust let out a yell, sword drawn and held defensively ahead of him.

"We're under attack!" Dannan yelled as he ran past each wagon, making sure to look under and around them to make sure no bandits had managed to sneak into the camp already. He could hear the sounds of metal on metal, and arrows striking wood.

As he approached the last of the seven wagons, where several of the wives and children slept inside bedrolls, he saw that three of the bandits had tried to sneak up from this side as well. The bandits, while expecting guards, weren't expecting a child.

For the closest bandit, that mistake was his last. Dannan quickly ran him through, not stopping to think about the disgusting sound that the sword made as it entered the man's stomach, or the even worse noise as he yanked it free.

Darting on to the second bandit, this one had the presence of mind to throw up his sword to block. He only managed to prolong his life for a moment longer, as Dannan slid his blade under the bandit's, slicing his stomach wide open. Dannan looked around for the third bandit, and saw that he was trying to get into the front of the wagon while Dannan was distracted.

Ignoring the still screaming bandit on the ground, Dannan lunged with a right-handed thrust, piercing the bandit's calf. With a cry, the bandit fell off the driver's seat of the wagon and on to the ground, where Dannan quickly dispatched him with another thrust to the neck.

Returning quickly to the still injured bandit, Dannan had to resist the twisting in his stomach as he looked at the man. Trying to clutch his guts in with one hand, and feebly waving his sword in the other to fend off attack, the man was as good as dead in a few minutes anyway.

Dannan swallowed hard, bile rising in his throat. He knocked the man's sword aside, and then dispatched him as mercifully as he could.

Striding quickly to the front of the wagon again, he hopped onto the seat, making sure that everyone inside was safe. Grabbing his bow and quiver from just inside the entrance, he ignored the terrified looks that the children and wives gave him, and leaped out, laying his sword in the dirt next to the wagon.

Peering right and left, he could still hear the sounds of combat coming from the other wagons ahead. He cursed, wishing he could see further through this mist, and thought of the scale. Pulling it out, he hesitated for a moment, thinking it might not be the best choice to use it here.

Suddenly he heard one of the guards scream.

Closing his eyes, the scale burst into light. The mist seemed to thin within the harsh purple light, and he grabbed his sword again, darting towards where the combat was still underway.

As he rounded one of the other wagons, he saw that Samust and two of the other guards were still fighting, back to back, with about seven bandits surrounding them in a loose circle. Hanging back were three bandits with bows, who looked like they were waiting for an opening. One more, who Dannan assumed was the leader, stood watching with them.

Everyone turned as they noticed the light, and Dannan dropped his sword to the ground. Quickly nocking an arrow, he let it fly. The arrow lodged itself in the shoulder of one of the archer's, who let out a cry of pain. His cry seemed to rouse everyone from their stupor, but unfortunately for the bandits, Samust was the first to react.

Dispatching the two in front of him in a single breath, he leaped through the opening, suffering a minor cut on his left arm where one of the bandit swords nicked him as he went. The bandits backed up, trying to guard against Samust, and abandoning their encirclement of the remaining two guards.

Dannan dove to the side, just as two arrows thudded into the dirt right where he had been. Scrambling behind the nearest wagon, he desperately tried to nock another arrow, when suddenly a shadow fell over him.

Looking up, he saw the bandit leader's sword descending, and for a moment, he was sure that he was done for. Suddenly sparks flew as another sword came up from below, flinging the bandit's sword upwards.

Dannan watched Samust move in front of him, and nodded gratefully, though he wasn't sure if Samust saw. Swinging out from the back of the wagon, he fired his arrow at the bandits clumped around the guards, the arrow eliciting a cry from one bandit as it struck him in the back.

Dropping his bow, Dannan dived towards his sword. He quickly grabbed the handle and pushed himself backwards even as he heard the twang of bowstrings. One of the arrows landed in front of him, and the other nicked him in the side of his calf. Letting out a hiss of pain, he moved so that the guards and bandits were between him and the archers.

Even as he tried to use the group as cover, he could see the bandit archers moving to either side. He could hear Samust desperately fighting off the leader, who, from the sounds of it, was quite skilled, and knew there would be no help from him.

Stepping forward so that he was just out of reach of the bandits surrounding the two remaining guards, he let out a yell, hoping to startle one of the bandits into losing his focus.

He didn't have time to be pleased when it worked, as one of the four bandits remaining spun towards him. Even as the bandit tried to swing wildly at where he thought Dannan was, the guard behind him stepped in quickly, running him through from behind.

The bandits began casting hesitant glances amongst themselves, now that more than half of their number had fallen. The two archers began backing towards the woods, where the third archer had run after being hit in the shoulder.

Dannan rushed to where his bow was on the ground and grabbed one of the bandit's arrows, dropping the sword in its place. Picking up his bow, he quickly nocked the arrow and pulled back. The archers looked at the fight, which their companions were starting to lose badly, and then at each other.

Grinning, he was glad they had given him a little more time to aim as he released the bowstring. He cursed when the arrow soared several feet over their heads, but this was the last straw for the two of them, as they suddenly took off into the woods. He quickly fired on the remaining bandit who was trying not to have his back to Dannan and the two guards.

As the bandit dodged backwards, the arrow shot past, narrowly missing the guards as well. Dropping the bow, Dannan stepped forward, picking his sword up as he went. The bandit, darting back further, managed to get a little distance between himself and the two guards. The moment he seemed to think he was safe, he turned around and ran, not looking back once.

Turning around, Dannan quickly rushed towards where Samust was fighting a losing battle with the bandit leader. Although neither of them had taken anything more than minor cuts, the bandit leader seemed like he had more power behind each swing than Samust did.

Extinguishing the light as he got close, Dannan dived forward, his sword up to deflect any incoming blows. The bandit leader kicked out and caught Dannan in the chin, but he kept pushing forward.

Unable to keep his balance and still swing at Samust, the bandit leader went down. Although he quickly threw Dannan off, he found himself with Samust's sword tip at his throat.

The other two guards hurried over after checking their fallen companions, grabbing some rope as they came. When they got there, they began to tie the leader's hands and feet. Although it was obvious in his face that he wanted to struggle, the bandit leader could also tell from Samust's glare that struggling would just get him killed. So he lay still, grumbling a little as he was hog tied by the two guards.

Samust dragged him by his arms over to the extinguished fire, and left him there as they covered the two fallen guardsmen and got them ready to be brought back and buried in the city. Dannan wiped off his blade in the grass, then walked back to check on the wives and children.

Seeing several of the merchants already there tending to the crying and wailing family members, he turned to leave. As he did, he noticed the corpses of the three men out of the corner of his eye, piled up next to each other. Staring at them for a moment, what had happened finally sank in.

Rushing over behind one of the other wagons where no one else could see, he vomited. After emptying his stomach, he gave a few dry heaves, and then looked down at the grass. Wiping his mouth on his sleeve, he saw that the dragon scale was hanging out, and he quickly tucked it away, worried that he might already have caused too many problems.

While the caravan master and Samust took stock of everything and loaded up the bodies and prisoner, Dannan circled the camp, bow drawn and arrow ready. No more bandits were forthcoming as the first rays of sunlight shown through and started to burn away the mist, but the scene was surreal enough by itself.

Dannan knew that there was no going back now, and he could also understand why his father wouldn't want him living this way. There was no feeling that explained what it was like to take everything from someone. All he could think of was the fact that he had killed, and would have to again if he continued on this path.

He heard footsteps in the grass behind him and spun about, arrow drawn back to his cheek, when he saw it was Samust. Samust had his hands held up, and when it finally registered to him, Dannan lowered the bow and let the string go slack.

"How many did we lose?" Dannan asked in a shaky voice. Samust grimaced, and shook his head. "While it's better not to dwell on that, I'll be honest. We only lost the two guards, Junner and Rork. From the sounds of it, that could have gone much worse." Dannan cocked his head to the side, and Samust chuckled.

"Those first three bandits you killed by the family wagon? They were probably planning to use the children as hostages. If you hadn't killed them when you did, we'd all have died, and they'd have only lost two."

Dannan shrugged, uncomfortable at being praised for killing. Samust, seeing his discomfort, shook his head. "That's what fighting is about. For now, just get past it. For me, relief came from knowing that at least I was merciful and fair in my fights. The fact that you had to fight three at once, and you killed them to save the life of someone else; you should let that feeling do it for you."

Shrugging uncomfortably again, Dannan looked around apprehensively. Samust motioned for Dannan to follow him back to the wagons so they could start off, and Dannan did so woodenly, still trying to wrap his mind around everything.

The caravan didn't waste much time leaving, and they made good time getting to Whitehaven, now that the handlers were spooked. Dannan rode the whole way on one of the horses the two dead guardsmen had ridden, and in some ways, it just made him feel that much worse.

Chapter 13

When they finally got within sight of the city, he was too morose to feel awe or anything else. Whitehaven had a population of several thousand, and it had been enriched for a long time by the lumber that flowed from his village through to the rest of the nation. Merchants regularly went through the gates, and a steady throng of traffic on foot did so as well.

Riding through the gates, Dannan looked around, wondering if any of the bandits they had fought had made their way here. With five surviving the ambush, a full third of the band that attacked them had escaped. Gripping his sword tightly, he kept a constant eye on everyone as the caravan pushed through the city. When they finally got to the wagon yard, Dannan was already exhausted from trying to watch too many people at once.

He noticed out of the corner of his eye that the caravan master sent Samust off on an errand at full speed, and for a moment, panic gripped him. Looking around at the exits, he wondered if they would bring him in because of the amulet, or if the guards would just cut him down, without trying to find out what it was. He started to move slowly towards one of the exits, forcibly releasing his hand from the sword hilt so that he wouldn't look as suspicious.

Suddenly he heard someone yell from behind him.

"Hey older brother!"

Whipping around to see who it was, he was caught off guard. One of the children, a girl of about five, ran up and hugged him around the legs as hard as she could. He was so surprised that she almost knocked him over. Looking down at her, he couldn't keep the surprise off of his face, while the little girl simply beamed up at him.

He heard someone calling her, and looked up to see one of the merchant's wives beckoning at her daughter and calling her name. "You should go to your mother, you know."

The little girl nodded, and then grinned. "The mommies said that you saved us when the bandits attacked. They were scared of you, but we're not. It's true, isn't it, older brother?"

Dannan looked down at her, unsure of what to say, then nodded. He wasn't sure which surprised him more, being thanked by one of the children, or being called 'older brother'.

"That means you're a good older brother! Thanks!" The little girl hugged his legs again, then ran back to her mother, who was looking worriedly over at him. Dannan chuckled, feeling much older all of a sudden. He found it amazingly funny how the kids trusted him fully with just one action.

He turned away and grimaced, hoping that he still had Samust's trust, or he could be in a heap of trouble. Shaking his head, he decided to wait near the wagon with the bandit leader in it, occasionally checking on him to make sure that he didn't make any moves to escape. Although obviously uncomfortable, the bandit leader just laid there, a calculating look on his face.

It wasn't long before Samust returned with the guards, and Dannan moved away from the wagon. He watched them for a moment before walking out a little to meet Samust. Taking a deep breath, he opened his mouth, but Samust shook his head for silence. Samust kept walking past, to where the bandit leader was.

One of the guards pulled out a piece of paper while the other looked at the bandit leader's face, and then they nodded at each other. "Alright. When he's executed tomorrow, you can pick up the bounty." Samust nodded, and stepped back as they each grabbed an arm, dragging the bandit leader out of sight and presumably to the last place he'd see before the chopping block.

Watching him get dragged away, Dannan momentarily forgot about his worry. Letting out the breath he had been unconsciously holding, he almost jumped when Samust touched his shoulder. "He'll be executed tomorrow, so don't worry about him. And don't worry, no one in the caravan will spill your secret, either. Whatever it is."

Dannan looked at him in alarm, then relaxed, seeing the sincerity in his eyes. "It would be one thing if you were a random stranger, but we owe you our lives, even if there are some who might not like that fact. So whatever that light was, that knowledge is safe with us." Dannan nodded after a moment, deciding that the only thing he could do was trust in Samust's words.

"Shall we go help keep an eye on things while the porter's move the goods out? We get tomorrow to ourselves, so I'll show you around the town then."

Dannan nodded again, then muttered "Thanks."

Samust shook his head, and a small smile briefly crossed his lips. "Like I said, I owe you a fairly large debt. Consider this payment towards that, if you want."

Chuckling a little, Dannan shrugged. "It's up to you to consider it a debt or not. To me, it was just a child doing what he was supposed to."

Looking at him, Samust just shook his head in disbelief. "Damn scary brat then if you ask me." Dannan looked at him in surprise, then scowled as Samust burst into laughter.

"Let's just go help with the unloading."

Samust nodded, still chuckling as Dannan stumped over towards the wagons to watch them unload the furs and other goods the caravan had picked up in his village.

The rest of the day passed by uneventfully, for which Dannan was extremely grateful. When he went to leave, the caravan master told him that he could bunk with the guards for free, since he had earned at least that much. Dannan gladly took the offer, and, after practicing his sword exercises, managed to fall into a deep sleep.

The next morning was busy, as they had to go attend the bandit's execution, which took place just after first light. When Dannan, Samust, and the caravan master got there, Dannan was surprised to see how many people had gathered before the execution platform.

It was a solidly built platform with five steps leading up to the top, where it held the chopping block, high enough so that even those at the back could see it. Although it made Dannan somewhat uneasy to see, he noticed that most of the crowd seemed excited.

Occasionally he overheard bits and pieces of conversation from where they stood at the back, and he gathered that the chopping block was only reserved for hardened criminals. He was surprised to find out how much of an event it was though. "Maybe we caught a bigger one than we thought." Dannan muttered to himself.

"His bounty was one hundred gold coins." Samust said softly next to him. Dannan looked over at him in surprise, and then looked back at the platform.

A few more minutes passed by, and the crowd grew hushed.

Although he couldn't see it, Dannan was certain the guards were walking the prisoner up to the block. Sure enough, after a few moments the top of the bandit's head appeared over the crowd, followed by the rest of his body, and the two guards.

His arms were securely tied behind him, and when they got up to the chopping block, they forced him to his knees. Holding him by the shoulders, they pressed down on his back to prevent him from moving. The crowd's excitement became palpable, and Dannan soon realized why.

The velvet hood of the executioner appeared over the top of the crowd, and his broad, bare shoulders followed. He was a large, well-muscled man, bearing an axe that anyone would think a giant would be wielding. The bandit leader waited patiently, and when the executioner was almost there, the bandit leader threw his body back. Although he struggled mightily, the guards holding him refused to be thrown off, managing to keep their grip on his arms even as the executioner raised his axe high.

Watching the bandit writhing around, Dannan almost felt pity for the man as the axe fell, but in an instant it was over. A fountain of blood erupted over the wooden deck of the platform, as the bandit's head fell to the wood and rolled several feet away. Closing his eyes for a moment, Dannan shook the image from his mind, trying not to picture himself up there.

As he turned to leave, he noticed Samust and the caravan master were still waiting. Sighing, he stopped and waited along with them, even though he wasn't sure exactly what they were waiting for.

Several minutes later, when the crowd was mostly clear, a guard approached the caravan master. The guard handed him a sack obviously heavy with coins, and shook his hand, leaving quickly for his post when he was finished. As they left the square where the execution platform was, Dannan took one last look back, watching as a guard casually tossed a pail of water to clear the blood away.

They walked back to the wagon yard in silence, each of them lost in their own thoughts. When they finally got there, the caravan master quickly opened the pouch and counted through it.

Nodding in satisfaction, he counted out twenty coins, which he handed to Samust. Samust nodded and took them, dropping them into his belt pouch with a small "thanks". The caravan master then counted out another twenty, which he held out to Dannan. Staring at the coins, Dannan couldn't seem to process what he was being offered.

After a few moments, the caravan master made a clucking noise with his tongue, shaking Dannan from his reverie. Taking the coins quickly, he dropped them into the small pouch containing his bowstrings, and tied it onto his belt. "I'm going to go deliver the death payment to the two guard's families. Samust, you have the day off, as you know. I'm going to go ask Tymol to accompany me before he takes the rest of the day off." Samust nodded, looking over at Dannan. Dannan met his eyes, and then they both looked at the caravan master.

Giving them each a curt nod, he walked further into the wagon yard, looking for one of the other two guards, Dannan wasn't really sure which. Laughing to himself, Dannan couldn't help but shake his head. He was great when it came to being aware in the outdoors, but being aware of other people was a whole different issue.

Suddenly he felt a light tap on his shoulder, and he looked up at Samust. "Here, I'll show you the three schools, and tell you about them. And a few of the landmarks while we go. Hopefully that should take your mind off of things." Dannan nodded, and followed him out of the wagon yard.

Chapter 14

What Dannan noticed immediately as they walked through the streets was that although Whitehaven was a fairly large town, it was very crowded. Dannan had to work hard to stay close to Samust, only getting a brief respite when Samust stepped over to the side of the road to point something out, or moved to avoid the throng.

The first section of the city Dannan got to see was the market section. The wagon yards of other merchant caravans were also housed here, as well as many of the general businesses. As they passed one store, Dannan looked at the sign curiously, before commenting on it to Samust.

Glancing over at it, Samust shrugged dismissively. "A printer's. The owner claims they've found a way to revolutionize the ability to make books using tools, and that making more people literate from now on will be easier."

Samust kept walking, ignoring the fact Dannan had stopped. "I personally doubt the claim. Despite the efforts of the kingdom's magistrate run schools, if a person doesn't want to learn, usually, they won't. On the other hand, for those who do want to learn, it seems nothing anyone ever does can stop them. Just a matter of choice and drive, I suppose."

Staring at it, Dannan pondered what that might mean for the future, having attended the magistrate run school of his village until he was eight. He had never really thought anything special about it, as they just taught basic reading, writing, and mathematics. Shrugging, he rushed after Samust, who had gone ahead already.

As they continued walking, the first of the sword schools came into view. Dannan immediately noticed that although the street was still fairly crowded, most people were avoiding the two guards near the front gate. Above the entryway to the walled compound was a large shield, bearing the crest of the school. Samust stopped on the opposite side of the street, and offered Dannan his hand. Dannan looked at him quizzically, but accepted it.

Suddenly he found himself lifted into the air, and he let out a small gasp of surprise as he found himself sitting on Samust's shoulders. Looking down at him incredulously, Dannan saw that Samust was wearing an ear-to-ear grin. "You couldn't exactly see from down there, could you?"

Dannan grumbled, then said softly. "I'm amazed you can stomach having a killer up on your shoulders."

Samust let out a hearty laugh, and shook his head. "I've never really thought about kids, being a mercenary and all, but if I had one, I'd definitely want one who could at least defend himself." Dannan looked down at him in shock, but quickly covered his reaction, turning back towards the school.

The crest on the shield was of extreme interest to Dannan, and he studied it intensely. An eagle, it's wings back, claws outstretched, and it's beak wide as it silently cried out in fury dominated the center. The background of green highlighted the white talons and the silver feathers, while a thin border of blue was traced around the edge of the shield.

After a moment, Dannan noticed the two guards were staring at him, and he quickly tapped Samust's shoulder. Kneeling down a little, Samust moved so Dannan had some room to get off. Jumping down quickly, Dannan found himself hidden between Samust and the building.

Waiting a moment, Dannan followed Samust as he began to walk again, talking just loud enough to be heard over the crowd. "The sword schools here are all based off of one of the previous lord's strongest retainers, a man named Galem Swiftstrike. While not his given name, nobody debated it because of the fact that he was the best in the area."

"During the fortieth year or so of the last lord's rule, three of Galem's apprentices began teaching their own apprentices, so that his memory would be immortalized in the fighting styles of their descendents. That particular school is called The Hawk's Fury."

Samust chuckled, his eyes on some distant memory. "Very much a straightforward fighting style, they believe in being strong enough to overpower their enemy, even enough to put their lives on the line without regard to the consequence. They also tend to be the most aggressive with their social interactions, which is why it was good we didn't linger too long. Some of the most loyal men I've met have been from there, but so have some of the most repulsive men, to. At least a few of them became bandits when the war was over."

Looking up at Samust in surprise, Dannan tried to figure out how old he must be on his fingers. Samust looked down and let out a little chuckle as he saw what Dannan was doing. "I'm thirty-five now. I enlisted in the last war when I was twenty, and it ended three to four years after it started. Some people fought longer, of course, and some quit early, but most of us fought for about four years."

Dannan made a face at him, then started mumbling to himself as he counted out the time. "So eleven years ago was when it officially ended?" Dannan said.

Nodding, Samust looked at him, a wide grin on his face. "You may be able to kill a full grown man with a sword, but you're definitely still a child in a lot of ways." Dannan scowled at him, though it came out looking more like a pout than angry grimace, and Samust burst out laughing. "Ahh, but I'm terrified! No more, please!" Dannan's scowl deepened, and he trudged along silently behind Samust as they entered the next section of the city.

This part of the city was much more residential, with barely any store fronts at all. The houses, many of them two stories, seemed to be made of brick and mortar, though occasionally Dannan did see one that had its front covered in plaster.

He commented on it, but Samust just shook his head. "The plastered houses are owned by those with a bit more money than the average citizen. And although many of these brick buildings look like they could fit numerous families, you'll find that the top floor and bottom floor are both owned by only two separate families. Usually they pay a fee to someone who owns one of the plaster houses. That's why there are so many more of the brick ones."

Dannan nodded, looking at each plaster house as they passed. He quickly noticed that the plaster, while white, was not the only color present. The houses all had outdoor shutters, and on the brick houses, they were white. Each of the plaster houses had one of three colors, varying between green, blue, and red. "Why are the shutters different, Samust?"

Samust ignored the question at first, but after Dannan asked again, he sighed. "It's about politics. Not something a kid like you has to worry about." Dannan shrugged and kept looking at the houses they passed, wondering why adults made everything so complicated.

Leaving the residential area behind, they found themselves near the eastern edge of town. Dannan looked around in surprise, not having expected to cross the town so quickly. Samust chuckled at the look on his face, then kept walking towards the walled compound that had just come into sight around the corner. As they got closer, Dannan noticed that though there were fewer people, they weren't avoiding the two guards at the gate like people had at the other school.

Walking past, Samust slowed his stride a little so that Dannan could examine the shield above the entrance as they went. A pair of fierce looking eyes stared out from the shield, seeming to follow the viewer as they passed by. Dannan shivered at the surreal effect, and rubbed his eyes with the back of his hand. Looking again, he saw that the eyes still seemed to follow him, and he moved slightly behind Samust. The background of blue that showed through the eyes didn't seem to help, and Dannan barely noticed the red stripe around the edge of the shield, as he couldn't wait to tear his eyes away.

Samust chuckled at Dannan's reaction, and Dannan relaxed as they turned a corner, leaving the staring eyes behind. "Those were The Hawk's Eyes. Fifteen years ago, what started the war was the barbarian hordes of the east deciding they wanted the rich resources of the central part of the continent. The main horde didn't reach as far as Whitehaven, but by the third year, some of their raiding parties, which could range from twenty men to two hundred, were reaching the town."

"After the war, The Hawk's Eyes decided to shift the location of the school to the eastern portion of town. They went from simply being cautious, to watching for the threat of raiders ever coming back. They actively train outriders, and their scouts are some of the deadliest and most skilled in the nation. Well, I might say they even rival some elves, though the elves have a natural talent for that sort of thing."

Dannan looked up at him in surprise, mouth wide open. "You've met elves?"

Samust nodded, smiling a little. "They weren't really interested in a tiny war between humans, but the fact is, we're their eastern border guardians for all intents and purposes. They knew that if we were overrun, they would have to deal with the barbarian hordes themselves. So I met at least a few elves during the war." Dannan gawked at him in awe, ignoring the houses they passed.

When he finally started paying attention again, he saw that

another walled compound had come into sight. As they approached, Dannan grinned. "Let me guess... The Hawk's Speed?"

Giving him an odd look, Samust laughed. "No, nothing as silly as that." Dannan frowned at him, then looked at the shield as they passed by. Dannan noticed Samust duck behind the crowd a little as they walked along, keeping his face obscured from the guards, but Dannan didn't comment.

He was too intent on the proud hawk standing on a mountain peak, his chest thrust out, his silver plumage ruffling slightly in a wind that never stopped. The red background seemed to highlight his pride even more, and a green line encircled the whole thing, similar to the border patterns of the other two. As they moved away from the compound, the crowd began to thin, and for a moment, Dannan thought he saw the guards watching them.

As they passed out of sight, he noticed that the buildings in this area were a bit more run down than the other neighborhoods had been. He glanced back as Samust took up a protective position slightly behind him and to the right, but couldn't figure out why.

Deciding it must be because there were bad people in the area, Dannan tried to make his strides more measured. Keeping his hands swinging by his sides, he resisted the urge to put his hand to his hilt, remembering what his father had said about drawing his sword. Taking slow, deliberate breaths, he hurried through with Samust, immediately aware of the change in houses when they were away from that section of town.

The houses in this area seemed well maintained, and Dannan noticed that there were more plaster houses once again. As they came to the corner of the main street, Dannan saw another walled area, and he looked up at Samust in confusion. "I thought you said there were only three sword schools, Samust." Samust looked at the compound, then nodded to Dannan.

"That's the compound that belongs to the town guard. While the three sword schools defend the town from any outside threat, the town guard keeps order in town. Although we just passed through what are effectively the 'slums' of Whitehaven, you noticed that there weren't too many people actively loitering about? The reason is because the two hundred town guards are able to keep order within the town without fear."

Chuckling, Samust eyed the compound with a mix of disdain

and amusement. "If an outside threat appears, the three schools could probably muster about two hundred trained guardsmen, one hundred Swordmasters in training, and I imagine at least fifteen trained Swordmasters. Combine that with the cities own defenses, and you'd have a hard time breaking in, or even causing any real damage without a significant force."

Dannan looked around as they passed by the town guard compound, not surprised to see there were a few more shops in this area. Looking up at Samust, Dannan cocked his head to the side. "Is it normal for a mercenary to know so much about the inner workings of a town's defenses?"

Samust looked down at him quickly, his surprise evident on his face, and he let out a strained laugh. "Knowing things like that as a mercenary will keep you alive, so I'd say yes, it's important to know."

Although he was calm now, Dannan could tell Samust hadn't been expecting him to notice that, and must have said something he didn't mean to.

Deciding it didn't matter, he looked around, and frowned slightly. "Doesn't Whitehaven have a keep?" Samust gazed down at him, laughing again.

"The keep and all the well-to-do's are in the center of the town, which we avoided. Compared to them, we're just riff-raff, so we don't have a free pass to go sightseeing through the area. But if you distinguish yourself as a Swordmaster, you might get to see inside the keep. You might even get to meet Lord Whitemane the Second, the current lord of Whitehaven."

Dannan snickered at the name, and Samust shook his head. "Don't laugh. It's not his fault. Every lord since the first has had 'white' somewhere in his name. Tradition, and all that." Samust paused for a moment, then added with a gleam in his eye. "Even if it is a stupid tradition." Dannan burst out laughing, and after a moment Samust joined him. The walk back to the wagon yard was peaceful, with the two of them making idle conversation as they went.

Chapter 15

It was an hour or so past noon when they finally got back to the wagon yard. Grabbing some bread, butter, and meat stew from the kitchen, they ate outside in the courtyard, perched on some covered rain barrels that were already filled to the brim for later use. "I know I should leave for one of the sword schools today if they'll accept me in, but which one do you think I should go to, Samust?" Dannan asked when they finished their food.

Dannan saw him tense up almost imperceptibly after asking, but said nothing. "Tomorrow is the actual date they have their entrance tests on." Samust said calmly.

After a few long moments of silence, Samust looked over at him. "Well, I've already told you a little about The Hawk's Fury school. The Hawk's Eyes tend to be more lenient in their tactics restrictions, as they believe that a trap or preemptive strike can be the difference between life and death."

"The Hawk's Honor believes that as long as you survive and protect your objective, which is usually the lives of yourselves, your comrades, and the people, then you have succeeded. To that end, they even accept retreat, as long as it's for a strategic reason, and not from cowardice. Although they are more lenient in that respect towards certain things, they are absolutely rigid when it comes to protecting the lives of others. Property is worthless, but lives cannot be rebuilt. I think they have a saying for it... 'You can always find a new nest, but you cannot find the same mate'."

Dannan stayed silent for a moment, and then nodded. "Which school do you think best suits me?"

Although he could tell Samust was dreading him asking for some reason, Dannan still wanted to know. Sighing, Samust shook his head. "You aren't as reckless as a Fury, and you might be a little too direct for an Eye. Though of the two, you'd like the Eyes more." Dannan nodded, and watched him quietly.

Scowling, Samust looked up at the sky. "You're most like an

Honor, but I hesitate to recommend them to you." Dannan looked at him curiously, waiting until he said more. Finally, Samust looked back at him. He wore a pained expression, and his unwillingness to talk was apparent. But still, he spoke once more. "The most repulsive man I ever met in Whitehaven, indeed the lowest man I have ever met in my life, was a member of The Hawk's Honor school. If I could, I would forget his face, but I can't. And as I am now, I'm not strong enough to kill him, or even beat him in a fight."

Dannan was surprised by the revulsion in Samust's voice, and opened his mouth slightly to speak. Shaking his head as Samust looked away, Dannan decided not to ask anymore for now, and they sat in silence, watching the crowds pass by.

An hour or so later, Dannan finally stood, stretching his arms and legs a little. "Do you think the caravan master will mind if I leave tomorrow?"

Samust shook his head. "Considering how much money you saved him, hell, that you earned him, since that bounty put an easy twenty gold in his pocket, I imagine he wouldn't mind letting you stay in the barracks with us." Dannan smiled, relieved, and followed Samust to the hall where everyone ate. That night passed quickly, and as Dannan prepared for bed, he wondered what tomorrow would bring.

Dannan let out a loud yawn as he woke up and looked around, seeing that only one of the guards was still asleep nearby.

Hopping quietly out of bed, he dressed quickly and went out into the yard, the smells of a city before dawn flooding his nose. After a few sneezes and sniffles, he decided that he much preferred the clean air of the forest to the road dust and people smells of the town.

Starting his sword exercises, he noticed as the daylight came up over the walls that he was getting a crowd of children. Smiling to himself, he started to add a little flare to his exercises. For a few moments he wondered if fighting like this was the same as the dancing teenagers and adults did at festivals. Clearing his head, he kept this up for a little while, much longer than it normally took to complete his practice swings.

When he finally finished, Dannan stopped, the sword and his right knee both nearly touching the ground from his downward slash. Unwrapping one hand from the hilt, he let the sword hang limply from his left hand and he panted, realizing that sweat was pouring off of his body. After a moment, a cheer sprang up from the children, startling him out of his reverie.

Sheathing his sword, he grinned idiotically at them, and they ran around him, most of them only barely coming up to his waist. Dannan briefly debated how the caravan master could justify bringing such young children along on the trips, but after a second he decided it might be better than leaving them alone in the city.

Stepping through the children, he walked towards the washing stalls located near the back when he remembered that he didn't have any clothes to change into. Stepping into the kitchen, he saw one of the merchant's wives standing next to a table, slicing up some bread for breakfast. Looking up at him, she eyed him warily as he came close, her grip on the knife tightening unconsciously.

Dannan noticed, and couldn't completely hide the sadness from his eyes at her reaction. He knew Samust said that it would be worth it, and he couldn't help but smile inwardly at the memory of the little girl thanking him. But at the same time, it still hurt when people had that kind of reaction to him.

Stopping at the end of the table, he gently cleared his throat, trying to think of what to say as she stared at him. Looking up at her, he took a deep breath to clear his thoughts, and nervously spoke. "Umm... I realized when I was going to the washing stalls that I didn't have any spare clothes, and then I realized I didn't even know where to get any in the city, and I was looking for someone who might know, and then I saw you slicing bread." Dannan rushed through, nervously gripping the edge of his pants as he finished.

The woman looked at him, and he saw her eyes soften as she set the knife down. "You're still just a child at heart, aren't you?" Dannan looked at her, confusion mixing in with his nervousness, and he nodded slightly.

She shook her head, then sighed. "Menfolk. Always pushing the children to start younger and younger. No wonder no one in the caravan understood you. You aren't even sure who you are yet." Dannan nodded slightly, his confusion now apparent. She smiled, the kind of smile he remembered so well on his mother, and he smiled back tentatively, unsure whether or not this meant she'd help him.

"Here, let me finish slicing the bread for toast, and then I'll get you some of my oldest sons' spare clothes. He outgrew them a number of years ago, but we kept them for when Junus grew into them. After what you did to protect us, I think we can spare you a set or two of clothes." Dannan smiled appreciatively and waited, watching her as she sliced the bread.

When she finished, she began to set a few plates, and set a metal tray across the top of one of the charcoal braziers next to the fireplace. As he watched her, Dannan began to nervously wring his hands, unused to standing around as someone else worked in front of him. After a minute or two, the woman noticed, giving him a curious glance. "What's the matter, child?"

Dannan realized he was wringing his hands and stopped, and looked to the side. Turning back, he looked over at the tray heating up over the brazier. "Is there anything I can do to help?"

Looking at him in surprise, the woman let out a soft chuckle, then shook her head. "You just have a seat on one of those stools, and then we'll get you some new clothes." Dannan nodded meekly and hopped up onto one of the stools, waiting as he watched her prepare breakfast.

It took about twenty minutes before she was done, but Dannan waited patiently, worried that if he went anywhere, she might change her mind. When she finally finished, she called out "Dora! The plates are all set for the table!"

A slightly younger woman came in, and started in surprise seeing Dannan sitting there. She quickly regained herself, however, and immediately began to ferry out plates for the merchants and others who would be eating in the actual dining hall.

Motioning for him to follow, the merchant's wife walked through the doorway, leading him past the table where people were just starting to sit down, and down a long hallway to a storage room at the end.

Opening it up, she stepped inside, motioning for him to wait there. He heard the creak of a chest opening, and a minute later, she came out with two sets of sturdy looking clothes, one made of cotton and one made of wool. The wool was dyed a deep brown, while the cotton was a light green. "They aren't fancy, but they're sturdy and will last a long time. That way, until you can get some more of your own, you'll have something."

Dannan smiled and gave her his best bow before taking them from her. She smiled at him, then shooed him. "Go get washed now.

You stink after all that exercising!" Dannan laughed and nodded, rushing to put the wool clothes in his carrying bag, and then running to the stalls with his cotton outfit.

Dannan stopped in surprise when he saw the washing area. The village only had a public bathhouse, so he had no experience with a private one. Looking at the one before him, he was almost unsure of what to do.

What stood before him looked almost like a stone stable, with stalls the size of outhouses built over a partially exposed cistern. The end closest to him was open to the air, so that rainwater could refill the cistern as necessary. On each side of the building there was a small drainage canal, leading away from the bathhouse and towards a dirt hole near the wall, where Dannan guessed the water ran back into the ground. Walking forward, he saw that there were cobblestones rather than ceramic tiles under each stall, and someone, most likely the servants, carefully maintained each stall.

Shaking his head in amazement, he stepped inside, closing the door behind him. Inside the stall, a stone lip rose a few inches from the floor, giving easy access to the water, while preventing it from draining right out into the drainage ditch near the door. The water trough was about a foot and a half wide, leaving plenty of room to dip a bucket in, but still leaving the stall spacious with a feeling of openness.

On the wall opposite the door were several hooks to hang clothes from, high enough that they wouldn't get wet as long as the person didn't fool around. On the other side Dannan was expecting to find a piece of pumice, but instead, an odd, chalk-like block had a rope running through it, anchoring it to the wall a few feet off the ground.

He tested the rope a little, and found that there was some give, but he couldn't figure out what the chalky substance was. Sniffing at it a little, he made a face as the scent of pine needles hit his nose. Shaking the smell away, he looked at it again, unsure of what to do with it. Finally he decided the smell couldn't be any worse than feeling dirty. Looking at the stool and bucket on the floor, Dannan laughed, feeling silly about being happy that something there looked like what he was used to.

Stripping quickly, he hung his sweat-drenched clothes on one of the hooks, and the cotton clothes on another. Dragging the bucket through the small trough of water, he sat down, pouring it over himself. He let out a little gasp as the cold water covered him from head to toe, and he flinched a little as he felt a small tug. Looking down at the dragon scale, he took hold of it gently, and felt it tugging him towards the north. Looking up, he wondered if the dragoness was safe, even as he was amazed at the distance she could cover in less than a fortnight's time.

Shaking his head, he quickly rubbed himself down with the chalk-like bar, gritting his teeth at the smell it left on him, before rinsing himself off with another bucket of water. Shaking his body to get rid of some of the water, he pulled on the cotton clothes, feeling exposed without anything covering the dragon scale. Slinging his dirty clothes over one arm, he quickly walked out, heading back to the room for his things.

When he arrived, he found the other guard was finally waking up, and looking just as tired as he had the night before. Nodding to him, Dannan quickly stuffed the dirty clothes in next to the clean wool clothes, and wrapped the bag and poncho in the bedroll. Pulling it over his shoulder, he grabbed the bow and quiver, wondering if he would find any use for them in a sword school.

Walking to the doorway, he stopped, looking back at the guard who was just now standing up and stretching. "When does the caravan next leave?"

Looking over at him sleepily, the guard scratched his chin, letting out another large yawn. "We leave halfway between noon and dinner. We always do. Day and a half at home, two to four days on the road, three to four in town, and then two to four back. Goes like that until snow or rain makes the roads too bad to travel."

Dannan nodded, disappointed that he wouldn't get the chance to tell Samust if he had been accepted into sword school or not. Shaking his head and sighing, he left the guard scratching his head, and went out into town.

Chapter 16

It was easier to walk quickly during the early morning, as the crowds had not yet started to form. This time, it only took Dannan an hour to reach The Hawk's Honor compound. Standing across the street from it, alone except for the two guards, he stared once again at the hawk perched so regally on the mountaintop. Meeting the eyes of the two guards, he walked forward, stopping about ten feet from them.

They looked at him for a moment, then each other, and finally one of them spoke. "What is it, child? The tests aren't until noon, if that is what you are here for." Dannan nodded slightly, and the two looked at each other again. "You'll have to go home until later. The grounds aren't open to any but school members."

Dannan shifted slightly, then took a deep breath. "I actually came in on a caravan. I don't have a place to stay in Whitehaven yet."

The guards looked at each other and sighed. "Alright, I'll take you to the breakfast hall, and you'll have to wait there until the testing starts."

Frowning, Dannan shook his head. "Is there someplace I could practice while I wait, please?"

The first guard raised an eyebrow at him, while the second just shrugged. "I suppose as long as one of the teachers is there, you can practice at the sparring field. They aren't used on testing days, only the regular training fields are."

The other guard pulled his helmet back to scratch his head, revealing curly brown hair that sprung up immediately after getting some room. "Jordain is usually there at this hour. He shouldn't have any issue with watching over a boy like this. Go ask him, Lucile."

The first guard nodded and motioned for Dannan to follow him. "I'll be back shortly, Tohmas. Just don't get into any trouble."

Tohmas grinned and flicked his nose at Lucile. "I'll be fine even without a whiner like you around to scare the enemies off." Dannan looked at both of them, glad that he hadn't chosen a school where they were too aloof.

As they walked through the gate, Dannan noticed a portcullis slot at the top, and saw a lever off to the side a little ways, allowing the guards to drop it quickly if need be.

From the inside, the compound looked even more like a keep. The walls seemed of uniform height and length, with crenelations on top to fire arrows through, and even a small ballista at each of the corner towers. Although compared to the town it looked small, Dannan was surprised at how spacious it was. There seemed to be enough room in the keep for a training field, a number of buildings, and possibly more fields at the back.

Following the guard further down the road, he saw that the main building dominated the center of the keep, while to the left side there were several dormitories. To the right there was a stable, with horses just starting to be prepped for their daily exercise, and a smithy that was already ringing with the sounds of hammers. As they approached closer to the main building, he saw past it, noting that there were indeed more fields on the other side.

When they finally got up to the entrance, Dannan turned his attention to the building itself. While the building was devoid of ornamentation, as far as practicality went, it was perfect. A single shield, each similar the one that hung over the front gate, decorated the sides of the doorway. Through the solid steel doors that hung open, plain hallways could be seen leading in several directions from a small antechamber, with the occasional tapestry breaking the monotony.

Moving through the halls behind the guard, for a little while Dannan felt intimidated, wondering how many Swordmasters had walked these stone halls before. Passing multiple wooden doors, he counted the metal numbers on each door as they passed by. As they approached another steel door that led out to what appeared to be a field with a number of dueling rings set up, a tapestry to his right caught his eye. Stopping, Dannan let out a gasp, trying to figure out what it meant.

Stepping out the door, the guard noticed that he was no longer being followed, and turned back. Grinning, he looked up at the tapestry with a mixture of pride and sadness. "That's Samust Nellinson, one of the greatest would-be Swordmasters to come from these halls since the inception of The Hawk's Honor. During the war, it was said that he turned back a barbarian raid of twenty by himself. That tapestry was created and given to us to celebrate that."

Dannan stared at the tapestry, then started running, taking off the way they had come. Although he heard the guard shouting after him, it barely registered as he ran out of the building. Students looked at him as he sprinted past, but he didn't care as he left the compound, running for the wagon yard.

Because of the crowds that had started to form, it took Dannan longer to get back to the wagon yard. When he finally did, he saw that the last goods were being loaded onto the wagons, and the drivers were finishing hooking up the horses.

Darting from wagon to wagon, he didn't see Samust anywhere among them, and for a moment, he wondered if Samust had left ahead of the caravan. As he passed by the last one, Dannan saw Samust emerge from the barracks, his pack over his shoulder.

Spotting Dannan, a resigned look came over his face.

Samust approached him, stopping several feet away. They stood there silently for a minute, the bustle around them seeming as if in a separate world. Scowling, Dannan took a deep breath, and suddenly realized he wasn't even sure what he wanted to say.

Although he thought he had gotten to know Samust fairly well, thinking back he realized he had met the man less than a week ago. What right did he have to judge?

Seeing the look on his face, Samust let out a sigh and shook his head. "So you found out then?" Dannan nodded slowly, trying to make his expression neutral again. "I won't ask how you found out, or how much. I also won't tell you the story now. I don't think you'd appreciate the gravity of what I did. If I'm still around when you've become a Swordmaster though, you can find me here. I'll tell you then."

"I'll ask that until you become a Swordmaster though, you let me have my peace here. I stayed away a long time until people forgot, and now, I'm just a simple mercenary. I don't want anyone thinking otherwise."

Nodding again, Dannan looked around at the caravan in a new light before turning back to Samust. "Just promise that you'll tell me if you decide to leave town permanently. Please? Even if it's by messenger, since I know you don't want them to know you're here."

Samust smiled wistfully, and nodded. "Never thought I'd

have a kid before I got married." Samust said with a chuckle. Ruffling Dannan's hair, Samust gave him a slightly more relaxed smile, and nodded. "I will. Don't worry."

Dannan took a deep breath, then nodded, a weak smile on his face.

"For now, you had better head back though, don't you think? The sooner you start, the sooner you can work on becoming a good Swordmaster." Dannan bobbed his head, then gave Samust a quick hug.

Samust jumped in surprise, his shocked face drawing a few laughs from one of the drivers who could see them. Giving Dannan a few gentle pats on the back, he stepped back a little as Dannan let go. "Don't worry, I'm sure we'll see each other sooner than you think. Hell, if there's another war, much sooner. Until then, work hard."

Dannan hesitantly took a step back. "Go on, get moving." Samust said as he made a shooing motion with one hand. Dannan turned around and started running, stopping briefly at the gates to the yard to wave at Samust once more, before disappearing from sight. "Life just never gets dull." Samust muttered, chuckling as he loaded his gear onto his horse.

Dannan stood sheepishly before the two guards at the gate to The Hawk's Honor. They looked him over, curiosity and skepticism mixing in their eyes. Bowing deeply, Dannan did his best to look apologetic.

"So, do you mind telling us why you ran off?" The guard named Lucile said.

After a few moments of hesitation, Dannan nodded. "I realized that I had forgotten to thank the people at the caravan who had taken care of me, and they'll be leaving town right in the middle of the sparring tests."

Looking at each other, the guards shrugged. "Alright, well, I'll take you back to the sparring field, then, since the test will take place in an hour or so. You'll be waiting with the others taking the test. As long as you don't get in their way, you can practice to your heart's content."

Dannan nodded and started following the guard again, no less awed by the compound, but this time sensing a grittiness to everything. The training ground in front was occupied as they passed this time, and Dannan watched with barely disguised envy as a group of about twenty students went through their sword drills.

Following the guard into the building once more, he looked at the door numbers again, seeing that these were in the mid-forties. He wondered just how many were in the building, and hoped he would be able to stay and find out.

When they finally passed the tapestry of Samust, Dannan lowered his eyes to avoid looking at it, his thoughts a jumbled mess.

Stepping out into the bright sunlight, Dannan had to shield his eyes with a hand to see. Looking around, he saw a number of other kids about his age, as well as several adults. Lowering his hand as his eyes adjusted, he looked at the guard, who was already heading back towards the front gate.

Turning towards the sparring field again, he realized that several people were looking at him, and he quickly retreated to a spot near the building away from anyone else. Setting his back against the wall, he looked around, seeing that a few of the others had started to warm up. Taking a deep breath, Dannan moved so he was about ten feet from the wall, and drew his sword slowly. As he began his regular exercises, he found it calmed him, and made it easier to concentrate.

He quickly lost track of time like this, and when he finally stopped swinging, he found that his breath was coming in pants. Sheathing his sword, he wiped his forehead dry on his sleeve, and was startled to see someone less than a half dozen feet from him to his right.

The man's brown hair was tinged with gray, and his hazel eyes looked like they could pierce steel. He was wearing a simple outfit made from cotton, with a small insignia on the collar of his vest. Although the spring was cool, Dannan still thought that the pants and shirt would have been enough without the vest.

Looking at his weather beaten face, Dannan suddenly realized the man was examining him, and had been for at least a few minutes. Turning bright red, Dannan gave him a small bow, unsure of what to do under the intense gaze of this total stranger.

After a few moments, the man nodded at him, then walked towards the center of the dueling circles. Dannan followed the man with his eyes, noticing briefly that several racks of practice swords had been brought out while he was concentrating on his sword work.

Glancing around, he saw that several of the others here for

the test were already paired up in dueling rings, though no one had started yet. Two other adults in outfits similar to the older man's were standing in the center of the area where he had walked to. Dannan guessed that they must be the judges. Looking back at the older man, Dannan noticed that he was being motioned towards one of the rings to the left.

Nodding, he headed for the practice swords, picking one up as he went by. Stopping momentarily in front of the judges, he removed his sheath from his belt, and gently set the sword and bedroll in the dirt at their feet.

Walking to the ring, he found that his opponent was one of the adults who had come earlier. For the first time, Dannan realized that several dozen more had come while he had not been paying attention as he faced towards the building.

He hadn't noticed at first, but seeing how wide a berth they had given him, he wondered what kind of impression they had. Shaking his head a little, he looked at his opponent, a man in his late twenties most likely. His copper hair was cut short, and he wore the garb of a trader's guard from the south, with the tan colored wool only slightly lighter than his bronzed skin.

Giving him a nod, Dannan wondered at first if the man would complain about having a child as an opponent. Meeting the man's gaze quickly convinced Dannan this wasn't the case though.

Shrugging, Dannan decided that might be for the best, since he didn't want to win because his opponent was careless. Letting the practice sword rest by his side, he watched the judges as everyone else was doing. It took another minute or so while they waited for the last four dueling rings to be filled. After they had filled those rings, the older man, who appeared to be the leader, raised his hand over his head for silence.

A hush quickly fell over those taking the test, and Dannan watched as the man slowly lowered his hand back down.

"We will announce the rules only once, so pay attention." Running his gaze over each and every one of them, the man seemed comfortable commanding large groups of people, and the steel in his voice said he was used to being obeyed as well.

"We will not be testing based on victory or defeat. Winners may lack what it takes to make a true Swordmaster, and losers may still have the qualities to be smelted into fine weapons. We are only interested in the quality of your swordsmanship, your ability to handle yourself, and your ability to deal with an opponent. All you have to do is show us every bit of skill you have. That is the only condition for success here today."

Taking a moment to make sure it sank in, he continued. "The conditions of a loss are as follows; if you leave the ring, you will be dismissed. If you kill your opponent, you will be dismissed, and, depending on the circumstances, brought to the town guard. If you take five solid hits to anywhere on your body, you will have lost the match, and must stop. If you surrender, you have will have lost the match, and must stop. If you are rendered unconscious, you will have lost the match. Disobeying the decision of a judge to continue or stop will result in dismissal."

Surveying the gathered entrants, his gaze occasionally stopped on someone as he pronounced each rule, the force behind his words like an executioner's axe. "We three judges will oversee each match, and when these first sixteen are finished, we will choose the fighters for the next sixteen. Until then, those on the sidelines are to wait patiently, and watch. You might learn something by doing so."

With that, the main judge nodded to the other two, and each went to a different ring. Dannan couldn't help but notice the main judge walking straight for his ring, and his stomach sank as he realized he would be one of the first to be tested.

Looking at his opponent, he saw that the man hadn't expected to be tested immediately either, but that he quickly fell into a readied stance. Taking a deep breath, Dannan took his stance as well, watching the man across from him. Concentrating, Dannan let the ring become his whole world.

"Begin." When the judge spoke, it seemed like it was from far away. Gazing into the eyes of the man across from him, Dannan calmly took a step forward, raising his sword. As his opponent lunged, Dannan wondered for a moment if he really thought that he could hit anyone moving that slowly.

Stepping forward again, Dannan brought his sword up quickly, deflecting the man's practice sword to the side. In response, his opponent spun, bringing his sword around at Dannan's head height. Looking at the sweeping motion, for a moment Dannan tensed his muscles to strike his foe in the back, but then decided against it.

Ducking down, he found that he was definitely much faster, and he listened to the sound his opponent's sword made as it harmlessly cut the air. Sweeping his sword in an upward stroke with both hands, Dannan felt some resistance as it struck against the man's outstretched forearm. Feeling the shiver along the wood as it tried to push through, Dannan suddenly jumped back, holding the sword sideways in front of him.

Staring down at the wood in surprise, Dannan was almost caught off guard by his opponent, who had leaped after him.

Deflecting several quick blows from the man, who was now only using one hand, Dannan tried to process what had just happened. As his opponent stabbed forward again, Dannan slid past and grabbed his foe's practice sword with one hand, making a small tug as if to pull it out from the man's grasp.

As his opponent jerked backwards to maintain a hold on the sword, Dannan released it and pushed forward with his sword positioned sideways, knocking his foe to the ground.

Moving back, Dannan took a moment again to look at his sword, when he finally realized what that feeling had been. He looked on as his opponent stood up, and wondered if the man's left arm was broken.

From the way he was holding it, Dannan guessed that it probably wasn't, but that the man wouldn't be able to use it again soon. Waiting patiently, Dannan continued watching his foe as he stood there, his sword slightly relaxed. The man began to circle him slowly, gripping his sword in one fist.

Although the man wasn't showing many outward signs of stress on his face, Dannan noticed from the corner of his eye that his opponent's knuckles were a stark white against the brown wood of the practice sword. Taking another deep breath, Dannan held his sword a little tighter and stepped towards the man again, raising the sword in a cross-block in front of him.

As the man started his swing, Dannan ducked forward, his practice sword angled to take the blow head on. Although his opponent could only use one arm, the man's swing was still enough to send a shudder through Dannan's arms and bring him up short.

Planting his feet, Dannan threw his weight forward, knocking the man's sword from his grasp, and out of the ring. Stepping in, he rapped the man across the ribs lightly three times before taking several steps back. Letting his practice sword fall to his side, he watched as the man stood there for a moment, apparently surprised at having no major wounds. "You have lost. You may leave."

Chapter 17

The judge's voice brought Dannan back to reality. Looking over at the judge, Dannan wondered for a moment which of them he was talking to.

Turning to follow the judge's gaze, he saw that the other man, now infuriated, had gone to pick up his practice sword. "Leave it, and leave. You have no need to think about it further." The man grabbed the practice sword and whirled, letting out a yell before charging towards Dannan.

Looking at the judge, Dannan waited, unsure of what he should do. Sighing, the judge met Dannan's eyes and gave him a small nod before crossing his arms.

Dropping his stance even lower than usual, Dannan gripped his sword in both hands, waiting until the man was almost on top of him. As the man's sword began to fall in a downward arc, Dannan jumped to the right, bringing his sword in sideways across his opponent's stomach. Letting out a loud, pained cough, the sword fell from the man's hands and he clutched his side, dropping to his knees with a soft thump.

Waiting a few moments, Dannan picked up the fallen practice sword and walked over to the judge, ignoring the man on his knees. Stopping in front of the judge, Dannan held both of the practice swords at arm's length.

Shaking his head, the judge motioned for Dannan to put the two swords back himself. Letting his head droop a little, Dannan set them both on the rack before he retrieved his own sword.

Grabbing his bedroll, he turned to leave when the judge called out to him "You're going the wrong way! The dorms are that way." Dannan turned and looked back at the judge, who was pointing off to Dannan's left. "Your full name?"

"Dannan Bellmen, sir."

"Report promptly to the waiting room in the first student's dorm, Dannan. You will wait there until the tests are over and the judges come to inform you of the next step. Understood?" Nodding eagerly, Dannan rushed off in the direction the judge had pointed, following several others he could see walking towards the same place.

Dannan slowed down as he approached the plain stone dormitory, hesitating as he looked at the open doors. Taking a deep breath, he walked into the two-story building, and immediately found himself inside a large waiting room.

There was a doorway on each side of the room leading further in, and a multitude of wooden chairs sat facing the entrance. Three others had arrived ahead of him, and were already seated. The first was a man of about twenty, whose platinum blonde hair would have made him stand out even in a crowd. The scars along his bare arms spoke to the number of fights he had been in, and his chiseled features made the walls seem soft.

The other two were about Dannan's age, and appeared to be close brothers. Each had hazel brown hair and green eyes, a combination that Dannan thought looked a little unusual. Although they didn't seem like they had a great deal of battle experience, Dannan had to remind himself that up until a few fortnights ago, he didn't either.

Sitting off to one side away from the others, Dannan did his best not to stare. At the same time, he was very curious about everything going on at this point. The two brothers didn't hesitate to stare at him, though, and he heard them whispering softly from where they sat towards the back.

It seemed like a lifetime before the next person came into the waiting room. Dannan was surprised to see it was a young woman, as he hadn't known they accepted women as students. Her brown hair hung down to her shoulders, and although she wasn't mature yet, she still had a very womanly figure. Her eyes were a dark blue, and the hard look that filled them was more similar to that of an experienced soldier than a trainee.

Dannan had to resist the urge to sigh as he turned away, making sure to avoid her gaze. "Why is it that I wound up in the same group as all the trained soldiers?" He muttered to himself.

"Well, no matter what group you're in, you'll find skilled people. Isn't it the same with you?" Dannan nearly leaped out of his seat as he heard the soft voice behind him. Spinning around, he saw that the blonde man had moved so he was sitting behind Dannan to the left, and he had leaned forward a little to whisper.

Sitting back, the blonde relaxed into his chair again, his arms crossed in front of him. Looking at the other three sheepishly as they stared at him, Dannan sat back down, his face bright red with embarrassment. "I suppose every group will have skilled people. But what do you mean it's the same as with me?"

The blonde chuckled a little. "Surely you're joking. You're one of the better ones that will be in this group. Everyone else has noticed it, to. With the number of years you've been training, you must be confident in your skills."

Looking down, Dannan shook his head. "I've been training less than a quarter of a year. I'm not confident at all." He said softly.

His eyes going wide, the blonde made a derisive snort. "I don't believe you. No one has skills like that after only a few months."

Dannan's smile turned sheepish again. "I practice a great deal. But that's all."

"Oh, you mean like the half an hour or so before the spars started?" Dannan nodded, ducking his head a little to try and hide his ever-growing embarrassment. "I came in about half an hour to noon, that's how I know. You were already completely in a trance while swinging your sword, and you didn't seem to notice anyone. Not even when the judge walked up to you."

Sitting there quietly, Dannan wished he could sink out of sight. "Well, that should prove it, then. I'm not very good. You should have been able to tell from my practice swings."

Chuckling again, the blonde shook his head. "Oh no. You're definitely skilled. That's what I got from watching you practice. And I certainly believe that you practice like mad."

Dannan shrugged. "Well, I needed to get better, so I practiced. Isn't that what everyone does?"

Shaking his head in amusement, the blonde just smiled. Suddenly, a look of surprise came over his face, and he grinned. "Sorry, I forgot to introduce myself. The name is Tannil. It's been a while since I've been in decent company, and you tend to forget your manners out in the field."

Tannil held out his hand, and Dannan shook it firmly. "Dannan. I'm from the town to the west of Whitehaven. Woodslock isn't very big, but its home."

"Hey, anyplace you can call home is someplace special. Plenty of mercenaries like me without homes, or even someplace that would let them put down roots. That's why being a Swordmaster is the best. Nothing like the stigma of being a mercenary."

Looking stone ceiling, a thoughtful expression crossed Dannan's face. "No stigma, huh…"

Tannil gave him a curious look. "There's still stigma to it, I'd say. Anyone who's afraid of a sword will still be afraid of the wielder, whether he's a good person or a bad one. It's just the nature of battle."

Dannan looked back at Tannil, shaking his head. "No, people are only afraid when they think something will happen to them. That's nature. People are still afraid of a 'good' man because they worry he's not like them. And if he's not like them, what if he decides that they are 'bad'? That wouldn't end well for them."

Raising an eyebrow, Tannil looked at Dannan, and for a moment, Dannan thought he might have said too much. All of a sudden, Tannil burst out laughing, and slapped Dannan hard on the back. "I'm the hardened mercenary, and you're the cynical one! Oh, but this is going to be a fun place!"

"I'm not cynical, just realistic." Dannan muttered under his breath. Turning away, he tried hard to ignore the others as they stared at the pair, and shook his head.

They waited for what must have been a few more hours, with a new person coming in every so often. By the time the main judge came in, there were ten of them seated there. Looking around at the empty chairs, Dannan estimated that they had only filled about one fifth of the seats. Shaking his head, he couldn't decide if that was a good sign, or a bad one.

Suddenly, the judge cleared his throat, and Dannan's eyes were drawn back to him. "Look closely at the people around you. These are the students who you will spend most of your time training with. Each class has ten to twenty students normally, and this one is no exception. You will spend approximately eight years as a student, assuming you are successful. What you do after that is up to you, though many take a noble as a patron and serve him for a number of years, before once again searching for battle."

Looking among them, the man's eyes held a glint that hadn't been there before. "And trust me, you will seek battle again, even in times of peace. Only those who seek war in its many forms ever try to become Swordmasters. Whatever their outward reason is, what isn't discussed is the lust for battle. I have taught here as a member of The Hawk's Honor for almost thirty years now, and I plan to finish teaching at least one more class. As for how that affects you? I will be your teacher and mentor for the next eight years... for those of you who keep up."

He let that sink in, the slight menace in his voice obvious. "It is not uncommon for those who cannot find the effort to leave, or for those who are afraid to run away. However, I will make sure that those of you who remain are among the strongest when it comes to sword techniques, and that every one of you will be prepared for at least the basic situations of war. Now, do any of you have any questions before I continue?"

Dannan watched as the teacher's steely gaze went over each of them, like a smith searching for impurities in the metal. After a moment, Tannil cleared his throat. "What about living quarters, meals, things like that? I'm assuming we're living here in the compound, but how does that restrict our movements?"

Looking Tannil up and down, the teacher waited a moment or two, as if appraising the blonde man, and nodded. "Your name?"

"Tannil, Sir. Formerly of the Wolves Brigade in the northern mountains."

Smiling, the teacher nodded approvingly. "You have some good mercenary experience under your belt then, Tannil. As to your question, yes, you will live in this dorm. For the first four years, at least. After four years, the entire class will be moved into the senior dorms. Do not believe the titles mean a thing about age, though. There are those in the senior dorm who have yet to see their fifteenth birthday, but in terms of ability, most of them are better swordsmen than you."

"And you will respect them as your seniors, even if they are half your age. There will come a time in every Swordmaster's life where they will have to deal with taking orders from someone younger than them and less experienced. For those times, it is necessary that every Swordmaster knows exactly how it feels, so that they are able to objectively advise in battle. Whether it is a noble's child, or a general seeing his first major battle, we will be there. That is why every single one of you will be prepared."

Stopping, he made sure they had absorbed what he said

before continuing. "You will be provided with three meals a day, assuming you show up for them. That is your responsibility. The mess hall is located at the back of the dorm. You will also be able to obtain two outfits per season of the appropriate quality. No matter how good you are as a Swordmaster, if you freeze to death in the winter, you're useless. Those you can obtain from the quartermaster, who maintains an office next to the supply room in the headquarters. Any clothes you brought with you or that you buy yourself you may keep in your dorm rooms."

A wry smile crossed his face. "I hope you like meeting new people, because each of you will share a room with one other student, depending on the number in each class. Most likely, you will each be sharing a room with someone from a different class, but it is not unheard of for classmates to wind up in the same room. Unless you have a serious issue with a bunk mate, you will spend the next four years with them. So get used to it, quick."

Scratching his chin, the teacher looked thoughtful for a moment. "The last part of your question was... Ah, yes. Movement restrictions. You will all practice daily. Every seventh day you will be allowed into town in the afternoon, but for the rest of the week, you must stay inside the compound. You will be briefed in the first week of each year on what classes you will be studying for the coming year. This first year you will study armor. You will learn the theories behind using it, the skills to effectively use each type of armor properly, and the skills to make your opponent's armor useless. You will also have the option to learn how to make it from our resident blacksmith. Some of our best armorers have come from our own ranks." After saying this, it seemed as if he expected some response.

After no response was forthcoming, however, he continued on. "You will find your room numbers, the names of those in your class and other classes, and the names of the teachers all posted in the mess hall. Are there any other questions?" Silence filled the room for several long moments, and he nodded. "Dismissed to your rooms, then. If you need to leave the grounds for any reason from now on, you will be escorted by a guardsman."

Chapter 18

With a nod, the teacher left down the hall to Dannan's right, which he assumed led towards the teacher's own room. Dannan stood slowly, looking at the others. After a moment, he shrugged slightly as he headed for the hallway that led towards the back of the dorm. He heard the movement of chairs as the others stood, and he found that Tannil was right behind him as he entered the hallway.

Smiling slightly back at him, Dannan was glad that while he might not have made a friend, he had at least met someone friendly. As they walked through the halls, Dannan couldn't help but notice the numbers carved into each door. "Forty four... Forty five..." He heard Tannil murmur softly behind him.

"If the highest numbered doors are downstairs, do you think that means the rest of the rooms are upstairs?"

Tannil nodded, though none of the others seemed to pay attention to the question. Turning his attention forward again, Dannan found that it was another forty or fifty feet to the large double doors that led to the mess hall, and there were more doors along the way.

Stepping through the open doors, Dannan was surprised to find a good number of students already inside the mess hall. Looking around nervously, he waited for a moment, unsure of what to do, when Tannil stepped in behind him, his heavier boots clicking on the stone floor. The students talking in the mess hall immediately went silent and turned towards the newcomers, and Dannan felt like he was the object of all their stares.

Cringing, he wished he could hide behind someone, or at least towards the back, when he felt a hand on his shoulder. Looking back, Dannan relaxed a little as Tannil gave him a small wink. Walking towards one of the empty tables near the entrance, Tannil pulled out one of the chairs surrounding the circular table, sitting down heavily.

Dannan held his breath. Tannil definitely seemed more relaxed than Dannan felt. As if Tannil making the first move had broken some sort of stalemate, the talking in the mess hall resumed, and the other students turned back to their food and friends quickly. Dannan hastily walked over to sit next to Tannil, trying not to look too nervous, or too confident.

Pulling out a chair, he sat down quickly, his body posture so stiff he wondered if he wasn't giving off the wrong impression. He noticed the others following them at a much more leisurely pace, and sighed. Several sat at the empty table adjacent to them, while the two brothers and the girl sat at their table. Dannan looked at the two brothers for a moment, watching them as they looked at Tannil, then him.

Turning to look at the girl, he found she was glaring at him, and he had to resist the urge to sit back. "Do you have a problem with me?!"

Dannan shook his head, wondering how it had gotten so bad so quickly, and turned as he heard Tannil start laughing. "Cool it there, little lady. We might not be friends, but we certainly aren't enemies. We don't know that we can say the same of our senior classmates. After all, some people are in here for more than just training."

He relaxed as she turned her glare on Tannil, and Tannil chuckled, holding up his hands as if to ward off a blow. "Alright, alright. I take back the 'little lady' part. But I wasn't joking about the fact that although we're training here, we don't know what reasons get someone dismissed from the compound. Competition is probably pretty fierce, and hazing is also very likely, I imagine."

"You'll have noticed, I'm sure, that there are only three other women here. That puts more pressure on you, obviously. I'm sure that's part of what makes your personality like a porcupine." Tannil winked at Dannan as he said the last part.

Dannan felt a twinge of nervousness, wondering if Tannil was going to get him into trouble, then decided it didn't matter. At least he'd know he had someone on his side. A shadow suddenly fell over the back of Dannan's chair, and he spun quickly, his hand going to the hilt of his sword.

A young man, probably just past the age of fifteen, stood over him, arms crossed. His black hair and pale skin seemed to contrast sharply with each other, and his blue eyes had the look of a hunting beast. Staring up at him, for a moment Dannan considered drawing his sword before the boy had a chance to attack, when suddenly he felt a hand on his shoulder.

"Now now Dannan, no need to be jumpy, even if it is the fault of our senior. I'm sure he didn't mean any harm. Right?" Tannil said quietly. The second part of that sentence, obviously aimed at the young man, drew his attention away from Dannan.

Releasing the hilt, Dannan let out a sigh as he felt the pressure leave him. After a few moments of glaring at Tannil, the boy turned and walked away, other students avoiding him as he made his way out of the mess hall. Dannan hadn't even realized that the conversations near them had stopped until they started up again, and he relaxed back into his chair.

"Thanks, Tannil. I was really worried there for a moment." Tannil patted him on the back, then sat forward, leaning his elbows on the table.

"Don't worry about it. Like I said, it's important to have each others backs in here. Remember what the teacher said, about everyone being here for 'war', after all. That can also mean to fight stronger opponents, not just fight in full-scale wars. And while I have confidence in my swordsmanship, I don't think I can beat the best out there. Which is why I came to learn."

Rubbing his eyes, Dannan sighed. "I liked living in the woods more. Bears will just try to kill you and eat you if they're hungry, but people will do it just because."

Dannan looked over at the sound of a girl's laugh, and saw her trying to hold in her laughter. "So you're a country bumpkin, then?!" She said, unable to contain her mirth any longer.

"If you mean I grew up in the country, then yes. But let me ask you this. Could you survive a week in the wilderness by yourself? Two? A month?" She looked at him uncomfortably as he spoke, and then looked away. "Just because you're older doesn't mean you've got a better chance of survival. And for where I want to end up, I'm going to need it." They all looked at him, and Dannan shut his mouth, worried he might say too much if he kept talking.

Tannil had no problem filling the conversation gap, telling them stories of the five campaigns he had already been in up north. Dannan listened halfheartedly to all the conversation, doing his best to pay attention while staying out of it at the same time.

Finally, as dinner wound down, a woman wearing the same

plain wool outfit as their teacher came into the mess hall. Using a hammer and some nails she produced from her vest, she posted a small piece of vellum to a board next to the doorway. Really noticing it for the first time, Dannan realized there were numerous other pieces, all with writing on them. Immediately after she had finished posting it, she glanced around at the gathered students, then turned and left without a word.

Dannan waited until the conversation had died down a little, then stood and walked straight for the board. The others looked at him as he stood, following him to the board with their eyes. Tannil followed him after a moment, and for a second, Dannan wanted to laugh. Tannil had said that he was nine years older, and yet Dannan kept leading the way.

Well, the teacher had said things would be different here. Now he just had to get used to how different. Wondering for a moment if being at the front was a bad thing, Dannan sighed to himself.

Stopping in front of the board, Dannan saw that there were five pieces of vellum in total, one for each class year, and one for the teachers. Looking at the piece that had their names on it, he glanced over the others, noticing that he and Tannil were sharing a room. Hearing someone directly behind him, he turned slightly, seeing Tannil grinning at him. "Well, at least we know we won't have to deal with annoying roommates. That's some relief."

Dannan grinned wryly, and nodded. "Shall we go see the room? Since apparently we won't get to eat until breakfast."

Tannil nodded, glancing at the others who were behind them, and chuckled. "Do you know where the stairway up is?"

Dannan shook his head, exhaustion overwhelming what little embarrassment he felt. "All I know is someone else should, and I want to get to sleep."

Tannil chuckled, then looked at their classmates. "Does anyone know where the stairway to the second floor is?"

One of the boys that had come in later, who was a much darker blonde than Tannil, nodded. "It's out of the mess hall that way." The boy pointed towards the doorway off to their left.

Nodding, Tannil grinned at Dannan. "See? Not hard at all. All you have to do is ask." Shaking his head, Dannan wasn't sure whether to laugh or sigh.

"Alright, let's go, then." Dannan started walking for the open doors, following the edge of the room so as to avoid walking too close to the older students. He wasn't sure if they were all like the one who had come up behind him. Now that he had noticed he was tired, however, it only seemed to make the idea of dealing with them worse. As he left the mess hall, he wondered if dealing with the senior trainees would always be like this.

The hallway from the mess hall to the second floor was much shorter than the hallway that came from the waiting room. Dannan noticed there were fewer doors in this corridor, as well. When he mentioned it, Tannil just shrugged. "Probably to make it more defensible. That's all."

Dannan grunted, continuing down the corridor until they hit a small corner staircase that led to the second floor. Although it was wide enough for two people to walk abreast, it felt quite cramped.

Torches shone down the staircase, and as Dannan walked up he wondered whether there were any windows on the second floor. As he reached the top of the stairs, Dannan paused momentarily. He looked down the two halls that met there, unsure of which way to go. "We're in room twenty one, Tannil. With the size of the floor, how many rooms do you think are up here?"

Staring down each hall, Tannil looked lost in thought for a moment, before pointing down the hallway to their right. "There are probably thirty or so rooms up here. I'm going to guess that we should go that way." Dannan nodded, and motioned for Tannil to lead the way.

After a second, Tannil laughed and started off. "What, tired of being in front?" Dannan's cheeks colored and he shook his head.

He was glad that with the shadows the torches cast, it would be less obvious. "I didn't mean to. It's just that no one else was going, and I didn't want to stay in the waiting room or the mess hall for too long. I'm uncomfortable around people."

Tannil laughed and shook his head. "It's alright, I'm just joking. There's nothing wrong with being uncomfortable around crowds." Dannan shrugged, following a few steps behind Tannil as they turned a corner and started down another hallway. "Here we are." Tannil pointed at a door with a metal twenty one nailed to the front. Pushing the door open, Tannil grabbed a torch from next to the door and stepped inside.

Dannan followed after a moment, waiting until Tannil had lit a candle using a flare stick that was sitting on a small table. Dannan held the door as Tannil replaced the torch back in the bracket next to the door, and surveyed the small room. It was about ten feet by ten feet, with two cots, a trunk at the foot of each, and a small stand table with a candle in between them. A drawer in the front of the stand table held two dozen flare sticks, and both trunks were completely empty. The cots were similarly barren, with a single blanket and a pillow on each, and no mattress or straw.

Sitting down on it, Dannan sighed, longing momentarily for the comfortable bed back at his parent's house. Setting his bedroll and sword on top of the trunk, he laid out on the bed, letting out another sigh. "Well, making a room like this is one way to make sure that the students stay outside. I imagine there are practical reasons to, but gods, it will take some getting used to."

Tannil laughed, then sat down on his own cot. "I've had worse. This is still preferable to sleeping outside in the rain and snow."

Dannan looked over at him, then shook his head. "I'd rather sleep outside. Even if it was in the rain. Maybe not the snow. But I like being able to see the stars at night, and animals are a great early warning system. If the forest is too quiet or too loud, then you know something's happening. Could we even hear fighting downstairs from up here?"

Tannil shook his head. "From what I've seen of these walls, we wouldn't hear a thing. I imagine they've got an alarm system of some sort to make up for that, though. You could probably still hear the town alarm bells, as well. Though I doubt we'd be involved. We'd probably be the last ones they pulled to fight, since we're just trainees."

Dannan shrugged in agreement, rolling onto his side facing the wall. "I'm going to get some sleep. I'll see you in the morning, alright, Tannil?" He assumed from the lack of response that Tannil agreed with him, and a few minutes later, the snoring confirmed it.

Reaching into his shirt, he gently took hold of the dragon scale, holding it tightly in his hand. The pulse that he felt through it was reassuring, and he couldn't help but feel a bit of elation that he had been accepted. "Wait for me… I'm on my way." He murmured softly, as sleep wrapped itself around him like a warm blanket.

Chapter 19

As Dannan slowly awoke to the darkness, he wondered at first if it was morning at all. Waiting until his eyes adjusted, he remembered finding their room, and falling asleep to the sound of Tannil's snores. Sitting up, he heard Tannil before he saw him, smiling at the snores of his still sleeping friend.

Shaking his head, he remembered that he had just met Tannil, and until he knew him better, it was best just to treat him as a possible enemy. Standing up carefully, he walked to the door. He opened it slowly, unable to remember if it creaked or not.

He let his breath out quietly when it didn't, not even realizing he had been holding it. Stepping into the corridor, he shut the door softly behind him, and he turned as he heard footsteps from down the hallway. Looking over, he saw another student, a little older than him, walking in his direction.

Standing back against the wall, Dannan waited until the older boy was past him, when suddenly the boy stopped a few feet away. "I haven't met you yet, so I'm assuming you're new. My name's Wyatt. I'm in my fourth year here, under Teacher Matthias. Breakfast will be served soon, and if you feel like it, you might want to hit the bath house behind the dorm. Just a tip; stay away from the girl's bath house. The teachers will punish you for causing trouble, and it will hurt."

Nodding meekly, Dannan didn't look up. After a few moments, he finally looked up, wondering why the boy hadn't walked away yet. Staring back at him, the boy's eyes were kind but firm. Dannan couldn't make out much in the dusk-like darkness of the hallway, but he could tell the boy was about a foot taller than him. "Don't lower your eyes to anyone. You're training to be a Swordmaster. That's something that no one can take away from you. And cowardice and subservience aren't things they teach here at The Hawk's Honor." Dannan nodded again, meeting his gaze without saying a word. After a few moments, Wyatt smiled slightly, and then started back down the hallway again, in the direction of the stairs.

Opening the door gently, Dannan looked over at where Tannil was still sleeping, and gently rapped a knuckle against the door a few times. "Tannil, they said it's near to breakfast time."

Soft muttering came from under the blanket, and after a moment or two Tannil stirred. "Why's it so dark in here?"

"We forgot to put out the candle before we fell asleep last night. And it doesn't seem like they replace many of the torches in the hallway except when night is coming."

Muttering, Tannil stood up, and Dannan heard the thunk of a leg striking wood. Cursing, Tannil walked up to Dannan, letting out a yawn. "Well? Why are we still standing here. There's food to be had!" Dannan chuckled and moved aside, letting Tannil walk past him, and shut the door as they started walking away.

"I see the cot didn't bother you as much as you complained it would." Shaking his head, Tannil stretched a little as they reached the stairs. "As much as it feels like a dungeon in here, it wasn't so bad, since we didn't get woken by a guard, after all. Ha ha."

Dannan smiled at his comment. "That would have been worse, yeah."

When they finally entered the mess hall, Dannan was suddenly blinded by sunlight. Covering his eyes, he waited until they had adjusted, and then looked to his right, where a large set of double doors stood open.

Sunlight streamed in from over the compound walls, and for a moment Dannan wondered how beautiful the sunrise must be from up there. Shaking his head, he saw that Tannil had already headed towards the cook, who was ladling some kind of soup out to students as they passed by. Dannan noticed that on a small cart, halves of bread sat, with each student taking one under the watchful eye of a cook's assistant.

Hurrying after Tannil, Dannan caught up before the students crowding together managed to get in between them. He had to resist the urge to grab onto the back of Tannil's vest to hold on, and simply pushed forward behind him, getting jostled as he went.

Finally, they reached the cook, who handed them each a bowl which she filled with soup. Staring at it for a moment, Dannan couldn't figure out what was in it, when the cook yelled at him to move on. Shaken from his thoughts, Dannan hurried after Tannil again, grabbing his portion of bread as he went by.

Following Tannil to a seat towards the far end of the mess hall, they both sat, grabbing wooden spoons from the center of the table. Dipping the spoon into the soup, Dannan swirled it around a little, trying once again to figure out what was in it. He heard Tannil munching away, and looked at the smug grin he was wearing. "What, the poor little baby is afraid of what might be in the soup?"

Grimacing, Dannan quickly started eating, glad to find that there seemed to be nothing other than noodles, carrots, and a few other vegetables. Chuckling, Tannil shook his head. "This isn't bad fare, compared to what you might eat in the field." Looking over at him from his bowl, Dannan raised an eyebrow. "Well, when you're in the field, at least in the north, you basically only eat what you can catch. There are noodles and other rations, but you usually save those for when you can't catch things. Of course, another reason you try to catch things is because after two weeks straight of salted jerky, you hope the enemy will be kind and put you out of your misery." Tannil ended with a laugh, and Dannan just shook his head.

"Are all mercenaries crazy, or just you? Or the Wolf Brigade?"

"Wolves Brigade. There is a difference. Slight, but there is one."

Cocking his head to the side, Dannan waited for him to elaborate. When it didn't seem like he would, Dannan coughed slightly. Tannil looked at him, raising an eyebrow. "Choke on some soup?" Dannan glowered at him.

"What's the difference between the Wolf Brigade, and the Wolves Brigade?" Tannil looked at him, and chuckled.

"Isn't it obvious? There's no 'ves' on the end of 'wolf.'" Dannan let out an exasperated sigh and bit off a chunk of his bread, shaking his head again.

"If I ever get used to your sense of humor, I'm going to get worried."

"You should. He sounds dumber than a goat when he makes jokes like that." Dannan and Tannil turned slightly, and saw the girl from their group approaching their table. Sitting down across from them, she set her soup and bread down, and grabbed a spoon.

Shrugging at each other, they watched her dig in voraciously, and Dannan opened his mouth to make a joke. Her glare quickly silenced him, and he shook his head, going back to eating quietly.

When he was finished with the soup, Dannan pushed his bowl a little forward, relaxing his chin on his arms as he leaned down on the table. "Hey Tannil, when did the teacher tell us we had to meet him for lessons? At noon?"

Tannil nodded, slurping up the last of his soup. "Yeah, but we have morning practice before that, remember?" Dannan shot up, almost knocking his chair over as he stood.

He looked around sheepishly as a number of people turned towards him, and sat down almost as quickly. "I totally forgot about that." He said sheepishly.

"We should probably head to the training fields after we finish with breakfast. You going to come with us, Carissa?" Tannil said, his tone concealing a smile. She turned towards him quickly and glared, almost as if she was seeing if she could will him dead. "Now now, your name was on the roster with all of ours. It's not like I had to dig up information on you, or something."

She kept glaring at him, causing Tannil to sigh and shrug. "Suit yourself. Well, ready to head over then, Dan?" Dannan looked over at him, unsure of his new nickname, then nodded.

"Alright. I'm all set with breakfast, so it can't hurt to go to the waiting room to check. Then we can see if we're supposed to meet at the training fields."

Tannil whacked him on the back, then grinned at Carissa. "See? Now there's someone with a head on his shoulders. Someone using it for something other than glaring, anyway." Tannil chuckled at the last bit and stood up, ignoring her continued glaring. Dannan followed suit, moving after Tannil as he quickly headed out of the mess hall and towards the waiting room.

The waiting room was empty except for two students who were walking out the front doors as Tannil and Dannan entered. Walking after them, they followed the pair at a discreet distance, trying to look like they knew where they were going.

After a short time, Dannan noticed a number of other students all heading in the same direction, and gently nudged Tannil. Tannil looked down at him, then glanced around. "It looks like everyone goes to the training fields at the same time in the morning. A good military regimen to beat into people. It'll serve us well in the long run, to."

Dannan nodded, and grimaced, suddenly noticing the difference in their heights. Although Dannan wasn't short for an eleven year old, at a little taller than four feet, he felt tiny next to Tannil, who was a little over six feet. Glancing at other students they passed, he noticed that Tannil was taller than them, as well, and wondered if it was because of where Tannil was from. Shaking his head to get rid of unnecessary thoughts, he decided he'd ask Tannil about it at a better time.

As they got close to the training fields, Dannan could see that many of the other students had already gathered there. He could see eight groups of students in total, ranging from the five of his classmates who were at the closest end, to the twelve waiting patiently that looked like they were in their last year. Behind the groups was a small shack with a large padlock on the door. Dannan and Tannil headed straight for their classmates, and as other students passed them, they heard snatches of conversation.

"…new blood, huh? Let's see how many make it to their second year."

"I'm betting none…" Dannan concentrated on trying not to listen, and wished that he could just block them all out.

A little while passed, and Carissa and two other boys Dannan vaguely recognized from yesterday joined them. Studying the others, for the first time Dannan noticed that Tannil was the only real adult among the group of them. Shrugging his shoulders, he decided it didn't matter.

Looking at the other groups, they were a more even mix. He wondered briefly if that brought more experience to the group, when his thoughts were interrupted by a loud whistle.

Turning to face forward, he saw that the teachers had all quietly walked to the front of their respective classes except for his. After a moment, Dannan saw something moving out of the corner of his eye, and he turned to see their teacher coming around the side to the front. Moving so he was standing in front of the class like the other teachers, he yelled out "Alright you lot. Class eight, get your practice swords!"

Dannan turned to look at the class mentioned, and saw the twelve of them and their teacher all head towards the shack. The padlock had been removed already, and the eighth class's teacher stepped inside.

A second later, practice swords came flying out to the left and right, and the students each caught them, waiting patiently to the side after they were armed. When the last student was holding a practice sword, the teacher walked out holding one as well.

As soon as they had returned to their position, the seventh class went, and then the sixth, though not every teacher threw the practice swords at their students. Finally, it was time for them to get their swords. They turned and followed the teacher to the shack, and Dannan heard some of the other students snickering. Glancing around, he quickly figured out that they were snickering at how unorganized his class was.

Where all the other groups had marched almost in unison, his class looked more like a small mob of people than a group. Shaking his head, he got the feeling this was another thing the older students would mock them for.

Each of them took a practice sword as it was handed back through the group. As soon as the teacher handed the tenth sword out, he closed the door behind him, and strode back towards their position.

They rushed after him as his long strides forced them to move quickly to keep up. After all the classes were back in position, the teachers took a stance with one foot slightly back, their dominant foot forward, and the sword gripped in both hands pointing forwards.

The sound of students shuffling into place filled the air, and Dannan quickly took the stance as well. Each student was about ten feet from the next, and Dannan glanced around, making sure he had enough room. He smiled momentarily to himself, remembering when his father had first shown him this practice stance, and he almost missed it as the teacher started to swing.

Dannan counted one hundred swings before they finally stopped, and although he heard the occasional pant from his classmates, the older classes seemed almost at ease.

Moving so they faced sideways, each teacher held their practice sword in their dominant hand, giving the students a few moments to catch up. As soon as they deemed the students ready enough, the teachers began to thrust straight ahead.

Dannan followed suit, but his attention was totally focused on their teacher. Each thrust was at chest height on an average man, perfectly suited for a stab straight through the heart. Every movement looked perfect, and if the thrusts were any more precise, Dannan was sure the teacher could have threaded a needle with the sword.

One hundred thrusts later, his arm was tired, even though he had barely been paying attention, so engrossed was he in watching the teacher. He could hear more panting coming from several of his classmates, and he was starting to feel the sweat on his own back as well.

Glancing to the side, he was glad to see that after two hundred the class next to them was starting to show signs of tiredness to. The teachers, some of whom were starting to sweat with the class, moved their arm so that the sword was facing sideways with their palm down. From this position, they began with a swiping motion, as if swinging a paint brush. Dannan had practiced this swing diagonally before, not across, but found that it used almost the exact same muscles.

Falling back into the rhythm of it, Dannan began to let his mind wander to the days he had spent in the wilderness. Although hunting for food had been somewhat of a chore, at the same time, he loved that freedom. He had truly enjoyed spending the days with Elvistir talking, hunting rabbits, and practicing his swordsmanship. Somehow, that relaxed atmosphere felt like a rejuvenation of his spirit, his will to move forward.

Lost in those thoughts, he almost missed the next stance change, until Tannil moved forward and poked him gently with the practice sword. The teacher glared at them momentarily, and they quickly switched into the new stance.

This one, Dannan was sure, was meant to be used with a shield. With both feet planted shoulder width apart, his practice sword gripped in one hand, he watched as their teacher brought his arm up and around, as if to toss something underhanded. As his arm came around the front he brought the sword blade straight up, his palm facing out.

Dannan quickly tried to mimic the movement, and found out the hard way that doing it incorrectly or too fast hurt his shoulder. When they hit fifty swings, he started to feel comfortable with the movement, and began to think of where this would normally hit his opponent.

Trying to imagine a person with a sword and a shield in front of him, Dannan was unsuccessful at first, when finally he started to get a mental image. Unfortunately, the first image that came to mind was one of the bandits he had killed en route to Whitehaven. As he brought the sword up, he could see how it slashed the image, adding a cut straight along the center to go with the sliced open stomach. Taking a deep breath as he continued to swing, Dannan tried to forcefully get rid of the image, but found that it was even worse with his eyes closed.

Opening them again, he was glad to see that the teacher had let his practice sword fall to his side, and was resting a moment. Looking at the others, Dannan was surprised to see some of his classmates sitting, trying desperately to catch their breaths. Only he, Tannil, Carissa, and the two brothers seemed to be able to stand at all, and the two brothers were both panting.

Turning towards Tannil, Dannan was surprised to see a manic glint in his eye, and Tannil gave him a quick wink and a grin. Glancing over at the other classes, he saw that some of them were beginning to get winded as well, and all of them were sweating.

Wiping his forehead off with his sleeve, he wondered why it had gotten so hot when he noticed the sky had grown lighter. Looking up, he saw the sun had fully come out now, and was starting to climb its way directly overhead. After resting for a number of minutes, the teachers switched hands with their practice swords, and repeated the same routine, but with the other arm.

Although Dannan had done a similar routine in the woods, he had allowed more rest between every hundred swings. His arms both felt heavy from using them so much in such a short period, and he could tell from how the other students were reacting, even the more experienced students, that this was a heavy practice menu.

The only groups who seemed relatively unfazed were those who had already been here for more than five years. Staring at them, Dannan spotted the senior, apparently from the seventh year, who had suddenly appeared behind him in the mess hall last night. He quickly turned away when he saw the senior notice him, and watched his classmates, most of who were in the same state he was.

Tannil was the only one who wasn't panting for breath at this point. Dannan couldn't help but wonder, if this wasn't enough to make him tired, what kind of exercise he had to do to survive in his campaigns.

Shaking his head, he turned back to the teacher. "Alright, break for lunch!" The teacher yelled.

As the students and teachers began to move away, Dannan moved to the front, waiting until the teacher noticed him. When he finally got the teacher's attention, Dannan hesitated a little, then spoke. "Where should we meet you for the class after lunch, sir?"

Looking at him for a moment, the teacher smiled slightly. "Glad to see some of you have voices other than Tannil. You'll be meeting me near the blacksmith. After all, when you're learning armor, it never hurts to have the advice of someone experienced in making it." Dannan nodded, and waited a moment. "Is that all?"

Dannan nodded again, remaining silent. "Very well then, I'll see you at the smith then after lunch. Go eat." Dannan nodded a third time, unsure of whether to bow or salute, and instead just rushed off after his classmates. He heard a soft chuckle from behind him, but he was too busy trying to catch up to Tannil.

He finally caught up just outside the mess hall. It was much more crowded for lunch than it had been for breakfast or dinner, and the line stretched from the cook to the door. Waiting behind Tannil, Dannan couldn't see much except for the crowd surrounding them.

When they finally reached the cook, Dannan took the bowl of soup eagerly, starving from all the exercise. As they grabbed the loaf of bread, Dannan concentrated on staying behind Tannil without having his soup spilled by the jostling of the other students.

Tannil led the way towards one of the few empty tables left, sitting down to his soup with an eager energy. Dannan took the chair next to him, trying to eat the soup a little slower, so that he would have a chance to enjoy the taste. After a few bites, he noticed there was beef in the soup, along with the noodles and vegetables.

Smiling, he eagerly finished it off, mimicking Tannil as they both slurped the remainder of the broth from the bowl. Setting the bowl down, he noticed that a number of their classmates had joined them at the table, and although they were tired, they still had the energy to give him an odd look.

Shrugging his shoulders at them, he turned to his bread, biting a chunk out of it. As he began to chew the slightly dry bread, he wished that he hadn't finished his broth off. Shaking his head, he turned to look around, listening to the conversation and rhythm of the other students as they enjoyed their meals.

Although they had all just worked so hard, a happy air seemed to pervade the room. Thinking about it, Dannan guessed that the fact they were still here meant something to them. "Well, if you're still here, you're good enough, I guess." Dannan murmured to himself. Tannil raised an eyebrow at him from over his bread as he tore another chunk out of it.

Swallowing hard, Tannil coughed a little and grabbed the pitcher of water and a cup from the center of the table. Filling the cup, he quickly gulped it down, coughing a little more. Laughing, Dannan couldn't help but grin at him, which drew a joking glare and a chuckle from Tannil.

Although the room was crowded, it quickly cleared out as people finished their lunch. When his classmates had finished off their lunches as well, Dannan stood, pushing the chair back in.

"Where are you off to?" Tannil asked, looking up at him.

"Our class on armor is at the blacksmiths. So I'm going to head there now."

Tannil nodded, a small smile coming to his lips. "See? If you work up the courage, you can gather information, to. Just takes some guts, that's all." Dannan laughed and shook his head, then moved out of the way so Tannil could stand.

Pushing his chair back, Tannil stretched his arms out, one of his shoulders making a small popping noise as he did. Dannan raised his eyebrows, and Tannil shrugged. "Stiff from exercise, that's all. Nothing to read into it."

Dannan took a deep breath, shaking his head again. Walking towards the door, he murmured "I'll never figure you out." Tannil, a step behind him to his left, chuckled.

"You're right there." Looking at him in surprise, Dannan almost walked into the door post. Darting to the side at the last second, he struck it hard with his shoulder, and let out a curse. Bursting out laughing, Tannil gave him a wide grin. "You plan to be a Swordmaster like that? The door almost won!" Dannan glared at him for a second while rubbing his shoulder, then gave up and laughed with him as they walked on.

Chapter 20

The smithy was a sturdy building. Four large wooden beams driven into the ground formed the corners, and the roof was formed from thick wooden planks. The brick forge sat dead center, with a metal roof over it to protect the building, and a chimney to let the smoke out through the roof. Rolls that looked like tanned leather hung from each side of the roof, with a pulley on the inside edge of each beam.

At the moment, racks of swords, spears, axes, and armor stood about, waiting as the blacksmith hammered away at each that came before him. His apprentice ran back and forth, setting weapons aside that had been quenched in the barrel of water, and bringing new ones to set next to the anvil.

Watching it, Dannan was fascinated, as it was nothing like the blacksmith back home. There, the largest thing he had seen was metal posts for doors, though far more common were horseshoes and household items.

Looking at the blacksmith, he got the feeling the smith here could easily wrestle down the smith from his village. The man was short, only about five feet tall, but he rippled with muscle. Soot had long since stained his skin and hair, and as such, it was hard to tell what color his hair or dirty gray skin really was. Even his age was hard to tell, as the years spent as a blacksmith had added many lines to his face.

His apprentice, a man who appeared to be in his late twenties, seemed much more new to smithing. His tan skin had yet to take on the soot-gray tone, and his hair was still solidly oak brown. Although a good head taller than his master, it was still obvious without a second glance from his posture who served who.

Dannan almost didn't notice the teacher arrive, so intent was his study of the blacksmith. The other students had been chatting amongst themselves before the teacher arrived, but immediately went silent when he got there.

Walking to the front of the group, the teacher nodded to the smith, who gave him a curt nod back. Turning towards them, the teacher looked them over, then nodded. "Good. You've learned how to act already. Although I am your teacher here, in most ways, you will treat me as you would your commanding officer. The Hawk's Honor does not just train Swordmasters, but generals, officers, mercenary leaders... Those who cannot adapt to the system quickly find that they are at a disadvantage when it comes to working within any military organization. Because at the end of the day, an undisciplined group is no better than a mob. That is why the barbarians lost the war. That is why we won, and why we will win again when they next range forth."

Smiling grimly at some recollection, the teacher continued. "But to defeat your enemy, you must know how to fight them. When the barbarians came forth, the Allied Cities had to figure out how to defeat the magic of their many shamans. Though the barbarians did not wear mail or plate armor, still their skin seemed to turn the points of blades, and resist the blows of maces. Without the assistance of our elven allies, we might have lost the war."

One of the boys at the back of the class raised a hand, and the teacher nodded to him. "What are the elves like, sir?"

Smiling, the teacher looked back at him. "Enigmatic... Disinterested in the petty squabbles that normally take place among humans... Skilled in many things, from magic and poetry to swordsmanship and stealth. You'll only ever meet an elf if they want you to meet them. But don't let that fool you. Very few of the elves are malicious, but when you live hundreds of years, why die in a fight over something that might not last a month?"

The boy looked back at him, and he chuckled. "When your grandchildren are born, see their grandchildren born, and then die themselves... That should give you an idea of how long the elves live. The dwarves don't live as long as the elves do, but they'll still outlive your grandchildren. More enigmatic races, like the fey and the dragons... it's said some of them never die."

A few of the boys in back laughed, and the teacher stared at them. They hunched their shoulders, trying to look anywhere but back at him. "What's the matter? Don't believe in the fey? Don't believe that just because you haven't seen something, it doesn't exist?"

The boys hunched their shoulders further, and he shook his head at all of them. "The remnants of ancient cultures are found in the furthest corners of the world. Trolls, dwarves, and orcs fight alongside and against men in the north. The elves and their allies occupy the western woods, where men aren't allowed to build. Barbarian hordes rampage to the east, and to the south, the nomads and halflings roam the plains following their herds. Yet somehow, you find it hard to believe that creatures you've never seen still exist."

Shaking his head, he let out an exasperated sigh. "Alright, let's move onto the basic armors that you'll find other humans wearing. Even the stupid among you can grasp that." The boys flinched slightly at his criticism, and they all hunkered down in the grass as he pulled over an armor stand with a suit of chain mail on it.

When the lecture had finally finished, Dannan was sore from sitting for so long. Standing up, he felt like a creaky old chair, and he winced at the how accurate the comparison felt. "Go use the bathhouses before dinner, then to bed. You'll want to adjust quickly, because this is what your next year will look like."

Several of them groaned, but Dannan knew that each and every one of them would fight to stay here. Walking back towards the dorm, he silently accepted as Tannil fell in step next to him. When they got to the dorm, they went straight through, ignoring the other students who were already in the mess hall. Heading through the double doors to the outside, they found themselves a scant hundred feet from the bathhouse.

Going inside, Dannan was glad to see it was more like he was used to back home. It was an open bath, with racks off to one side for personal belongings, and stools and buckets to one side for when you needed to rinse off quickly.

Deciding he would enjoy it more when they got their first afternoon to relax, he quickly hung his clothes on a rack, sliding the scale off inside his shirt so no one would see it. Noticing Tannil follow suit, he had to hold in a gasp as he saw the scars covering Tannil's body.

He couldn't help but wonder how Tannil had survived many of them, some of which ran the length of his back. Sliding the scale into his pants pocket under the shirt, he wondered how he would manage to avoid having the scale seen while staying here.

Letting out a sigh, he realized especially with the teacher, there could be trouble if it was found. Washing quickly, he rushed a little more than usual, to make sure he had plenty of time to get in the dinner line.

As he pulled his clothes back on, he noticed several of the students arguing on the other side of the bathhouse. Glancing over, he saw two boys, a few years older than him, coming to blows. Quickly turning away so he wouldn't get caught up, he glanced over and saw that Tannil was watching him.

He shrugged his shoulders at Tannil and slid his shirt on, putting his hand in his pocket to make sure the scale stayed secure. Meeting Tannil's eyes, Dannan was surprised to see disappointment in them. Turning away, Dannan scowled and walked out, unsure of why Tannil's reaction bothered him so much.

Stepping out of the bathhouse, he saw that the sun had fallen almost to the compound walls, and now cast long shadows over everything. Glancing around quickly, Dannan made sure no one was around before sliding the dragon scale back up onto his neck. Tucking it securely back into his shirt, he breathed a little easier feeling its comfortable weight over his heart once more. Walking back towards the mess hall, he tried to push off the memory of Tannil's eyes, but somehow, he couldn't escape the feeling behind them.

Dinner seemed unappetizing that night, as Tannil's eyes kept appearing in his mind. It seemed even more pronounced as Tannil hadn't followed him to dinner, and so Dannan quietly sat off by himself, none of his other classmates having returned from the bathhouse yet.

Finishing his dinner, Dannan sat there for a few moments when one of the older boys came up to him. Dannan thought he might be from the fourth or fifth year, but he wasn't entirely certain. The boy emitted an almost palpable aura of mischief, and Dannan sighed, sure that this was going to be the crowning moment of a bad night.

After waiting a few moments for the boy to say something, Dannan decided to speak first. "Can I help you?"

"It's can I help you, sir." Dannan's patience, already grown thin, started fraying the moment the older boy opened his mouth.

"Can I help you, sir?"

The boy smirked before speaking again. "Yes, you can. Some

Huntress of the Sky

of my friends want to meet you, and you're going to oblige them. Come with me." Shrugging, Dannan stood, and he followed several feet behind the boy.

It only took a minute for Dannan to realize the boy was leading him to a secluded part of the compound behind the dorm. Although it was relatively wide open, you could only see it if you came all the way around behind the dorm and past the bathhouse.

As they got closer, Dannan saw that three other boys, all about the same age as the one leading him, were waiting there. When they were close enough, the three boys spread out, moving to form a net that he was sure they thought they could catch him in. Shaking his head, he resisted the urge to sigh, hoping he could leave without antagonizing them. Turning around, the boy grinned at him, and for a moment, Dannan really wished that Tannil hadn't chosen this particular night to throw a tantrum.

Watching them, Dannan just stood there, knowing when they were ready, they would tell him whatever reason they were going to make up for attacking him. As he expected, after a few moments the boy spoke. "Now, this is nothing against you personally, but it's something that every new trainee has to go through. The girls have their own method, though I don't know if it's quite as… kind, as ours. We're just going to give you a small beating, and if you manage to escape, then we don't attack you ever again. If you don't, then you'll have some bruises and memories to use as a reason to get better while you're here. Any questions?"

Dannan smirked for a moment, then nodded. "What happens if I beat you?"

The four boys, all taller and two of them more muscular than him, burst out laughing. "Well, then you'd also have something to use as a reason for growth." The one who brought him here got out between laughs.

The boys moved closer around him, so that there was one on each side, and the leader of the group grinned. "And don't think that by refusing to resist, we'll go easy on you. Any coward who thinks playing pacifist would work at a sword school is a fool. We're especially gentle with them."

The others laughed again, and suddenly, the boy behind Dannan jumped at him. Stepping to the side, Dannan grabbed the boy's shoulder and pushed him past. Immediately, he took a few short steps backwards so that he wasn't in the square they had formed any more. As the boys to each side of him moved closer once more, Dannan rushed the boy on the right, catching him off guard with a solid right punch to the jaw.

He knocked the boy down and moved to go past him when the second boy tackled his legs from behind. Dropping on top of the one he had knocked down, he struggled to get out from under the heavier boy, but to no avail. As they dragged him to his feet, he allowed his body to go slack, letting them hold his weight up. The leader moved in front of him, still grinning, and the other boy moved behind him again and held his shoulders.

As the leader wound up to take a swing at his face, Dannan threw his weight to the left, managing to keep the punch glancing. His cheek still hurt like hell, but he was glad he didn't take it head on. Laughing, the boys held him tighter, and the leader began to strike him in the stomach like a punching bag.

After a few moments, the leader stopped, and he got a curious look on his face. Looking down, Dannan realized that the outline of the scale was slightly visible through his shirt, and he paled. "Well well, what's this? Something from your mommy? Or maybe a girl you like back home?"

The leader reached out and grasped the scale through his shirt, and grinned wider. "It's a necklace, huh. I wonder how it would look on me?" Dannan got even paler, and started throwing himself about wildly with all his might, desperate that they not see it.

The boys were caught off guard, but he wasn't able to shake them loose more than a little. Reaching out, the older boy took hold of the chain, and Dannan suddenly felt a chill, as if someone were gripping his neck tightly. As the boy removed it, a laughing look on his face, Dannan struggled as hard as he could, at one point hearing his shoulder pop in the socket.

He didn't see the worried look of the boy holding his right arm, though. All he could concentrate on was the leader, holding the dragon scale, his dragon scale, so mockingly. "Well, let's see how I look guys." The leader said as he went to slide the chain over his head.

Wrenching his arm free from the distracted boy on his right, Dannan grabbed the leader's wrist in a vice grip, and for a moment, he saw the boy's eyes register fear. The boy didn't have a chance to react though.

Dannan threw his body forward as he pulled the boy towards him, his forehead slamming into the leader's nose with a sickening crunch. The other boys looked on in surprise, and only the boy behind Dannan had the presence of mind to try to hold on.

Pulling forward even further, Dannan grabbed the wrist of the boy still holding him and pulled his arm forward, sinking his teeth into the soft flesh of his forearm. The boy let out a shriek of agony, but Dannan didn't even notice as he spit the chunk of flesh out and leaped for the leader.

Grabbing the amulet, he darted past, ignoring the blood flowing freely from the fallen boy's face. Spinning on his heels, he turned to face them, and he felt his vision narrowing as his senses captured everything around him.

Suddenly, he could taste the metallic tang of the blood in his mouth, and although it bothered him, all he could think of was the dragon scale amulet, and that they were trying to take it away. The cool night air did nothing to hide the pervading smell of blood coming from the two boys, and Dannan snarled.

He watched as one of the two uninjured boys tried to help the boy bleeding from the arm, even as the other charged at Dannan, his fear apparent.

As he closed with Dannan, the boy leaned back to take a swing, and Dannan barreled forward at that moment, headbutting the boy in the chest. His head stung from the impact as he and the boy both went down, but Dannan ignored it, quickly pulling himself into a sitting position.

Gripping the dragon scale in his right hand, he drove it point downwards towards the boy, who threw up his arms to ward it off. Dannan felt the resistance as the point drove through skin and into the boy's arm, and he felt sickened even as he struck, the boy's shriek ringing out through the air.

He could hear a commotion coming from the dorm now, and he slammed his fist into the side of the boy's head, still holding the scale. The boy's eyes rolled back even as he went limp, and Dannan turned to the last uninjured boy. Jumping from where he knelt, Dannan stood over him, the dragon scale held upright, the blood shining softly in the moonlight.

The boy looked enthralled even as he looked terrified, and

Dannan slammed the dragon scale flat side down on the boy's shoulder. There was a soft crack, and Dannan's hand shivered from the resistance as he pulled the scale back. The boy slumped to the ground with a soft cry.

Quickly looping the dragon scale over his neck, he looked around, his vision slowly returning to normal. The sudden sensation of the blood once more made him spit, and could feel the warm blood on the scale against his chest. He tried to wipe the blood off his lips with the back of his hand, but this only succeeded in smearing it over his face. The two boys still conscious could only stare at him in terror as they held their wounded arms. "Don't tell anyone about this!" Dannan hissed quietly.

They nodded quickly, a mute appeal for mercy in their eyes. Dannan shook his head in disgust, though he wasn't sure if it was for himself or for them. He started running, just as he saw people start to come out of the mess hall to investigate.

Chapter 21

Dannan ran past the side of the bathhouse when suddenly he felt a hand cover his mouth, and an arm surround his chest. He found himself practically flying through the air as he was yanked into the back entrance of the bathhouse, and he tried to get a look at who had grabbed him. He was carried quickly into the bathhouse, and out of sight behind one of the pillars.

The shouting continued for about a dozen minutes, before finally moving further away. Dannan wanted to relax, but at the same time, he still didn't know who was holding him. All he could tell was that the person had pale skin. Unfortunately, that could have been any number of the older students, many who came from the central and northern lands.

After a few more minutes, he felt the person release their grip, and he darted forward, his left hand clutching the dragon scale tightly as he clenched his right into a fist. He spun around on his heels, almost slipping on the stone floor, and lowered his fist in surprise as he saw Tannil standing there, his hands opened with his palms forward. "Tannil?!" Dannan tried to whisper, though it came out louder than he wanted.

Tannil immediately reached out and covered his mouth with his hand, and held up a finger for silence. After a few moments, he removed his hand, then grabbed a bucket. Quickly dunking it in the bath, he set it in front of Dannan, pulling out a cloth. "Rinse your face and hand, quickly. And roll up your sleeves. Don't get any water on you." Dannan nodded, dumbstruck, and slowly did as he was told.

When both sleeves were up around his elbows, he gently cupped some water, washing the back of his hand and his face thoroughly. He watched as the bloody water drained into the corner, and went through a small hole at the base of the wall. When he had finished doing that several times, Tannil stopped him. "Let me see your mouth."

Dannan opened his mouth obediently, unsure of what to do, and Tannil nodded. "Rinse and spit." He said softly. Dannan nodded, taking another handful of water and swirling it around in his mouth before spitting it out next to the hole. After a moment of checking, Tannil nodded. "We won't be able to get rid of the scent entirely, but for a human nose, that should be good enough to mask it." Dannan gave him a curious look, and darted back as Tannil poured the rest of the water hurriedly towards the hole, washing away the evidence.

Setting the stool and bucket where they had been, he motioned at Dannan to follow him. As Tannil started walking towards the entrance, Dannan quickly dipped the scale in the water, trying to be as inconspicuous as he could. Glancing at it to make sure it was clean, he followed after Tannil.

As they walked quietly out of the bathhouse, Tannil checked left and right, then motioned for Dannan to follow him again. Looking both ways as they walked towards the girl's bathhouse, Tannil spoke so softly Dannan almost couldn't hear him. "You won't tell anyone that you got in the fight. You'll say they hit you a few times, and then you managed to break free and get away. If you tell them you were the one fighting, they'll definitely ask questions, especially about that scale."

Dannan drew back in surprise and fear, and Tannil spun quickly, grabbing him by the shoulder. "We don't have time for this." He hissed. "Do you want to stay in The Hawk's Honor, or run now? Because those will be your only options if you're found out. And from the looks of that scale, they might not let you keep it when they send you packing." Dannan nodded slightly, trying to take everything in at once. Staring into Tannil's eyes, Dannan relaxed a little, unable to find a trace of malice or the disappointment from earlier. "Good. Now, keep following me."

He nodded as Tannil released him, and they started slowly back towards the girl's bathhouse, slouching as low to the ground as they could while moving at a reasonable speed. Dannan constantly looked around, as there was no cover, and anyone who came outside would be able to see their shadows in the moonlight. "We were spying on the girls. That's why you were alone at dinner. I went first, and was waiting ahead of you, and those boys brought you out to haze you. You managed to get away after getting punched around a little, and took off running towards where I was peeping. When you got to the bathhouse and saw the boys weren't following you, you thanked your good fortune and ran all the way to me. I made you wait with me, so that they wouldn't catch you on your way back to the building. We heard the yelling, and were afraid to come back right away, and waited by the bathhouse until it had stopped. That's when we tried to sneak back into our room. Got it?"

Hesitating a moment, Dannan nodded silently again. They finally reached the corner of the girl's bathhouse, and he let out a small sigh of relief as it obscured the dorm from view. "Don't relax just yet. The hardest part comes now. Just be prepared, because the teachers will catch us, and will question us. Do you have the story straight?" Dannan grunted an affirmative, and Tannil smiled a little.

"Good. Now, don't worry if you don't remember those exact words. You shouldn't. That would be too suspicious. Just remember it as best you can, and as you talk, just keep thinking 'this is the truth'. Just convince yourself of that, and answer."

Reaching out a hand, Tannil gently set it on Dannan's shoulder. "Are you ready? This is going to be hard." Dannan nodded, the fear apparent in his eyes, and Tannil shook his head. "That fear is good, just don't let it control your actions. Remember, we're in this together, and I've got your back." Dannan nodded and took a deep breath, and they began sneaking back from the girl's bathhouse towards the dorm.

As they got close, Tannil stopped them by the door, and peaked around the edge. After a few seconds, he nodded at Dannan, and they crept inside. "Hold it." They both froze, and Dannan and Tannil looked to their right, where the voice had come from.

Their teacher was sitting about ten feet back from the door, a chair up against the wall, a sword resting across his lap. "You two, Carissa, and Haddin from your class are the only ones unaccounted for in this dorm. The teachers recognized those four from class five, and are going to check if there are any more missing from the other dorm. Now."

He paused, his words hanging heavily in the air. "Where have you two been?" Dannan turned to Tannil, and was about to say something when Tannil bowed down at the waist.

"I apologize sir, it's my fault!" The teacher looked at them, then back at Tannil. "Dannan and me got to talking, and he told me that he had never seen a girl naked before. I decided to take him to peep on the girl's bathhouse, to celebrate his entrance as a Swordmaster trainee, but I never expected anything like this to happen!"

Dannan turned bright red as Tannil talked and lowered his eyes to the floor, unable to meet his teacher's gaze. "Why did you stay out so long? And did you hear the yelling?"

Tannil nodded, not raising his head. "Yes sir, I did! I assumed it was just a regular fist fight between some students, and seeing as how I'm only a student myself, decided I didn't have the right to stop it. By the time the screams started, we had already hidden in the boy's bathhouse." Dannan was sure the teacher could see right through them, and he clenched his teeth quietly.

"Alright. Why did you wait so long before coming back in?" Tannil took a deep breath, then shook his head. "We were going to come back in earlier, but when the screams started, we got worried. Fist fights don't usually involve screams. And when they finally stopped, I was worried if we ran inside, people would think that we attacked the other students. It's bad enough to get busted for peeping, but I don't want to get thrown out for injuring another student!"

The teacher looked them over again, and Dannan felt like the silence stretched for eternity. "Alright, head back up to your room immediately, then. We're certain to get to the bottom of this tomorrow, if nothing else. You won't be confined to quarters for peeping, because as bad a pervert as you might be, it's unimportant in comparison to what happened tonight. Neither of you, however, will get to leave the compound for a month or two. It will be up to a group decision of the teacher's to determine how long you will stay confined for. Dismissed." They bowed and nodded, then walked at a hurried pace towards the second floor staircase, and their room.

When they got back to their room, Tannil looked both ways to make sure no one was looking, and then quickly shoved Dannan in without taking the torch from the bracket.

Dannan protested softly as Tannil shut the door, and then he heard the sound of a flare stick being struck against stone. The small stick brought a tiny amount of illumination to the cell-like room, and he was suddenly struck again by Tannil's comparison to a dungeon.

Lighting the candle, Tannil quickly blew out the flare stick, setting it on the stand table. Standing in front of his cot, he looked over at Dannan. "You're going to bruise up in the morning something awful from how he was hitting you, but first, let me check your shoulder." Dannan stared at Tannil as he moved closer, and as Tannil gently pressed on his shoulder, Dannan let out a little yelp of pain. "You're going to have to grit your teeth. This is going to hurt a little." Dannan looked at Tannil again, and he suddenly realized what Tannil had said about being struck.

At that moment, Tannil gave Dannan's shoulder a sharp push, forcing it back into its socket. Letting out a cry of pain, Dannan immediately gritted his teeth, holding in the urge to yell as Tannil stepped back. Moving his shoulder a little, he grimaced at the pain, then looked at Tannil. "You were watching the whole time?" Tannil nodded, and Dannan wished eagerly that he could throw a punch, but decided it would be worthless. "How are we going to explain my bruises, then? Since you told the teacher that we had both been peeping."

Tannil shook his head, smiling sadly. "I'm going to have to hit you a few times." Dannan scowled at him, and growled a little. "And why would they believe that?"

"Because I'm going to say you got mad at me and tried to hit me a few times, and I gave you some bruises to put you back in your place."

He grimaced, unable to deny the logic. "So that yelp of pain I just let out was you beating the stuffing out of me?" Tannil smiled sadly.

"Believe me, this brings me no pleasure. And it will hurt." Dannan nodded and sighed, resigning himself to it. Gritting his teeth, he closed his eyes, and Tannil clucked his tongue. "Don't close your eyes. If you see it coming, you can prepare yourself for the pain better. Don't worry; I won't be using my full strength." Dannan smiled wryly and opened his eyes to a fist flying straight at him.

Moving to dodge, he felt Tannil's knuckles clip the cheek he had been struck on, but he barely had time to register it, as Tannil's right fist clipped him on the left side of the chin.

Staggering back down onto his cot, Dannan put his hand on the edge to try and hold his balance, and Tannil looked down at him. "There, that should do it. That's going to be sore in the morning, but at least it will be believable. Sorry."

Dannan grimaced at him, then shook his head. "Why'd you just watch the whole time, if you knew I was going to get beaten? And what was with that look you gave me earlier?"

Tannil sat on his cot, silent for a few moments, before meeting Dannan's eyes with that sad smile again. "If you tell me the secret of that scale you have, I'll tell you my secret, which will also answer both of those questions."

Dannan stared at him for a moment, then finally let out a sigh. "You've already seen it, so what more is there to tell?" Tannil scratched the side of his nose lightly, then shook his head.

"Why do you have the scale of a giant lizard? There's plenty to tell there."

Dannan looked annoyed, and snapped. "Dragon. Not lizard. Dragon." Tannil looked at him in disbelief for a moment, and his jaw dropped.

"Damn it all." He murmured to himself. "That's... a real dragon scale?"

Letting out a sigh, Dannan nodded. "I might as well start from the beginning. There's no way you're going to believe all of it if I start from the middle." Tannil nodded and leaned forward intently, and Dannan noticed his smile had disappeared, and now he just had a look of insatiable curiosity. "Well, about a month ago, I was in the forest…"

It took at least an hour for Dannan to finish his story, and by the time he finished, he felt exhausted. At the same time, he felt relieved, having shared his story with someone. Even if he was sure to be cast out for being crazy, or lynched to get to the dragoness.

Staring at Tannil, he waited for a reaction, unsure of whether to bother trying to run. He was caught off guard when Tannil burst out laughing, but his anger quickly overcame his shock. "What?! So you think I'm a liar?!"

Tannil shook his head, and quickly tried to regain control of himself. One look at Dannan made him start laughing again however. It was several minutes before he finally managed to calm himself down, and then he took several deep breaths, to avoid laughing more.

Staring back at Dannan, Tannil grinned, and shook his head. "Well, I thought you smelled like a kindred spirit, and not like a regular human, and this explains why." Dannan looked at him, confused, and opened his mouth to speak. Cutting him off with a gesture, Tannil shook his head. "I have to show you something first, then I'll answer your questions. Just promise not to scream, alright?" Dannan met his eyes and nodded, his eyebrows furrowed as he watched Tannil.

Taking a deep breath Tannil closed his eyes, and his breathing slowed to a very even rate. As Dannan stared, his eyes began to water a little, and he rubbed them, sure he was seeing things. After a moment though, he could tell he wasn't imagining it.

Tannil's platinum blonde hair seemed to be moving, and more was growing from every visible portion of his body. After a few moments, he was nearly covered with a soft white fur, and then his body began to change even more. His face began to lengthen into a snout, and his forehead sloped back slightly. His fingers and arms began to lengthen, and his nails began to grow as long as the claws on a bear.

Even through the pants, Dannan could tell that his legs had gotten leaner but more muscular. As the hair on his body went from a soft fur to the longer, coarser fur of a dog, Dannan's mouth dropped open.

After a short time, it seemed like he had stopped changing, and Dannan could only gape in wonder. His face had become the muzzle of a wolf, with a fang protruding down from each side. His ears had become long and pointed, measuring at least a few inches, and his eyes were more in line with his muzzle than with the human face he had possessed just a minute ago. The hair covering his body obscured the scars, and his limbs had lengthened, giving him at least a few extra inches of height. When Tannil opened his eyes, Dannan saw they had gone from a misty blue-gray to the golden yellow of a wolf's.

Holding his gaze for a few minutes, Tannil just sat there, before finally he opened his mouth to speak. Dannan had the urge to flinch back when he saw the mouthful of fangs, but he resisted, knowing that if Tannil had wanted him dead, it would be over already.

Tannil's expression was unreadable, but Dannan felt a sense of sadness from his eyes once again. Shaking his head, Tannil closed his eyes once more, and started taking deep breaths. It took around a minute for the changes to fully reverse, the muzzle slowly shrinking back into a normal human mouth and nose, and the fur receding back until it was only regular human hair.

All the scars on his arms were still there, and when he opened his eyes, they were once again a misty blue-gray. "You asked why I seemed disappointed, and why I only watched. When at first I met you, you smelled like a kindred spirit to me. Most likely because of the magic from your amulet. It would easily explain why you smelled like you had been touched by the supernatural. That's why when you had such a typical reaction to those boys fighting in the bathhouse, I was saddened."

Taking a deep breath, he sighed. "I had been hoping that somewhere out here, far from my pack, I had met someone else to keep me company. I didn't step into the fight because I wanted to see what you could do on your own. You certainly displayed the will to survive of a werewolf. I was caught off guard when you bit that other boy, but considering how precious that dragon scale is to you, I understand now." Tannil grew silent and met his gaze, and they sat there and stared at each other for minutes on end.

Shrugging, Tannil shook his head. "Now we're even. I've got something about you that you want kept secret, and you've got something about me that I need kept secret. What now?"

Dannan looked at him for a moment, and understanding truly hit him. Now they were even. "You said pack. There are more like you where you're from?"

Tannil nodded, smiling a little. "Yes, the whole Wolves Brigade, in fact. About fifty members strong. I'm sure there are other werewolves out there, but that is my pack. The children travel with the pack in a wolf's form, watching and learning from the adults. As they grow old enough to mimic the form of a child of the appropriate age to be an apprentice, they begin to practice the form that will be their personal form throughout their life. But that is also why the Wolves Brigade fights alone, and never with an army. If the secret got out, we would all be hunted down, even though we are not cursed."

Looking at him curiously, Dannan shook his head. "Cursed?"

Wearing a grim expression, Tannil nodded. "There are two types of were-creatures. I do not know how many kinds there are throughout the world. There may be one kind for every form of animal spirit out there. But for all of them, it is the same. There are those, like the members of the Wolves Brigade, who are born with it as both a gift and a burden. We have the ability to change our forms by our own will, and we can control it. Those who are cursed, though... They have no control. The curse that transforms them into a beast takes control of their mind, and they become a beast completely."

With a growl, he continued. "They are the 'were-beasts' you have heard about in legends and myths. Just as dragons are not the rampaging monsters you had heard about, they have the power to be. And just as werewolves are creatures of the night, those who are not cursed are also creatures of the day. It is one of the missions of those with the gift to hunt those who are cursed. Because the curse cannot be passed along to us or by us, if we hunt them down, the curse ends with its owner. But for those who do not bear the gift, they will be transformed, and will murder." Tannil's last words sent a shiver up Dannan's spine, and he remembered the vicious fangs that Tannil had in his other form.

Dannan wasn't sure how long they sat silently before he shook his head. "You don't have to worry about your secret, Tannil. At least not with me. I'm not letting this scale out of my sight. Not until I see her again. Even if she kills me, I have to meet her. And I'm already aware she's being hunted, and I imagine anyone who finds out will likely join in. And I won't let them endanger her. So I know what it's like, having a secret that you can't let people find out. You can trust me."

A half-smile crossed Dannan's lips, and he shrugged slightly. "Besides, if you ever feel that I'm untrustworthy, you can just eat my face while I'm asleep. Especially if we share rooms for the next eight years, ha ha."

Tannil chuckled at that, and shook his head. "It's not my style. People taste bad. I don't care what trolls tell you about them tasting like chickens, people taste dirty and sweaty." Dannan stared at him for a moment, unsure if he was joking, when Tannil burst out laughing.

After a few moments, Dannan joined him. Extinguishing the candle, Dannan laid out flat on his cot. "I'll be curious to hear your stories, since you've heard some of mine now. But that can wait. For now, I'm tired, and we still have practice tomorrow." He didn't hear any response from Tannil, so Dannan quietly rolled over onto his side, and closed his eyes. "Goodnight, Tannil."

"Goodnight, Dannan." Dannan smiled slightly, wondering if that was a slight quiver he heard in his friend's voice. Closing his eyes, he nodded to himself and drifted off, glad that he had indeed made a friend out in this harsh place.

Chapter 22

The next morning, the mess hall was filled with rumors. Everyone who had an opinion had come up with a different reason why the students had been injured last night, and no one had any real facts. Dannan did his best to cheerfully ignore it all while conversing with Tannil, though he let out an involuntary little shudder whenever a rumor sounded too accurate.

Morning practice was uneventful, and although the gossip mill was in full swing, by the time lunch rolled around, Dannan had gotten used to the noise. He relaxed even more when they finally got to afternoon classes, and even his teacher's stern glares couldn't dampen his mood.

When night finally came, Dannan was relieved to get back to his room. Although it was tiny and cell-like, it still felt like a safe haven from the woes of the world. Sitting down on the cot, Dannan idly played with the dragon scale, luxuriating in the tug he felt. Even in this tiny room, he could tell which way was north, because of the scale. And the dragoness was still there.

Closing his eyes, Dannan lost himself in that feeling. He was suddenly pulled from it by the sound of the door opening and closing quickly. Opening his eyes, he looked up at Tannil, who had just walked in, a semi-serious look on his face. "What's the matter, Tannil?"

Tannil sat down on his cot, and looked over at Dannan. "Nothing important. The teacher just talked to me on the way back after class, wanted to make sure 'I'd never pull something like that again'."

Dannan chuckled. "I'm just glad no one inquired about my bruises. I guess they just assumed whoever beat the others beat me as well." Tannil smiled wryly, and shook his head.

"The teacher asked, and I got a lecture on responsibility because of it. But that was all."

Shrugging, Dannan let out a laugh. "So your pride is

wounded, but nothing else. That's not that bad."

Scowling at him, Tannil shook his head. "You're lucky I'm not one of the vindictive types."

Dannan laughed, throwing his pillow at Tannil. "As if you'd hurt a hair on my head for anything other than one of your plans. You're far too much of a schemer for that." Dannan said with a smile.

Tannil looked hurt for a moment, and Dannan quickly spoke up. "You know I don't mean that in a bad way. If it weren't for that tendency of yours, I wouldn't be able to continue my training as a Swordmaster anymore. I doubt that after being dismissed from the compound, I'd be able to get into any other sword school in town." Tannil shrugged slightly, and Dannan sighed.

Perking up, Dannan grinned. "Here, let me show you something. This will take your mind off of my comment." Looking down at the dragon scale, Dannan concentrated, mentally commanding it to brighten slightly. The scale immediately reacted, a soft purple glow beginning to emit from it and fill the room. Gradually raising the light level, Dannan managed to get it until the light filled the room as if it were regular daylight.

Grinning at Tannil, Dannan was pleased to see the shocked look on his roommates face. "See? I told you that would distract you."

Tannil shook his head in surprise, still staring at the scale. "I didn't realize that you have some control over it."

Meeting Dannan's eyes, Tannil looked thoughtful for a moment. "Come to think of it, you haven't told me much about what the scale actually does, just how you got it. Which is quite a tale in and of itself."

Dannan laughed softly. Looking down at the scale, he felt a little scared talking about it, then shook his head. "I'll only tell you this because I trust you, because honestly, I don't know how much harm the scale would do in the wrong hands. It is magically attuned to me, at least that is what Elvistir said, and I think that means that as long as I'm alive, only I can use it to its full potential."

Tannil nodded, looking down at the scale, then back at Dannan. "I can make it glow like you saw. At first, I could only make it as bright as a torch. I think that's all Elvistir really intended for it to do. But I've noticed the more aware I become of it, and the harder I concentrate, I can make the light level change depending on my feelings and by how hard I concentrate on it. For example, if I'm happy, the light is soft. If I'm angry, I think it's going to be a sharper light. I haven't really had much time for experimentation, since it's a very noticeable thing when I do. But when I fought the bandits on the way to Whitehaven, the light was very harsh."

He looked thoughtful for a moment. "I'm pretty certain only Samust and the other two guards saw it. And I know they won't tell. Not since I saved their lives." Tannil chuckled, shaking his head.

Giving him an odd look, Dannan waited for a moment. "What's so funny?"

Tannil grinned at him, his visible teeth nowhere near as threatening in this form. "You'd easily fit in with the Wolves Brigade. We fight from the time we're apprentices, about eight to ten years old for humans, and at your age, most of the children have killed. But it's very rare to see that among regular humans."

Dannan shrugged, his discomfort showing on his face, and Tannil shook his head. "Don't be upset about that. The fact is, you killed protecting the lives of others. There's very little as noble as that, except for perhaps fighting for a just cause. So don't feel bad about that at all." Dannan nodded slightly, his mouth twisted with worry.

"I just hate seeing how people react once they know I've killed. Most of them won't be as forgiving as you are."

Tannil sighed, and smiled. "Once you're in the field, you'll find people have a distinctly different attitude about that. But for now, get back to telling me about the scale. That seems to make you happier. Look, even the light has changed."

Dannan took notice of the light filling the room once more, and he was surprised to see that Tannil was right. The soft, enveloping purple glow had turned into a hazy, mist-like shroud that hung in the air, giving the room a haunting aura.

Taking deep breaths, Dannan closed his eyes and tried to concentrate on getting his emotions under control. After a few moments, he opened his eyes again, only to find that there had been no change. Frowning slightly, he shrugged at Tannil.

"Think of the dragoness. Close your eyes and picture her, and then try to calm yourself."

Dannan nodded and closed his eyes, letting his mind wander

back to that day. He could feel himself smiling as he once again saw her gracefully ascending into the sky.

Opening his eyes after a little bit, he saw that the light had once again gone back to a soft, enveloping purple glow. Tannil covered his mouth, trying unsuccessfully to hold in all his laughter. Looking at him, Dannan grimaced wryly, and shook his head.

Once Tannil's laughter finally stopped, he looked at Dannan again, still grinning. "Oh, but the look on your face was priceless." Dannan raised an eyebrow at him, and Tannil shook his head. "I'm sorry, it's just that I've very rarely seen a look that lovestruck admiration on anyone, much less someone your age. You really meant it when you said you had to meet her even if it killed you."

Dannan nodded, and Tannil's grin relaxed into a smile. "Well, I'll do my best to see you get through this training along with me, then. I'd love to see how a dragoness looks being escorted to a ball on your arm." Dannan scowled at him, and Tannil began to howl with laughter, clutching his sides.

Grabbing his pillow, Dannan covered Tannil's head playfully, until finally Tannil pushed him off, gasping for air from laughing too hard. "I'd love to see her, but with how in love you are, you might kill me out of jealousy." Dannan lifted the pillow again, and Tannil covered his mouth with a hand, trying hard to contain more laughter as tears came to his eyes.

After a few more minutes, Tannil shook his head and took a calm, deep breath. Finally able to speak without laughing anymore, he looked at Dannan again. "You said it has other abilities?" Dannan nodded, and concentrated on making the light from the scale softer and dimmer. After a moment, its' glow became more like that of a small lantern than that of a bonfire.

"The most dangerous ability it has, at least for her, is that as long as I'm wearing it, I can find her. It will always point me in the right direction to her, though I don't know if I could tell distance with it. Maybe if I became more skilled in its use. But I can always feel a slight tug on my heart, leading me in the direction towards her. I can also tell, to some extent, that she's alright. Maybe I'd be able to tell how she's feeling, to, if I tried. I won't even pretend to understand magic, much less this world I jumped headfirst into."

Tannil chuckled, and smiled sadly. "Just remember that, and you'll be safer. This world isn't all fun and games. And when you're dealing with the fey, they don't much care about people who mean no harm to them or their woods. But with that scale, they'll either react better or worse immediately to you."

Scratching his cheek, Tannil's smile faded. "Since fey magic is definitely present, the good fey will probably welcome you. But those fey who are fueled by negative emotions will probably seek to kill you whenever they find you."

Dannan shrugged, then grinned slightly. "As opposed to human bandits, who will try to kill me just for sport? Ha ha." Tannil shrugged and nodded, conceding the point.

"Magic can be a wonderful and fascinating thing, but it can also be amazingly dangerous. Just remember that. A gift, or a curse."

"Don't worry, I'll keep that in mind."

Grinning once more, Tannil nodded. "Good. You can practice at night with your scale in here, and I'll keep a watch at the door. Who knows, maybe some day I'll need the help of you and your dragoness. It can't hurt to have friends in high places. Especially for scouting." Tannil added with a small laugh.

Dannan rolled his eyes and rolled onto his side, concentrating on extinguishing the light, and suddenly the world was dark before his eyes again. Sliding the dragon scale back inside his shirt, he gripped it gently. Drifting off to sleep, he felt it pulse in time with his own heart, and he smiled.

Chapter 23

The next day Dannan barely noticed his bruises during practice, and he found it easier to smile without pain as well. Afternoon practice was interesting, as they started studying the practical applications of learning about chain mail. Specifically, how it felt to be hit in it, as well as how best to dodge to change a fatal blow into an injury that they could survive.

Each person was paired up, one as a defender, one as an attacker, and they spent the whole afternoon swinging practice swords and blunted maces at each other and dodging. "Enjoy working your frustrations out on your classmates, because tomorrow, they get the chance to return the favor! And remember, only aim at the chain mail. We'll be practicing how to dodge someone aiming for your head later on in the course." The teacher told them with a smile.

Dannan was paired up with Carissa, and although he would've preferred Tannil as his partner, he didn't complain. As they began the lesson, Dannan wondered if he'd be able to hit a girl when the time came tomorrow. By the time she was finished adding bruises to his ribs, he was sure he would have no problem.

When he was finally able to take the chain mail off again, Dannan winced and gingerly pulled it off, so sore he was barely able to lift his arms over his head. While he didn't mind the beating, the smug little smirk on Carissa's face irked him greatly. As they all turned to return to the dorms, the teacher stopped them. "Yes, Teacher Kalaman?" Said one of the two brunette brothers.

"The other teachers and I had a meeting last night. While the investigation as to whether someone outside attacked those students or not is going on, no one will be allowed outside the compound. If someone is targeting students, we can't allow anyone else to be injured." The students all traded looks with each other, and Tannil and Dannan exchanged wary looks. "That is all. Back to your dorm rooms." They all nodded and turned, heading straight for the dorms.

After dinner that night, Dannan nervously paced their room from end to end, counting each step as he went. "Maybe we should tell them, Tannil. I mean, if they find out without us telling them, I'm guaranteed to be dismissed. And you heard the teacher, they're practically closing the compound down, to make sure they catch whoever did it."

"Are you willing to risk that they'll accept that you caused that kind of damage defending yourself from four bullies? That they won't ask why you hurt them that badly?" Dannan stared at his feet for a moment, then went back to pacing.

Shaking his head, Tannil growled. "There's a chance they already know, but that's the problem. If they already know, they don't plan to dismiss you. The chances that my lie was seen through are not high, but it does exist. And if our teacher did see through me, then they've known since that night. Which presents us with another problem. If they've known since that night, then the teachers have already formed opinions, without ever hearing your side of the story."

Dannan frowned, scratching at his upper arm nervously. "So the issue is we don't know how much they know, and without knowing that, hiding might or might not be useless?"

Tannil nodded, a discouraged look on his face. "I don't know how much experience the teacher's have with magic, but if they recognize that your dragon scale is magical, you may have to leave before they can take it from you." Dannan's expression grew even more worried, and Tannil shook his head. "In the worst case scenario, you'll have to run, and you won't be able to return to Whitehaven. You might not even be able to return home. Are you willing to take that risk, just to do 'the right thing'?"

Taking a deep breath, he nodded. "I have to this time, so that no other students suffer for something that isn't their fault. Not when I know the truth. You already pointed that out to me." Tannil sighed and stood up, shaking his head.

"You know we have no idea where to find the teachers right now, right?"

Dannan looked at the door. "I have a general idea where the teacher's rooms are, and isn't one patrolling right now? We should run into whichever one is patrolling in the mess hall if we wait a little while."

Tannil shook his head and grinned. "That's probably not the best idea. Using my nose, maybe we can sniff out our teacher's room. You said you know the general direction to their rooms, so if we just go that way, I should be able to tell which room is his. The teacher's probably have real doors on their rooms, to, not these silly things we have that wouldn't stop a stiff breeze."

"Alright, do you want to carry the torch, or should I? You can see in the dark better than I can, but if we're walking around in total darkness, it would be really suspicious."

Sighing, Tannil shrugged. "I'll carry it. It will feel odd, since normally I aim for darker areas in night time missions, but you're right. It would look more suspicious to not have a torch." Looking up at Dannan, Tannil smiled. "So, ready to go jump off a cliff and hope there's a lake below?"

Dannan winced at his comparison, then grinned back. "I hope there's one. If not, I'm going to be gone from here very quickly." Tannil nodded solemnly and stood, grabbing a flare stick from the end table. "Alright, let's go before we realize that this might not be even a remotely good idea." Dannan chuckled, and gripped the door handle.

Stepping out into the dimly lit hall, Dannan looked left and right, surprised how eerie the silence was inside a solid stone structure. Moving aside, he looked over as Tannil exited behind him.

Taking the torch, Tannil gently pressed his hand to the door as it began to swing shut on its hinges, easing it closed to avoid noise. They slowly began their trek through the halls, Tannil a few feet in front, Dannan casting worried glances behind them every so often.

When they finally made it to the stairway without interruption, Dannan let out a small sigh of relief, quickly covering his mouth as Tannil made a shushing motion at him. Handing the torch to him, Tannil quickly walked down the stairs, his boots making almost no noise as he went down.

Coming back up a moment later, Tannil took the torch from him again, motioning for Dannan to follow. As they walked downstairs, Dannan couldn't help but marvel at how it felt like they were going deeper underground. Trying to shake off the feeling of being trapped, Dannan gently gripped the dragon scale through his shirt, drawing comfort in the feeling of it in his hand. As they walked down the hallway towards the mess hall, Tannil held up a hand for them to stop. After around a minute of standing there silently, he nodded, and they began walking forward once more.

Standing at the doorway to the mess hall, Tannil looked

around before finally motioning to Dannan to come after him. Glancing around quietly, Tannil pointed at the doorway that led towards the waiting room, and then across to the hall, before pointing back to Dannan.

Dannan nodded silently, then pointed at the door towards the waiting room. Although the building was basically rectangular from the outside, Dannan didn't want to accidentally wind up taking a set of stairs down to a real dungeon. Heading towards the waiting room, Dannan suddenly had the feeling that something or someone was waiting there for them.

Lightly tapping Tannil on the shoulder, he shook his head at Tannil and gently gripped his shoulder. Tannil nodded at him, then looked down the hallway, motioning with his eyes. Dannan shook his head once more, and gently took hold of the torch. Tannil grinned, then nodded, gently tapping his eyes. Dannan nodded back at him, then walked a little bit away with the torch, so that the light wouldn't give Tannil away as he continued forward.

Disappearing into the darkness, Tannil didn't glance back at all, and for a moment, Dannan felt utterly alone. Trapped by darkness and stone, he felt his breathing begin to quicken and his blood race, and although he knew how to get out of the building, he felt completely isolated.

Closing his eyes, he concentrated on a mental image of the dragoness, using that to calm himself, and he opened them again. Looking around, he kept a constant vigil on both sides of the hallway, waiting for Tannil to come back.

The minutes seemed to stretch on forever as he waited, and when Tannil finally came back into view, Dannan almost jumped with glee. Tannil motioned for Dannan to come, and Dannan followed after him as Tannil set a quick pace towards the waiting room.

As the torchlight entered the room, Dannan saw that their teacher was waiting there, seated in the most advantageous spot to see all four entrances. He looked up at the sudden intrusion of the light, seeming unsurprised, and stood. "What are you two doing down here at this hour?"

Dannan looked at Tannil, then spoke softly. "I have something I have to tell you, sir."

"About the attack the other night?" Dannan nodded slightly,

trying to conceal the tremor that ran through him. "You were the one they attacked, am I right?" Dannan lowered his head, and the teacher sighed. "So this was a regular hazing gone wrong, then?"

Dannan nodded again, unable to speak for fear of giving away his nervousness. "And the bite mark?" Dannan was glad that the torchlight distorted colors, as it hid some of his embarrassment. He lowered his head further, until he was staring at the ground. "Alright." Dannan looked up at his teacher in surprise, and waited, unsure of how to react.

"We were fairly certain it was a hazing that got out of hand. These things happen every so often when the seniors get… over-excited. However, since we weren't absolutely sure who they had been fighting, we wanted to be certain. When I saw you two, I had a feeling that you had been the one they had been hazing. Tannil, after all, would have been able to beat them without using both arms."

Tannil grinned at the compliment, and the teacher glared at him. "Lying to a superior, however, is a very serious infraction. You two will be held inside for the mandatory punishment period, which is two full seasons. After those two seasons, you will be allowed to leave the compound on the afternoons off, though under the same restrictions as the other students. Since this isn't an entirely unexpected development, there will be no other punishment, unless you are caught lying to a teacher or one of the guards here again. Have I made myself clear?"

Tannil saluted, and Dannan imitated him quickly, unsure of what else to do. After a moment, their teacher nodded, and made a dismissive motion towards them. "Get back to bed. Practice won't wait because you're tired." They both nodded and headed back to the room, tomorrow promising to be an interesting day.

Chapter 24

Despite Dannan and Tannil's expectations, the next day was completely normal. Practice went as planned, and Dannan enjoyed giving Carissa a number of bruises to match his own. When the day finally came to an end, Dannan was relieved that nothing had occurred other than the teacher seeming to keep a more watchful eye on them.

That night, Dannan practiced harmonizing with the scale for the first time, spending hours simply exploring every inch of it with his hands in the dark. He didn't know how long it was, but when he drifted off to sleep, he felt that comfortable tug at the front of his thoughts.

The rest of the fortnight went quickly for Dannan. He spent each day with sword exercises and studying armor, and each night studying the scale, yet he still felt well rested by the end of it.

When the rest of the students went out for their afternoons in groups, Dannan was happy to stay in the dorm and study the dragon scale further. Tannil spent the time relaxing in their room with him, occasionally trading stories about the campaigns he had fought in, or about his pack back home.

The next fortnight was the first time that Dannan saw any of the boys who had attacked him again, but the moment they saw him they turned pale with fear and went the other way.

Although normally such a reaction would have bothered him, Dannan was more than happy that they were avoiding him. He was pretty certain that he wouldn't have to worry too much about getting any more trouble from senior students, as his name had been included in some of the rumors that had been going around the compound.

His main concern was staying out of trouble from now on, so that he could continue his studies here. These thoughts and the stories Tannil shared with him occupied his time as summer approached.

The first two fortnight's of summer, Dannan wasn't sure if he should get clothes from the quartermaster. However, by the third fortnight, summer was in full swing, and practice was becoming harder in the spring outfit.

He was glad that they got two full outfits as part of their student allotment, because it was an unreasonably hot summer. He even heard some of the teachers complaining about the heat. Dannan was most surprised by Tannil's lack of a reaction, since he was from the much colder northlands.

Tannil just laughed his curiosity off, saying "When you're in the mountains, you find all sorts of strange things. And once you've dealt with caverns with magma in them, summer heat really isn't that bad." Dannan wanted to believe Tannil was jesting with him, yet after everything he had seen, he wasn't so sure.

As the summer came to a close, Dannan thought about how the hunters and others back home would be doing, and how they would be preparing for the fall logging season. He wondered how the farmers were doing, and if his mother was starting to make the pies she baked every year.

Smiling to himself, Dannan briefly wondered how long it would be before he returned home. Indeed, if he would ever get the chance. Shaking his head, Dannan pushed that line of thinking away, deciding that would come when he finished his training.

Before he knew it, the heat of summer gave way to the wonderful breezes of fall, bringing with them the burnished bronze, rust-red, and yellow gold leaves that made the forests so beautiful in his opinion. As the temperatures finally started to return to more reasonable levels, they changed from studying chain mail to full plate armor.

Dannan was amazed that they used such an expensive suit of armor for practice, but given that they were being trained to be the best, he accepted it on some level. They spent almost the entire season sparring against Teacher Kalaman while he wore the armor.

Towards the end, he also trained Tannil in its use, since he was the only one tall enough. Dannan spent that whole fortnight laughing, as Tannil constantly complained about how itchy and heavy the armor was. Dannan was in agreement with Tannil on one major point, though. No matter how good the protection was, if it made you too slow to reach your enemy, it was useless.

At the end of the fall, the wind grew cold, and with it, the first snows came. Dannan loved how the new snow lightly coated the whole world. Although it chilled him to the bone most nights, he still thought it made the world look so peaceful before people began to dirty the snow with their boots.

The first night after it snowed, Dannan and Tannil crept up onto the battlements, staying far enough from the towers that they wouldn't be spotted. Placing a blanket down on a spot they cleared of snow, they sat and looked out over the city, blanketed with the soft white fluff.

Grinning over at Tannil, Dannan couldn't help but feel at peace. "Were the northlands ever like this for you, Tannil?" Tannil nodded, still staring out over the city, and for a moment, Dannan thought he saw him begin to tear up.

Clearing his throat, Tannil turned to Dannan, his characteristic grin back once more. "The day before a fight, sometimes, the snow was this wonderful. Some of the older members of the pack used to say 'the snow promises new beginnings as it makes everything equal'. I often wondered what they had meant by that, but staring at the peace and tranquility of it, I usually forgot. For some reason, I can't help but remember it now."

Dannan smiled a little. "It's called homesickness. It's alright to feel it, even if you are a big, bad mercenary." Tannil snorted at him, and Dannan had to hold back a laugh as his smile grew. Turning back out to the city, Dannan let out a small sigh. "My mother and father will be sitting on a rug in front of the fire right now, their backs up against several cushions and blankets we keep for the winter. Most likely, father will be reading one of the books he loves; ma-mann will be knitting something for one of the village elder's young grandchildren. Sometimes, she'll work on a quilt for a year or so. The ones she first made for me went to them."

He went silent for a moment, letting his eyes rest on the occasional plume of smoke rising from the sleeping houses. "Although I have no other relatives that I know of, my father was always close with the village elder. I never found out how they met, but if the village elder believed something needed to happen, my father always supported him. Come to think of it, I don't know how my mother met my father, either. I've always wondered, but never asked."

Tannil chuckled softly, shaking his head. "Sometimes, it's something special, sometimes it's not. While the children of a pack are raised communally, I knew who my parents were. Harkig Wolfbrother was my father, and my mother was Selena Moonmistress. My father was a very typical werewolf of the Wolves Brigade, and my mother came from a line of elven werewolves from the western woods. Apparently, they hadn't suffered the same way my ancestors had, because when the first cursed ones appeared, the elven lines dealt with them, and their creators, swiftly."

Dannan glanced sideways at Tannil, then let out a soft "hmm".

Looking over at Dannan, Tannil cocked his head to the side. "What?"

"Well, you said the cursed ones appeared after the elven line was already established. The legends say that what you call the cursed ones appeared first, and their descendants started to be born that way after a few generations."

Tannil chuckled and shook his head. "The legends also say all werewolves are ravenous, bloodthirsty monsters with no control over themselves. We've proven that one wrong, haven't we?" Dannan turned slightly, his embarrassment showing on his face.

"I'm curious, though. Where do your people say they come from?"

Taking a deep breath, Tannil raised his eyes, staring out over the city, and far beyond its walls. "This is actually the reason the natural born hunt the cursed. You see, the lines of werewolves for each race that harbors them were established at least several thousand years ago. Maybe even since the first human-like creatures walked the land. But about two thousand years ago, after humans had discovered magic, the darker side of magic began to show up."

Grimacing, he seemed like he wouldn't continue, when finally he sighed. "One of the things that came from human wizards was the Curse of Transformation. The curse didn't specifically seek to create werewolves, from what I understand. It simply turned the cursed being into a bloodthirsty monster. So even if you were to be cursed into the form of say, a rabbit, you would be a flesh-eating one, who wouldn't stop until killed. It was most likely developed for war."

Tannil let this sink in for a moment, ignoring Dannan's chuckling at the idea of a flesh-eating rabbit. "I suppose a wizard of that time saw how strong, fast, and deadly werewolves could be. My people don't record his name, I think because they didn't want to immortalize what our culture essentially considers a living 'sin'. The reason for this, as the story goes, is that he took the curse, and fashioned it into a disease-like thing, so that anyone who survived the attacks of a cursed being would be transformed into the same thing."

"Because he copied werewolves so accurately, however, the cursed copies couldn't maintain their form all the time. Most likely because of the tremendous magic that it requires. So only when the lunar magic that werewolves use is at its strongest, during the full moon, are they forced to transform. Some werewolves, the more spiritual ones, believe it is the moon goddess' way of exposing the aberrations that were modeled after her children. I'm not particularly religious, but I can understand how they would see some truth in that."

Pausing for a few moments, a wistful look came over Tannil's face, and a small smile curled the edges of his mouth. "I remember Joingur, our storyteller, always used to tell these stories to the small children and adults who would gather around on the full moon and new moon. In many ways, I think he felt that he was leaving us a part of himself as a legacy, not just the legacy of our people."

Dannan watched Tannil silently as he sat there for a few moments, remembering a far off land. "What was your mother like?"

Tannil shook himself from his reverie, and turned back to Dannan. "Oh, she was a strict one. But she was also very kind and loving. She felt it was her responsibility to act as the second in command. To always keep her wits about her when my father got overly excited."

He grinned to himself slightly. "My father was the kind who got excited about a hunt, a battle, or a game of catch-the-pig. The only time I ever really saw my father serious, truly serious, was when we had to fight the cursed ones. The Wolves Brigade made a reputation as being 'bloodthirsty' and 'savage', that way, commander's hired us based on the idea that we would simply kill whatever came our way. Under that cover, whenever we went hunting cursed ones, it didn't look as strange to be abandoning our posts."

A pensive look came over his face, and he lowered his gaze. "The most notable fight I remember was when we were in the northern mountains, and we had heard rumors of a wizard's valley. We were fighting orcs there, and some of the ones we ran into turned out to be cursed. Using magic, our... 'priest' as you would call him captured one of the cursed ones. After interrogating him, we found out that the wizard had rediscovered the curse of transformation, and he had created the cursed ones we fought."

"The pack immediately took off towards the valley, abandoning the hunt of the orc tribe we had been on. As a wolf runs, it took us less than a day to reach it, though some of the children were tired. They stayed by the valley entrance while the fighters moved in for the kill. The valley had been affected by strong magic, as it was closer to a forest here during the spring than a frozen windswept valley. I was seventeen at the time, and so I was with the death hunt. There were a number of cursed ones guarding the tower, and one almost got me, but thanks to the more experienced members they were all killed."

Tannil's eyes glazed over as he remembered, and he spoke with a tremor of awe in his voice. "Cursed ones are almost as strong as the natural born, but the ten hunters who came with us, my father included, slew them like you would calves. Single blows normally are not enough to kill a cursed one, yet my father, with his great ax Klimdor, rent them apart in a single strike."

"Although I have never seen him fight as ferociously, I have never seen him as upset, either. He takes his duties as a hunter very seriously, and that is what first attracted my mother to him, who has similar ideals."

He shook his head, as if to rid himself of an unpleasant memory, and he smiled wanly. "I have killed before, but I can safely say that what the hunters did to the wizard when we found him... that was murder, not killing. It was like watching a rabbit try to fight a pack of hounds. He had powerful spells at his disposal, yes, but something about my father's ax rendered them useless against him. And when he was finally exhausted, they transformed and tore him apart with their fangs. I accept that he needed death because of what he did, but at the same time, there was so much malice in what they did that I had a hard time stomaching it."

"I think for my father, as for many of my people, they take the existence of the cursed as an affront to everything they stand for. It can be hard to watch the... retribution, though."

Shaking his head again, Tannil met Dannan's eyes for a moment, and Dannan was sure he saw guilt in them. "Are you worried that you might be more monstrous than what you're hunting? Or that you enjoy destroying them too much?"

At the second part of Dannan's statement, Tannil flinched a little, and then shook his head. "So it is that you're afraid of enjoying it." Tannil met his gaze, and the guilt was clearer now.

"You aren't a monster, Tannil. Not like they are. It's one thing to hunt your enemies, and another to enjoy destroying them. It's an entirely different thing to hunt others simply for the enjoyment of killing. You have a purpose when you hunt those who are cursed. Even if that purpose is to kill them, you have a purpose. Not only that, but if you don't hunt them, they will hurt innocent people. Tell me, has there ever been mention of a cursed one maintaining enough control to not hunt humans?"

Tannil shook his head after a moment, and he sighed. "I just worry about becoming too much like them."

Trying to smile as comfortingly as he could, Dannan patted him on the shoulder. "That's a good thing, though. You should worry about becoming too much like them. It's when you've stopped worrying about the consequences that you'll have truly become like them. Until that happens, do what your heart feels is right, even if it's granting them a merciful death that you don't necessarily think they deserve."

Tannil nodded, then took a deep breath. Chuckling a little, he looked out over the city, and then looked back at Dannan. "Here I am being told how to live by someone, what, nine years my junior?"

"Eight, actually. I celebrate my naming day at the beginning of the fall."

"Congratulations. You survived another year."

Dannan chuckled, then stopped when he realized Tannil was serious. "Oh, that's right. That is something of an accomplishment in the northlands, isn't it?"

Letting out a yawn, Dannan leaned his back against one of the merlons. Looking up at the sky, Dannan smiled a little. "I just hope I live enough to see the dragoness again."

Tannil chuckled, then nodded. "I'm sure you will. Not many ever see a dragon; much less have the strength of will to make finding the dragon again their life's purpose. I think you'll succeed. And if you're having too much trouble on your own, you can always call on your friend for help."

Dannan looked over at him in surprise, and Tannil nodded.

Dannan looked over at him in surprise and Tannil nodded. Grinning, Dannan nodded after a moment. "Thanks, Tannil. I appreciate that. I really do."

Tannil shrugged, and then smiled. "You can only survive in this world with a pack. And all packs are formed from just such bonds. So why is it surprising, when you guard my secret and I guard yours, that we should be friends?"

Shrugging, Dannan realized he had never thought of it from such a practical viewpoint. After a few minutes of silence, Dannan rose to his knees, casting one last look out over the silent town. "Let's return to our room. Tomorrow's practice won't wait because we're tired." Tannil laughed at Dannan's mimicry of the teacher, and they folded up the blanket before sneaking back to their rooms for sleep.

Chapter 25

Despite enjoying how the snow looked, Dannan found that practicing in it was extremely tiring. Trying to maintain his balance in the mud and packed snow of the training field, he was exhausted by the time they finished. He saw that many of the other students had run into the same problem, and he hoped that it would get better in time.

Lunch was a wonderful respite from the cold, with hot beef stew warming them right up, and Dannan went to the afternoon class full of energy. The class switched from plate armor to leather today, and Dannan found that not only was it interesting, it was warmer.

He was surprised to find out just how many different types of leather there were, as he had just assumed all leather armor was made from standard hides, like cow. After the class was over, the teacher stopped Dannan and Tannil while the rest of their classmates went back to the dorm. Standing in front of him patiently, they waited in silence as he looked them up and down.

"You both know what you did wrong, correct?" They nodded, never letting their eyes leave his. "Good. You will be allowed to leave on the rest days like the others, with the same restrictions. Your punishment is ended, and so is your house arrest. I will be harsher next time, however. So do not let this happen again. Am I making myself clear?"

They both nodded, and answered with a quick "Yes Sir!"

Looking them each in the eye, he waited for a few moments before nodding. "Go get washed off, and get to sleep. The winter has only just started. It's too early for you to get pneumonia." They both saluted before taking off towards the dorm. They could feel their teacher's eyes on them as they left, and Dannan silently thanked whoever was watching out for them that they had only been punished lightly.

The constant fight to adjust to the snow during practice

slackened some during that fortnight, as they all finally began to get used to the slush and mud. Another fortnight passed, and they began to fall into an easy rhythm, until the snow storms started up.

On mornings when the snow wasn't falling too heavily they practiced in the falling snow, the icy flakes cooling their sweating bodies. On the mornings where the snow was too heavy, they practiced inside wherever they could. As the third fortnight of winter passed, the storms became more frequent, sometimes dropping ten inches of snow in a single night.

Although Dannan was used to the snow, two of the boys had come from the south, and this was the first winter they had ever seen snow. Dannan felt bad for them, but at the same time, he couldn't help but laugh at them as they constantly walked around complaining about the cold.

Tannil seemed amused by all of them, as he could sometimes be seen walking around without even a coat on. "It's another benefit of being a werewolf." Tannil said when Dannan inquired about it. "I'm less affected by regular cold like this."

Dannan sometimes made fun of Tannil, saying there was little that actually affected him. The first time that Dannan had made the joke, Tannil had grown deadly serious, and shook his head.

"Silver, certain rare ores, and magic tend to be the only things that cause serious harm to a werewolf. Otherwise, anything other than a fatal wound or a lost limb will heal." Dannan was reminded of Tannil's scars, and he could understand how that would help a warrior.

The classes were never held up by the snow. If there was too much snow outside, the teachers with the two smallest classes shared the waiting room, while the two larger classes used opposite sides of the mess hall. The first few times, this had been uncomfortable for some of the students, including Dannan, but after a while, they got used to seeing each other.

A few times, he even saw some of the senior students from their dorm flirting with Carissa, though she was merciless in her rejections. The first time she saw Dannan laughing, she had come straight for him, though he had retreated for fear of being struck. After that, she simply glared at him whenever she caught him laughing.

The winter progressed peacefully like this, until finally the snows began to melt, and the days began to lengthen once more. On the last day of winter, their teacher took them all into the waiting room on their afternoon off, where he made sure they waited until the last student had arrived.

Finally, when the last boy, one of the two dark olive-skinned southerners had arrived, the teacher nodded at them. "Congratulations. You have officially passed your first year of training. Starting tomorrow, we will make sure that you have mastered the basics of the armorers' class. After you have all either internalized the knowledge or been dismissed for ineptitude, we will begin your second year preparations. In sixty days, you will all begin your second year as students here. If you succeed. I will not make these tests easy on you. The life of a Swordmaster is a harsh one, and I would be doing you more of a disservice to send you out, unskilled and unready, than refusing you this path. You will receive two tries on each test. Fail both, and you will be dismissed. Succeed either time, and you will move on."

He let that sink in a moment before continuing. "You will be tested on the basic forms that you have learned in practice, to make sure that you can do them on your own. Those will be the easiest tests. The harder tests will be on what I have taught you about armor. You will need to be able to demonstrate the ability to fight an opponent who is wearing it, as well as remember any special dangers about wearing particular armors. Now, are there any questions?"

Looking around, he waited several moments before finally nodding. "Alright. Tomorrow after practice, instead of regular class, you will all come here, and your tests will be conducted as a group. You are forbidden from helping each other during the tests, and you will be expected to remain polite. Are those rules clear?"

They all nodded, replying with a clear "Yes Sir!" Making a dismissive motion at them, he turned towards the hallway that Dannan thought led to the teacher's quarters, and strode out of sight.

They quickly began talking amongst each other, several of them wondering if they shouldn't study the armors together as a group. Carissa snorted at the idea, and several of the boys looked embarrassed by her scorn, until Dannan spoke up. "I think it's a great idea. What do we have to lose from acting as a unit? If you look at the older classes, what is it they have that we lack? It's cohesiveness as a military unit. Something that our teacher has been nagging us about almost since he first met us."

Several of his classmates murmured in agreement. "This is the perfect time to make use of that. After all, we're all here to succeed as Swordmasters, right? And he never said that anyone has to pass. Who knows, maybe we could all fail out by our eighth year. And where would that leave us? I say we work together, whatever our reasons, so that we can accomplish what we came here for."

Several of them were staring at him in surprise, while Carissa was staring at him with contempt. Glancing over at Tannil, Dannan was surprised to see a small smirk on his lips, but could tell from Tannil's face that he approved.

"What the hell, why not." Tannil said casually. "It's like he said. This isn't a 'one person is the best' situation. We could all fail if we're not careful. I, for one, would rather not fail because of a stupid mistake. I'm all for it."

Carissa snorted, and Tannil turned to look at her. "Do you have something to say?"

Sneering at him derisively, she laughed. "You two are such friends, is it any surprise you'd support him?"

The others were starting to look back and forth from Carissa to Tannil, but Dannan sat back, unworried. "You think there's a problem with having allies, Carissa?"

Sneering again, she stood up. "Oh please, as if allies are all that important."

Glaring out at her from under lowered eyelids, Tannil's look stopped her cold. "Those without any allies are just curs, trying to get scraps from whatever table they can find. Even hyenas have allies, disgusting as they might be. And no one outside of this compound can help you during the tests."

Carissa turned crimson with embarrassment and opened her mouth to speak, but Tannil cut her off. "So, are you willing to join us, or do you want to leave? After all, you're welcome to make your own decision. But those of us who choose to stay are also welcome to make our own decisions."

Tannil said this in such a way that although they could feel the pressure of his words, Dannan was sure no one felt pressed upon by them.

After a moment or two of uncomfortable silence, she sat down again, her face less beet red, but no less angry. Tannil nodded at her, then turned and smiled at the others. "I say we form a circle, so that we can see who's talking more easily. We only have this afternoon to study, after all."

Nodding in agreement, Dannan and a number of the other boys stood up, rearranging ten of the chairs so that they could all sit in a circle. Carissa grumbled something about "overly emotional people" but a quick glare from Tannil silenced her. The others seemed glad to have some direction, and after quickly figuring out how to go about it, they began a round-robin question and answer style, to make sure that everyone was completely set when it came to each type of armor.

By the time they finished, Dannan had memorized the names of the rest of his classmates, even though he was only really getting to know them now. Glancing over at the two brothers, Symon and Tymon, Dannan couldn't help but be surprised at how well they complemented each other in terms of personality. Although Symon was more outgoing, with Tymon's support, they had forgotten almost nothing the teacher told them.

Ahminel, one of the southerners, had remembered the weakness of each armor down to which joints were easiest to hit, and which were most likely to be exposed in certain attacks. Careel, the other southerner, wasn't very skilled when it came to these things.

They did find out that he absolutely loved various siege engines, and had a very strong understanding of fortifications. Carissa, although ornery, had a strong grasp of basic swordsmanship, and also the other weapons they had practiced with, like the spear and axe.

Dannan was surprised to find out that Hale and Uthul both came from near the Great Cities, further east, where the barbarian hordes had first struck. Their last classmate, Ramme, had come from the north, like Tannil. He was a smaller boy, even by their standards. Dannan was sure that Ramme was probably only a year or two younger than him, but at three and a half feet, Dannan was sure the boy would need a lot of growing to catch up.

Although they had only spent the time between lunch and dinner studying, even Carissa acknowledged that it was unlikely that any of them would fail the tests tomorrow. Dannan couldn't help feeling a bit of pride when he thought of them not just as other students, but as his classmates. He caught himself grinning like an idiot as they replaced the chairs and went on their way to dinner, and he was glad to lose himself in the idle conversation and gossip that was traded.

The next day came fast, and practice seemed done even before it began. Dannan knew that like him, his classmates were all extremely nervous. When the teacher finally arrived, they were all starting to show signs of their anxiety, from Tymon's hand wringing to Carissa's angry pacing.

Looking them over, a small smile flitted across their teacher's face before it became impassive once more. "Move the chairs to the outside of the room, stacking all but ten so that you can sit." They nodded and immediately set about doing so, and in short order the center of the room was unmarred by any object.

When this was done, the teacher whistled, and the blacksmith's apprentice came in through the front door carrying a stack of ten practice swords. Setting them down in the center of the room, he nodded to each of them, and then saluted the teacher.

Saluting back, the teacher nodded a curt dismissal, and the young man exited quickly. Motioning for them to take the swords, the teacher waited patiently until each had armed themselves and fallen in line. "Now, I'm going to walk one by one between each of you, and you will demonstrate ten of each practice swing. If your posture or form is off for any of the ten swings, you will have failed that chance. Any questions?" After a few moments of silence, he nodded. Walking down to the end Dannan stood at, the teacher stared at him. Assuming the practice position, Dannan took a few deep breaths. "Begin."

Each swing felt like he was trying to lift an anvil, and Dannan was curious why he had never been so aware of how heavy his body really was. Keeping his eyes closed, he concentrated on the mental image of the sword work, switching smoothly from each practice stance after the tenth swing, until he had done all four forms.

Opening his eyes, he looked at the teacher, whose face was a picture of surprise. Dannan turned a little red from embarrassment, and the teacher turned from him to look at the others. "Do the forms that well, and you will pass." Looking back at Dannan, the teacher seemed to be appraising him in a new light, and Dannan wondered what he had done right to inspire such a reaction from his teacher.

Moving on to Tannil, who was the next student, the teacher

waited momentarily as he assumed the first stance. Studying him, the teacher gave a small nod. "Begin!"

The moment the word was out of his mouth, Tannil began his swings. Methodically he went through the first ten, before switching to the second stance. Taking what seemed like seconds in that stance, he once again went through the swings. Stopping once more for a moment, he switched to the third stance, the swipe, and executed it with a fairly good form. Switching to the last stance, Tannil made each swing count, the sound of the practice sword cutting the air in the room. The moment Tannil finished, the teacher nodded. "Nicely done. Pass."

Tannil murmured his thanks and winked at Dannan, who smiled. Moving from one student to the next, the teacher repeated the process, until he reached Careel. While executing the fourth stance, the teacher shook his head. Careel stopped so suddenly he almost hurt his arm, and he grabbed the sword with his other hand as well to stop from losing his grip. "You will have to try again after I finish with Ramme and Carissa. Wait patiently until then."

Careel nodded, downcast, and Dannan gave Tannil a worried glance. Ramme and Carissa both passed with ease and the teacher returned to Careel. Taking a deep breath, Careel slowly started to go through the forms again, going without issue.

Taking the fourth stance, Careel got visibly nervous, when Tannil called out "We know you can do it Careel, don't worry!" Careel looked over at him, and Tannil smiled back. Careel looked at the others, then took another deep breath, relaxing his shoulders.

The instructor gave Tannil a warning glare, then turned back to Careel as he began to swing. After the tenth swing, they all waited with baited breath, and the instructor nodded. "You pass." Careel startled them all as he leaped into the air with a small whoop, and his grin said it all.

Turning quickly back to the teacher, they all fell into line once more, waiting patiently and silently for his next instructions. The teacher glanced from one to the next, and then nodded. "Tomorrow you will all take the armorers' test, and we will see how many of you successfully make it to your second year. Until then, you are dismissed."

They all saluted, then quietly filed out of the room towards the mess hall. The sun had already fallen out of sight, and they were sure dinner was probably starting by now. Dannan, the last one out, was the only one to notice the small smile on the teacher's face as they left.

The evening went by quickly, and Dannan was pleased to see that the excitement from passing the first round of tests had even gotten Carissa to open up. By the time they got to bed, Dannan was almost too excited to sleep.

Gripping the dragon scale, he calmed himself down, smiling as he thought of the dragoness, when suddenly he felt a harsh tug on his heart. Staring at the scale in horror, he couldn't figure out what was wrong, but he also couldn't get rid of the feeling of impending danger.

Rolling onto his side so Tannil wouldn't see his face in the darkness, Dannan held the dragon scale tightly. He heard Tannil grunt, and he flinched when he felt a hand gently shake his shoulder. "What's wrong, Dannan? What's going on?"

Dannan rolled onto his back, unable to see through the pitch black, but still sure of where his friend was. "I don't know. Suddenly, the dragon scale... I've got this horrible feeling coming through, like there's danger right outside. I don't think it's me. I think it's her."

Tannil put his hand on Dannan's and gently pried his fingers off, and for the first time Dannan noticed his hand was bleeding. He heard the sound of cloth ripping, and he felt Tannil gently binding his hand. He was surprised that his friend could be so gentle, knowing full well Tannil had the power to crush a grown man with his bare hands.

After gently testing it, Tannil made a small murmur of approval. "There's nothing we can do right now. You just need to get through the tests tomorrow, and keep moving forward. I hate to sound funny, but she is a full grown dragoness. I don't think you have to worry about her too much. She'll get through this."

Dannan nodded slightly, his heart unconvinced by his friend's words, and he rolled onto his side. "I just need to get through this, then tomorrow night, when the tests are done, I can see if I still feel it. That's all I can do."

"Don't worry, nothing will happen to her. Just sleep for now." Tannil murmured softly. Dannan nodded, trying his hardest to fall asleep, and after a short while, a fitful darkness claimed him.

Chapter 26

When morning finally came, Dannan awoke slowly, his hand aching, and his head pounding. He didn't feel much better than last night, and he was sure from the intake of breath he heard from Tannil that he didn't look much better, either.

Dannan resisted the urge to skip breakfast, knowing the rest of the day would be worse if he did. As his classmates began to comment and ask questions about how he was feeling, he started to regret it though. After a few minutes of questions, Tannil motioned for silence. "He was just a little sick last night from nervousness, that's all. We're at a very important point in the beginning of our journey for all of us, after all. He's just worried about doing well this afternoon."

The others seemed to accept that without too much trouble, though Dannan could tell that Carissa wasn't completely satisfied with Tannil's story. He shrugged, not caring, and ate his breakfast in silence as the others chatted about the class, and how they had done yesterday. For his part, Dannan just couldn't wait for tonight to come.

Morning practice came and went, and lunch went equally quickly. The beef stew sat heavily in Dannan's stomach, and he wondered for a little while before the test if he wouldn't be sick when sparring with the teacher.

When the teacher got there, he walked in carrying a suit of leather and a suit of chain mail. Moving to the front, he motioned for them to move the chairs once more, and they did so hastily. When that was complete, he set the chain mail off to one side, and quickly slid the leather armor on over his wool outfit.

Standing in the center of the room, he ran his eyes over each of them, finally stopping on Ahminel. "Alright, this first spar will be between Ahminel and I. The spar is simply to determine if you can aim for the weak spots of the armor. We will only use leather and chain mail this time, as you have all proved adequately that you can fight someone in plate mail during the practices. I will stop the spar when I have judged whether or not you are able to do well enough by my standards. For your part, I'd say aim to make three successful hits. I'll also be fighting at about half strength, so that you have a fair chance. Any questions on the rules of the test?"

They all shook their heads, and he nodded, motioning for Ahminel to join him at the center of the room. Ahminel took one of the practice swords from the corner where they were propped up, and strode to the middle of the room where the teacher was waiting. Giving a small salute to each other, Teacher Kalaman took a two-handed stance, and Ahminel gripped the handle of the sword in his left hand.

Dannan was slightly surprised to notice that Ahminel was left-handed, but even his surprise barely broke through the feelings overwhelming him from within the dragon scale against his chest.

As he watched the spar begin, it was like watching it from a great distance. A sudden feeling of lightness startled him, and it felt like he was losing his grip on his body. Looking down as he felt himself rise towards the ceiling, he was surprised to find himself staring at his own body.

His slightly ruffled auburn hair, lightly tanned skin, and brown wool outfit almost seemed like they belonged to someone else, or a shell on a mannequin. As he felt himself pulled through the ceiling, he noticed the only thing he could feel anymore was the scale.

For some reason, he wasn't as bothered as he thought he should be. As he felt himself pulled north by the tugging of the scale, he wondered for a little bit if he had died.

Although it seemed like he was floating serenely through the air, he could tell by the land flying by beneath him that he was moving at a great speed. Passing over some mountains, he realized he was probably entering the northlands now, and wondered if that's where the dragoness was.

Suddenly, he began to fall towards the ground, and for a few moments he panicked, certain that if he wasn't dead, he would be shortly. As he fell, he saw some humans climbing a steep slope, and he gritted his teeth as he recognized Calkon, the hunter's raven black hair easily recognizable even at a distance.

Just as suddenly they were gone, as he felt himself float

through solid rock, disappearing into a giant cavern that had a light of its own. Looking at the walls, he saw the lamplight moss that Elvistir had mentioned, and he grinned to himself for a moment, remembering the pixie.

Turning his gaze downwards, he saw the dragoness, curled up in apparent sleep, her tail wrapped around her. As he got close, he saw her open her eyes, and he saw that they were just as deep as he remembered them.

Floating about fifty feet away from her at head height, he suddenly remembered the hunters. Trying to speak, he found he had no voice. Desperate, he did his best to mime 'danger', but he was uncertain if she received his meaning. Staring at her, he stopped, wondering how he could warn her, when he saw her open her mouth. Gazing down her throat, he saw a swirl of ice gathering in its depths and begin to rise, when all of a sudden he felt himself yanked back to his body.

Dannan sat forward so suddenly that Tannil almost fell backwards from where he had been sitting on the floor. Looking around, he saw the others staring at him, and the teacher glaring at him with annoyance.

Standing up quickly, he bowed in apology, and rushed over to get a practice sword. Picking it up, he walked meekly to the center of the floor, where the teacher was standing, watching him. Taking his stance, he inhaled deeply, finding it hard to concentrate after that strange experience.

The teacher seemed to notice that something was off, as he waited for a few moments before finally taking his own stance. "Alright. Come at me." Dannan nodded, stepping forward slowly.

When he was just outside of sword range, he shuddered as he felt a wave of anger crash over him. The teacher noticed and his stance relaxed a little, and Dannan lunged forward, the teacher just barely deflecting the sword tip away from his shoulder.

Back peddling quickly, Dannan managed to just barely dodge a simple swing at his waist, and the teacher grimaced, concern and disappointment warring on his face with anger.

Dannan moved to take a solid stance when he felt another wave of anger crash over him, but this time he was better able to handle it. Maintaining his stance, he began to deflect each one of the teacher's thrusts, maintaining a steady rhythm. As the teacher began to speed up, the sound of the practice swords slamming together echoing through the room like drums, Dannan felt an even heavier wave of anger strike him like a physical force, and the world went black.

He opened his eyes, not sure what he was staring at. As he slowly focused, he saw that Tannil was sitting next to him on his left, and Symon and Tymon were sitting several feet away to his right. He heard the sound of practice swords striking each other and leaned up a little. Tannil put a hand behind his shoulder and helped him sit up, and he looked around to see that Carissa was fighting the teacher, who was now wearing chain mail.

The others were sitting in chairs nearby, alternating between watching the fight, and occasionally looking over at Dannan. After a few moments, the teacher called for a halt, and Carissa stopped, panting. The teacher let out a deep breath, and nodded. "You pass."

Smiling, Carissa nodded at Tannil, as if to say 'I told you so'. Tannil nodded back at her, then turned back to Dannan, who was staring at the teacher. The teacher looked them all over, and then smiled slightly. "You've done well for your first set of tests. You are all now second year students of The Hawk's Honor. Be proud of yourselves. You will have four days of rest, with only morning practice, and you will be permitted to go into town. With an escort, of course. After that, we will begin your second year studies."

Waiting to see if there was any response, he continued when they remained silent. "Now, since you have made it to your second year, I will tell you how sword training will progress. Every year, you will learn one new technique. You will practice it while I talk to you about fortifications, and fighting in enclosed quarters, such as a small house, or a hallway. Now, are there any questions?"

When they all remained predictably silent, he shook his head, then sighed. "Alright. In five days, we'll meet here, not the blacksmith's. Dismissed." The students, including Dannan, all saluted, and the teacher strode into the hallway without looking back.

Looking around at them, Dannan met Tannil's worried eyes, and then looked at the others. "What happened?" He said after a few moments of silence.

No one said anything for a bit, when finally Carissa spoke. "You went berserk." Dannan looked over at her curiously, and Tannil cleared his throat.

"Let's start from the beginning. How much do you remember of sparring with the teacher?"

Dannan scratched his chin a little, thinking. "Up to the point when I was only deflecting his sword, and he was just starting to speed up."

Tannil grimaced, then looked at the roof. "Alright. We'll start from the beginning, then. Several of us noticed you shudder the first time when you were closing with the teacher, and then again when you were taking your second stance. A few moments later, you started attacking him like you were possessed. When that happened, he retreated a little, and called for the spar to halt. Except you didn't stop. You were pursuing him like a madman, and he was simply blocking all your swings. That's when I tackled you down. When I got off you, we tried to wake you up, but you were out cold. No response, and barely breathing. We were getting pretty worried for a bit." He continued watching Dannan with a concerned expression.

Dannan listened through the whole story, and was flush with shame by the end. "I don't remember any of it." He murmured timidly. He glanced at the other students, worried, but they seemed relatively impassive.

After a moment, Symon slapped him on the back. "Hey, don't worry! It seems like you got caught in the moment. It was pretty amazing to see you actually get the teacher to put his guard up like that. After all, he's been teaching swordsmanship for longer than any of us have ever been alive. That counts for something." Dannan smiled wanly, and several of the other students nodded.

"Don't worry, Dan. We've got your back. Even if you go insane, we'll keep you from doing anything stupid. That's what friends are for, right?" Tannil said.

Nodding his thanks, Dannan stood, Tannil supporting him with one arm as he rose. Dannan ignored Carissa's look, a cross between distaste, contempt, and fear, and started walking towards the mess hall.

After a few moments of walking in silence, the students began talking once again, going over the details of Dannan's fight with the teacher. "Just think about it this way." Tannil whispered to Dannan as they walked on. "The teacher was impressed enough with your swordsmanship that even though you only fought him in one of the two tests, he passed you for both. That has to count for something."

Dannan nodded after a moment, then smiled wanly at Tannil again.

"Just as long as I never hurt someone by accident because of it, I'm happy. That's my only fear now." Tannil grew solemn, and smiled consolingly after a moment, and for once, Dannan thought he truly knew how Tannil felt.

Later on that night, Dannan noticed that the dragon scale was gently humming to itself, but the feelings of dread and anger were gone. Staring at it as he lay in bed, he heard Tannil sitting up. Turning to the right, Dannan was unable to see anything in the darkness, but knew his friend could see him. After a few minutes, Tannil spoke. "What happened today?"

Dannan stayed silent for a minute or two, then sighed. "You remember how I said I had felt danger through the scale?" Tannil nodded slightly.

"Well, while we were sitting, waiting to take the test, something... happened. I don't really understand what. But it felt like I left my body. I went north, really far, to where the dragoness was hiding in some caverns, and I saw the hunters who had been chasing her before. I think she might have been able to see me. I mean, if I was really there at all."

Pausing to take a breath, he continued in a shaky voice. "She had opened her mouth to do something. I saw ice crystals gathering. Maybe she breathes ice instead of fire. Dragons do that, don't they? But then I disappeared. I think you brought me back to my body. Then, when I was fighting the teacher, I felt her anger through the dragon scale. That's what made me black out. I don't know if she was fighting the hunters, or something else happened. I just... don't know." Dannan tried hard not to sound desperate as he said the last part, or to choke up, but he was sure Tannil could hear it in his voice.

After a moment he felt Tannil pat his shoulder hesitantly, his friend's discomfort obvious. "I'm not good at comforting people. I'm a mercenary at heart, regardless of what humanity I might or might not have. But I don't think you have to worry. You can still feel her, right?"

Dannan nodded slightly, tearing up even as he tried to concentrate on the feelings from the scale. After managing to reign in his sniffling, Dannan successfully found the dragoness once more, and he could tell she was alright, at least for the moment.

Shaking a little, he let out a shuddering sigh of relief, and he heard Tannil chuckle. "See? She's safe, am I right?" Dannan nodded slightly, unable to stop the smile that came to his lips.

"Then rest for now, Dan. Apologize to the teacher, and work even harder to get strong. You'll need to be to protect her from the sounds of it. Or to even survive reaching her." Dannan murmured softly and rolled over, a feeling of comfort washing over him as he closed his eyes. He heard Tannil get back into bed, and he relaxed, falling into a deep sleep.

Chapter 27

Dannan couldn't wait for practice to finish the next morning, and the moment it did, he immediately approached the teacher. Teacher Kalaman was watching him warily as he approached, and Dannan sighed a little, worried that he might have damaged his chances of success here.

Waiting until the teacher acknowledged to him, Dannan tried to appear as nonthreatening as possible. When the teacher finally gave him a nod, Dannan immediately bowed at the waist, both arms at his side. It was hard to ignore the stares of the other students as they walked by, but Dannan knew that he had to.

"Sir. I am terribly sorry for my behavior yesterday. I don't know what came over me. I will readily accept whatever punishment you feel is necessary, as I went fully beyond the bounds of the spar. Please accept this as my apology." Dannan smiled internally, thinking that sounded fairly similar to what Tannil might say, and he waited for a response without standing back up.

After about half a minute, he heard a murmur, and looked up to see the teacher smiling. "Well, you're honest sometimes, at least. Though it seems you've picked up some habits from your friend Tannil. Apology accepted. And do not be ashamed of performing that well. It was wrong of me to underestimate every one of my students, and that was an insult to you as a swordsman. Whether you're training or not, a swordsman is still a swordsman, with his own pride. Next time, I'll just make sure to go all out from the beginning."

Dannan nodded slightly, remaining bowed down, waiting. After a few moments, he saw the teacher's hand just at the edge of his vision, motioning for him to stand up. "Let's see if you can apply the same energy to the classroom learning portion of your studies in a few days." Dannan gave another quick bow before heading off to his room.

The days passed uneventfully, as Dannan did his best to

forget about what had happened. He was relieved that most of his classmates were out enjoying their freedom, enabling him to hide in his room without arousing too much suspicion. His nights were the worst part, as the anger haunted his dreams, and Calkon's dead gray eyes seemed to endlessly stare at him.

When classes finally came, it was a relief.

Dannan wasn't completely surprised to find that he had no head for fortifications. The teacher spent several hours going over the basic types, from mud walls and stake pits to crenelated walls. He also noticed that with the teacher more relaxed around him, his classmates seemed to have an easier time dismissing the events of the test.

Over the span of the fortnight, Dannan noticed that the eighth year class wasn't at morning practices anymore. Mentioning it to the teacher, Dannan was surprised at the mischievous smile he got in return. "They're off on a training mission. You'll find out more when you get your chance as an eighth year." Dannan tried to get more out of his teacher unsuccessfully, and eventually was forced to concede.

At the beginning of the next fortnight, they entered the waiting room to find the practice swords propped in one corner, and next to them, a number of small wooden daggers and shortswords. Murmuring over them, the students didn't have long to examine the weapons before Teacher Kalaman arrived.

They each quickly took a sword and went to their spots, and the teacher shook his head at them. "Each of you, grab a dagger or shortsword as well. In the third year, you'll learn how to use a sword and a shield, but for now, you'll learn how to block and fight with a dagger or shortsword in your hand. If you're good enough, you'll be able to get a feel for both of them before the year ends." They nodded, each going back to retrieve a different weapon.

Dannan chose a dagger, which was slightly more suited to his current size, and saw that Tannil chose a shortsword. Chuckling, he saluted Tannil jokingly with his dagger, and Tannil gave him a grin as he saluted back.

Although it didn't take any time at all for the teacher to start scolding them about their handling of the two weapons simultaneously, Dannan was confident he could master the style. His thoughts occasionally went back to the eighth years and the new scars that he had seen on some of them when they returned, but more often than not, he was too involved in practicing with the sword and dagger.

He didn't have long to contemplate the eighth classes new found scars, though, as seven days later, the eighth class graduated. Apparently, the ceremony was held in the meeting room of the headquarters in the morning, while the other students were at practice.

Dannan saw a number of people he didn't recognize that morning, when suddenly he realized that today was the testing day for the students who would once again make up the newest class. Somehow, this truly hit home the fact that he had already spent a year here, and more than a year away from home. A sudden pang of homesickness hit him, and he wondered how his parents were doing.

They held their class out on the training fields that afternoon, and when they finished, they were told to walk the back way to reach the mess hall. Grumbling a little about having to walk further to get to the bathhouses and dinner, they still obeyed, knowing their teacher had a reason for any orders he gave them.

When they finally got to the mess hall, they saw that the new students hadn't yet come in for dinner, and Dannan had sudden flashbacks to when they first entered The Hawk's Honor. As he and his classmates sat around two of the corner tables closer to the waiting room hallway, he couldn't help but smile as they chatted amiably among themselves.

Just a year ago, most of them were too shy to speak at all, much less hold a conversation. He felt privileged in some ways to be a part of this, and he was looking forward to the coming year as he dug into his soup.

He was pulled from his thoughts by the noise of multiple people coming down the hall.

Dannan looked up in curiosity at the newcomers who entered the room. The first five all looked like they were from the Great Cities, like Hale and Uthul were. There were four from the north, and two more from the south. The last two were the ones that caught Dannan's attention.

The boy was a year or two older than Dannan, with an unusual gray-red hair, a chiseled face, and a stocky body. Although he was about the same height as Dannan, who had grown several inches, he still looked like a more intimidating opponent.

Behind him to his right a girl walked a little bit slower, seeming like she was trying to hide in his shadow, which immediately struck Dannan as odd. After a moment, they had all gotten into the line for dinner, which made Dannan chuckle slightly. Although they would certainly get a meal, Dannan had to wonder if it was worth it for the pressure of all the students staring from the side.

A slight murmur went through the crowd as they got closer to the cook, though Dannan couldn't see what was causing it.

As the last of the new students exited the crowd, he realized what it was. The girl who had been hiding at the back was now easily visible as the two of them quickly tried to walk to their own table, apart from their classmates. Her ears were what first drew Dannan's notice.

They reminded him of Elvistir's, and his eyes immediately went wide with shock. He hadn't been expecting to see an elf anytime soon, much less at the sword school. Studying her more closely, he could see why the other boys were both surprised and taken with her.

There was an unearthly beauty to her, as her skin seemed too smooth, her features too fine and too well sculpted. Her hair color didn't stand out unless you looked; when you paid close attention you could see it shimmered, despite being the color of fresh soil. Even her movements were inhuman, with a fluidity that made one think of a river.

Shaking his head, Dannan turned to look at his classmates, to see what how they reacted. He noticed all of them except for Tannil were focused on the elf girl and her companion, and Dannan chuckled, drawing a sharp glare from Carissa. Shrugging at her, he set down his soup with a sigh of contentment, and chuckled slightly again.

He never thought he'd be content with vegetable and noodle soup. But it certainly hit the spot when he was hungry. Dannan glanced over at Tannil, who had turned to look at the pair from earlier, and Dannan followed his gaze, then sighed.

Standing across the table from the pair were four of the recently promoted fourth year students, at least one of the older boys wearing a mischievous grin on his face. The redhead and the girl had both sat down to their soup before the boys had come over, and were now forced to look up at the fourth years.

A whisper ran through the room as people started to notice something was going on, and Dannan sighed again, looking over at Tannil. Tannil was looking back at him, wearing a huge grin, and Dannan just shook his head. Carissa glanced back at them, and Dannan took a deep breath, whispering to Tannil "What are you planning?"

Tannil shook his head, the grin still plastered over his face. "What are you planning?" Dannan rolled his eyes and exhaled, shaking his head.

"This won't end well for me, will it?" He whispered softly.

One of his classmates looked at him, but Tannil remained unfazed. "Doing the right thing never does. Isn't that why people stopped doing it?" Muttering to himself, Dannan had to admit that Tannil had him there. As the room finally became completely silent, the head of the four boys, a brunette that Dannan didn't recognize very well could be heard talking. Leaning over the table with a smirk, the boy reeked of self-confidence, and Dannan wondered where he got it.

"C'mon, we're just asking nicely that you'll spend the first rest afternoon with us. You can even come back to your stumpy friend here after. We just want to spend some time with you." The leader said.

The elf girl sighed, shaking her head. "And how many times must I refuse you? I have no interest in boring human children."

The brunette grimaced at her, then smiled again. "You say that as if you yourself are not a child."

Staring at him icily, the girl spoke with clear contempt. "By elven standards, I might be considered a child at one hundred and twenty, but I've already been alive longer than the first time your grandfather crawled out of a ditch to find your grandmother."

Dannan covered his face with a hand and sighed at that, unable to hold in his exasperation. Several of his classmates glanced at him, and he just shook his head.

Looking over at the cook, Dannan was surprised to find that he was studiously looking everywhere but at the students who seemed about to fight as he stirred his pot of soup. "So rather than spend time with us, you'd rather spend time with your friend who looks like the bastard child of a dwarf and a giant?" The boy yelled.

Turning back to the brewing fight, Dannan was unsurprised

to see that the fourth year was becoming flush with anger. His three compatriots had moved so they were a little bit further away from him, though they remained on the same side of the table.

"Yes, although you'd do well to keep a civil tongue in your mouth, wretch. He's a far better fighter than you are."

The boy grinned maliciously at her, then shook his head. "What, so I should be polite to a wench who doesn't know her place, so as not to offend her misbegotten friend?"

As soon as the boy finished saying it, the redhead sat up fast, knocking his chair over in the process.

Muttering under his breath, Dannan looked around for something he could use, knowing full well that he was useless without a weapon in hand. Finding nothing but the dinner utensils and plates, Dannan let out a disappointed sigh. Picking up one of the large, thick wooden soup spoons, he hefted it slightly, nodding when it seemed like it might be heavy enough to stop a fist if used right.

Standing up slowly, he mentally berated himself even as he rose, ignoring the glances from his classmates and several other students nearby. Walking towards the impending fight, he grimaced slightly, shaking his head.

None of them paid attention to him until he was at the edge of their vision. At that point, the rest of the mess hall had turned to watch what most were certain was going to be a fight.

When they finally turned to him, he stood there, relaxed, the wooden spoon hanging lazily from his hand. He wasn't sure if this would actually work, but he figured it was worth a shot to see if he could stop it from coming to blows.

Ignoring the glances from the angry redhead and the elf girl, he paid most of his attention to the senior students. The leader was grimacing at him fiercely, and the other boys moved behind him, trying to lend support without getting in the way of his wrath. "What do you want, shorty?"

Dannan shrugged a little, stretching his arms out to the sides with a small yawn. "C'mon, you're the smart leader here. Dinner time is halfway over, it's late at night, and everyone is looking to finish their food. The teachers won't go easy on us at practice just because there was a fight. In fact, they might even be harder on us. They'll certainly punish whoever started the fight, as well as whoever participated. Right now, the only one who can stop that would be the smartest person in the situation. And at the moment, I'd say that's you."

The leader narrowed his eyes at Dannan, his face doubtful and grim as he tried to figure out what motivation Dannan had to interfere. The other students were all watching with bated breath as the leader seemed to consider what Dannan said.

He could see the pride that was beginning to war with the anger on the boy's face, and he was sure that a little push would do it. "It takes a stronger and more mature man to walk away, and prove that he's in the right." Dannan chuckled inside, remembering his father using that line after he had gotten into a fistfight as a little boy.

After a few moments, the leader shook his head, looking slightly calmer than he had before. "You're right. I will be the bigger man here. After all, we are the senior students. We need to set a good example." The other three nodded at him as the leader looked back over his shoulder, and he grinned widely. "C'mon, guys. Let's get back to our dinner. They always come around eventually."

The others nodded and followed the brunette as he walked away, eying Dannan and the others with an air of superiority and condescension. The redhead opened his mouth to say something, but Dannan silenced him with a quick glare that said exactly what would happen if he started the fight.

Conversation broke out in the mess hall again as Dannan started to turn away from the table, a fake smile plastered on his face. The elf girl reached up and grabbed him by the wrist as he started to move away, her eyes icy. "Don't interfe…"

"Shut up." Dannan said, cutting her off more harshly than he intended. The elf girl looked at him in surprise, her eyes wide with shock. The redhead glared at Dannan, but picked his seat back up, setting it down none too gently.

"This is a military training ground. Whether we like them or not, whether we are out of line or not, superiors need to be accorded at least some modicum of respect. And that whole line about 'his grandfather crawling out of a ditch' only served to throw fuel on the fire. Yes, he was out of line in the first place. Then you had to go and make the situation worse. How can you lead men, or elves in battle if you can't keep a cool head?"

Looking over at the redhead, Dannan let his face relax a little. "Don't let them bait you so. If you need to smash them, do so after they take the first punch and justify it. But don't put yourself at a disadvantage. Because then, after you're punished and out of the way, you'll be leaving her by herself."

Dannan pulled his wrist from her slack fingers and started walking away.

He took a deep breath and looked down, noticing he had unconsciously gripped the wooden spoon the way you would a dagger with no guard. Relaxing his grip, he got all the way back to his table and nodded at Tannil. "I'm tired. I'll be heading up to the room first."

"Goodnight" Tannil replied, as Dannan looked at his classmates. They nodded to him, and he ignored Carissa giving him a questioning look.

Only Tannil seemed outwardly approving of his actions, but the grin he wore seemed like his face would break in half as he made a goodnight gesture at Dannan. Setting the spoon on the table, Dannan walked out of the mess hall, leaving the noise and the students behind.

Dannan was awoken from sleep by the light from the hallway coming in. Looking up, he saw Tannil standing in the doorway, grinning. Letting the door swing shut behind him, Tannil sat on his cot, causing it to creak a little. Dannan waited for a few minutes in the silence, sure Tannil would speak first.

It only took a few minutes before he finally heard Tannil chuckling. "Oh, but that was amusing. And well done, I must say. I assumed you'd probably have to strike him once or twice to get him to see reason, but you managed to do it without ever using that wooden spoon you took. I'm thoroughly impressed. With that kind of conviction, if you don't sweep that dragoness off of her feet, I'll be amazed."

Dannan laughed at the mental image, picturing himself trying to get his arms around even one of her legs.

"I'm surprised, though; an elf, and from the smell of him, someone with dwarves in his blood. I wasn't expecting such… unusual students at the same time I was here. You must just bring this kind of luck with you." Dannan grimaced, causing Tannil to let out another laugh. "It could be worse. At least they're not trying to kill you. Though I'm curious how the hazing will go."

Shaking his head, Dannan sighed. "I'm really not sure. But

private fights, I don't think I can step into. When they're out in the open like that, not only is it easier, but it's possible to do without getting in the way of already existing authority. If I went out looking for trouble, I'd be more likely to cause a disturbance than solve it." Dannan shrugged, smiling at where he thought Tannil was.

"I'll do my best to affect what I can see and what I can stop. There is no sense contributing to the problem if it won't stop it from escalating."

Hearing Tannil's chuckle, Dannan felt pleased by his own response. "A very practical, very mercenary response. I like it."

Dannan laughed softly, and rolled over on his side. "Let's see how they adjust before we decide that it was the practical response. I may have made myself some unnecessary enemies, after all." Tannil laughed, and a thought popped into Dannan's head. "You were already making a living as a mercenary with your family, so why attend a sword school?" Tannil grew silent, and as time slowly passed, sleep crept up on Dannan.

Chapter 28

The next several days were extremely uneventful, though he did notice a glimmer in his teacher's eye that Dannan hadn't seen there before. Dannan noticed a marked improvement in his own dagger handling skills after he started paying attention to how he was gripping it, and Teacher Kalaman even commented. "Pick up some new tricks somewhere, did you?" His teacher said jokingly. Dannan shook his head, unsure how to respond, and the teacher let it lie.

Nothing was different for Dannan until the day of rest. Deciding that he wasn't getting better fast enough while listening to the lectures, he went behind the dorm, to the semi-secluded area where the boys had tried to haze him.

Although he got looks from the few students who he passed because of the practice sword and dagger he was carrying, he ignored them, concentrating on his training.

When he arrived, he found it peacefully empty, with no one even in ear shot it seemed.

Taking the appropriate stance, he began to practice the swings. He concentrated on making his mental image of himself as close to that of the teacher's form as possible. After an hour or so, he was sure that he had the appropriate form in his mind.

The sun was just starting to fall when he started, and he lost himself in the hours of practice. The sound of someone clearing their throat woke him from his reverie, and he looked over to see Tannil leaning against the wall with his arms folded. "I thought I saw you here. Not content with only class practice?"

Dannan grinned and shook his head, sweat covering his body. "You don't become the best by doing what everyone else does." He quipped.

Tannil laughed, shaking his head in amusement, and he motioned for Dannan to follow him. "Let's go, dinner's ready. I figured you'd practice the whole night if I left you here." Dannan frowned, and then pretended to adopt a petulant look.

"I'm not that bad."

Bursting out laughing, Tannil grinned. "You're getting taller, but not more mature, that's for sure." Dannan cocked his head to the side, and Tannil chuckled. "What, you didn't notice that you're getting taller?"

Dannan shook his head as they walked towards the bathhouse, and Tannil smiled. "Yep. You've grown a few inches since I first met you. Who knows, some day you'll be as tall as me... maybe." Dannan laughed.

"My father is only five feet and a half feet or so, so I doubt I'll ever reach your height."

Tannil shrugged, chuckling. "You never know. A lot of children outgrow their parents."

"Sure, sure. Let's get to dinner quickly then. I'm starved." Dannan commented wryly. As they walked back, he could tell Tannil was slightly uncomfortable, and he stopped a little way from the mess hall doors. "What's the matter?"

Tannil started slightly as Dannan pulled up short in front of him. "You remember the question you asked me a few days ago? About why I"m here?"

Dannan nodded, meeting his friends gaze with an impassive look. "I told you about how I was worried I was becoming like the... the ones I mentioned to you. I left the Wolves Brigade to see if I could control myself better. I didn't want to get swallowed up by those feelings."

Dannan shifted slightly from one foot to the other, unsure of what to say, then gave Tannil a lopsided grin. "Well, it doesn't seem like life here will be too hectic, so maybe this is the best time to get those feelings under control."

Tannil met his eyes, and his usual confidence seemed to return a little. "Now, I'm still starving, so let's go enjoy our oh so boring life as trainees." Tannil laughed at Dannan's obvious sarcasm, and they started walking the rest of the way to the mess hall.

The rest of the evening was uneventful, as was the rest of the fortnight. The only difference in Dannan's routine was that now he went out to the space behind the dorm to practice each day of rest. He made sure that he practiced the stance with both hands, remembering what his father said about being the best. Although he wasn't sure if he could do it, Dannan knew for a fact that if he didn't try, he would always regret it.

As summer approached, the heat quickly began to affect the students at practice. On one particularly hot day, the teachers had all the students practicing inside.

Looking out through the front door of the waiting room, Dannan noticed the redheaded first year, especially the fact that he wasn't sweating. Shaking his head, he assumed it was just one of those things, like the fact that Tannil was used to the heat. He didn't think on it any more at the time, and was more than happy to fall back into his routine.

With the last days of summer came the cool winds of fall once more, and Dannan was eager to be able to leave the compound this fall, even if it was only for an hour or two. He hadn't been outside in a year and a half, and he wondered if Samust was still in Whitehaven.

Although he knew it hadn't been that long, it still felt almost like a lifetime ago. If Samust hadn't asked him not to visit, he would have stopped by the wagon yard, but as it is, he would be guarded, and Samust would never forgive him, or tell him what happened, for that matter.

So when the first day of rest came, he contented himself with leaving the city for an hour or so with Tannil. The guard, while not particularly friendly, did not interrupt their conversations, though he always stayed within about fifteen feet. The town was too far from the woods to do much except enjoy a nice walk outside, but it was enough that Dannan felt refreshed when they went back to the compound for dinner.

Dannan and Tannil went outside the city several more times during the fall, finally stopping when the first snow came.

Although the regimen was harsh in many ways, Dannan found that just like in the forest, he was slowly finding a niche that he truly enjoyed. The practice, the people, even the unpleasant ones, and the scenery all combined to create something that, in so many ways, was uniquely his, even as it was theirs. He almost regretted that he would have to leave someday. But he knew in his heart that the thing he wanted more than anything was to see the dragoness, and that he wouldn't let anything, even regret, stop him from that.

During the winter, things began to get uncomfortable as the easily irritable redhead began to butt heads with just about everyone.

It didn't come to blows, but it came close a number of times. Dannan was surprised once to see that even the redhead's teacher, a woman in her late thirties of northern descent, rebuked him for his temper. He had rarely seen the teachers intervene in the student affairs, except when it got too violent.

Once, when they were sharing the waiting room as a classroom due to the snow, Dannan caught the elf girl staring at him, while the redhead glared at him. He had ignored them and attended to his class work, but sometimes he wondered if helping people was really worth it.

Finally, the last day of the winter came. This year, Dannan was looking forward to the tests, and was sure that they would all pass them. Once again, the teacher had let them know the day before, and they were sitting in a circle on their afternoon off.

"Why don't we make sure everyone has the stance and form right? That's one of the things we had an issue with last year." Dannan said as they started off the study meeting.

Careel looked down in embarrassment, and Dannan quickly shook his head. "None of us did perfectly, Careel, so don't feel bad. This year, we just have to make sure that we all pass without issue. After all, I'm probably going to do the worst when it comes to the fortifications, and that's where I'll need your help."

Brightening visibly at that, Careel nodded. "You do have a tendency to lose yourself in your sword practice. I would not be surprised if you had missed something the teacher said while so engaged." Dannan grinned, still not used to Careel's manner of speaking, but glad that he had managed to cheer him up.

Unlike the others here, Careel came from a merchant family. He was the only one who didn't have some form of combat in his background. It was also part of why he was one of the more skilled when it came to things like fortifications, and Dannan imagined he'd be pretty good at tactics, as well.

"Why don't I go first?" Symon said in his usual, cheerful, baritone voice. Dannan nodded then looked around at his classmates, who also nodded in agreement.

Symon took the first stance, holding his sword out in front of him as if to thrust, and the dagger at an angle facing towards the center of his imaginary opponents body. They each took a turn going around front, and making a thrust, slash, or swipe at him, and Symon parried each one fairly well, making a return thrust with his sword after each.

They repeated this until each person was confident in their ability to do it, even Careel. It took an hour or two at a steady pace, but once they had finished, they all began to get hungry. "Why don't I go see if dinner is ready?" Hale offered. They all looked at the stocky son of a smith, with his smiling eyes and his black hair, and nodded eagerly.

"We'll resume talking about fortifications and everything when Hale gets back, then?" Dannan said questioningly. The others nodded, and Hale started walking down the hall without another word.

Dannan looked among his classmates after Hale left, and he was surprised to find that although he had only picked up bits and pieces about each, they were truly starting to resemble a unit.

Careel, although from a merchant family, had defied his father to come to a sword school in the north. Whitehaven, being well known for the Swordmasters who it now produced, had been the obvious choice.

Hale, who had just left, had come with Uthul to support him as a friend and brother in arms, after they had both gone on two campaigns as smith's assistants. Dannan still wasn't entirely sure why they hadn't decided to become full-fledged smiths, but he thought it had something to do with the scar that stretched from one end of Hale's back to the other.

Carissa had found herself forced into mercenary work as a matter of survival. Her village had been raided by bandits, and with nothing left there, her choices were try to find work in a city, or join up with a mercenary group that had passed by. With how women were treated in the city from what Dannan saw, there was no chance of a villager, even a man like himself, getting any real work.

Symon and Tymon interested Dannan more though, as they were actually from Whitehaven, and had become squires for the town guard, only to get thrown out after an incident with an officer bullying Tymon. Dannan wasn't sure what exactly Symon had done to the man, but apparently they had only avoided time in the local dungeon because of another squires help.

Other than Tannil, Ahminel seemed to have the most experience. Both of his parents were active mercenaries working in the Scarlet Deserts, which, according to Ahminel, were actually bright crimson, due to ore below the sands. This made it a very profitable, but very dangerous place to work. Because of this, his parents had sent him here, to learn the "northern" fighting style, though Ahminel seemed more confident in the skills of the southerners.

Turning to look at Ramme, Dannan still wondered about his background sometimes. The boy had yet to open up to any of them, and all they had found out was that he was Dannan's age, thirteen. Sometimes, when he thought no one was looking, Dannan saw him move in ways that were definitely the result of training, though.

He often wondered if Ramme wasn't running from someone, but was worried if he pried, that Ramme would never open up.

They heard someone running towards them from the mess hall, and they all turned almost at the same time as Hale burst into the waiting room. "There's a fight in the mess hall! A big one!" Dannan cursed, wondering who it was, and he looked at Tannil.

"Bring the practice swords, or bad idea?"

Tannil shrugged, shaking his head. "I wouldn't recommend it, because then it would be swords against fists, which would be kind of unfair. Means that next time someone gave you trouble, they'd probably bring a real one. At the same time, it'll be us against who knows how many. We can't count on 'what might happen'. In the end, it's up to you."

Sighing, Dannan grimaced at him. "What a great big help you are." Tannil shrugged, a 'I can't help you, sorry' look on his face. Sighing again, Dannan walked over and picked up one of the practice swords, holding it lightly in his hands.

He looked at the others, but between the shrugs, unresponsive faces, and Carissa's cold stare, he found no suggestions there, either. Setting it back down, he grabbed one of the small daggers, sliding it through a belt loop on his pants.

Walking into the hall, he shook his head. "Won't do me any good to be dead." He muttered as he passed Tannil. Tannil grinned and shrugged, following a step or two behind him. The others, uncertain as to what to do, followed further behind.

They could hear the fighting in the mess hall long before they reached it.

When they could finally see what was going on, they witnessed a tangled mess of people fighting in the center of the room. Several of the tables in the center had been overturned, and chairs were everywhere.

As they entered the room, they saw that all the students not involved had moved to the outside walls. Some were cheering, some were jeering, but many more had sullen faces on.

Only a few of them looked at the students that entered, and for a moment, Dannan was glad for the respite. The brawl was directly between the cook and the class, which immediately gave Dannan an idea.

Motioning for the others to wait there, he started walking forward. Tannil followed him for a moment, but Dannan shook his head. "This is going to get even messier." He said, grinning.

Tannil stood back, a look of concern on his face, and Dannan turned back towards the fighting students. Taking a deep breath, he strode forward, sliding the practice knife from his belt loop as he reached the seething mass of people.

The first students near him didn't even see him as he walked forward.

Stopping before the group of people, he took another deep breath, before letting out a great yell. The students closest to him stopped fighting so suddenly that some of them were still mid-grapple, and others looked up from where they lay.

Scowling at them, Dannan let his glare travel over each and every one. "How the hell is anyone supposed to eat dinner with you all acting like idiots?! Who started this mess?!"

The students closest to him pointed back to the middle, still too surprised to realize that it was one of their juniors speaking to them this way.

Dannan saw that the redhead was still trying to throw punches even as the brunette tried to wrestle him to the ground. Walking forward, Dannan stopped as one of the taller fourth years who had been with the brunette earlier stepped in front of him.

Looking up at him coldly, Dannan's glare made most of the students near them back away. "Move. Now."

The fourth year laughed at Dannan, bringing his fists up into a fighting pose, one slightly ahead of the other. "You should be polite to your seniors. Remember?"

Dannan took a deep breath, and in the blink of an eye, slammed the butt of the practice dagger into the side of the boy's head.

The boy dropped heavily to the ground, and the other students nearby who had been looking nervous immediately scrambled away, not stopping till they were with the group on the edge of the room.

Walking forward, Dannan smiled inwardly as he saw the other students were more than happy to get out of his way now.

When he reached the two boys who were still fighting, Dannan immediately darted forward, slamming the butt of the practice dagger into each of their sides once. Both of them immediately curled forward and turned to see who interrupted them, even as Dannan kept moving forward.

Bringing his hand up, he drove the butt of the dagger up into the brunette's chin, and even as it rose over the brunette's head, brought it down like lightning at an angle, striking the redhead on the forehead.

Both boys looked at him for a moment, stunned, as the brunette toppled onto his back, and the redhead fell onto his face. Looking up, Dannan saw that the elf girl was being held by the other two fourth years that had been with the brunette when they made trouble before.

They quickly glanced at each other, and one made a move to say something, but Dannan didn't give him a chance to speak.

Darting up and under, he used his low stature to get behind the boy, and slam the butt of the practice dagger into his side. Spinning as he brought himself to face back towards the other boy, he drove his knuckles behind the elf girl's head, and straight into the remaining boy's cheek.

Reeling back, the boy grabbed his cheek, even as his lip immediately started to bleed. Taking a few quick steps back, Dannan relaxed his stance a little, making sure there was no one nearby him, and let his practice dagger fall to his side.

Looking over at his classmates, he had to resist the urge to grin, as all but Ahminel, Carissa, and Tannil stood there, gaping. "Tannil, come help me move these idiots so we can get the tables back in place and eat. Carissa, I hate to ask, but would you go get Teacher Kalaman and the fourth year teacher please? I think they need to know about this immediately."

Carissa gave him a curious look, then nodded, even as Tannil strode forward to help him.

Dannan started walking forward to help Tannil move the first boy Dannan had dropped, and as he walked past the redhead, he felt a slight movement behind him more than heard it.

Ducking his head and rolling back on his heels, he watched as the elf girl's arm sailed right over his head, and she stumbled past, obviously not expecting him to dodge. He allowed her to regain her footing, and then walked past her, ignoring the angry glare she gave him.

"We'll find out what started this once the teachers get here. Until then, behave. Or, you can wait unconscious. Like them." Dannan motioned at the boys who were all still splayed out on the floor. Grimacing at him, she spit, hitting him on the cheek. Shrugging, he continued past, wiping his cheek with his sleeve.

It only took a minute or two to move the unconscious boys to the wall near the entrance, though it took several more to get the tables back into order. Two of them were unsteady, as they had received damage to one or both of their legs during the fight.

Dannan shrugged mentally as they put the tables back, deciding he'd leave it alone and simply let Teacher Kalaman know when he got there.

Chapter 29

By the time they had finished putting the tables back in place, both teacher's had arrived, and the other students had gone back to eating dinner and chatting.

He wasn't surprised to find that he recognized the fourth year teacher from when they had first arrived. She had been the woman posting the room assignments, if he recalled correctly.

Shrugging slightly, he walked towards them as they entered, noticing that although she wasn't as tall as Teacher Kalaman, she still had a strong presence. Her shoulder length brown hair was well-maintained, and although somewhat tan from exposure to the sun, she was still fairly light-skinned.

She seemed slightly annoyed as she looked at the students propped up against the wall, then turned to look at Dannan and Tannil.

Teacher Kalaman watched them as they walked up, ignoring the students unconscious on the floor, and Dannan immediately noticed his stare was cold and penetrating.

Resisting the urge to sigh, Dannan stood at attention, feeling slightly better when he saw Carissa come out from behind the two teachers. "Carissa has explained a little of the situation to us. Hopefully you know more of what happened." Their teacher said, his calm voice in disagreement with his stern gaze.

Dannan nodded, then looked around, seeing if he could spot the elf girl. He noticed her sitting at one of the tables in the corner, a little bit away from where her redheaded friend lay unconscious.

"I do not have the best understanding of the situation, unfortunately. We were studying for the tests tomorrow as a group, to make sure we would do well, and Hale came down to the mess hall to see if they had started serving dinner. I'm not sure exactly what he heard at the time, but he came running back to the waiting room, and said that a fight had broken out in the mess hall. It would be hard to eat dinner while others fought around us, so I decided to stop it."

The teachers both looked at him for a moment, as if to try and determine the truth of his words by staring a hole in him, and Dannan had to resist the urge to shift uncomfortably.

After a little bit longer, his teacher nodded, and Dannan let his breath out a little. "The others who are here will say the same things?" The fourth year teacher said, slightly skeptical.

Dannan nodded, and looked over at the unconscious students. "I didn't really wish to hurt them, however, they were unwilling to stop. There were many more than these three unconscious boys fighting, however, these were the only ones unwilling to stop when challenged. I do not know who started the fight, but the redhead's friend; the elf girl, she might."

Both of them glanced over at where she was sitting, and then turned back to Dannan. "I will accept whatever punishment you deem is necessary, as I did participate in a fight between students." The teachers looked at him, slightly surprised, and for a moment Dannan thought he saw the faintest glimmer of amusement in his teacher's eye.

Shaking her head, the woman glanced at the boys. "I want to find out what happened here, so that these idiots don't keep fighting until we're forced to throw them out. You were not incorrect in your actions. I will leave it up to Kalaman as to whether he would like to punish you or not."

Dannan nodded, giving a small bow of acknowledgment as she turned and walked towards the elf girl and the unconscious boys.

"You do not seem all that bothered by this, sir." Dannan commented softly when the fourth year teacher was out of earshot.

"What, the fact that you are an idiot, or the fact that those fools were fighting?"

Dannan turned bright red with embarrassment, and shook his head. "That I am an idiot who sticks his nose into places it doesn't necessarily belong."

Teacher Kalaman chuckled a little, and shook his head. "No, I am not surprised. No one who gets anywhere got there by sitting on their hands and waiting for good fortune. Especially not among Swordmasters. It's amusing to me, however, that you seem to attract trouble wherever you go. Something that could be both a good trait and a bad trait in a Swordmaster."

He wasn't sure whether to be insulted or proud, so Dannan

simply kept his mouth shut, though he was sure Tannil was struggling to hold in a laugh next to him. Dannan noticed Carissa looking at him oddly, and shrugged at her, certain that he was just as confused with the whole situation as she was.

They were surprised suddenly by a loud cursing and they all looked over to see that the brunette was awake, apparently after a few slaps from the teacher.

Gripping his chin, he stared daggers at Dannan, and for a moment, Dannan thought the boy might attack him even with the teachers there. The fourth year teacher never gave him a chance though, grabbing him by his vest collar, and lifting him up.

"Now, what the hell were you thinking, starting a brawl in here?! You can't be a respected senior student if you act like some bar room thug! And explain quickly, or I'll give you some bruises that'll make you forget all about that bump on your chin!"

The brunette flinched from her words, and lowered his head. "It was just an argument between me and the first year. He said some things he shouldn't have, and I was calling him to task for it. That was all."

The teacher shook him so hard for a moment Dannan thought she would knock him out again. "I know you, Kulin! You're dumber than a post when it comes to lying, and less convincing than one, to. Now, what'd you do to start the fight? You're going to get house arrest for a month at least, now don't make it harder, or it will only get worse on you. I've yet to decide what to do with your flunkies, since I'm sure they were involved." She said, aiming a glare at his friends.

"This is actually the second time he's made trouble with them. The first time, also in the mess hall, I managed to diffuse the situation without too much trouble. No fights. That was the entrance day for the new class. He said some things that he probably shouldn't have, the elf girl said a few things she shouldn't have, and I managed to convince him to do the smart thing and not make a scene." Dannan said, involuntarily flinching a little as the fourth year teacher glared at him.

"Now now, Presala, it's not Dannan's fault. Save your glare for your own idiot student. My idiot student will have plenty of his own problems." Teacher Kalaman said with a grin. Dannan felt slightly relieved that he wouldn't have to deal with both teachers, but wondered what his had in store for him.

Turning back to Kulin, Presala grimaced. "Alright, so what did you say this time?" After a few moments of silence, she shook him again, and he grumbled.

"The redhead said something to me first."

The teacher shook her head, growling a little. "I don't care what he said. What did you say?"

The brunette scowled at Dannan slightly until she shook him again, and he muttered. "I said that his head was either so red because he couldn't control his temper tantrums... or because of the frustration since the elf girl must be so frigid in bed."

A loud slap rang through the mess hall, hushing all conversation, and Dannan didn't even have time to flinch before the brunette's back hit the floor.

Dannan gaped at the teacher, then glanced over at Tannil, who he saw was also trying to swallow his tongue, which made Dannan feel a little better. He hadn't even seen her hand move; much less what had actually knocked the brunette to the ground. A moment later, she hauled him back to his feet and forcefully walked him towards the table where the elf girl was sitting.

The girl looked like she wanted to flee, but one look from the teacher and she stayed still as the boy was marched up to the table.

Dannan and the others walked behind at a distance that they thought was both respectful, and safe for them, and stopped about ten feet away.

Slamming the boy's cheek flat to the wooden table, he let out a grunt as the teacher leaned on his back. Although she didn't seem like she weighed a great deal, she certainly knew how to throw her weight around.

"Now, I've put up with this behavior from you for a while due to your skills, but you're getting too arrogant. You cannot be a respected leader if you can't respect your subordinates. All that would make you is a pathetic worm and a bully."

Continuing in a voice that sounded like steel sheathed in silk, she wore a vicious expression. "Now, you are going to apologize to her, and if there is another issue, you will be dismissed from The Hawk's Honor. Is that understood?"

Kulin turned pale in her grip and nodded, and for a split second, Dannan almost felt sorry for him. Almost. Then he thought about how much trouble that Kulin must have caused other than this, and he had to wonder if this wasn't fate's way of getting back at him.

Shrugging a little, Dannan watched as the brunette stammered out an apology and was released. Rubbing his neck, he grumbled and saluted, before speeding out of the mess hall.

A few of the other students began to cheer, only to be silenced by a glare from the teacher that froze the air itself. They immediately turned back to their food, leaving the group once more to their own devices.

Inspecting Dannan, the teacher gave a small nod of approval, then turned to Teacher Kalaman. "You've got a good pupil here, with a head on his shoulders, even if he doesn't know well enough to get his superiors before trying to stop a fight."

Kalaman smiled and chuckled deep in his belly, then glanced over at Dannan. "Let's just see if he keeps it on his shoulders for all eight years."

She nodded, and Dannan had the feeling of a horse being inspected for sale that had just gotten approval. "I'm going to wake up the other two, and then deal with sorting out the punishments. I don't know where Otis is, but he should hear about the problem with his student's temper."

Kalaman nodded, then motioned dismissively at Carissa, Dannan, and Tannil. "You three eat dinner. I don't want you whining you failed the tests tomorrow because you were hungry."

They bowed quickly and saluted, heading straight for the cook, who was serving hungry students as they wandered in.

During the entire time they got their food, sat, and ate it, Tannil couldn't stop laughing or retelling how Dannan had thrashed the fourth years. Although it was amusing to Dannan how Tannil played it up, at the same time, he wondered if he hadn't gotten himself more trouble than it was worth.

When they finally finished dinner and went to go upstairs, Dannan caught the elf girl staring at him, with the redhead nursing a bump on his forehead next to her. Sighing, he decided it definitely hadn't been worth all the trouble he had gotten himself.

The tests went smoothly the next day, even after the interruption of their studying yesterday. Dannan was a little worried when it came time to remember what fortifications were the most useful against which type of siege engine, but he managed to succeed, even if it was only by a hair.

Chapter 30

The day after the tests, they found themselves in the waiting room once more, but this time there were wooden shields instead of shortswords and daggers. The teacher actually looked happy to see them all there that morning, and for a little while, Dannan was nervous.

Having not received a punishment last night, he was still waiting to see what would happen after the incident with the fourth years. Shaking his head, he decided to wait and see what would happen. As it turned out, he was in for a surprise.

"Congratulations! You are all officially third year students of The Hawk's Honor now. This means you have passed the first half of the beginner's courses; so to speak. While nowhere near being a Swordmaster, you are now probably better swordsmen then the average bandit. You all saw someone who let this go to their head, so let that be a good example to you. It's time for you to start learning what it means to be a soldier. This year, you will be learning how to use a shield effectively with a sword."

Inspecting each of them, Teacher Kalaman seemed genuinely pleased for once. "Now, remember. A shield is not just a tool for defense. A good swordsman can attack freely with his shield as well, keeping his opponent off balance. Just like how a wall is a place to defend and attack from, a shield can be the start of your defense, or the beginning of your attack. Now, who here has used a shield before? Raise your right hand."

Dannan looked around, expecting Tannil and maybe Carissa to raise their hands. He was surprised to see that among them, only he and Ramme hadn't used shields before.

Staring at them, the teacher shook his head. "Alright, then. I'm going to show the entire class the maneuver that we'll be practicing during the lectures, and after that I'll be training you two individually during the lecture. Hopefully, I'll be able to bring you up to a level where I can teach you some other techniques for fighting with a shield. Understood?"

"Yes sir!" They all replied in unison. Dannan felt a little embarrassed to be behind the class, even if he had no reason to ever have used a shield.

"At least I'm not the only one." Dannan murmured to himself.

He didn't pay much attention to his classmates after he was handed his shield. The instructor pulled Ramme and him off to the side, where he immediately began trying to get them to grip the shield properly. He had been surprised by how heavy the shield actually was, but by the end of the lecture, which had been consistently punctuated with curses the teacher aimed at them, he only noticed his sore arm.

When they finally finished up, Dannan was glad to take the rest of the evening off until dinner, doing his best simply to rest his left arm. He had been quite proud of his muscles from constantly practicing with his sword, but it seemed like when he used a shield, he just couldn't get the hang of it.

Shaking his head, he looked across the table at Tannil, who was grinning like a cat that caught a bird. "Sore for once, huh?" Tannil said with a laugh.

Scowling at him, Dannan shrugged. "Is that so surprising? Those shields have to be what, twenty stone's weight?"

"Fifteen, actually."

Dannan's scowl deepened as Tannil's grin widened, and he sighed. After a moment, Dannan went back to his soup, and they finished their food in relative silence, ignoring the noise of the surrounding students.

After finishing his soup, Tannil leaned back into his chair, letting out a relaxed sigh. "Although this is a tough life in a lot of ways, I see how people could get soft like this. Three good, guaranteed meals a day. A roof over their heads. And enough excitement and admirer's staring a hole in the back of their skull to keep life from getting dull."

With the last comment, Tannil motioned with his eyes over Dannan's shoulder, and Dannan turned to see what was interesting. Glaring from across the room at him were the elven girl and her friend, and Dannan let out an exasperated sigh.

Turning back to Tannil, he shook his head. "Why? Why do I

have to put up with this? It seems like every time I stick my nose out for some reason or another, life seems determined to snap it off."

Tannil let out a raucous laugh, ignoring the looks from the nearby students, and leaned forward. "That's what makes life interesting though, don't you think? After all, if you hadn't stuck your nose in, you wouldn't be here today."

Dannan gave Tannil a sharp glare, and Tannil leaned back again, holding his hands up as if to ward off the look. "Hey, it's not my fault that you seem to draw all the trouble that happens within a mile of you. Curse the fates or something, not me."

Grumbling, Dannan sighed. "I just hope this passes soon. I'm already sick of dealing with it." Tannil chuckled again, and they spent a little bit longer relaxing in the mess hall before going to their room.

As it turned out, it continued this way for quite a while. Although Dannan would describe his third year there as uneventful, in the background he was always waiting for either the elf girl or her friend to start a fight with him.

Although he soon became accustomed to using the shield, neither he nor Ramme ever became good enough to ever draw anything but a grimace from their teacher. When the third year tests finally ended, Dannan was more than happy to let loose a sigh of relief.

With the fourth year, they began to train in wielding spears, both short and long, and Dannan finally let his mind wander during the lessons. While not particularly easy, he found nothing interesting about the spear lessons, and wound up spending more and more time with his head in the clouds.

Teacher Kalaman never really brought him to task over the issue, but he was sure that the teacher was annoyed with him over it. As the year passed by, he found himself becoming more relaxed in the harsh training sessions. Dannan found that he was happy in this routine, but it changed again when they finally graduated from their fourth year.

Chapter 31

They were all excited from the night before, knowing that they had all passed the tests easily this time around. So no one was surprised when they followed the teacher to the waiting room of the junior student dorm, and he was wearing a smile on his face.

"Normally, I'd have lost at least one or two students by now. So I'm going to congratulate you seriously on completing your fourth year as students of The Hawk's Honor." They murmured happily for a moment, before he made a motion for them to quiet down.

"But that's no reason to relax. You still have four years ahead of you, and I've only had one class other than you that graduated with all of its starting members. So this is going to get tougher from now on. I am going to give you one fortnight to spend time on yourselves, as well as a small stipend of money to spend on clothes, amusements, or practical items. It's up to you."

Careel began to let out a whoop, but the teacher cut him off with a glance. "Don't celebrate just yet. This fortnight off is unusual, and most likely, the other students will avoid you for quite some time after they realize what's really going on."

They quickly glanced amongst themselves, unsure of how to take that, when he continued on. "After that fortnight is over, there will be no more afternoons of rest for you. I will drill absolutely everything I know into you in these last four years. They will most likely feel like an eternity, but I don't give a damn about that. If you want to be the strongest of my classes and all survive this training, then I'm going to make it training that will help you survive on any savannah surrounded by barbarians. On any mountain, knee deep in orc guts with a hundred more chasing you down. Or in the harshest desert, that would bake a regular man's skin right off his bones."

He punctuated each statement with a glare as he spoke. "If you have any issues with that, tell me now. You passed the first test on the road to being a Swordmaster, but I have no intention of raising any children here. You're potential Swordsmasters, and as my students, that means a lot more than some of these younger teachers."

Matching eyes with each of them, he went on. "You might never be as famous as Kron, the barbarian warlord who led the hordes against our walls, or Andros Bellmen, one of the strongest mercenaries to ever fight alongside Galem's apprentices. You might never even become as notable as some of the teachers here when it comes down to it. But every one of you will be the strongest where you fight. I'll make damn sure of that." Dannan tried unsuccessfully to hide his shock at hearing his father's name, and quickly looked at Tannil, so as to hide his expression from the others.

He heard murmuring from his classmates, and when he finally managed to get his emotions in check and turned, he saw Carissa standing a step in front of the others. "Is there a particular reason for this extremely harsh training, Teacher Kalaman? There is no point in breaking us before we graduate, especially not for pride."

The glare he gave her made them all sit back, and for a second Dannan thought Carissa would drop to the floor right then and there.

After a moment the teacher's face softened a little, though, and his eyes became thoughtful. "Is that how you see this, then? As simple pride? An old man trying to regain his glory?"

Carissa looked at the others, unsure of how to proceed, and their teacher sighed. "Whether you see it this way or not, I am still fifty nine. You are my last class because of my age, not because of my will. As such, that means all of you will be the legacy of my teachings. That is the reason I will forcefully try to pass on everything that I would not normally try and teach in these next four years."

His voice became softer, and took on a sad tone. "Is that answer acceptable to you? Or do you still question my motives? Because no one here with any doubt in their heart will be able to succeed at what I plan to push onto you."

Dannan and his classmates all looked back and forth amongst each other, and for a moment, Dannan wasn't sure what the right choice was. Meeting Tannil's eyes, he saw an unshakable resolve there, and he grinned a little.

After a few seconds, Tannil grinned as well, and they both turned towards the others. Careel and Ahminel were the first two to nod after them, followed by Symon and Tymon. Carissa was next, followed by Ramme, and then Uthul.

They all turned to look at Hale, and for the first time, Dannan saw that Hale was sweating from nervousness. Looking around at all of them, Hale had the look of a rabbit caught in a trap, rather than a would-be Swordmaster.

Dannan waited until Hale met his eyes, and then he nodded, giving Hale his most confident and supportive smile. After a moment, Hale sighed and nodded as well. Looking at the the new found resolve in their eyes, the teacher smiled slightly, and nodded.

"Good. You'll need that kind of support to make it through this. I plan to make sure that when you leave here in four more years, there won't be another sword school on this continent that has students with skills comparable to yours."

The teacher looked at each one of them for a few moments, and took a deep breath. "I will not be doing the end of the year tests anymore, even though they are the normal method. Instead, as we move on to new things, I will double check to make sure that you have at least a rudimentary grasp of what I taught you."

Shaking his head, the smile slipped from the teacher's face. "For now, don't think about that, though. You have one fortnight. When we next meet here after that fortnight is done, I will tell you where the training will start. Understood?" They all nodded quickly, and the teacher let his breath out. "Dismissed. See you in one fortnight."

Dannan couldn't contain his surprise after the teacher left, and he could hear the conversations picking up among the others almost immediately.

"Do you think we did the right thing?" Hale said out loud, causing all the others to fall silent.

"There is no reason to worry, Hale. We have succeeded this far together, this final push will just be the same. Certainly it will be hard, but with our combined efforts, I am confident we could win against any senior class. We can do this." Careel said with a smile.

The others nodded in agreement. Carissa commented, smirking. "I'm surprised you're the nervous one, Hale. You and Uthul have real experience as campaigners. A little thing like this shouldn't bother you."

Carissa sat back when Uthul glared at her, and Hale shook his head at Uthul. "No, I should probably talk about it, since we're all going to go through hell together." Uthul grimaced and sat back, then nodded.

Hale took a deep breath, and let it out slowly, seemingly trying to hold in his emotions. He opened his mouth again, then closed it, unable to force his way past his discomfort.

"I'll tell it, alright? You just sit there." Uthul grumbled after a moment. They all looked at him questioningly, and he sighed.

"It was our second campaign. That's where Hale got that scar on his back. We were working at the camp smithy, assisting the blacksmith, when for some reason the blacksmith went insane. They still weren't sure if it was from the pressure to fix all the broken blades and armor so quickly, or if he was suffering from being under the sun too long at the temporary open air forge."

Scowling, he continued. "But after we brought in a new load of broken down swords, he took one of the ones that seemed relatively undamaged. I don't even remember why it was there. It didn't look like any of the other broken pieces of trash we were told to repair. Anyway, after a few seconds with the sword, he just turned and looked at us. Now, he was a bastard. I'll never deny that. But he had never abused us. So when he came at us with the sword like he was ready to kill, we were completely unprepared. Hale and I started running and yelling for help, but before the nearby guards could reach us, or even figure out what was going on, the smith had struck Hale down from behind."

Hale flinched, and Uthul looked over sympathetically. "He was fortunate that it wasn't deep enough to sever his spine, or he wouldn't be walking now, but it was still pretty severe. After the guards saw him go down, they drew their swords and called for the smith to drop his weapon, but he just went straight for them. He was no match for trained soldiers, but once he died, we were left with no idea as to why he went berserk. Hale was nervous even back then about extended campaigns and long drawn out fights, but as you can see, he's even worse now."

Uthul looked at Hale as he finished, his eyes filled with a mixture of sadness and pity. Hale closed his eyes and let his head droop, while the other students stared at each other.

After a minute or two, Tannil cleared his throat. Looking at the others who were all now staring at him, he shrugged his shoulders. "No one here is here because they've got an easy past. Or maybe even a legal or sane past. But we're here. And while I've said to Dannan before that whoever is watching your back when it comes to things like this is your friend, I'm sure we don't all consider each other friends. I'm especially sure that some here aren't even certain about the intentions of the others. But we are a fighting unit now, when it comes down to it."

He met each of their eyes, then continued. "Just as the more experienced classes act like military units, now we're one, to. Even if it's only for those four remaining years, we'll be the only ones to watch each others backs. And I don't think any of our pasts are likely to be something we're ashamed about. Whether it's because of past traumas, past crimes, past campaigns, or lack thereof, every single person here has gone forward as part of our little group. So I say, why worry about it?"

Dannan nodded at that, and glanced around, glad to see the others nodding in agreement as well. "Well, now that that's settled, anyone already have any plans for their fortnight?" Dannan saw a couple of shrugs, and then turned when he heard Tannil sigh.

"I suppose we already know Dannan's. He's going to practice like the madman he is, but does anyone else want to go out for a night on the town?" Dannan made a huffing noise, and Tannil just laughed, refusing to look him in the eye.

No one spoke up, and after a few moments, a playful scowl made it's way onto Tannil's face. "Geez, and I thought he could be boring sometimes."

"We are still having to report to our morning practice, Tannil." Ahminel said, his smooth accent sounding as relaxed as always.

Tannil grumbled, and shrugged his shoulders in resignation. "Fine, fine. I'll just try and drag Dannan out, then. See each other at morning practice." Everyone murmured in agreement, and Dannan and Tannil went to their room to rest, while the others each went their separate ways.

Chapter 32

Dannan awoke the next morning to the sound of someone rapping on the door with their knuckles.

Grumbling as he slowly sat up, he looked over to see that Tannil was still sound asleep on his cot. Sliding his legs out onto the cold stone floor, Dannan winced, grumbling a little louder about being woken up earlier than morning practice.

Opening the door, he looked out to find Teacher Kalaman standing there, a scowl on his face. Immediately standing up straight, Dannan saluted, unsure of what he did wrong, but hoping it wasn't too bad.

"Why aren't you in the other dorms already? You should have changed dorms last night like the others did."

Dannan's jaw dropped as his eyes went wide, and he looked over at Tannil, who was muttering in his sleep. Rushing over, he quickly shook Tannil awake, and Tannil opened his eyes slowly, grumbling even louder.

Taking in the panicked look on Dannan's face, and the scowl on the teacher's, he immediately bolted upright. "What's wrong, Dan?"

"We forgot to switch dorms!" Tannil gave him a quizzical look, then his eyes shot wide open.

"Oh! That was this year! Right!" Looking over at the teacher, Tannil gave him a lazy grin. "So, uh... where are we moving in the other dorm?"

"You're both going to be on the first floor, in the thirtieth room. You'd still be here when the new trainees arrived, if I hadn't come to give you each your stipend. But you only have a little while before the sun starts to rise and morning training starts, so you'd better hurry."

They both nodded and quickly rushed to get their things as the teacher tossed a small pouch onto each of their beds. The pouches struck with a jingle, and Dannan and Tannil both glanced at the pouches quickly, before tossing them into their respective bags.

Looking at each other, Dannan turned and gazed at the open

door where the teacher had just stood, and shook his head. "It's stunning to think our entire life for four years can be fit in a sack like this."

Tannil let out a laugh, and started walking out, leading the way as they went towards the senior dorm they had avoided so studiously for all these years.

Poking their heads in through the double doors, Dannan and Tannil immediately noticed that the dorm looked almost identical to the junior student dorm, though with a few more tapestries.

Thinking the numbering might be identical, Tannil immediately moved them towards where room thirty would be in their dorm. It took them only a minute or two to reach the room, and when Tannil knocked on the door and pushed it open, they found it was already empty.

Stepping inside, they both looked at their new cots, which, while not what could be considered comfortable, were significantly sturdier than the cots in the junior dorms.

Setting his things in the chest at the foot of the bed, Dannan sat on the cot with a sigh. Tannil chuckled and dropped his bag in the other chest, stopping momentarily to grab the coin purse they had received before sitting down as well.

Opening it up, he quickly counted through it, and a small smile crept onto his face. "Good. Ten silver pieces is easily enough to get drunk and cause some trouble with." Dannan made a face, and Tannil laughed. "I'm not really planning to go and cause trouble. After all, the teacher was serious that this will be our last fortnight free for four years. I don't want to spend three of those nights in a jail."

Dannan chuckled and shook his head, then went to the chest, grabbing both his bowstring pouch and the new coin bag. Counting out five gold coins, he dropped them into the coin purse, and set the bowstring pouch back into the bag.

Raising an eyebrow at him, Tannil waited a few moments before saying "You're kind of rich for being from a small village."

Grimacing, Dannan looked at the pouch. "Blood money. Every gold coin."

Waiting for an explanation, Tannil finally sighed. "What, it's not like you murdered someone for it."

Dannan looked over at him, and his grimace deepened. "I got

it because we brought in a bandit to be executed. So yes, it is money I got because I killed someone. I didn't swing the sword, but it is my fault he's dead."

Tannil raised an eyebrow, then shook his head. "A bandit? Really? That's what you're losing sleep over?" Dannan cocked his head to the side, and Tannil chuckled dryly. "I can guarantee you that he wouldn't be losing a second over murdering you. And he died for breaking the laws and, if you got that much gold for him, killing people."

Sighing, Dannan conceded the point.

Rolling his eyes, Tannil grinned a little. "Five gold coins is the standard bounty for one murder. So chances are, the fool you brought in was part of a larger troop, but not important enough to warrant a significant pouch of coins."

Shaking his head, Dannan met his eyes. "You don't get it. That was only part of the bounty."

Raising an eyebrow, Tannil smiled slightly. "Oh, so you brought down someone important, then? Worth fifteen or twenty gold coins?"

Shaking his head again, Dannan stared at his feet. "One hundred."

Tannil's face went blank, and he stared at Dannan expressionless for a few moments, before bursting out laughing. "So you brought down a band leader, then? That's something to be celebrated by a round of beers, not by somber faces."

Unsure of whether to grimace or to smile, Dannan looked up at his friend. Clucking his tongue, Tannil smiled. "Well, I'm still not interested in getting drunk, but I'm definitely taking you out for a beer in celebration. After all, it's things like that which put you on the map for other mercenaries, and prove that you're well on your way to being a strong fighter."

Dannan shrugged, and then gave a small, embarrassed smile. "I wasn't the one fighting him. I just distracted him while he was fighting someone else, and they managed to capture him."

Chuckling, Tannil's grin didn't fade in the slightest. "And he didn't manage to kill you while you distracted him, so you must have done something right."

Dannan looked away, then back at Tannil. "Can we celebrate some other way? Truth be told, I've never been drinking. And I don't know what my mother and father back home would say, either."

Tannil burst out laughing, and for a moment, Dannan had the urge to smack his friend hard. After a few moments, the urge, and Tannil's laughter, both subsided. "Besides, I've got other things that I need to do. I haven't written anything to my parents in the four years since I got here, and they must be worried about me. And I need new clothes, not the ones from the quartermaster, because the ones I've got now are starting to get too small. You might not have to deal with growing any bigger, but I do."

"That's fine. We'll just finish all of that first, and then we can go drinking. But you're not getting out of me treating you to your first time. Whether you consider it a rite of passage, or just a laugh for me, I will get you into a tavern over our rest period." Tannil finished with an even wider grin, and Dannan dropped his head with a sigh, sure this wouldn't end well.

Morning practice was a blessing for Dannan today, as he was sure that afterward Tannil was going to drag him through the city. And while Dannan was hoping that the guard escorting them would help keep some of Tannil's antics in check, he got the feeling it wouldn't stop his friend from all of his trouble making.

Dannan was surprised by the speed his classmates went their separate ways after morning practice finished. Only he and Tannil were left standing there a few minutes later, and Dannan couldn't resist the urge to scowl at Tannil's mischievous grin. "You are supposed to be the older, more responsible one. You know that, right?"

Laughing, Tannil made a 'tsk tsk' sound with his tongue. "You can be the boring one. I'll keep laughing until someone finally runs me through. And speaking of putting things in our bellies, shall we get your errands done so I can see how you handle your ale?"

Sighing, Dannan nodded. "Let's go get a guardsman who can escort us, then. I want to get that letter sent out to my parents today. Maybe I'll even get to hear a reply by the time we have to be ready for more training." Tannil smiled wistfully, and they went off towards the gate.

It only took a few minutes of waiting for a guardsman to show up at the gate to escort them. After that, Dannan let Tannil lead the way, as he knew that his friend had spent some time in the city before joining the school.

After about an hour of steady walking they found the shop Tannil was looking for. A large open book on the sign gave away what was inside, and beautifully embossed gold letters beneath it spelled out 'Words of Wisdom'. Looking through the windows, Dannan noticed for the first time there was actual glass inside of them. He had never really noticed it before when he had been in the city four years ago, but for a moment, he just marveled at it.

Tannil stopped at the door and looked at him, then at the windows. "Ahh. Just noticed the glass now, huh? It's still a bit rarer up here for those poor folk like us." Tannil said with a wink. "But from what I've heard, Ahminel's people down south have been practicing glass blowing for a few hundred years now. In the past fifty or so, those goods have started to show up in the north more often. Of course, the elves did much of that first, but who's going to see elven goods on display in a place like this?" Tannil finished with a chuckle.

Opening the door, Tannil stepped inside, with Dannan a step behind him, and their escort a few steps further back.

Glancing around, Dannan was amazed to see books of all sizes and colors on the shelves. Some had Kranth, the common alphabet, on the spines, while many more had strange markings that Dannan couldn't begin to fathom.

After a moment, he heard the guardsman behind him clearing his throat, and he jumped a little, startled.

Realizing they had fallen behind Tannil, Dannan rushed after him, just in time for him to notice a young man, a little older than himself, off in one corner behind a desk.

Stopping behind Tannil quickly, he was caught off guard by the glare from the man behind the counter. Slightly past his fortieth year, his graying hair and the wrinkles of his sun-browned skin did nothing to detract from his angry blue eyes. "I'd appreciate if you'd control your friend, before he knocks over one of my bookshelves."

Tannil nodded politely, and motioned for Dannan to step back a little. Grumbling, Dannan obliged, looking everywhere but at the old bookseller.

"Now, I remember when I was here several years ago you ran a small courier service for personal letters." Tannil said, a humble tone to his voice. "Is that still true?"

The old man finally stopped glaring, and gave Tannil a nod.

"Jeremi over there can write fairly well. So any letters you need written can just be dictated to him. The cost is four silver per day of travel, since I employ my own messenger. That's there and back, mind you. You pay what I expect it should take up front, and if it's a shorter trip, I'll give back the extra. If it takes longer, then I'll send him to collect the difference. Does that sound agreeable? Since I'm assuming you want to send a few letters."

Looking over at Dannan, Tannil nodded. "We're only sending one letter, to a village a few days away, but that sounds fine by me."

Dannan gave a hasty nod, then looked at the bookseller, trying not to get overwhelmed by the hard look in the man's eyes. After a moment, Dannan took a deep breath. "You know where Woodslock is, sir?"

The bookseller's eyes bored into him, and for a second, Dannan was tempted to abandon the whole idea. "I know where it is. That's where you want the letter to go?" The bookseller's voice was a little gruffer than when he was speaking to Tannil, but his tone was much more businesslike than earlier. Dannan nodded, resisting the urge to look away.

"Alright. Go talk to Jeremi, then. He'll handle it from there. You can pay me when the letter is fully scribed." Dannan nodded and turned quickly, trying to hide his enthusiasm to get away from the old man.

Tannil chuckled at him as they walked around a bookshelf and approached the oversized writing desk in the corner, drawing a small grimace from Dannan.

A boy of about Dannan's age looked up from behind the desk, his overly-wide eyes taking in the three of them. "I heard Master Orvis. I've never been to Woodslock, but it sounds like an easy trip. About how many days travel was it for you?"

The boy's eyes were much softer, and Dannan smiled as he relaxed. "I think it was a two day trip to get to Whitehaven? I was with a caravan, though. So we probably weren't very fast."

Scribbling something on a piece of parchment, the boy cocked his head to the side. "Alright. Now, tell me what you want written, and I'll put it to parchment exactly as you say it. Whenever you're ready, that is."

Dannan nodded, taking a moment to put his thoughts in order, then took a deep breath. "Dear mother and father. I know it's taken me longer to write to you than I said it would, but things have been busy. Unbelievably busy. I have made some friends in my training class already, and I have seen more of the city than I ever thought I would. Though most of the time I'm practicing my sword skills in the compound."

Clearing his throat, he continued. "I was accepted into The Hawk's Honor after I arrived. I should have said that, first, I think. I have a good friend here who watches my back, named Tannil. I hope after the training finishes, you get to meet him face to face. I think you'd like his sense of humor, ma-mann."

Biting his lip a little, he paused for a moment. "I know you didn't really approve of this when I left father, but I still think I'm doing the right thing by being here. I feel like I'm walking forward, even if I don't know where I'm going. I'll tell you more when I see you after I graduate. I hope the messenger finds you well, and I hope everyone else in the village is doing alright. I love you both very much, and I miss you."

Dannan stopped briefly to take a breath, and found that the lump in his throat made swallowing hard.

Thinking about the other children who had been in the village, he wondered if he would recognize any of them when he went back, or if they would remember him.

Shaking his head, he tried to throw off his worries about the village, and he took another deep breath to steady himself. Looking back at the boy, Dannan nodded. "That's all. Should I place my signature on it? Or do you do that as well?"

The boy shrugged, meeting his eyes. "If you have a seal of your own, you can sign it and place your seal in the wax. Or, I can. It's up to you."

Dannan moved over to the boy's side and looked down at the letter. "I'd like to sign it myself. I don't have a seal, though."

Making a dismissive gesture, the boy quickly dipped the quill pen's tip into the inkwell next to him. Holding the quill out between two fingers, the boy looked expectantly at Dannan.

Giving him a small smile of gratitude, Dannan took the quill hesitantly, realizing it had been years since he last held one.

Writing his name down on the open portion at the bottom of the parchment, he handed the quill back to the boy, who quickly stood it up in the inkwell before it leaked too much.

Blowing on the paper gently, the boy looked over the letter, then turned his eyes toward Dannan. "Does everything look to be in order in your letter?"

Dannan scanned it briefly, then nodded.

"Alright, then. It will go out tomorrow, with the other letters. That just leaves the payment, which Master Orvis will handle." He nodded dismissively at them with a small smile, and Dannan looked at Tannil, who motioned for him to go first.

He walked around the bookshelf and back in front of the bookseller, who looked up from a book he had in front of him. Closing it lightly and setting it on the counter, he looked Dannan over. "So, it will be two days there, and likely two days back. All told, that means sixteen silver pieces."

The old man held out his hand, and Dannan quickly fished out two gold coins from his pouch. Dropping it into the bookseller's hand, Dannan shrugged. "There were bandits on the road, so two gold seems fair." The old man nodded after a moment.

"Very well, then. I'll tell the messenger to be extra careful. I'll also tell him to take a reply down from the recipient, if that is to your satisfaction?"

He looked at the bookseller oddly for a moment, before he realized what the man was asking. "Oh. That would work very well, then. Does that cost any extra? And do you know where to send Jeremi to find us?"

The old man chuckled dryly. "I imagine everyone in the city would know where to find you when asked where The Hawk's Honor is. As to costing extra? No, it will not in this case." Dannan nodded after a moment, then looked at Tannil.

"Do you want to send anything to your family?"

Tannil shook his head, then grinned. "I doubt that a messenger from here would reach them any time soon. It's a long ways from here."

Dannan shrugged, then looked back at the bookseller. "Farewell, then."

Picking up the book, the old man nodded. "It was good doing business with you." He said over the top of the book. Dannan pursed his lips, then looked at Tannil, who had already started towards the door. Following after him, Dannan quickly fell into step behind Tannil as they exited the shop.

Shopping for clothes went quickly, as Tannil seemed to know exactly what Dannan would need, and was just as good at finding it. Finally, Tannil lead them to a tavern near the merchant district that seemed fairly clean, and led the way in.

Dannan grimaced as they entered, looking around at the few other patrons who were inside. "I really don't feel comfortable doing this. Can we not do this, and I'll do something stupid to give you a laugh another way?"

"It sounds like you're afraid of a mere pint of ale. That won't do, Dan."

He shrugged, then followed Tannil to one of the tables. "I'm not afraid... just, not comfortable with the idea. That's all. I don't like the idea of not being in full control of myself."

Tannil chuckled as they sat, and looked over at the guard, who remained standing. "Well, think of it this way. One or two beers shouldn't get you drunk, and if they do, you have a problem. After all, there are plenty of places where ale is almost more common than water."

His grimace deepened, and he let out a sigh. "Alright, fine. But only one or two, alright? And then we go back to the compound." Tannil smiled widely, and Dannan sighed again. "And promise me if I start doing anything stupid, that you'll prevent me from causing too much trouble?"

Tannil nodded, his smile not shrinking in the slightest, then looked up as he heard a serving maid approach.

"What will it be for you three?"

Looking over at the guard and Dannan, Tannil shrugged. "Just two ales. That should be more than enough. Something strong, though."

The serving maid, who had obviously seen her fair share of winters, held out her hand. "That'll be three silver each."

He grumbled about the price, but dropped the coins in her hand without any real fuss, then gave Dannan a wink as she walked away. Coming back from the bar a few minutes later, she plunked both drinks on the table. After a few moments, she walked back towards where she had been standing when they first came in.

"Now, drink up, Dan. The guard will help me carry you home." Tannil said with a grin. Dannan sighed and gave the guard a pleading look, then turned back to the ales after no help was forthcoming.

Taking one tankard by the handle, he lifted it up, a smell like axle grease assaulting his nose the closer the drink got. Taking a deep breath, he lifted it up to his lips, then tossed his head back, pouring the ale down his throat as fast as he could.

He had to resist the urge to cough as the noxious stuff hit his throat, and he swallowed hard, trying to get through it as quickly as possible.

After what felt like several minutes, it was finally empty, and he slammed the mug to the table, letting out his breath. He ignored the looks from the other patrons and glared at Tannil, the foul taste coating his tongue. "There, are you happy? Maybe that was the best ale I'll ever taste, I don't know, but god did it taste awful. Can we go now?"

Tannil shook his head, then gestured at the second tankard. "You've still got one more to down. Then we can go."

Scowling at him, Dannan picked up the other tankard. "I will get you back for this, you realize." He said with a growl.

"Oh, I'm sure. But for now, I get to laugh. Now let's see if two is the magic number." Tannil said, his grin unshaken.

Dannan sighed and looked at the tankard, hoping he didn't vomit after drinking more of the foul smelling brew.

Taking a deep breath, he downed the second drink as quickly as the first, and set the tankard down gently before breathing a sigh of relief. They waited a few minutes in silence before Tannil scowled and said. "What, no reaction?" Dannan shrugged his shoulders and looked around, pleasantly surprised.

"I guess not. Does that mean we can go?"

Tannil cursed softly, then stood. "Yes, that means we can go. God, even your drinking is boring! Did you ever have any fun as a child?" Dannan shrugged and stood as well.

Following Tannil out, he smiled a little. "I had plenty of fun. Just not at my own expense."

"Bah, so that's why you're so boring." Tannil said with a huff.

"Yes, but that's also why I'm not drunk right now, and you're disappointed." Tannil scowled at him as they walked out onto the street, and with a shake of his head and a laugh, they headed back towards the compound.

Chapter 33

The next five days passed uneventfully, with Tannil and Dannan going out of the city for short rides after practice, and returning each night. On the sixth day, one of the guardsmen approached after the morning practice finished and handed Dannan a letter, drawing glances from some of the others as they went off. Glancing at Tannil briefly, Dannan rushed off towards their room, leaving his friend to catch up.

As soon as the door closed behind him, he tore the wax seal open, moving to light the candle so he could read.

It was addressed simply 'Dannan', and he wasn't sure if the handwriting was his father's, or belonged to some one else.

"Your mother is furious with you for not writing earlier." It began, and Dannan winced. "But, she is glad that you arrived safely. The merchant caravan told us about the bandit attack, and Samust, the guardsman you seem to have made the biggest impression on, told us that you handled yourself admirably."

Dannan winced even harder, wondering just what Samust had told his parents.

He looked up as he heard the door swing open, then looked back at the letter when he saw that it was only Tannil. "The merchant speaks highly of you, though I doubt he said a word of it in your presence. He's hoping to hire you as a guard, with our permission, when you get back. We pointed out that you would be a man capable of making your own decisions at that time, but he said, and your mother agreed, that as parents, we'd probably have our say. I wasn't so sure though."

Dannan ignored the sound of the door closing, but looked over at Tannil at the creaking of the cot. Tannil waved at him to keep reading, and Dannan nodded, quickly turning back to the letter.

"We regret that we won't be able to make a trip to Whitehaven to see you, but since you said you'll be back after your training, we accepted that. I'd be lying to say that your mother isn't worried stiff, but she seemed slightly reassured when you said you had someone watching your back."

He smiled a little, picturing his mother's face, her brow furrowed, wearing a small scowl.

"Speaking of having someone watching your back, I met a friend of mine in the woods about two years ago that I hadn't seen in a while, and he said you two had met."

Dannan's face went pale, and Tannil moved over to his side, trying to read the letter over his shoulder.

"I'm not bothered, of course. I should have thought of the fact that he would still be there. More amused, I think, that we both wound up meeting him. He of course will be ecstatic to hear you're in good health, and will probably ask if you've been eating enough mushrooms. He didn't seem to know why you went to sword school… or maybe he just wouldn't tell me. I'm not sure, and I don't care."

He laughed, hearing his father's stern but aloof voice in his head. "I just know that with your penchant for getting yourself into things, you'll need all the friends you can get. So be careful, and come home safely when you're done. We look forward to your return."

Dannan didn't notice the tears that had formed in his eyes until several of them hit the vellum. Wiping them away as fast as he could, he handed it to Tannil, and rubbed his sleeve across his eyes.

Sniffling a few times, he waited until the ache in his chest had subsided before he reached for the letter again.

Tannil handed it over, and Dannan re-read it, finally reaching the last line. "Love, your mother and father." Dannan looked at the signature's they had placed on the parchment and smiled, before handing the letter to Tannil again.

"Good news, I take it?" Tannil said, more than a little concern apparent in his voice.

"Great news. Great news. I just didn't realize how much I missed them until I read the letter. That was all."

Grinning a little, Tannil patted him softly on the shoulder. "No worries, there. Everyone gets more than a little homesick the first time they leave. The ones who get it bad enough never leave again. How do you think little villages like yours keep most of the people there?"

Dannan chuckled and shook his head at his friend. "I'm sure there are plenty of people who would hate to live in a big city like this. But you're right, I'm not worried." Tannil nodded sagely, then started reading the letter.

"Of course I'm right. Aren't I always?"

He looked up briefly with a grin, and Dannan grinned back, resisting the urge to punch him.

After a minute or two of reading, Tannil handed the letter back to Dannan. "We can buy a parchment holder for that, so that it won't get worn down. After all, we don't get to keep many things from home on our trips, and it would be a shame to let it get ruined because of something silly like negligence."

Dannan smiled, then went with Tannil to get the case. Though the crowds were the same size as usual, Dannan didn't notice them at all, and Tannil even commented on the fact that he seemed lost in thought.

He didn't mind though, as his thoughts kept going back over the few years since he had come to Whitehaven. His head was still in the clouds even when they went to bed, and his sleep was filled with dreams of home

Chapter 34

The next seven days passed without much change, though he noticed some of the teachers watching them as their fortnight of rest ended.

When the first day of their training finally came, Dannan noticed that the others were just as eager as he was. Arriving in the waiting room, they saw that their teacher was already there.

Looking up at them from where he was sitting, he smiled a little. Dannan didn't have time to take in the fact Teacher Kalaman seemed more energized, as he immediately started barking out orders. "Alright, listen closely! From here on, you're going to see a hell that no one else in all of Whitehaven has experienced! When you are not asleep or eating, I will make you train."

Glancing from one person to the next, his eyes had a strange fire in them. "The first thing you will learn about is traps. Making them, spotting them, and disarming them. After that will come riding, since just being able to stay on a horse won't keep you alive in a battle. Those will fill the first year. Then, if you've survived all that, we'll move on. For now, we're heading to the southeast corner of the compound. The other teacher's know to keep their students away from there, as I've trapped the entire field. That's where we'll start. Any questions?"

Tannil raised a hand, a grin on his face. "So, you're honestly trying to kill us?" Smiling, the teacher walked past without a word, and Tannil's grin faded.

Following their teacher at a modest distance, they arrived at the corner field he had mentioned. It looked fairly inconspicuous, and there were certainly no signs of any traps.

Stopping suddenly, their teacher turned to them, and his smile was just as wide, if not wider, than it had been. "Now, who here sees any signs of danger?"

Tannil raised his hand a little, as did Ahminel and Carissa. Dannan looked between the three of them, unsure of what to do, then shrugged.

After waiting a few more moments, the teacher nodded. "Alright. What traps can you three see from here?"

"There's disturbed grass about fifteen feet to the right. It humps up a little more than the rest, so maybe you planted spikes there?" Tannil said calmly.

Teacher Kalaman nodded, then looked at Carissa, who lowered her hand. Turning towards Ahminel, the teacher raised an eyebrow at him. "There is probably a pit trap twenty feet ahead of us. The grass is lying flat in a patch, even though around it all the grass is healthy."

"Good, glad to see at least a few of you have experience spotting traps. Because the compound doesn't have the resources, I can't train you on the kinds of traps you'd find indoors. We will be able to practice with the kinds of traps you'd find out in the plains though. And while I mentioned disarming them, in the case of most traps outdoors, it comes down to triggering them without getting hit. They don't really get 'disarmed'. Any questions?"

They all shook their heads, and their teacher's smile faded. "Good. Start walking around, then."

Exchanging glances, they looked at each other, surprise on more than a few of their faces, and then Dannan shrugged and sighed.

Walking directly towards the patch of grass that Ahminel had pointed out, he felt something catch on the front of his foot. He caught a glimpse of metal spikes as they pulled free from the ground, and he threw himself to the side.

With a loud whoosh, a lattice-work of garden rakes whipped up, slamming down into the ground next to him. Staring at it, his face whiter than snow, it sunk in that their teacher might not have been joking about trying to kill them.

Yells erupted from the others as they rushed over to his side, and Tannil stood over him, a look of surprise on his face.

Holding his hand up, Dannan looked at Tannil, before his friend helped pull him to his feet. They all looked at the teacher, who had a wide grin on his face. "Just remember. An obvious trap might actually be the trap itself. As Dannan just showed everyone, being light on your feet and aware is how you survive traps. Now, stop standing around and get moving again! There are twenty five traps here, so find and trigger them all."

They grumbled as they looked amongst themselves, then Dannan shook his head. "Let's look in pairs. That way, we've got a better chance of surviving a pit trap with spikes in the bottom. They work on bears, so he probably put a few out here for us, to."

The others looked at him, and Tannil grinned. "Alright, then. Let's hurry and split up. Maybe we can be finished in time for an early dinner."

Spreading out, they began to search, and almost immediately Careel let out a yell as he stepped on a grass covered pit. Ahminel pulled him back from the edge by the back of his vest, dropping Careel to the grass next to him, and everyone looked over again. Careel's coughing was the only noise that penetrated the silence for a few moments, and then they resumed their silent search.

It took the better part of several hours to find most of the traps, which were a mixture of pits and spring-loaded contraptions. Dannan quickly noticed that although Carissa and Ramme were moving quickly, it seemed that Ramme was finding most of the traps. Tucking that piece of information away for later, he decided to ask if Ramme could help them figure out better ways to spot traps without getting so close to them.

Uthul found the last trap, a small ditch hidden by a cover of grass, with wooden spikes driven into the ground on one side.

Letting out sighs of relief after counting the traps, they relaxed. "Good. It took you quite a while, but none of you are really injured. And when it comes to traps, that's what counts for success. Now, once at the end of every fortnight, I'm going to bring you back here. The traps will be in different spots, and you will have to find them all over again. There will only ever be twenty five traps, though."

Fixing each of them with stare, his tone grew harsh. "You are absolutely forbidden from coming to this field until I bring you here from the waiting room, where we will meet. The rest of the fortnight we will be borrowing horses from one of the local stables. Unless there are any questions, go to dinner. Things are only going to get tougher from here." Teacher Kalaman had a small smile when they walked away, and as Dannan and the others walked past, he couldn't help but think it was full of pride.

Dinner was a somber affair that night. The other students were having their normal meal, but at the two tables their class occupied, the silence was almost palpable. He almost laughed to himself as he saw some students walking near their table, and then turn to take a longer route.

After their dinner was finished, Dannan turned to Ramme, who was sitting at the other table, and tapped the back of his chair. Ramme turned towards him quickly, then relaxed. Meeting Dannan's gaze for a few moments, he blinked then turned back towards his empty bowl.

"Ramme, you seem to be more familiar with traps." Dannan said, a little surprised by his classmates sudden reaction. Ramme flinched a little, and Dannan quickly spoke up. "That's not a bad thing. I was just wondering how you spotted some of those traps so quickly. I think it's best if we learn from what you know, so that we can better survive this training. That's all."

Ramme sighed a little, his shoulders relaxing, and he shook his head. "I don't really know much about traps. I just got lucky."

Dannan shook his head, and looked over at Tannil. "He found how many of them, Tannil? Seven?" Tannil nodded, and Dannan looked back at Ramme, who had shrunken down into his seat.

"Like I said, I think it's a good thing that we have someone who's skilled when it comes to traps. It would be a shame for us to be successful Swordmasters and get killed because some stupid orc managed to get the better of us with a pit trap."

Ramme shook his head. "There aren't many good places for a pit trap in the mountains. It'd be more like them to rig an avalanche." Ramme shook like he'd been hit when he realized he spoke, and he shrank further back into his seat.

Looking at the others, Dannan sighed. "There's no reason for you to be afraid of us here. We've all known each other for four years now. There's no one judging you here."

For a few moments, it seemed like Ramme might respond, but finally he moved so that his back was to Dannan.

No matter how Dannan tried to coax Ramme to talk after that, he didn't say another word the rest of the night.

The next day's morning practice was uneventful, and when they met in the waiting room, the teacher was dressed in a heavier coat than usual. "For today, you won't be dressed for it, but we're going to spend about three hours on horse back this afternoon. So remember to dress in slightly warmer clothes. Because we'll be doing it every day, even once the leaves and the snow fall."

Their silence was his answer, and a small smile flashed across his face. "Now follow me. The guards will not be going with us, so I expect you to behave yourselves like professional soldiers on duty. There will be no fighting with outsiders, there will be no unsightly behavior, and there will be no abuse of the name of this sword school. Is that all clear?"

They all nodded, and Dannan raised a hand. "I'm curious, Teacher. What exactly is 'unsightly behavior'?"

Teacher Kalaman laughed and shook his head. "You don't have to worry too much about that, but I'll tell you honestly. Any conduct I deem to be unfit for a member of The Hawk's Honor or a Swordmaster of Whitehaven. Clear enough?" Dannan shrugged. "Good. Follow me."

Forming a single file line behind him, they followed as he walked towards the gate. They could see a class sitting near the smithy with one of the younger teachers talking with the blacksmith. Dannan smiled a little as they passed by, remembering when they had done the very same thing.

When they got to the gate, the guards took one look at the students before saluting Teacher Kalaman. Nodding to each of them, the teacher walked through the open gates.

Looking back over his shoulder, he called out "You should walk side by side. Probably with the partners you worked with on the traps. I don't want to lose anyone in the crowds." They all saluted quickly, and then fell into a smaller line made up of pairs.

The crowds were indeed thick, as it was a little past noon, and there were many people out and about after lunch.

Winding through the crowds while keeping the teacher in sight was a challenge for them at first. As they got the hang of just following the pair in front of them though, things became easier.

Chapter 35

Although it took them a while, the teacher led them to a large stable near the edge of the Noble's Quarter. When they finally got there, Teacher Kalaman banged a fist on one of the open doors at the entrance to the stable. "Gor! Are you in here?"

As the teacher kept banging, a huge figure emerged from the shadows in one of the furthest corners of the stable.

Dannan gaped openly as the man, if he could be called that, walked closer to them. He seemed like his enormous body would block out their view, and although the stable door was ten feet tall, his head almost brushed it. A well-groomed beard hung down to the middle of his chest, and his chestnut brown hair seemed to accent his tan face well. His clothes were that of an average courier, made to stand up to the wear and tear of constant travel. His clear blue eyes sparkled with mischief as he saw their teacher, and the huge man swung him up in a hug.

Dannan's jaw fell further at this spectacle.

"Gor, you can put me down now. I saw you less than a fortnight ago, after all." Their teacher's irritation was apparent to all of them, and Dannan glanced over his shoulder as he heard Tannil snickering.

Closing his mouth, he was about to say something when a booming laugh almost made him jump back.

Setting Teacher Kalaman down, the enormous man smiled down at him. "Ahh, but Kal, you know I never get sick of seeing my old comrade! You seem to spend less and less time outside of that compound of yours, and that's compared to how little you spent outside after the war."

Teacher Kalaman shook his head, a wry smile on his face. "Well, you'll be seeing a lot more of me for a while. As I told you, these are the students I want to borrow your horses for. I'm hoping to make them into decent riders in the next year."

Turning to look at them, their teacher nodded over his shoulder. "This giant is Gormund Shovelhands. Don't ask me what his real name is, I don't speak the language. And the nickname stuck well enough. Don't you think, Gor?"

Gormund chuckled again, this time the sound like drums being struck. "Who'd have thought those idiot soldiers would come up with something useful?" Dannan looked at Tannil, who shrugged.

"Are you a real giant?" Careel asked, his eyes wide.

Gormund looked at Careel, and a fierce look crossed his face. Letting out a small yelp of surprise, Careel hid behind Ahminel, and Gormund burst out laughing again. "Yes, I am. I'm an average example of what you might call... what was the name, Kal? 'Hillock Giant'?"

Teacher Kalaman nodded, and Gormund looked back at Careel. "In the giant language, we're called runtling giants, but Hill Giant seems a fair enough description to me. Where other giants are mountains tall, we're only as tall as the hills."

Careel peeked out from behind Ahminel's slightly taller shoulders, his eyes even wider. "There are bigger giants?" Gormund's chuckle shook his whole body, and he smiled down at them.

"Yes, there are, but if you ever meet them, you probably won't realize it. Not unless they're actually moving when you see them. And you'd have to go much further north than you'll probably ever go to do that."

Looking at Tannil, Dannan was about to say something, when he saw their teacher punch Gormund in the leg out of the corner of his eye.

"He means you'll likely never see one, that's all." Their teacher said calmly. Glaring up, he quickly added. "Now, are the horses ready for us? I know you said that you wouldn't be using your hired hands for a few sets of horses while we borrowed them and put them through their paces. But you always liked to take your time when you were off duty." Gormund chuckled, and motioned for them to follow him in.

As they walked through the doors, Dannan gasped as he was assaulted by the smells of such a huge stable. He quickly glanced at Tannil, who was looking a little queasy, and he patted his friend on the back.

The overwhelming smell of so many horses seemed to be

affecting all of them except for Ahminel, Careel, and Gormund. Even their teacher had scrunched his nose up at the smell.

"As you can see, Kal, it's even bigger than last time you were here!" Letting out a small chuckle of his own, Teacher Kalaman shook his head.

"You certainly are obsessed with collecting and breeding horses. How many do you have now? A hundred and fifty? I think that's what your goal was when I saw you a few years back."

Gormund shook his head, a wide smile on his face. "I passed that goal a few months after I saw you. You are now looking at one of the largest stables on the continent. It's getting to the point where I almost can't spend even a few minutes each day seeing every one of my beauties."

His eyes sparkled as he looked over stall after stall filled by horses. "I've passed two hundred."

Dannan cocked his head to the side, and looked at Ahminel and Careel, who looked like their jaws could fall off at any moment.

"I've got a few foals who should be born soon, and I'm hoping they come out fine. But for horses older than one year, I've got two hundred in the stable. That's pretty much as big as I could get it without having to buy any houses to knock down for more space."

Turning, Gormund looked back at them. "You remember my land outside the city, right, Kal?" Their teacher nodded, even as he rolled his eyes. "I've got another thirty five old horses out there in the field by my house."

Gormund let out a sigh, his eyes misting over a little as he seemed to look far away. Shaking his head, Teacher Kalaman let out an annoyed sigh. "As you've all noticed, Gormund is absolutely obsessed with horses." Glancing up, he added. "I still think that paladin's charger knocked your brain about in that hollow head of yours."

Grinning down at him, Gormund led them a little further in. "All that horse knocked into my head was love for such a beautiful, loyal, and intelligent creature. No, not beautiful, statuesque!"

Their teacher punctuated his next head shake with a sigh as they walked on. "He's obsessed with horses. Even spent his whole damn fortune from the war on creating this stable. And still he wants more!" Chuckling, he looked at several of the horses they passed by.

Ahminel sped up a little, almost walking directly next to their teacher and the giant. Careel hurried after him, hanging back a little further from them. "But... with this many horses, you must be one of the richest men on this part of the continent. Why is it we have never heard of you in the south?"

Gormund stopped and looked down at Ahminel, and for a moment, the hairs on the back of Dannan's neck stood up. "I don't trade with the cities of the south." The look in his eyes was so sharp, Dannan was worried Ahminel might get hurt. "And if you treat any of my horses the way I saw the nomads and other southerners treat their horses, even as Kalaman's student, I will grind your bones into dust beneath my heels. Understand me?"

Ahminel gaped at him, his eyes almost as wide as his mouth, and he nodded, almost desperately, before falling back a few steps.

Looking at Careel, Gormund's eyes seemed to carry the same message, but to Dannan's surprise, Careel's back stiffened and he stood up straighter. "Not all the families of the south treat their horses like chattel or currency. And I'll challenge you on that any day. I don't know what nomads you met... after all, the Kilush nomads treat their horses abominably. But I will not be likened to those savages!"

A dark smile slowly grew along Gormund's lips, and he turned to face Careel. Though perhaps face was the wrong word. He towered over Careel so much that Careel had to crane his neck just to meet Gormund's eyes. "You'd challenge me when it comes to horses, you say?"

Careel nodded stiffly, and the giant let out a small laugh, then looked over at their teacher. "At least you've taught them a little backbone. Even if they haven't got the brains to back it up."

Teacher Kalaman shrugged, and Dannan breathed a sigh of relief as Gormund's smile relaxed. "As for you, I'm glad to see you'll stand up for them. And I'll refrain from insulting you accidentally again. Is that acceptable?" Careel nodded, and as the giant turned away and started walking again, Dannan noticed Careel's knees were visibly shaking.

Patting Careel on the shoulder as he walked past, Dannan heard Tannil whisper from behind. "Nicely done."

Finally, Gormund stopped in front of a number of stalls that had saddled horses inside them. "These eleven are for your use today.

I remember you said you'll be using them for thirteen days out of each fortnight, so I've rotated my helpers so that you'll always get horses in need of some exercise. Unless someone takes to a particular horse, though, I'm going to rotate them till you stop coming and use you as free labor. That's alright with you, Kal?"

A small nod from their teacher confirmed it, and Gormund smiled. "Alright then, these ones are all yours."

Gormund went from stall to stall, giving each horse a small pat and a few kind words as he led them out to the group. For the first time, Dannan noticed how wide the stable really was, as three horses were easily able to fit side by side in the aisle. They all mounted up quickly, and Dannan was surprised to see how comfortable their teacher looked in the saddle. He also noticed that Tannil's mount seemed less than pleased to have him, and Dannan cast his friend a sympathetic glance.

As they left the stable astride their horses, Gormund gave them a cheerful wave, and winked at their teacher, who grumbled again. Dannan let out a little snicker, and pretended to look innocent when their teacher shot him a sharp glare.

Avoiding Teacher Kalaman's eyes, Dannan immediately noticed that everyone else in the crowd was watching their party. He immediately began to feel uncomfortable, and he saw that the others were feeling the same way.

As they continued trotting their horses after the teacher, they noticed that although the crowd was parting to give them plenty of room, more people were gathering to see what was going on.

By the time they had gotten halfway towards the edge of the city, there was a sizable crowd, and Dannan had noticed a few city guards starting to gather along the route as well. When they noticed Teacher Kalaman, they gave him a nod, and started paying attention to the crowd more than the students.

Dannan assumed they were keeping an eye out for pickpockets. He remembered Samust had said the city guard had the luxury of only paying attention to what went on inside the city.

Thinking about it like that, he looked out over the crowd again, and he realized their looks weren't of suspicion. Some of them looked anxious, most were curious, and a few of the older citizens even had proud smiles on their faces. Exchanging glances with Tannil, Dannan let a small smile creep onto his face, and he felt his back get a little straighter.

By the time they reached the city gates, the crowds had dissipated a little, the remainder largely composed of the older citizens. As the Northern gate guards gave the group the nod to go on through, some of the people still left began to clap.

The noise was so sudden, Dannan was completely caught off guard, and he spun to the sides, looking at the people. After he quickly realized what it was, he sat up straight again, his face a little flushed with embarrassment.

He caught Tannil chuckling at him, and gave him a little grimace. Dannan hid it quickly though, so that no one would notice as they started to walk through the gateway under the wall.

Dannan marveled as he looked up at the walls as they walked under, remembering how it had looked four years ago. He smiled to himself, thinking about how nervous and scared he had been at the time, and looked at his classmates.

Although they were all young, he felt so much more confident, knowing that they had his back this time. Riding behind the teacher, he felt less like a follower this time, and more like he was moving forward on his own.

The teacher led them a fair distance from the city on horseback. Dannan thought they must have gone at least five to ten miles, when they finally saw a walled home in the distance.

It took them another hour or so of riding to reach it, and Dannan glanced back over his shoulders to see that the city walls had gotten much smaller behind them. Looking over the wall that surrounded the house, Dannan couldn't help but gape as they approached.

The wall itself must have extended for several miles in its course around the home, and the house itself was by no means small.

Built from what must have been hundreds of trees, the size was indeed fit for a giant of Gormund's size. It was certainly the most impressive log home that Dannan had ever seen.

As their teacher walked his horse up to the gate that led through the seven foot wall, a guard popped his head over the side. The man looked them over for a moment, and then disappeared from sight again.

They heard the groaning of wooden gears, and the gate swung to the left slowly, revealing small, four foot fences drawing a maze through the inner pastures.

Teacher Kalaman flipped his reins gently, and his horse started walking forward again. They followed after him, winding their way through the corridor like space the fences created.

Dannan was amazed to see all the horses gently grazing inside the fenced in portions of the inner area, and he was so distracted he almost didn't realize when the teacher stopped.

Looking forward, he let his eyes go up as his mouth fell down. The house towered over them much like Gormund had, and for a moment, Dannan wondered how they were going to do anything in a house with doors almost twice their size.

He received his answer when the door swung inwards. Looking inside, they could see a man in his early twenties dressed in a plain wool tunic and pants pulling on what looked like a net. Following the ropes with his eyes, Dannan saw that they were attached to the door handle, which was about six feet up the door.

When the door was most of the way open, the man, who Dannan guessed was a servant, bowed to them. "Master Gormund told us to expect you, Sir Kalaman."

Teacher Kalaman nodded to the man, and then looked around at the furniture, which, while obviously high quality, was more notable for its size. Almost everything in the front room was made for someone of Gormund's size. Dannan was glad that this time he wasn't the one gawking, like several of his classmates were.

"Now, Gormund said that someone named Arek would show us around?" Their teacher said, not wasting any time. The servant nodded and bowed again, his face impassive.

"Yes, I will be showing you around the master's home. If you will follow me?" Nodding, their teacher began walking after the servant, who had already begun to move.

Hurrying after them, the students looked around, trying not to remember the legends about the homes of giants. Even though it looked like a regular log home in many ways, it was as if they had all shrunken down to the size of small children once more.

The enormous tapestries depicted scenes of great battles, endless plains, and a lone stallion. The stallion shown in the tapestries was beyond regal. The look in his eyes, which seemed to follow them as they moved, was one of absolute authority and dignity.

"No king I've ever seen looks that strong." Tannil murmured

to himself. He almost seemed surprised when they looked at him, as if he hadn't realized he had spoken aloud.

Dannan nodded slightly in silent agreement, and they all turned when they heard someone clearing his throat loudly. Realizing they had stopped, they looked at their teacher, embarrassment clear on most of their faces.

"You'll most likely get a chance to see the tapestries of Morning Sun in the little bit of rest time when we're here. We're going to be staying here whenever the weather is too bad to make the ride back to town."

Careel raised his hand, and the teacher looked at him, one eyebrow raised. "Yes?"

"Teacher, why is he called Morning Sun? It seems kind of silly, as his fur is jet black."

Teacher Kalaman sighed, and scowled. "How should I know why an idiot paladin would name his horse that?"

Waiting a little bit longer, he sighed again when Careel continued staring inquisitively. "The reason I heard from the man was this. And trust me, when I say that it is an idiotic reason. Perfectly suited to an idiot like him."

Looking over at the tapestry, a wry smile appeared on his face. "He said he named the horse Morning Sun because, just like how the dark of night gives way to the morning, his jet black horse brought the light along with it. And yes, he did think he was some sort of 'savior'. But then again, most paladins do."

Grimacing slightly, he turned back towards Careel. "Does that answer your question?" Careel nodded, looking less curious, but no less in awe of the magnificent horse in the tapestry. "Now, we need to keep following Arek if we want to leave and get back before dark." Looking at the servant, Teacher Kalaman nodded to him, and Arek began walking again.

Other than the awe-inspiring tapestries, Dannan felt surprisingly let down by the rest of the home. It looked like a normal house you might see in some villages, simply with more rooms, and on a larger scale. There were several guest rooms made to fit human guests, as well as a single large chair and table in each.

When they arrived at the front door again, another servant quickly spoke to Arek.

Arek bowed to them once more. "The horses have been fed

and watered, and should be ready to take you back to town. I look forward to serving you all again."

Teacher Kalaman nodded, his face slightly sour, and waited patiently as Arek opened the door. When it had swung fully open, he motioned for them to follow, and walked out to where the horses were waiting.

After an uneventful trip back, Dannan was tired. It had been a long time since he had sat in a saddle for so long, and riding in the dark required more skill than during the day.

He was extremely glad to find out that they had not missed dinner, even though they were so late. Dannan could tell from the reaction of his classmates as they ate their dinner that they were all exhausted as well.

All of them except for Ahminel and Careel, anyway. He gave them a half-hearted grimace as the two of them had a few laughs at their tired classmates. When he finally bid goodnight to his classmates and he and Tannil went back to their room, he was ecstatic to fall onto his cot. Sleep took him quickly, and for once, he had no dreams.

Chapter 36

The next few fortnights went by quickly, and although they were uneventful, Dannan had no chance to enjoy a moment of peace.

True to his word, their teacher was working hard to run them ragged, and any time they didn't spend in their cots or the dining hall was spent training. Dannan was even getting used to missing meals every few days, as when they were too slow riding back, they wound up heading straight to their rooms hungry.

He could see as time went on that several of his classmates had started to lose some weight from the intense training. Every few days he asked himself if it was worth it, but every time, he found solace in the fact they were all enduring it together.

It continued uneventfully like this into early fall. When the rain started coming more frequently, they would occasionally stay at Gormund's home rather than ride back through the downpour.

The guest beds that Gormund had apparently bought in anticipation of them staying were more comfortable than their cots back at the compound by far. That was the most relief that they had when there, though. The morning drills that Teacher Kalaman put them through when they were in Gormund's great hall were harsher than the ones back at the school.

Each time, they would ride back when the rain stopped, or, if it continued through the day, stay another night at Gormund's ranch and practice.

One fortnight in fall was particularly heavy, and they were stuck at the ranch for seven days straight. When it finally stopped and they rode back to the city, Dannan was quite sad. On one hand, the training was harsher, but on the other, at the end of the day, there was a far more comfortable bed to look forward to.

More often now than before, Dannan noticed Tannil was making jokes about being out on campaign to keep up their spirits, and Dannan would smile to himself.

Although Tannil claimed when asked not to care about

others, Dannan knew his friend had a good heart. It was this weary yet relaxed atmosphere that saw them returning to the compound that particular day.

Dannan had stopped noticing the crowds once he realized they weren't interested particularly in the group. So he was unsurprised to have an easy, uninterrupted ride back to the stable. The walk back from the stable seemed equally quiet, when suddenly Dannan felt a tingle at the back of his neck.

Looking over his shoulder, he was unsure of what was bothering him when he realized that several men in well-worn laborer's clothes were following them. Turning so he was staring straight ahead, he made a quiet hissing noise to get Tannil's attention.

It took a few tries, but finally Tannil looked over at him, one eyebrow raised. "There are some people following us. They're not part of the crowd; they've been behind us far too long." Tannil moved to glance over his shoulder, and Dannan made another hissing noise.

Tannil grimaced at him slightly, then sighed and looked ahead again. "How many did you see? What were they wearing? Are they armed?" Dannan made a show of looking up at one of the plaster houses they were passing, and took that opportunity to glance back over his shoulder again.

He noticed they were much closer now, almost up to where Carissa and Ramme were walking behind him. Looking forward again, he grimaced. "They don't seem to have any large weapons on them. Probably shortswords and knives. They're wearing dark brown laborer's clothes. It looks like they're pretending to be warehouse workers. I could only see three, but I'm pretty sure there are more."

Nodding, Tannil let out a yawn, stretching his arms over his head. He slowed down a little as he did this, so that he was moving back towards Carissa and Ramme.

Dannan heard a quick shuffling, and noticed Tannil spinning on his heel suddenly. Turning to look at his friend, Dannan saw Tannil take off down an alley, and he looked around worriedly, realizing he couldn't see Carissa or Ramme.

Stepping to the front of the alley, he saw Tannil running after someone, though he couldn't hear much. Sprinting down the alley after his friend, Dannan watched Tannil round the corner at the end of the alley, and disappear out of sight once more.

Running around the corner, Dannan saw that the next part of the alley broke off in two directions. He was just in time to see Tannil go to the left, and he pushed his body harder, trying to catch up just a little bit more.

"They're just ahead in this warehouse!" Dannan heard Tannil's voice carry back through the alley to him, and when he came around the corner he saw a door in the side of the alley hanging open.

He ran almost all the way up to it, and slowed down just before he got to the open doorway. Pulling his sword out, he looked at the sturdy wooden door, shaking his head at the spot where Tannil had forcefully ripped the hinge off. Dannan could hear the sounds of movement inside, and poked his head slightly around the corner before grimacing.

There seemed to be about ten men in laborer's clothing. On the far side of the room, two men each were holding Carissa and Ramme by the arms. A third man had a dagger against Ramme's chest, and Dannan could see that the man's intent gaze was on Tannil, who had rushed into the middle of the room without thinking.

Although Tannil hadn't drawn his sword, Dannan could feel the palpable aura of menace that he was emanating, and Dannan had to hold in a sigh. "There's no way this won't turn bloody." He muttered under his breath with a fierce grimace.

Looking over, he saw that there was a window high on the other side of the warehouse that had been shattered, and he got an idea.

Moving low to the ground, he waited until Tannil started to talk and attract all the attention to himself, and then darted past, not even stopping to listen to what Tannil was saying.

Following the alley quickly, for once, he was glad the soft leather boots he was wearing weren't strong enough to really insulate his feet from the ground. He breathed a small sigh of relief as he continued following the side of the warehouse, and found that there was enough room to get to the window he had seen.

Sheathing his sword, Dannan looked at the wall of relatively sturdy, dark brown bricks. The cracks where the mortar had deteriorated were just barely thick enough to get his fingers in, but he thought with a little effort he might be able to climb up.

Taking a deep breath, he reached up and pushed his fingers into one of the cracks, and slowly began climbing up, worried that if he moved too fast, something might fall and give him away.

It seemed like it took him forever to climb the fifteen or so feet up to the window, but finally he made it.

Peering over the edge, he saw that Tannil was still standing there and staring down the leader, and from the looks of it, the leader was speaking. Craning his neck a little more, he was glad to see that all of the thugs were still intent on Tannil, and none had looked his way.

Gently he pulled himself up, trying his hardest to avoid any of the small shards of glass still left in the window sill from when someone had broken it.

Finally he managed to raise himself high enough that he could put his leg through the window. Looking down, he prayed with all his might that none of them would turn around, because there was no way they could miss him there, exposed as he was.

After a few seconds, no one had turned around, and he inwardly breathed a sigh of relief. Looking down, he saw that there were precious few footholds on the inside, as the cracks on the inside were a little smaller than the ones on the outside.

Slowly taking another deep breath, he pulled his other leg up so that he was sitting on the frame. He could feel the pressure from the shards of glass pressed against his bottom, and he tried not to think of how many ways this could go wrong. Lightly lifting his sword, he removed the scabbard from his belt and pulled it through the window.

Moving his left leg until he found a crack that seemed like it would support his weight, he swung his body over slowly, trying to hold onto the frame with both arms, even as he held his sword in his hand. Inwardly, he cursed himself for taking the hard route, but then he shook his head. "If it works, it works." He murmured under his breath

Dannan could hear them talking clearly now, and was glad that they hadn't noticed him. It seemed like the leader didn't even realize that Tannil had someone with him.

"Listen, I don't care if you fools are from a sword school or from the lord's own household. You're not getting them back, and the more you push, the further my blade pushes into this traitor's chest. I don't want to have to keep repeating myself."

The leader's voice seemed a little too smooth for a common criminal, and Dannan had the sinking feeling that they had a big problem. "You keep calling Ramme a traitor. But you still won't tell me who you are, or even if you have the right person." Tannil said, a slight tone of annoyance.

"And you won't find out who we are. It's in your best interest to turn around now, and leave him to us."

Dannan was about halfway down the wall when he saw from the corner of his eye that one of the thugs was turning towards the back wall. "How about we make a deal, then?!" Tannil yelled. Dannan could tell the anger was feigned, and just hoped that they couldn't.

He saw the thug jump and turn back towards Tannil, and Dannan breathed a small thank you. "I'm a mercenary, and I can tell that it's not worth it to you to fight me. But it's not worth it to me to just leave, either. You give me the girl back, and we'll both leave. Yes, you know we'll chase later, but for now, it's my duty to get as many of us out as possible. And I don't know what Ramme did to you, but he must have done something to get you to chase him as hard as you have."

Dannan's foot gently hit the ground as Tannil was talking, and he was glad that Tannil's voice covered up the small scuffing noise it made. Lowering himself down, he turned, glad to see that he was right next to a large stack of boxes around five feet high.

"That deal still isn't worth much to me." Dannan could tell from the man's cold tone that he didn't seem interested in budging, and he let out a little shudder.

Ducking behind the large stack of boxes, he peered out from behind the corner of one, just enough that he could see with one eye what was going on.

"Well, how many of your men's lives is it worth to you? You aren't common thugs. Probably thieves. You hold that dagger far too well to be just a thug. And while you might kill Ramme, and you might kill Carissa to, I'm fairly certain I can kill at least eight of your men. I might even be able to kill you, first."

The tone Tannil delivered that last threat in seemed to do the trick, as Dannan could see the leader's body stiffen significantly.

Watching silently, Dannan saw the man turn towards Ramme,

and Dannan quickly pulled back behind the boxes further. After a few moments, he heard a shove and the sound of boots stumbling on stone. "Take her, then. You get her, we get Ramme, and you'll never see us again. Deal?"

Silence persisted for a few moments, and Dannan began to get worried. "Alright. That deal sounds fine to me."

He could hear Carissa begin to start arguing even as Tannil finished. "Enough! Our first priority is to report back." Tannil said, cutting her off sharply. "I'm assuming one of your men is going to follow us to the end of the alley we chased you down?"

"Of course. And if you kill him him, we'll find you."

Dannan heard Tannil's dry chuckle, and he swallowed a little. "Like I said, if I wanted you dead, I would do it. But I've got other priorities."

After what seemed like an eternity of silence, Tannil spoke again. "There's no reason for us to stay, so we're going to back out of here, and leave. And if you tell your lackey to stab us from behind as we go, you'll never see him again. Got it?" Dannan couldn't see what the leader did, but he heard Tannil begin to walk out slowly.

More precisely, he heard Tannil dragging Carissa behind him, struggling and cursing as they went. Peering around the edge of the box, he quickly ducked back as he saw one of the thugs looking in his direction.

Moments later, he heard the leader. "Jik, make sure that they do as the merc said. I don't want to make more corpses than we need to, but I don't want any trouble while we're in the city, either. We'll wait five minutes." Dannan heard the sound of soft leather quickly hitting stone, and then the sound was gone.

Peeking around the other side of the boxes, Dannan was glad to see that the leader had moved away from Ramme, leaving him held by two of the thugs.

Clucking his tongue, the leader grimaced at Ramme. "You should know that no one ever leaves the guild. Especially not ones like you. I'll give you a minute or two to explain yourself, if you feel like trying to save your miserable hide. But when Jik gets back, I'm going to gut you, and we're going to take your corpse back to the boss."

Ramme murmured something that Dannan couldn't quite hear, then Dannan flinched as he heard a ringing slap echo through the now silent warehouse. "You've still got quite the mouth on you. It's a shame, really. You were destined to go so far."

The leader walked further into Dannan's view, and Dannan studied his hard features. A few days of stubble didn't detract from his almost handsome face, but the scar straight across his nose wasn't helping. His hair was dyed dark brown, and his eyes were a very light blue that would stand out in Whitehaven. His mouth was twisted into a cruel smile, and Dannan shivered as the man turned back to Ramme.

"I'd say it pains me to be the one to kill you, but we both know that's a lie." Ramme remained silent, and after a few moments of waiting for a response, the man continued. "I'm not going to miss this chance to gloat, though. I would've loved to kill you in a much slower, and much more painful manner. But the boss's orders are the law. You should know that."

Dannan heard the man's footsteps move further away, and he slowly withdrew his sword, working hard to make sure that it made no sound as it left the scabbard.

Sighing, Dannan saw the man move towards one of the other thugs. "What do you bet, Lonnie, that he screams when I cut him open?" The thug's harsh laugh made Dannan shiver again, and he slid a little bit closer to the left side of the stack of boxes.

"I'd wager five gold pieces he doesn't. The boss used to hit him too often for a little pain to make him cry."

Several of the other thugs chuckled, and Dannan felt his blood boil a little. Glancing around the edge of a box, Dannan saw that the leader was standing at the doorway, looking down the alley.

Chapter 37

Taking a deep breath, Dannan said one last prayer, and hoped the surprise would be enough of an edge to win. Moving in a crouch just past the edge of the box, he quickly memorized where the thugs were standing.

He didn't get more than a moment, as one of the thugs off to his left could see him.

Even as the thug opened his mouth to say something, Dannan rushed forward. Coming up into a standing position, he brought his sword up at an angle with both hands.

Dannan felt resistance as the sword started to cut into the head of the man holding Ramme's left arm, and he stubbornly pushed forward with all his might, praying that his sword didn't get stuck.

A chunk of the man's head went flying forward as Dannan's sword sliced through on the top, and Dannan let go with his left hand, letting the momentum carry the sword a little higher.

The first thug was finally yelling a warning, and the others were turning towards Dannan and Ramme quickly.

Surging forwards still, Dannan threw his right leg out in a kick, striking the thug on Ramme's right in the side. The kick knocked the wind out of the man even as it sent him stumbling a several feet away, and Dannan grabbed Ramme's left shoulder with his left hand.

Tugging hard, he pulled Ramme back towards the wall as he stepped forward himself, and he was glad he had. Although most of them were slow to react, the leader wasn't.

He charged towards Dannan, a murderous glint in his eyes, and it was all Dannan could do to deflect the first knife thrust.

The leader's thrusts started to speed up as he fell into a rhythm, and the blur of metal between him and Dannan was enough that Dannan could feel the wind moving.

He could see the other thugs slowly moving to encircle them, and he tried to back up a little. He felt himself trip a little on the corpse of the first thug, and he fell back, surprise on his face.

The gloating look in the leader's eyes showed strongly as he stepped in, but it quickly turned to surprise as his knife tip struck the dragon scale hanging against Dannan's chest. Dannan continued his fall, and he pushed one hand against the ground to make himself fall back further.

The leader moved after him quickly, and Dannan spun towards the boxes, hitting the stack with his shoulder as he tried to stand and sending them spinning outwards.

One of the boxes struck the leader in the shin, even as the rest hindered the thugs off to his right. Retreating a little further so that his back was to Ramme and the wall, Dannan faced the crowd again, waving his sword lightly back and forth as he slowly edged the two of them into a corner.

As the thugs on the left got closer, Dannan made a sharp step in and let out a loud yell, before quickly retreating. The men held their ground about fifteen feet from him, even as the others moved to block off his escape route.

Cursing silently to himself, Dannan stared at the seven remaining men, and for a moment, he was worried there was no way out.

Glancing over his shoulder at Ramme, he saw that his classmate had a despairing look in his eyes, and Dannan grew a little more afraid. "It will be impossible to escape if you give up now, Ramme." Dannan muttered quietly.

A slight noise brought Dannan back to the fight, and he brought his sword up just in time to deflect a knife thrust skyward. Instinctively kicking towards where it came from, he felt his foot meet resistance as it hit the leader in the stomach. Just as suddenly, a sharp pain bloomed in his upper thigh, and he stumbled back against Ramme a little, a knife about five inches long stuck in his leg.

Cursing fiercely, he glared at the leader, who had a smug look on his face, and spit.

The man laughed as he dodged back slightly, his grin widening. "You've never fought thieves, have you, boy? It's a good thing for us, to. That merc you were with, now he would have been trouble. But you're still too green."

Moving so that he was standing against the wall next to

Dannan, he grinned. "You still don't know how to handle this many people. Or fight dirty, do you?"

He laughed as he whipped a knife up from his left hand, throwing it towards Ramme's head. Dannan swiped it aside with his sword, and he threw up his hand to stop the leader's knife, even as it entered through his palm and went right through.

He gritted his teeth, holding in a scream as the knife blade exited the back of his hand, and he threw his head forward. As his forehead smashed into the thief's face, he pulled with his arm, yanking the knife from the man's hand.

Spitting towards the leader as he stumbled back, Dannan grimaced. "I know enough to beat you, scum."

Holding his left hand underneath him so that the handle was facing Ramme, he quietly said. "Take it. Quickly. We need you armed as well."

A moment or two passed, and Dannan felt a hand gingerly take hold of the knife. He could hear the sounds of some of the thugs off to the left moving, and he grunted.

"Do it now!" He yelled at the top of his lungs, and the thugs all leapt forward, their leader standing back, trying to stem the waterfall of blood from his nose. Dannan felt a slight tug on the knife, and it refused to move.

He pulled his arm forward as he felt a harder tug on it. Holding in the scream as it ripped free from his hand, he barely managed to get his sword up in time to deflect the knives of the first two men.

The sound of metal rapidly striking metal rang out from behind him, and he said a small prayer in thanks for Ramme's skill with a knife.

The third man got in closer, and Dannan swung at the man's legs, his slightly longer reach forcing the man to stop his rush abruptly.

Taking the chance, Dannan moved, crouching down a little and throwing himself forward a step. Using the momentum, he managed to bring his sword back to the right, and he felt it slice through the front of the thug's thighs, and a spray of blood let him know that it was a good strike.

Trying to step back quickly, Dannan stumbled a little, but managed to keep his sword in front of him as the thug he had cut fell backwards.

He heard a hiss of pain and a yell from behind him, and wished he could see what was going on.

The thugs backed off, and the leader yelled something unintelligible through the blood pouring down his face. The other thugs looked to the leader, and Dannan backed up, feeling his back hit Ramme's. Sucking in a breath, he started gasping a little, his body finally realizing just how much energy he had used up in that initial rush.

Looking at the men as they stood back, their nervousness obvious, Dannan grinned a little. Mastering his breathing, he chuckled. "There's only what, five of you left that can really fight? We can take them all, Ramme."

He heard Ramme laugh softly from behind him, and Dannan chuckled a little, glad to see the other boy had regained his will to fight. "We probably won't, but you know we'll kill a few. That's some consolation, right?" Ramme said.

Dannan got the feeling that his classmate was grinning, and his own grin widened. Moving slightly to tighten his stance, he flinched as a wave of pain emanated up from his leg.

Hearing a chuckle, he glared at the leader, who was grinning through the blood on his face. "Well, it looks like I underestimated you. You're officially a runt, not wet behind the ears. Too bad that still won't be enough to save you. It looks like you're bleeding pretty badly from that leg wound. And your left hand certainly isn't going to help you. You can still leave if you want, but if you wait any longer, it will be as a corpse."

Chuckling a little, the man pulled another dagger from behind his back, and Dannan grumbled to himself. He knew he wouldn't be able to deflect all those dagger thrusts as he leaned against Ramme's back, and he glanced over his shoulder at Ramme.

He could see a little blood coming from his classmate's shoulder, but it looked like one of the other thugs was down on the ground in a pool of blood.

Sighing, he readied his sword, trying hard to grip it with both hands. He could feel the heat of the blood pouring from his left hand onto the handle, and he grimaced, wondering if the men he had killed before had lived long enough to experience the unpleasant sensation.

Dannan was sure that he wouldn't have long to ponder it, but surprisingly, the thugs stood back and waited. And waited.

After several minutes of waiting, he moved a little, grimacing again at the pain. "What, I thought you were coming at us? Did you suddenly get scared?" He said with a forced smirk.

"Nothing so silly." Putting his dagger in the crook of his arm, the leader pulled what appeared to be an eye patch out from a pocket, and tucked a piece of cloth behind it.

Dannan raised an eyebrow at it, and the leader laughed. "It is actually an eye patch. Nothing sinister." Wrapping the thong around his head, he moved it so that it held the piece of cloth over his nose. "You see, we're both bleeding. But you're bleeding worse. I just need to wait a few minutes, and you might just bleed into unconsciousness for me."

Stepping forward a little so that he was next to the thug on the ground who's legs were bleeding, the leader looked down. "Well, we might be able to salvage your legs, Getter. You did good not screaming, though."

The thug on the ground murmured something, and the leader sliced off the arms of the thug's shirt with his knife. Moving quickly, his deft fingers wove them into seemingly solid bandages around the two cuts.

Though they quickly became soaked in blood, they seemed to slow the flow a little. Grimacing, Dannan felt a small twinge in the back of his head, and he wondered how much blood he had lost. Hearing a noise, they all looked towards the door, where the thug who had been tailing Tannil and Carissa was standing.

Dannan let out a groan, even as the leader turned and smiled broadly at him. "Well, Jik, you're just in time for the party. What took you so long?"

When no reply was forthcoming, the man grimaced and turned towards the thug, who Dannan noticed seemed a little pale. "S... Sorry boss..." The man stumbled forward, a knife sticking out of his back, and he hit the ground with a solid thump.

The leader's mouth fell open, but he had no time to comment as Tannil stepped through the door. Stepping over the corpse like just so much trash, Tannil seemed to stalk forward. "You didn't really think I'd let you go, did you? Gutter trash like you would never disappears just because you got threatened a little." The leader scowled deeply, his anger seeming more laughable than scary because of the eye patch over his nose.

Pointing his dagger at Tannil, he yelled. "You bastard! Don't think I'll roll over just because a few of my men are dead!"

Tannil laughed harshly, a grating, nasty sound that seemed completely unlike him. "You don't have to roll over. You just have to fall down." Dannan grinned at his friend, and Tannil gave him a small wink. Dannan watched Tannil keep moving forward, and he blinked hard as the edges of his sight grew dark.

Cursing, he tried to push himself up so that he was leaning against Ramme's back more heavily, but found that his legs wouldn't support him. Grimacing, he laughed harshly inside. "I always seem to be out cold at the worst times." He murmured.

He tried to turn to say something to Ramme, but found that the world was falling away even as he started to move. He could see the floor coming up sideways, and he saw Tannil's face.

It felt like so far away, and he realized he couldn't hear any noise as he started to slip into unconscious. He saw a look of horror cross onto Tannil's face, which turned into a mask of rage. The last thing he saw was Tannil's features begin to change as he rushed forward, and then it was gone.

Chapter 38

Dannan wasn't sure how long it had been when he finally opened his eyes, but he distinctly heard the sigh of relief. Looking up, he met Tannil's eyes, and grinned a little. "Hiya."

Tannil scowled at him for a moment, then grinned. "Hi yourself, idiot. I let you try something on your own, and you go and almost get yourself killed. Some Swordmaster you are."

"Apprentice Swordmaster." Tannil cocked his head to the side, and Dannan grinned. "Just correcting you. I'm an apprentice Swordmaster." Tannil rolled his eyes.

"If you weren't injured, I would smack you for that one." Dannan kept grinning, and tried to sit up a little. He grimaced as he noticed his chest hurt, and then shrugged. Tannil put a hand behind his shoulder to help him sit up, and Dannan looked around.

They were still in the warehouse, but it looked almost completely different from before.

Most of the stacks of boxes had been knocked over, and bodies were lying all over. There were large blood splatters covering most of the back wall, and Dannan could see that the leader's body was laying on the ground right below one of the thugs. Or at least, right below the thug's legs, which were hanging out of a box.

The rest of him seemed to be stuffed inside, though Dannan couldn't see him from this angle. Glancing to the left, he noticed Ramme was sitting on a box near the door, a piece of cloth covering his right shoulder as an improvised bandage.

Grimacing, Dannan felt a small surge of pain as he took a deep breath and tried to sit up further, and he felt Tannil's hand pushing him back down. "I'll help you up in a minute. For now, I just want to make sure that you're alright." Dannan grumbled a little, but nodded.

"I'm mostly alright." Looking at his leg and his hand, he grinned a little. "You already bandaged up the two big bleeders. Other than that, it's just muscle pain."

"And a big bruise on your chest. You got lucky there." Dannan raised an eyebrow, then remembered the dragon scale saving his life.

Smiling softly, he closed his eyes and shook his head. "It wasn't luck. She's always watched over me." Tannil made a noise in his throat and rolled his eyes, looking over at Ramme.

Turning back to Dannan, he grinned. "If I didn't know you better, you'd look so damn silly when you get that content look on your face." After a moment, Tannil shook his head. "Nope, even injured, you still look like a lovestruck fool with that smile on your face."

Dannan laughed, then looked over at Ramme. "How are you doing, Ramme?" Ramme nodded his head slightly, and kept his eyes averted from them.

Looking at Tannil, Dannan raised an eyebrow, and Tannil sighed. "I had to change to save you two. He's still a little... shocked."

Dannan let out a little "ah" and they turned towards Ramme as he jumped to his feet. "Shocked?! You're not human! I'm terrified, not shocked!"

Tannil looked over at him, his eyes cool, and Dannan put a hand on his arm. Tannil met his eyes, and then sighed. "Here, help me up, Tannil. We need to get back to the compound."

Nodding, Tannil helped him up as they both ignored Ramme fuming over by the door. "Why aren't you bothered, Dannan?! He's a monster!" As Tannil started helping Dannan towards the door, he let out a hiss of pain, drawing a glance from Tannil.

Shaking his head, he stopped momentarily in front of Ramme. "Because, Ramme. Unlike you, who's so busy worrying about your own hide right now, Tannil is only concerned about the fact we're alive and alright. He's been our classmate for almost five years now, and he's never given us any reason not to trust him. He might not be human, but he's one of us."

Glaring at Ramme, he scowled. "And he's not a monster." Nodding to Tannil, they started walking forwards again. "But he is! I don't care if he saved us, he doesn't belong near humans! He'll kill us just like he killed those Black Knives!"

Dannan whirled so suddenly that Tannil lost his grip on Dannan's shoulder. He stepped towards Ramme as he lost his balance, but it wasn't enough to stop his momentum as he fell forward and struck Ramme in the cheek with his fist.

Ramme landed on his backside hard as Tannil reached out quickly and caught Dannan before he hit the floor, to. Pulling him up a little, Tannil grumbled, even as Dannan glared down at Ramme.

Ignoring the shocked look on Ramme's face, Dannan growled. "I don't care what kind of idiot idea's you have about others, but don't you dare comment about someone who saved your life like that. You got us into this damn mess, and has he said anything about it being your fault? NO! He just ran after you and Carissa, not even checking to see if I kept up with him, because he was interested in making sure that you were both alright. And you dare say he's a monster?! He's got a more human heart than you seem to! You won't even tell us what all of this is about! So stop judging him, and start thinking about your own actions! Because whether you like it or not, we're all classmates, and we're stuck with each other. And I don't want you around if you're going to stab us in the back like you stabbed them in the back."

Grimacing again in pain, Dannan grumbled. "Let's go, Tannil. Who knows when someone will come looking for us."

Tannil took a deep breath and nodded, his surprise and discomfort still obvious on his face. As they stepped out through the door and started walking, Dannan heard Ramme stand up, but he didn't hear any footsteps following them.

They walked a little further down the alley and turned the first corner, the uncomfortable silence a very palpable pressure.

After a little bit further, Tannil let out his breath. "Well, someone should come back soon. I sent Carissa to tell the teacher we were in trouble. Who knows if there will be reinforcements, or if he'll just bring our classmates."

Dannan nodded, trying not to seem as sullen as he felt. He was sure it still showed on his face, though.

As they got halfway down the second alley, they heard footsteps approaching them quickly. Turning, they looked over their shoulders to see Ramme running towards them.

Stopping a short distance away, Ramme took a deep breath and leaned forward, his hands on his knees, his head bowed. "I'm sorry!"

He waited for several long uncomfortable moments, and then looked up at them. "I apologize. I was scared, but like Tannil said, I was also shocked."

Taking another deep breath, he took a moment to try and calm himself. "I didn't betray them, though. And I don't want you to think I betrayed you, either."

Looking at him, they waited, and he stood up straight, his face contorted from embarrassment and discomfort. Finally, seeing they weren't going to say anything, he continued. "I used to know them. But they were never friends or comrades. I won't betray your secret, either."

Ramme looked right at Tannil as he said this, and Tannil shrugged.

"Tell us the whole story, and then we'll tell you whether we'll still consider you one of us." Dannan said, a steely edge to his voice. Ramme grimaced and shifted his feet, then finally nodded.

"The Black Knives are a guild of thieves, based loosely around four or five of the northern cities. Tannil has probably heard of them as a mercenary." Ramme started off, his face finally returning to its usual placid mask.

Dannan looked at Tannil, who nodded grimly, his face saying everything Dannan needed to know.

Turning back to Ramme, Dannan grimaced slightly. "So what did they want with you?"

Ramme shifted slightly, and looked down. "I used to be a member."

Dannan's grimace deepened, and when Ramme didn't go on, he let out a grunt. "So you did betray them." Looking over at Tannil, he nodded. "Alright, let's go."

Shrugging, Tannil looked back at Ramme, then started to turn to help Dannan leave. "I didn't betray them!" Ramme said forcefully. "I never got a choice! I didn't want anything to do with the gang."

Stopping, they looked at him, and Ramme swallowed hard. "My father is the head of the Black Knives. Even if he barely acknowledged me until about six years ago."

Dannan raised an eyebrow, and Ramme shook his head. "What you've got to understand is that I'm an illegitimate son. He only ever really had one wife, but he had plenty of dalliances. And I wasn't born to his wife."

Sighing, Ramme looked up at the sky, the dark walls of the warehouses boxing them in. The reddish sky loomed over them, like some sinister ceiling, and Dannan could see how trapped Ramme felt from the look on his face.

"I looked at alleys like this all the time when I was young. My mother was a prostitute, and the Black Knives tend to keep all the street urchins, pickpockets, and streetwalkers under their thumb." He swallowed, unpleasant memories showing on his face.

"My mother was one of the prettier exceptions, and so my father, Klybold, took a liking to her. That of course only lasted a few months at best, but that was enough time for her to conceive me. And after I was born, she wasn't able to go back to work for several years, so they forgot about her. She went back to the guild though, after that. She told my father about me. That's when I first entered the guild. Around the age of three or four."

The skin around Ramme's eyes tightened, and he lowered his gaze to meet theirs again. "Klybold had me trained as a pickpocket from then on. All the really young children are. 'No one looks for young children in a marketplace'. That was his favorite saying about pickpockets our age."

Taking a deep breath, Ramme closed his eyes. After a few more breaths, he opened them and continued on. "At the age of six, my mother had an accident with a carriage. From what I've heard, it came barreling down the street because the horses were out of control, and it ran her over."

Grimacing, Ramme shook his head. "Knowing Klybold's wife though, my mother's death probably wasn't an accident. At that time, I didn't know any better, so I turned to the only thing I had left, though. Him."

Ramme shifted uncomfortably and rubbed at his shoulder with his hand. "After that, things got worse for me. I was good at what I did, but I never brought back a lot of money. He expected more from me, because my mother had always been a steady source of gold for him. She was pretty enough that the merchants with expensive tastes paid for her services, but she didn't always try to take advantage of that fact. Not until the end, at least. I don't know why she got greedy, either. That's part of what bothered me."

Shaking his head, Ramme sighed. "That doesn't matter anymore, though. What does matter is that the less gold I brought back, the more I got beaten. That's where most of the old bruises and scars on my back and upper arms come from. I'm sure you've seen them in the bathhouse."

Looking at them, he let his words sink in for a moment before continuing. "When I turned ten, I decided I wanted more from life. I had had enough. The thing is, people don't leave the Black Knives. Especially not people who know the guild leaders real identity. And I knew more than that. After I turned eight, my father decided to try and groom me to become his right hand. So I knew the names and faces of many of the higher ups. I also know old safe-houses, and at least a few old treasure vaults, though he didn't know that at the time."

Ramme cracked a smile, and for a moment, Dannan was surprised to see how normal it looked on him. "But that's the reason they were after me. It's also the reason I didn't bother to get too close to any of you. After all, being on the run doesn't allow for liberties like that."

Sighing, he shook his head. "Not that that's going to end. He'll find out they're dead, and send another squad. Hurrik was just a mid-level lieutenant. He hated me for the special treatment I got at the end, probably because he thought I was going to take his position. Who knows now, though."

Looking from Tannil to Dannan, he shrugged his shoulders. "And that's the whole story." After a few seconds, he sighed. "Are you going to tell the others?" Tannil opened his mouth to say something, but Dannan spoke first.

"It's up to you to decide what you want to tell them. We're a cohesive unit, but that doesn't mean we can't keep some secrets. It's just a matter of making sure that there are no secrets that will get each other killed. That's all." Ramme perked up a little at this, and Dannan smiled.

"Now let's get back. I know I hurt, and I'm pretty sure that you do, to." Sighing, Dannan grinned. "I don't think Teacher Kalaman will be very happy. Come to think of it, he probably won't go any easier on us just because we're injured, either." Ramme and Tannil both laughed at that, and they started walking towards the main street again.

They had walked until they were a few hundred feet from the entrance of the alleyway when they ran into their classmates. Teacher Kalaman was at the head of the group, walking at a quick pace, and he stopped when he saw them.

Dannan saw several of the others gaping, and he almost flinched at the hard stare in the teacher's eyes. After several moments, the teacher finally crossed the last twenty feet or so to them, and proceeded to scrutinize them further, his eyes inspecting every last inch.

After he seemed satisfied that there were no immediate injuries that needed tending, he grimaced and looked Dannan right in the eye. "What happened?"

Dannan was surprised to hear a level of concern in his teacher's voice, then mentally reprimanded himself. Teacher Kalaman had put a great deal of effort into their growth as Swordmasters, and it made sense that he would be worried.

Standing up a little straighter with Tannil's help, Dannan saluted. "We ran into some ruffians. They grabbed Carissa and Ramme originally, and with a little help from Tannil, we got Carissa out of there. I was unsuccessful in my attempt to get Ramme out without a fight, and I wasn't good enough to beat their leader. Well, at least, not with his cronies at his side. Ramme and I proceeded to engage them until Tannil returned, at which point he assisted us in wiping out the last of them. That is all, sir."

Teacher Kalaman's steady gaze seemed to bore into him, but Dannan managed to hold fast under his eyes. Nodding, the teacher looked at Ramme and Tannil, then back at Dannan. "You're the most injured. Any particular reason for that?"

Dannan nodded, and grinned slightly. "I was the first one to attack of the three of us." The teacher nodded, and looked over.

"Hale! Give Tannil a hand in helping support Dannan back to the compound. He won't be able to walk on his own for a day or two at least."

Hale nodded and rushed up, and his sympathetic glance told Dannan everything he needed to know. He gave Hale a nod of thanks as he took his shoulder, and Dannan breathed a sigh of relief as even more of his weight was taken off of his injured leg.

The walk back to the compound seemed to take forever, although Dannan knew it was only because his leg hurt so much. His classmates questioned him and Ramme relentlessly, and finally, Tannil made them give up. Dannan murmured a soft "thanks" to him, but Tannil didn't acknowledge it accept for a small smile at the corner of his mouth.

Chapter 39

When they finally got back to the compound, Teacher Kalaman spoke to one of the guards briefly. "Alright, all of you head back to the dormitory. Dannan and Ramme, I expect both of you to go straight back to your rooms, where you will wait for food and treatment. I'm going to go get one of the other teachers; she's got some experience as a field surgeon as well. While your leg might bother you some in the long run, I'm more concerned there's no damage to your hand. I don't want to lose a student because he can't use a sword with his left hand anymore."

With that, their teacher strode off, leaving them standing in front of the gates once more.

Sighing, Dannan grinned at his classmates. "Sorry to cause so many problems for all of you."

Ahminel laughed and shook his head, his eyes gleaming with mischief. "I don't believe anyone here blames you for being attacked. That is beside the point though. Life seems a lot more interesting with you around, so I think we are all glad for that on some level. Even if some of us wouldn't admit it out loud."

Dannan smiled a little as Careel and Uthul nodded, and he gave Tannil and Hale a half-hearted squeeze with his arms. "With friends like all of you, I could never go wrong." Carissa let out an exaggerated groan, and they all laughed as they walked back to their dorm.

As they got closer to the entrance to the dorm, Dannan saw the redhead who had caused all the problems when he had first joined the school. Dannan sighed, wishing that the time spent there had made the boy a little calmer, but sincerely doubting that it had.

The redhead looked at him in surprise, but it quickly turned to a look of disappointment. As they got closer, Dannan's classmates moved so that they were circled around him, with no gaps to move closer to him.

When they were almost to the door, the redhead moved in

front of them, his face relatively impassive, but with a small amount of disappointment showing through. Dannan wasn't sure if the boy expected them to part for him or not, but the redhead didn't seem too surprised either when the group stopped in front of him and stood there, simply staring.

After almost a full minute passed, Dannan sighed a little, and murmured softly "Let him through. Let's just get this over with and get on to eating. I'm sure you're all as hungry as I am."

They looked at him for a moment, and although they moved to the side, Tannil and Hale continued to support him. The corners of the boy's mouth turned upwards in a small smile, and he walked forward until he was standing in front of Dannan.

"I was going to challenge you to an official duel, but in your state, it seems like that won't be possible. Do get better soon though. I look forward to our meeting."

The boy tried his best to imitate Dannan's voice from when they had first met, and although he was fairly unsuccessful, the mocking tone was unmistakable. As the boy's grin widened, he straightened with an obvious air of superiority.

Dannan sighed inside, deciding he would have to deal with this problem sooner than later, when he suddenly felt the weight of his left side sink towards the ground. Glancing over, he almost didn't have time to catch Tannil's movement as he stepped forward, standing in front of the redhead.

The boy tried to take a step back, but Tannil's right hand settled on top of his shoulder, and try as he could, he was unable to escape Tannil's grasp. Dannan could hear the growl that was starting in Tannil's chest, and for a moment, worry flashed through his eyes.

He caught Ramme looking at him, and saw the same nervousness in his classmate. "You will not bother him again." The sound of Tannil's voice drew Dannan's attention back to him.

It sounded less like a human voice then what might be growled out by some sort of beast. "I don't care how your insignificant honor has been offended, or what purpose you think you're trying to accomplish here. If you continue to bother him, especially while he's injured, I am going to break both of your arms."

Dannan stood up straighter, the alarm on his face obvious to all the others now, and he saw several of his classmates move closer, probably, like him, to restrain Tannil if things got out of hand.

He noticed that although the boy was starting to become unsure of himself, Tannil seemed to be looming over him, and the hand on his shoulder seemed to be pushing him to his knees. "You will not be worried about becoming a Swordmaster. Do you know why?" Tannil said menacingly, leaning his face in closer.

When the redhead didn't respond, Tannil let a small growl boil forth from his throat. "When I say I will break your arms, I mean I will destroy them. You will never lift a spoon again, much less a sword. If you understand, nod your head."

The boy looked at him, trying to maintain a calm mask even though the terror was obvious in his eyes.

"Nod." Tannil's growl was much deeper this time, and they all moved in further as they saw his fingers begin to dig into the boy's shoulder. The redhead nodded quickly several times, and Tannil gave him a shove, propelling him off to the side, and away from the door.

The others moved out of the way quickly as he stumbled past, and when he stopped to look back, the rumbling growl in Tannil's chest deepened. Stopping to straighten his shirt, the redhead grimaced, then started walking off quickly.

Dannan watched until the boy was out of sight, then let out a deep sigh. "Just don't break his arms before you graduate, alright, Tannil? I don't want the class to lose a member because you lost your temper."

Tannil let out a snort before sliding back under Dannan's arm.

Symon and Tymon moved off to the side, and Dannan cast a glance after them. "We're just going to go see that this is reported to his teacher. After all, this type of behavior has never been acceptable. And if he intends to keep giving you grief, it would be better to just have him thrown out of the sword school for repeat insubordination, don't you think?" Symon said matter of factly.

Shaking his head, Dannan smiled. "I appreciate you helping, I really do. But I don't think it will be that helpful if he's waiting outside the gate to stab me in the back, either. And maybe in here, that tempestuous nature of his will finally be curbed enough that he won't be a problem for me."

Symon shrugged and looked at Tymon, who shook his head. "You're the boss, boss." Tymon said jokingly.

Dannan glared at him, and Tymon sat back on his heels,

surprise on his face. "Never call me boss."

After Tymon nodded, Dannan grinned at him. "After all, aren't we all equals here? You'd make me feel more like I'm not one of you than anything else." Tymon burst out laughing at this, as did Carissa, Tannil, and Hale. The others just shook their heads.

"I'm glad you're feeling well enough to be glib, but let's get you up to your room, alright Dan?" Tannil chimed in. The others all nodded, grabbing Ramme by the arm as well, and rushed them off to their rooms.

It was a while before Teacher Kalaman and one of the other teachers came into his room. "Teacher Yamara will check your wounds, so be cooperative. Understood?" Dannan nodded, looking at the woman standing next to his teacher.

Her shoulder length black hair made a striking contrast to her pale skin, and Dannan was surprised to see her skin so snow-white, knowing full well all the time the teachers spent in the sun. He immediately noticed her well toned hands as she began undoing the dressing from his hand, and he grimaced as he felt her press firmly.

Several students brushed past Teacher Kalaman who was standing against the door, setting several bowls of water and a variety of first aid equipment next to Teacher Yamara. She looked over his hand, and began to wash it gently, tossing aside the dirty bandages.

It took several minutes before she was finished and he was fully bandaged again, and then she moved on to his leg. Although he was somewhat embarrassed when she pulled his pants off and began to inspect the wound, she seemed to completely ignore the fact he was in his shirt and undergarments.

Her inspection of his leg was equally quick, and she ordered him to remove his shirt.

Panic gripped him as he thought about the scale, and he worked hard to pull it over his head wrapped inside his shirt. He breathed a small sigh of relief when he saw that he had succeeded in hiding it in the folds of the shirt, and was caught of guard as she grabbed it and tossed it to the side of the cot.

Looking over his chest and back, she nodded to herself, then turned to Teacher Kalaman. "Only those two injuries, though he took a nasty strike to the chest. Not sure with what. He should be fine as long as he stays off that leg for at least four or five days. The hand he can start really using after half a fortnight to a full fortnight.

Anything earlier than that, and he risks making the damage permanent."

Teacher Kalaman scowled, his eyebrows creasing as his thoughts played out across his face.

"What about Ramme, Teacher Yamara?" Looking back at Dannan, she shrugged.

"He got off easier than you did, that's for certain. Not a deep wound to his shoulder, and it missed the joint. You need to worry about yourself more right now. And make sure that you or someone else changes those bandages regularly. Understood?"

Dannan nodded, and she yelled for the students, who came back in and grabbed the used bandages and water bowls. "This one's all yours again, Instructor." She said as she walked out, her helpers in tow.

Dannan watched her leave, letting out a small sigh of relief. Teacher Kalaman stood there a moment longer, a variety of emotions warring on his face.

"I'll be at practice tomorrow, sir. I just need a good night's rest and I'll be fine."

Teacher Kalaman looked at him, almost as if he had forgotten that Dannan was sitting there, and his lips twitched into a small smile. "If you cause yourself permanent injury while practicing, I'm going to make your training load twice as heavy." Dannan shook his head, a resolute look on his face.

"Even if I can only barely keep up, I'll do it. After all, when I'm out on campaign or in the wilderness, no one will coddle me because of the fact that I'm injured."

The look of surprise that quickly crossed his teacher's face was replaced by a wide smile, and Teacher Kalaman shook his head. "Ahh... always so young, eager, and stupid." Dannan blushed in embarrassment, and tried to ignore his teacher's laughter. "Alright. I'll let you train. But if it seems you're causing yourself more harm than good, I will stop you. Understood?"

Dannan nodded, and the teacher chuckled again. "Get some sleep then. That's an order." Dannan saluted and grabbed his pants and shirt, and listened as the door swung shut. Lying down, he set his clothes to the side and slipped the dragon scale back around his neck before pulling the blanket up. He slipped into a light sleep, and tried to rest a little.

The click of the door opening woke him up, and he opened one eye, trying to make out the figure in the doorway.

When the person finally stepped into the light, Dannan was relieved to see Tannil carrying a tray of food. "I figured you would be starving after all that. So I got permission to be the one to bring your food up from dinner."

Dannan nodded his thanks and sat up, reaching out for the tray of food with both hands. He winced in pain as Tannil let him take it, and Tannil made a move to pull the tray back.

Shaking his head, Dannan gripped the tray with both hands, and grinned. "If you make me tug it out of your hand, you'll spill the stew." Tannil chuckled, the door closing with a quiet click as he let go of the tray and sat down on his cot. Dannan eagerly dug into the meat stew, only occasionally letting out a small grunt of pain when his hand throbbed.

Minutes passed in silence as he ate, and when Dannan was finished, he set the tray on the small table with a sigh of satisfaction. "It may only be basic fare, but now I know what you meant about it being something one could get comfy with. After being all beaten up then bandaged up, it tasted amazing."

Tannil chuckled, a half-smile on his face. "We'll turn you into a regular mercenary soldier yet."

"I'd never settle for anything less than being as good as the Wolves Brigade." He said with a wink at his friend. Tannil grinned somberly, and shook his head.

"You're probably better than a lot of pack members already. I'd hate to see you go at them with a silver sword."

Dannan shrugged. "Not something any of your pack will ever have to worry about."

Tannil chuckled, his back slightly hunched. Dannan laid out flat on his back, trying to get comfy again as Tannil blew out the candle.

Wriggling around, he finally rolled onto his side, and gripped the dragon scale with his injured hand. Although it hurt a little, he found that the small, thrumming warmth that was suddenly emanating from the scale was comforting.

Dannan grinned a little in the darkness, thinking it would be nice to pretend it was the dragoness's concern for him. As he drifted off to sleep, he murmured good night to Tannil.

He almost didn't hear Tannil's reply as he drifted off to sleep, but for a moment Dannan thought he heard him say "Good night, pack brother."

Chapter 40

The next several days of training were agonizing for Dannan as he tried to practice the sword with his injuries, and the riding training was excruciatingly painful due to his leg injury. After half a fortnight had passed, he almost wished that he had begged out of practice for a little while.

By the time a full fortnight had gone by, he was beginning to feel a little better, and he was glad that he hadn't let his muscles grow any weaker by spending all those days in bed.

Days began to get shorter again as the onset of winter approached, and Dannan was glad to have the exercise. The chill this year was almost unbearable, but he was happy to find that the heat practice generated was a welcome way of keeping warm.

Dannan was even happier that the redhead left him alone after Tannil threatened him. The peace it provided him was well worth any minor amount of guilt he felt.

As spring came around, Teacher Kalaman switched their training to tactics. He taught them all about small group tactics, and about individuals fighting groups.

He prodded Dannan with jokes during that time, and Dannan was glad to see that except for Tannil having an occasional relapse, no one but he and Ramme even seemed to remember the incident.

The spring turned into summer, and even the summer was uneventful until about halfway through, when Ramme came into their room nursing a bruise on his cheek.

Dannan let out a small yelp of surprise and stood up, looking at the bruise which seemed to cover half of Ramme's face. "What happened, Ramme?!" He said as he stepped forward to inspect the injury.

Ramme let out a little hiss as Dannan gently pressed a finger against it, and Dannan quickly let his finger fall back. "Carissa gave this to me."

Tannil, who still been resting when Ramme came in, sat up

with a yawn. Rubbing his eyes wearily, he looked over, then let out a little yell. His eyes shot wide open, and then his eyebrows came down. "What the hell happened to you?!" He said, his tone one of shock.

Ramme grinned slightly then winced when it aggravated his bruise. Dannan motioned for him to sit down on the edge of the cot, and then sat down himself.

"Well, the thing is, I've been telling everybody slowly since the incident about what caused it. I've gotten yelled at some by the others. Especially Hale and Careel. But Carissa is the only one who's hit me." Ramme sighed and grimaced. "She's the last one I told, to."

Tannil scrunched up his face, then shook his head. "You didn't tell her that, did you?" Ramme nodded, a resigned look on his face. "Oh... my... gods... You're an idiot. What were you thinking?!"

Sighing, Ramme shrugged. "Well, it seemed like being honest with both of you was a good thing. And like I had said to you, I won't betray our class. I don't want anyone to think that later on, either, so I started telling people slowly. I told Carissa last because I didn't want to hurt her feelings, and it was also my fault she got involved in that mess. I thought it was the best way to be considerate of her as a friend."

They both chuckled at him, and then Dannan met Tannil's eyes. "Do you want to tell him what he did wrong, or shall I?" Tannil shook his head, and motioned for Dannan to speak first. "I don't know a thing about women." Dannan started, and Tannil let out a small snort.

Dannan gave him a joking glare, and Tannil grinned widely back at him. Shaking his head, Dannan chuckled and continued. "I don't know a thing about women, but telling her that you wanted to tell her last seems more like you're afraid of her than like you're treating her as an equal."

Chiming in, Tannil interrupted him. "And you've got to remember; she's not just a regular woman. Many times, they're like flowers. They need to be gently tended to, cared for, and showered with love. But she's a mercenary."

Tannil grinned, then continued. "Yes, the same treatment sometimes works with them. But more often than not, you need to treat her like the strong individual she is. Which means swallowing your pride as a man and apologizing when you screw up. The rest of the time, it means getting out of her way." Tannil finished with a laugh.

Shaking his head, Dannan laughed at his friend. "I'll skip the first part, because I can't imagine the woman willing to sleep with you."

Tannil feigned injury, and Dannan just laughed harder. "The biggest thing you have to remember Ramme is that Carissa is not a very trusting person to begin with. You remember how hard it was to get her to open up to the class in the first place. Just like you. And what you did goes beyond just screwing up."

He took a deep breath, then let it out. "You damaged that bond, because she doesn't know if you have her back. And from the fact that she was nicer to you than the rest of us, I assume it was because she trusted you to have her back even more than we would." Ramme looked down, a chagrined look on his face, and Dannan shook his head.

"So you've got to find some way to apologize to her. If not for your sake, think about us. She gets cranky!" Tannil burst out laughing and fell backwards onto his bed, and Dannan grinned when he saw a small smile creep onto Ramme's face.

"That's the spirit. Wait a few days, and then try to apologize. Whatever it takes, it's up to you. No one else here has held your past against you, and you've seen what some of the rest of us have to carry. So don't worry, alright? She'll forgive you. Eventually."

Ramme gave him a piteous look, and Dannan had to hold in another laugh.

They continued to talk for quite a while, before finally Ramme went back to his own room. Dannan was glad to see that Ramme was finally opening up and getting comfortable with the rest of the class, and he went to sleep that night with dreams of his whole class together out on the battlefield.

The next morning, the teacher didn't comment on Ramme's bruise, but they could all tell Carissa was in a foul mood. The next three days continued like this, with her snapping at Ramme whenever he spoke to her, and being relatively cordial to everyone else.

On the fourth day, she seemed to be in a better mood. Dannan later found out from Ramme that she had finally accepted his apology, though after she beat Ramme black and blue during the tactics practice later, Dannan sincerely wondered if that was true.

As the summer continued on, Dannan was glad that the routine finally felt easier. The morning practices seemed almost like second nature, and sometimes, when Dannan thought of his life before joining the school, Samust came to mind. He wondered if Samust still committed himself to morning practice most days.

He also found himself wondering if what he was doing was similar to his father, or if his father had learned sword fighting a different way. He thought about the fact that his father must have made many enemies, and slain just as many.

Yet somehow, whenever Dannan pictured him, sitting in his favorite chair with a book in his lap and an absent minded look on his face, he just couldn't see it.

The rest of his sixth year as a student at The Hawk's Honor passed this way. Even as his seventh year started, he felt in a kind of daze, where everything they were doing was just so natural that he no longer noticed it.

They had begun weapons training in the spring, with spears, both short and long. In the summer, they worked with axes, from the two-handed versions, to hatchets and battleaxes. The fall brought with it bows, slings, and javelins, while the winter brought on more training with swords and shields exclusively.

The winter of their seventh year brought the first real change. They began to hear rumors of unrest to the east, from the plains where the barbarians had come from so many years ago. Teacher Kalaman only ever replied with a grim smile, but they were sure he thought another war was coming.

This unease continued for several seasons, when in the summer of their eighth year, news came from the east that the man who had been trying to gather the barbarian hordes was assassinated. No one knew how or why, but many people could guess. This was not the biggest news to affect them, though.

Chapter 41

Several fortnights into the summer, Teacher Kalaman ordered them to meet him in the waiting room when they finished their meal.

When they arrived, he was waiting for them, a wide smile on his face. "Well, you've made it to your eighth year. And I have to say, I'm impressed, proud, and more than a little happy. There are a number of reasons I'm happy about it, but one of the main reasons is this year will see you go on your first real mission."

They all looked around at each other, the surprise registering clearly on every face. "But I thought we weren't going on any missions until we had actually graduated, sir." Tymon said softly.

His smile showing every tooth, Teacher Kalaman grinned at his student. "Well, then that is a misunderstanding on your part. I'm sure you have all noticed that each year, some of the eighth year students disappear, or come back with new scars."

Nodding in response as he swept his eyes over them, they remained silent.

"The reason for this is because in your eighth year as students here, you will go on a supply delivery mission." They groaned, certain that this meant a boring trip somewhere.

Glaring at them to cut them off, he continued. "While I'm sure all of you have your ideas about what that will entail, scrap them. Immediately. This will be a supply mission to a fortress on our northern border, past where the northern cities are and into the mountains themselves."

Dannan's heart leaped a little as he heard this news, and he immediately thought of the dragon scale, which for so many years now had pulled him towards the north.

"The fort, which some of you might actually know by name, is Fort Winterfang. So named because it's one of the main fort's that prevent the orcs from boiling down from the mountains and killing us all. Now, for those of you who have never fought an orc, let me tell you now. The stories of their savagery are not to be underestimated."

"But don't assume that savage means stupid. The reason we have a permanent presence in those mountains is because every fifty or so years, one of the orcs is born smart enough to actually take charge of a true horde. They are dangerous, brutal, and will not hesitate once they are down in the grasslands to ravage anything in their path."

"Those of you with any real knowledge of history know quite well that it happened two-hundred and forty-three years ago. It was the decade after that Fort Winterfang was built, and we have helped maintain it since I founded this school years ago. And before we did, the northern cities themselves did. Still do, for that matter."

Looking around as realization crept onto their faces, he smiled slightly. "Good, didn't think any of you were stupid enough not to realize it yet. Yes, I am one of Galem Swiftstrike's apprentices. One of the remaining two, anyway. But those questions can wait till after this mission is successful."

Taking a deep breath, he looked them over again, and for a moment, he almost seemed hesitant. "We sometimes lose one or two wagons from the supply train, and almost every year we lose at least one student."

"I want this year to end flawlessly! You have survived some of the worst I can throw at you, and pressed forward."

"Each year, we leave one or two fortnights into the fall. So you have about four fortnights left in those cozy dorms you're sleeping in before we go out into the wide world beyond these walls."

Exhaling, he let out a small chuckle. "And then we'll see if you're really as tough as you've tried to show me." Looking at each other, they couldn't help but feel there was some menace in his tone.

After the teacher left them in the room by themselves, conversations immediately sprang up.

Dannan was too elated to really pay attention, until Carissa poked him in the arm, hard. Turning to face her, he was sure he looked as startled as he felt. He also felt a little sheepish. "Sorry?"

She sighed heavily and shook her head. "I asked, what do you think about the fact that we're going into hostile territory for the first time?"

Dannan shrugged. "I thought I was in hostile territory the first time I met you." She raised her hand to smack him as the others burst out laughing, and he leaned back with a grin.

"But in all seriousness, I'm not too worried. While we might only be apprentice Swordmasters in terms of experience, we'll still have Teacher Kalaman with us. And even if he wasn't one of Galem's apprentices, I'd still trust him with my life any day."

Scratching his chin for a second, Dannan shook his head. "Never mind that. I'd trust him with my life any day I was sure he wasn't the one trying to kill me." He drew a few chuckles from the others with that, then looked at her.

"I think we'd be wise to heed his warnings and keep training, but I'm not too afraid. I think we have more to worry about if the barbarians actually manage to organize. You heard the rumors about their leader being assassinated, but what happens if his second in command manages to take charge?"

Several of them nodded their heads, and the conversation turned towards the plains to the east, and what little they each knew about the area.

Later that night, when they all finally returned to their rooms, Dannan tried to settle onto his cot, but found that nothing was working. Looking over, he saw Tannil's eyes glowing slightly in the dark, and he grinned.

"I can guess why you're grinning like an idiot, but I'll ask anyway. Why?" Tannil said with an obvious smirk in his voice.

"It's been so long... I've almost lost count of the days since I saw her. I know it's been about eight years now, but still... She's always there now, in the back of my thoughts. It's that kind of warm feeling like when you're holding a small animal or a child... it's comforting."

"More and more often as time passed, I wondered if she could feel me to. I know she's aware of me, at least in some way, but I don't know if she realizes who it is."

Taking a deep breath, Dannan closed his eyes. "And I'm nervous. I mean, yes dragons are supposed to have memories longer than our lifespan, but... what if I wasn't important enough to remember? She was running away at the time, trying to find shelter. She obviously found some in the north, but how much?"

Continuing on, his words came more rapidly. "And what if we meet her with the class? There's no way to explain that, and if she attacks us, how could I possibly stop her? Could I even stop her? I don't think that I could attack her, even if she were going to kill me."

Tannil burst out laughing, and Dannan looked back at him, grimacing. "It's not that funny." Dannan saw Tannil's eyes wink shut briefly, and then open again.

"You sound like a lovestruck fool, that's all. And yes, it is just that funny. We're talking about a dragoness who's probably two stories tall and who knows how many tons. And you're acting like she's some lady in a court, who you can fall to one knee under her balcony and try to court her."

Dannan blushed at the comparison, then snorted in laughter when he tried to picture a balcony big enough for a dragoness to sit on. "I just want everything to go well in the end. And that's what I'm terrified of. What if we leave and I never get the chance to search for her?" Tannil clicked his tongue, and Dannan stopped talking, his face a mask of worry.

"If you keep obsessing over it, eventually someone is going to notice something. Just take out the dragon scale like you used to in the first few years. I'm sure the light with sooth your worries. It always has when you were struggling."

Dannan nodded and smiled, taking hold of the dragon scale gently under the blanket. It felt warm in his grasp, and the smooth surface made his fingertips tingle slightly as he gently traced the edges.

Smiling a little, he grinned over at Tannil, and suddenly light flared up from under the blanket, illuminating the whole room.

Tannil's grin was the first thing Dannan saw, and he had to laugh at his friend.

"You know me too well, I'd say." He said with a smile.

"Hey, that's what friends do. Besides, you do get whiny an awful lot."

Dannan twisted his face up, pretending to be offended, and Tannil just laughed harder. "Now get some sleep. We're going to be training even harder I bet, and we'll have to get things prepared to go, as well."

Murmuring in agreement, Dannan concentrated, and after a moment the warm pink glow winked out, leaving the room dark once more. Dannan blinked away the little glow spots left from the light disappearing so suddenly, and then closed his eyes.

"Well, at least it will get interesting again." Dannan said softly.

"Hopefully not too interesting. I like being bored every so often." Tannil muttered. Dannan laughed a little before rolling onto his side, and he fell asleep, clutching the scale as he always did.

Tannil had been right, like he was so often when it came to military matters. They got even busier after the announcement, and Dannan barely had time to stop and think before it seemed like three fortnights had passed.

They found out at the end of the third fortnight that they were indeed going to leave on the second fortnight of the fall. That way, they would hopefully miss the first snow on their way back to the compound.

When the fourth fortnight came and went, Dannan and his classmates were practically buzzing with anticipation. They had left the compound for the riding training, but at the same time, that hadn't really gotten them very far from the city. So when they finally followed their teacher on foot to where the supply caravan was waiting outside the city gates, it was with an air of quiet excitement.

Chapter 42

It had been a long time since Dannan had spent any time around a caravan. Seeing the wagon drivers working hard to pull together their horses while merchants shouted out questions to each other brought a smile to his face.

Following after the teacher, they approached the last several wagons, where a man dressed in fine chain mail was yelling at several men dressed like guards. As soon as he noticed Teacher Kalaman, he stopped yelling to turn and bow. "Welcome, sir. We will be leaving on time, and should be well on the road by noontime. The caravan leader is just making sure that everyone has made their last minute preparations before we start our journey."

Teacher Kalaman nodded after a second, then looked them over. "If you need any assistance, just ask one of my students. They should be more than capable of anything you need. Other than that, I'll leave it to you, captain." The guard captain saluted, then turned and started barking orders right over their heads, catching Dannan off guard.

Looking over at Teacher Kalaman, he saw that their teacher was already headed towards one of the wagons at the back. Turning to follow him, he was brought up short by the captain's yell. "You! Where do you think you're wandering off to?! There's plenty to do without anyone lazing about! If you have nothing else to do, go assist one of the merchants who's slow loading things up!" When Dannan seemed slow to respond, the captain growled out. "Get to it!" Dannan turned quickly and saluted, noticing that all the others had already split up and gone to different parts of the caravan.

Sighing, Dannan went to work helping get the caravan ready along with the others. Although it was tedious work, he was glad to be doing something to pass the time while they waited to leave.

It wasn't until at least an hour after their arrival that the caravan finally seemed ready to go. As the last of the merchants finished loading up their goods and the wagon driver's began to curse and start the horses at the front moving, Dannan hopped into the nearest wagon. Looking around at the few strangers sitting there he didn't recognize, Dannan held in a sigh, and hoped it wouldn't be too long before they stopped and reorganized.

As chance would have it, Dannan was in the last wagon. Looking out the the back window, he had the chance to watch the city get smaller and smaller as they continued on throughout the day. The road seemed to roll away behind them, and the plains carpeted the landscape for as far as the eye could see to either side. Dannan couldn't help but feel slightly at peace as time just seemed to slowly slip away, and before he knew it, dusk was starting to fall.

Moving to the front of the wagon, he looked out from behind the wagon driver, who grumbled something as Dannan came up behind him. The sun was starting to set off the left, and it had given the grasslands a beautiful orange glow, with the backs of the clouds a magnificent purple. Dannan grinned to himself as he watched the sun steadily sink, and finally, he looked straight up, enjoying the relatively clear view of the stars.

When they finally made camp that night, Dannan walked around a little, looking for his classmates and his teacher. Although there were fifteen wagons, when they were all set up for the night, it seemed like there were more. He spent several minutes searching before finally he spotted Tannil, who motioned for him to follow.

Following a few feet behind his friend, he saw his other classmates gathered around a fire at their teacher's feet. Looking over at the two arrivals, Teacher Kalaman smiled, then nodded. "Alright, now listen well. You are all going to assist on guard duty while we are on this trip. That will be the only real work you will have to do, unless one of the caravan members asks you for help. The order will be Dannan, Careel, Uthul, Ramme, Ahminel, Hale, Carissa, Tannil, Symon, then finally Tymon. Any questions?" Looking around, he smiled slightly when there were none. "Good. I expect to you to report to duty on your own until we reach the fort. Then, things will be a little different. Dismissed." They all saluted, and although Dannan wanted to stay around and talk to Tannil for a little, he sighed, shrugged, and started on his rounds.

The first hour of the night passed uneventfully, until finally one of the caravan guardsmen approached him.

Looking over at the man as he walked up, Dannan immediately noticed his poise. His sword, although hanging at his side, seemed like it could lash out at any moment, and his smile was cool but friendly. Dannan met the man's eyes, and in the dark, it was hard to tell if they were brown or dark green. He slowed his pace a little, stopping several feet out of sword reach. "Can I help you?" Dannan said, his tone cautious.

"I'm going to be joining you on patrol. Captain's orders. Always go in pairs, in case of an attack." Dannan nodded slightly, unsurprised at such a common sense order.

Walking up to the man, Dannan reached his hand out to shake hands. "My name is Dannan. Dannan Bellmen."

The man raised an eyebrow for a moment, then shrugged and took his hand. "Nemon. Nemon Janek." Dannan gave Nemon's hand a firm shake, then stepped back a little. Meeting each others gaze for a few moments, he was unsure of how to proceed, when Nemon motioned to the side with his head. "Shall we resume patrolling?" Dannan nodded, relieved the decision was taken out of his hands, and began following a few steps back and to the side.

The night passed slowly, and Dannan found it hard to keep his eyes open after being awake all day in the wagon. Finally, when he felt like he was starting to drift off as they walked, he heard Nemon clear his throat.

Looking over in surprise, Dannan stopped quickly. Nemon looked over his shoulder at Dannan, then raised an eyebrow. "Falling asleep already?" He commented with a small chuckle. Dannan shrugged, trying to hide his embarrassment, and Nemon shook his head. "I still can't figure out why someone as young as you would be a trained Swordmaster. You're barely older than my little brother. Have you ever even been forced to kill to defend yourself?"

Dannan grimaced at the question, turning his eyes outwards from the wagons towards the sea of grass that surrounded them. As the silence stretched on, Dannan could feel Nemon's eyes on him, and he finally turned back to meet Nemon's gaze. "Yes. I have."

Dannan's deadpan tone set Nemon back on his heels for a moment, then Nemon sighed. "Alright, so I won't call into question whether or not you can fight. But is this really worth it?" Dannan didn't hesitate a single second before nodding, and Nemon cocked his head to the side, his penetrating eyes filled with curiosity.

When Dannan remained silent, Nemon shook his head, and they resumed their patrol. The silence stretched on and on, when finally Dannan spoke. "So why are you working as a caravan guard?"

Nemon chuckled, then looked over his shoulder at Dannan. "It's easy work, it gives me the chance to flex my muscles every so often, and it pays well since I'm risking my life."

Dannan raised an eyebrow. "That reason seems kind of... cheap."

Nemon stopped suddenly, and Dannan had to take a step back so as not to accidentally walk into him. Glaring at him, Nemon's relatively impassive face was twisted up into a scowl. "Just because you've never had to do dirty work, don't act like that makes you any better than the average mercenary."

Shaking his head, Dannan held up his hands in front of him as if to ward off a blow. "I didn't mean it that way. I just meant that it seemed like a small thing to risk your life for. That was all."

Nemon continued glaring for a few seconds, then shrugged, letting out a small chuckle. "That's how the world works sometimes. It's not always grand ideas and righteous causes. Sometimes, simple greed or hunger can drive someone as effectively as a just cause."

Dannan lowered his hands. "I guess it's really my first time running into it, though."

Turning around, Nemon started walking again, shaking his head. "Don't worry about things like that. And remember, when it comes to people with simple reasons, they can be stubborn, to. So if you let them go, they will come back to haunt you."

He watched Nemon walk a little further away, then hurried after him to catch up. Although there were long patches of silence, they made small talk the rest of the night until two guardsmen came to relieve them.

Dannan spent almost the whole day asleep in the wagon, and when he finally woke up, it was nice to relax and just watch the world pass by. Although the others in his wagon didn't say a word again to him today, Dannan wasn't worried. Resting and just staring listlessly out the window, he enjoyed the beautiful scenery, knowing full well that the mountains they were heading to wouldn't be as pleasant.

Dannan enjoyed the trip for the next fortnight and a half, relishing being able to practice, eat, and sleep, without a care in the world. It was hard to imagine that they were probably going to have to fight when they got there, but he spent most of his time watching the beautiful scenery, and daydreaming about finally seeing the dragoness again.

Every so often during the trip, the dragon scale would gently vibrate against his chest, almost like it was humming, and he could tell he was getting closer. The more he concentrated on the scale, the easier it was to bring forth the mental picture he had of her from when he had left his body. He wondered every so often if she was still in the cave that he had seen her in, but decided that it didn't matter. One way or another, he would find her.

Three days passed when they came within sight of an outpost along their route. Looking it over thoroughly, Dannan had to resist a shudder. Although he knew that the outpost was supposed to be allied with them, it looked dirty, rough, and most importantly, inhospitable. The closer he got, the more strongly he had the feeling that they wouldn't really be welcomed there. When they camped that third night within sight of it, Dannan was relieved when Tannil delivered their teacher's order to stay away. Looking at the uninviting log walls, their tops sharpened into spikes, Dannan couldn't shake the feeling of a beast, baring it's fangs at the sky.

The next day, Dannan was finally able to get his first glimpse of the mountains around the wagons on the road ahead. Staring at them, he was awed by their size, their magnificent gray girth beyond anything he had ever imagined. Allowing his eyes to roam over the mountain range that seemed to spread out in either direction ahead of them, he found it breathtaking. Their peaks seemed to extend into the clouds, and the dark gray stone only seemed to enhance the mystery of the peaks, shrouded in white clouds. Whenever the clouds moved enough, Dannan could swear that the peaks themselves were white, but he couldn't be certain.

Chapter 43

They arrived at the foot of the mountains two days later. Dannan had thought he might not be as awed when they changed from gradual slope to steep mountain road, but he was wrong. The rocky, crumbling sides of the road that seemed to lead up to both sides of them were as impressive as they were massive. Although he knew that they were likely to be ambushed, he couldn't help but enjoy the majesty of the almost barren terrain. Even as the day wore on and they seemed to climb higher and higher up the steep road, Dannan marveled at their surroundings. The occasional mountain goat leaping from ledge to ledge seemed to enhance the solitude of the mountain, even as the occasional rumbling of a landslide made the mountain sound alive.

That night, Dannan had a hard time falling asleep because of the excitement. He could feel the scale against his chest almost as a heart, pulsing in time with his.

Wandering around the edges of the caravan, he resisted the urge to put a tunic on, enjoying the feel of the chill wind on his bare arms, it's soft caress giving him goosebumps. Closing his eyes every so often, it promised an almost primal joy as it swirled around him, capturing his breath, and whisking it away from him.

Hearing the crunch of a boot behind him, he spun around, his sword flying from it's sheath. Looking down the blade, he stared at Nemon for a moment, before lowering it.

Grinning a little, Nemon shook his head, then looked around. "In a spring shirt like that, you're going to freeze to death in these nights."

Dannan shrugged, then quickly sheathed his sword, enjoying the slight metallic ring it produced. Hearing it echo softly over the rocks nearby, he enjoyed it as it faded, carried away by the wind. "I'm not worried. Besides, it feels too good to put on a tunic, even if I should." Dannan said, closing his eyes once more.

He opened them as he heard Nemon start laughing softly,

and he shook his head. "What?"

Nemon's grin grew even wider, and he stopped laughing. "Very rarely do you see someone from the south get this comfortable in the mountains. Mainly it's us northerners who think there's beauty in these barren rocks. Well, at least in the rocks those ugly orcs aren't hiding under."

Dannan chuckled at that, and Nemon shrugged. "But who knows. That friend of yours... Tannil, is it? If you've been hanging around him long enough, then that's probably why you're so used to this kind of weather. I'd bet you spent a lot of time out in the snow when you were training."

Shaking his head, a small smile played across Dannan's lips. "While I do have to admit that some of the time I spent in the snow was because of Tannil, it was more because of all the training we had to endure as Swordmasters that made it so we could bear these temperatures. The teachers probably felt that if we couldn't deal with extreme heat or extreme cold, then there was no way we could survive on some of our campaigns."

Nemon nodded at that, his face thoughtful. "Smart teachers you have then."

Dannan nodded, feeling almost like he had been complimented, then shrugged. "After all, as my teacher has said before, it doesn't matter if you survive the battlefield to be killed by something like the cold, or sickness."

Chuckling a little, Nemon looked out over the mountains. "That's the way it is. I've seen people who seemed able to survive any horde of orcs, but a small landslide beneath them, and the mountains would claim another victim."

Dannan looked down, pensively. "Life happens that way sometimes. It's horrible when it happens, but loss is loss. The best thing to do is to survive as best as we can."

Yawning, Nemon stretched his arms a little. "Well, don't freeze to death out here. We've got guard duty again in two more days, and in three, we'll reach Fort Winterfang. It would be nice to have a trip with no nasty surprises for once, but I'm not going to count on it. The approach to the fort has always been the worst, and everyone is expecting an ambush there." Dannan murmured an acknowledgment, then turned around to stare at the mountain walls again as he heard Nemon walk away.

The next two days passed without a single incident, and even though Dannan kept Nemon's warning close to his heart, he couldn't help but feel a little elated. His heart sank when he saw the next part of their journey, though.

The morning of the third day, snow had begun to fall at a steady pace. The temperature had dropped enough now that they had gone so high, and even though there wasn't a great deal of moisture in the air, it seemed to be enough. The horses pulling the wagons were slowed greatly by the slick stones underneath, and their pace slowed to a crawl. Tension filled the air, and Dannan had to resist keeping his hand on the hilt of his sword all morning, as everyone was so wound up. By what he was sure was noontime, they had reached what the driver warned was the most dangerous part of their trip. Looking out the window, Dannan had to agree.

To their left, the mountains rose up in a steady slope, not steep enough that it was impassable, but only in certain places could you really climb up or down. To their right, the road gave way to a steep slope, a yawning abyss that seemed like it would swallow anything that fell off. Dannan wasn't sure how far the fall was, but he was sure anyone who fell would be battered to death against the slope before they ever hit the bottom, if they were lucky.

As the snow began to build up, the feeling in Dannan's gut worsened. Time seemed to stretch on, and the gray mist that surrounded them and filled the valley to their right enveloped them like a heavy woolen blanket. As the mist began to darken a little, Dannan wondered if they would ever get off this terrible stretch of road. That's when he heard what he thought might be one of the worst noises in his life.

A low, flat note resounded through the mist like a dying animal crying out with it's final breath. A few seconds of silence followed it, and then Dannan heard the animals begin to scream. The drivers were quick to work at calming them, and all of a sudden Dannan heard yelling and the crash of steel sound out ahead of them. Their wagon jolted to a sudden stop, and he was thrown against a bag of rations that he had been sitting near.

Leaping to his feet, he ran to the front, where he saw the wagon driver cursing and trying to gain control of the horses, who had tangled the reins up as they began to panic and mill about. Jumping down from behind the driver's bench, Dannan almost slipped on the snowy rock, but managed not to fall over by dropping to one knee. Standing up slowly, he looked up, and was taken aback by what he saw.

The wagons ahead of them were in chaos as dark forms surged down from the misty wall next to them.

He couldn't make out what they looked like, but he could hear the lust for blood in the roars that accompanied them. He could hear people screaming, and he drew his sword, preparing to rush into the fray.

All of a sudden, his attention was drawn off to his left, and he turned, his sword out in one hand. A dark shape barreled towards him, seeming to loom over him as it got closer, and in the mist, he could see it's dark red eyes staring at him, hungry. Throwing himself to the side, Dannan slid along the snow covered stone, and quickly tried to pick himself up.

Looking up, he found himself staring at what he was sure was an orc. Having never met one in person, he wasn't sure, but the description of how horrifying they could be stuck in his head.

Pale gray skin covered in a fine coating of sweat and water shown through where the gleaming steel chain mail didn't cover. Dirty leather gloves gripped the handle of an axe that seemed far too large to be wielded, and a heavy steam, smelling like the worst trash heap he had ever approached, came down towards him.

Staring up at his foe's face, Dannan couldn't help but think how inhuman it looked. Tusks the length of his fingers stood up from the corner of the orc's mouth, and it's bristly, greasy black hair seemed to stand at attention, it's poorly maintained beard framing an even worse face. It's squat nose, that in some cases might seem silly, did nothing to detract from the malice in it's solid red eyes.

Dannan took all this in during the moment he laid eyes on the orc, and indeed, that was all he had. Throwing himself back again, he barely managed to dodge as the orc brought it's axe in sideways, the heavy weapon easily burying itself in the wood of the wagon next to them.

He heard the driver yell something, but barely registered it as he tried to regain his footing. Even as he rose to his feet though, the orc ripped it's axe free, letting loose another roar that only served to propel it's disgustingly bad breath towards him again. Stepping back, it took all he had to maintain his footing as the orc began to swing wildly at him, each swipe of the axe seeming like it could split him in half.

All of a sudden Dannan felt his back hit the wagon that had been just ahead of them in the line, and he felt helpless as he watched the orc's axe, raised high over it's head, slowly start to descend.

A slight whistling sound came to Dannan's ear, and instantly a crossbow bolt appeared in the orc's throat. Letting out a choked gasp, the orc dropped it's axe heavily, grasping at the bloody waterfall that was it's neck. Dannan peeked around the side of the wagon, then grinned at Nemon, who winked back at him.

Taking a deep breath, Dannan looked at the orc for a few moment, then made sure it was dead with a quick thrust of his sword to it's back. Looking up from the corpse, he listened to the sound of the screams coming from the front, and ran around the side to see Nemon and several other guardsmen engaged in combat with more orcs.

Rushing up, Dannan slid on the snow, skidding in close on one knee. The orc closest to him, who was engaging Nemon sword swing for sword swing, glanced down at him briefly just before Dannan's sword skewered it through the thigh.

Letting out a roar, it turned slightly, the noise becoming a gurgle as Nemon's sword ripped open it's throat. Dannan stood up, throwing himself forward and to the left, trying to flank the remaining two orcs who were fighting the three guardsmen.

Even as he got into position, Dannan heard Nemon yell "Get down!" Throwing himself to the ground, Dannan heard the whistle of arrows falling down around them, and he covered his head with his arms, hoping none would hit him. As the volley of arrows finished, he swung out to his right with his sword, hearing a grunt as he felt it slash through leather and flesh. Looking over, he heard another grunt as he saw the orc begin to fall, a guardsman's sword being withdrawn from it's chest.

Pulling himself to his knees, he saw that the guardsman in front of him had been hit in the shoulder, the orc he had been fighting dispatched by an unlucky arrow to the back.

The other orc, who had been fighting an uninjured guardsman and was taken down with Dannan's help, lay on the ground next to Dannan. Ignoring him, Dannan looked over to Nemon, and his heart sank.

Kneeling on the ground, he was at the same height as Nemon, who was slouched against the wagon. Dannan's eyes immediately went to the arrow that had pierced his eye, pinning his body to the wagon behind him. Dannan sucked in his breath, almost unable to take in the sight before him, and he crawled over the corpse of the orc, trying to get closer to Nemon.

The noises of battle seemed to fade around him, as Dannan's concentration seemed almost sharper than his sword. All he could feel was the the chill of the snow under his hands as he crawled up to Nemon, and the warmth of his now-dead companion's body. Taking hold of Nemon's limp hand, Dannan gave it a squeeze, trying somehow to get Nemon's attention, sure that he could do something. Certain that he had to do something. Squeezing harder, he began to mutter to himself, and then began to yell, grabbing hold of Nemon's shoulders. Shaking Nemon as hard as he could, Dannan could feel the heat of the tears streaming down his face, but at the same time, it felt like someone else.

He didn't even really notice as he felt the pulse of the dragon scale grow stronger, until it felt like it was thrumming against his chest, creating an unbearable heat.

Something crashed into him, knocking him against the wagon next to Nemon, and Dannan suddenly remembered where he was. Glancing down, he let out a small gasp of surprise at the dead guardsman who was now laying against one of his legs.

Startled out of his reverie, Dannan looked up to see an orc, wearing the most horrible grin he had ever seen, wielding a giant sword. Something inside seemed to click, and suddenly Dannan felt overwhelmed with a rush of fury.

Pushing his hand under the inch or two of snow, Dannan quickly whipped his arm up, throwing the dirty snow into the orc's face. The orc let out a holler of surprise, and Dannan pulled his feet under himself. Bunching up his leg muscles, he grabbed the sword laying in front of him, not even sure who's it was, and pushed upwards.

Dannan felt the sword connect, and felt it slide in up to the hilt, even as warm blood spurted all over his hands and lower arms. Yanking it out, he threw his shoulder into the orc in front of him, knocking it backwards onto the ground. Dannan was unsure if it was dead, but he didn't have a chance to check as he heard more roaring closer through the mist. Darting to the left, he was forced to hop over Nemon's unmoving legs, and he let out a shudder.

He only had that one moment before his concentration was fully back on the battle, as three orcs barreled out of the mist towards him. Using the side of the wagon as cover, he ducked under the swing of the first orc, and jabbed upwards, feeling his sword strike something solid.

Stepping back, he heard the neighing of the horses, and he glanced further left, to see them backing away from the orcs. Dannan wondered for an instant why the driver wasn't handling them, then cursed when he saw the driver laying across the seat, an arrow in his chest.

He returned his attention to the orcs just in time to dodge an axe swing. The axe swing, so close that he felt the wind on his face, was hard enough to chip the axe blade on the stone road. Even as Dannan heard the axe make contact with the ground, he punched out with his fist, striking the orc right in the cheek.

Stumbling to the side, the orc cursed and tried to bring it's axe up, but it wasn't in time to block Dannan's swing. Dannan felt something guttural and dark inside him rejoice as he saw the orc's head leave it's body, and he turned towards the only remaining orc he could see, who was now watching him cautiously from a few feet away.

Taking a deep breath, Dannan surged towards the orc, who desperately threw his axe up, trying to catch Dannan's blade with the handle. Snaking the blade around it, Dannan's sword buried itself deep in the orc's stomach, and for a moment, Dannan and the orc were eye to eye, the beast's face filled with surprise.

Getting a solid footing, Dannan put one foot against the orc's thigh, and shoved hard. Stumbling back, the orc dropped it's axe as it tried to hold in it's guts, to no avail. Staring up at Dannan, it was hard to tell which the orc felt more strongly; disbelief, or anger.

Looking at his fallen opponent for a few moments, Dannan's attention was captured by the sound of the horses neighing, a much more terrified noise now. Turning around, he saw that one corner of the wagon had fallen over the edge as the horses had tried to get away from the fighting. Dannan was momentarily unsure of what to do, when he heard voices crying out from inside the wagon.

Making a sudden decision, he jumped forward, trying hard to

calm the horses and gently pull them away from the edge.

It was hard work, trying to convince the horses there was no danger, with the sound of steel on steel still echoing through the mist. Finally though, he was able to convince the horse that seemed to be the leader of the six to move forward, gently, and oh so slowly, pulling the wagon back up onto the road.

As soon as the wagon seemed to be on stable ground again, Dannan hopped up onto the seat to look inside. The merchantman who he had been traveling with, as well as the man's wife and daughter, were huddled in the back corner, their eyes filled with terror.

Sheathing his sword, he moved into the wagon slowly, worried that it might slide in the snow. "Come on. We need you to get out of the wagon for now! There's no time!" He yelled at them. The three of them stared at him, terror painted across every face, and Dannan cursed his luck.

Darting forward, he grabbed the man's arm, which was wrapped around his wife, and tugged. The man resisted a little, when suddenly they all heard a slight groan and felt the wagon shift. Dannan felt the man begin to move under his grasp and continued to pull until the man was moving past him, almost dragging his wife and daughter with him.

As soon as they were on the other side of him, Dannan turned and followed them, giving them a solid push from behind. They got to the driver's bench and stumbled out over it, each of them falling into the bloody snow next to the wagon. Dannan cursed as he heard the wagon groan again, and his face went pale as he felt it shift backwards even more.

Jumping after them, he almost made it off of the wagon when he felt his foot get tangled in the reins holding the horses to the wagon. As he felt it sliding even further backwards, he looked back with horror as he tried helplessly to get the leather ropes from around his ankle. He could hear the horses neighing in terror as they struggled for their lives against the wagon, and he tore at the leather reins, trying to get free.

After a moment of sheer terror, he felt the wagon slide free, and he managed to unwind his foot from the reins. Trying to leap from the wagon even as it slid off the snowy road and into the valley, he saw the reins tying the horses to the wagon snap, and the horses surge forwards, away from the edge.

Reaching out, he tried to grasp at the broken leather as it passed under his hand, and he felt it slide out from under his fingers. His last view as he disappeared over the edge after the cart was of the horrified faces as the merchantman, his wife, and his daughter all watched Dannan fall out of view.

Chapter 44

Dannan bounced and skidded down the slope, and he felt his tunic tear in several places as rocks seemed to bite through and dig into his unprotected skin. He wasn't sure how long he fell, when suddenly he struck a ledge, fetching up hard against a large rock. The impact stunned him, even as he felt several ribs break, and he began to cough hard as the wind was knocked out of him.

As he lay there, coughing and trying desperately to catch his breath, Dannan tried to figure out how far he had fallen. Although he knew he had to, he was having a hard time concentrating, and he wondered briefly what he had stopped against.

Glancing down, he saw that he had fallen to a small ledge, and had been stopped by a huge stone partially buried in the edge. Struggling to lift his head up, he found that he could barely move from the pain, and he closed his eyes with a shudder and a gasp.

After a short while, he felt his breathing stabilize, even as he felt the cold creeping in. Looking at the rock wall in front of him, he saw it darken momentarily with a shadow, and wondered what it was that would kill him.

In the darkness that seemed to cover his mind, Dannan struggled to think. He couldn't tell if he was alive or dead, but all he could feel was an almost searing heat on his chest, as if someone were holding a burning coal there.

Suddenly, he felt a chime ringing inside his ears, and his eyes popped open. Staring straight ahead, all he could see was a shining mirror of steel, like a shield, his reflection gazing back at him.

As he lay there, trying to understand what had happened, he felt the dragon scale on his chest suddenly go cold. Attempting to raise his arm to it, he winced as he felt a stinging pain in his ribs, and remembered about falling down the cliff.

Looking around, he couldn't figure out where he was. There was a huge leather curtain hanging just a few feet over his head, and it seemed to lay all the way down to the floor. Letting his eyes adjust to the dim lighting, he finally picked his head off the floor slightly with a groan. As he moved, the leather curtain seemed to fold back towards the steel mirror, and for a moment, he didn't understand.

As he tilted his head back, he saw another steel mirror slightly above the other, one seamlessly covering the top of the other. As he turned over slightly, groaning in pain as his broken ribs complained, he saw another, and another. Something finally clicked, and he let out a gasp.

Trying to push himself away from the silver scales he had been laying against, he saw the enormous arm move, and he shuddered. He closed his eyes as he felt the scaly hand wrap around his torso, and he winced in pain at the slight pressure as he was lifted.

He kept his eyes shut tightly, afraid of what he would see, when he felt the slight pressure of the floor underneath him as he was set down. Letting his body remain limp, he felt his back hit a wall, and he opened his eyes as a burst of pain shot through his body.

With his eyes open once more, he was forced to take in a sight that he had thought he might never see again. Looking up, he saw the long snout, followed by the sloped back horns, which just seemed to lead into the long, elegant neck that extended so far above him. But above all, what captured his gaze were her eyes. He had seen them for years in his sleep now, and he would recognize them anywhere. Just like the first time, he felt like he was drowning in those pools, and he felt good.

A sudden loud snap brought him back to reality, and suddenly he got the feeling of a rabbit, being eyed by a very large, very hungry wolf. Swallowing hard, he grimaced at the pain this caused him.

Watching her movements, he waited as he saw her open her mouth slightly. "I will give you one chance to live. You will do that by answering my question honestly. Lie, and I will know it." She waited patiently for a few moments, then, assuming his silence meant he understood, continued. "Why do you have one of my scales?"

Dannan remained silent for a moment under her forceful glare, and then took as deep a breath as he could muster without pain. "I do not know if you remember me, oh mighty dragoness... but we have met before." Her glare intensified, and for a moment, Dannan was worried that had been the wrong thing to say. "We met in a forest, about eight and a half years ago. I was hiding in the trees..." As he finished saying this, the dragoness leaned close, her mouth closed, her face feet away from him.

Staring into the only eye he could really see, Dannan was captivated. His reflection stared back at him, his gaping mouth revealing his awe at her presence. Try as he might to control himself though, all he could feel was an unbearably strong sense of awe and excitement, like nothing he had ever felt in his life.

After a minute or two of staring, she sat back again, her scales moving like masterfully crafted armor. She let out a small snort, and for a moment, Dannan wasn't sure what to think, when she threw her head back, and a booming laugh echoed forth from deep in her chest. Her laughter continued for several minutes, when finally she looked back down at him, her lips twisted in what he hoped was a smile. "You expect me to believe that you are the young boy from the Forest of Ek'vir?"

He shrugged. "I don't know a forest by that name, but if that is the true name of the Forbidden Forest, then yes, that was me."

She stared at him, her eyes seeming like they could swallow him up, and then she shook her head slightly. "Surely you can come up with a better lie than that to save your life. Now, quickly, before I grow bored of this and eat you. How did you get my scale?"

Dannan scowled a little, then winced at the pain as his ribs throbbed. "Have you ever met a pixie named Elvistir? He is a friend of my father's. I met him in the forest while training to chase after you, and he gave it to me. He seemed to think it was entertaining that I would go after you."

The dragoness's eyes darkened, and for a moment, Dannan felt the slightest rush of fear in his veins as he met her gaze. "That meddling pixie gave you the scale I gave him as payment for staying there?!" She roared angrily. Swallowing hard, Dannan nodded his head the slightly, unsure of how to respond.

Moving so she was looking almost straight down at him, her eyes tightened in an almost human squint, and her lips pulled back to reveal her teeth. "So tell me, human child, why have you chased me, then? Decided to be a dragonkiller, have you?"

Dannan vehemently shook his head, letting out a small grunt of pain as he aggravated his ribs. Lifting himself with his arms, he moved so that he was kneeling before her, trying to ignore the feeling of her breath down the back of his neck.

Wincing slightly at the pain, he moved to one knee, and looked up as best as he could. "You are the most beautiful creature in all of creation. I have no desire to hurt you, and I have seen those who hunt you. My most ardent wish, the reason I trained so hard for so many years... My wish is only that you allow me to serve you in whatever way you see fit, and that I be allowed to remain by your side until my death."

The dragoness sat back slightly on her haunches, her lower jaw hanging slightly, and Dannan couldn't help but notice that every one of her teeth was the size of a shortsword. Seconds turned into a minute, and then several, and finally her lips twisted into what looked like a harsh smile. "So be it. I was hungry already. This could not have come at a better moment. Is that acceptable to you?"

Dannan swallowed a little. Closing his eyes, he nodded. Lowering his head a little, he tried unsuccessfully to resist the urge to smile.

"Why are you smiling, human? You are about to die, after all."

Keeping his head lowered, Dannan forced his expression to become impassive. "Be that as it may... I spent years dreaming of this moment... This in and of itself feels somewhat fulfilling." The dragoness's roaring laughter once again filled the cavern, and Dannan waited patiently, trying to breath lightly so as not to hurt his ribs.

"Very well then, you have proven that you have bravery, at least. You know that I am being chased by hunters, and you are willing to kill your own kind to protect me?"

Dannan looked up quickly, his eyes wide with happiness at the realization that he might survive, and bobbed his head. "I have seen them more than just in the Forbidden Forest. I saw them once when the magic of the scale brought me to you here in the mountains."

She stared at him, her scrutiny that of a cat watching a mouse. Nodding to herself, she dug her claws into the stone softly, leaving furrows in the cavern floor. "Yes... I know of the event you speak of." Closing her eyes for a moment, she nodded, a wisp of frost escaping from her mouth as she sighed. "It has been a long time since a human swore his services to a dragon out of adoration. If you are willing to abandon everything at my command, then I will accept you."

Dannan nodded eagerly, wincing a little as his ribs resisted the motion. "I do so solemnly swear. Upon my name, Dannan Bellmen, son of Andros Bellmen, and upon whatever soul I may have. I will serve you loyally, with my life, and with my death, until whatever time you see fit. My sword arm and life are both yours, my mistress." Dannan met her eyes as he spoke, his chest bursting with a mixture of emotions. Pride warred with awe, and sheer joy fought them both.

Staring down at him, her expression was unreadable "Your oath is heard, and hereby binding. I, Aofe, accept you as mine." As she pronounced each word, an almost electric tension filled the air, and a sudden crash of thunder filled the cavern as she finished. The floor felt like it rocked under Dannan's knee, and he had to brace himself with his arms to stop himself from falling. It only lasted a few seconds, but it seemed to him that it must have rocked the entire world with how it felt.

When she finally motioned for him to stand, he did so slowly, the pain from his ribs receding even as he rose. Even standing at his full height, she towered over him.

Gazing down at him for a few moments, she sat backwards on her haunches, her body's position looking more like that of a cat than a lizard. "You have much to tell me, and I have much that I will have to explain, and we have less time than I would like." She said with a solemn tone.

Giving her a bow, Dannan immediately began to speak.

Chapter 45

It took hours for Dannan to relate everything, but he left nothing of the time between their two meetings out. For her part, she stared at him silently, seeming to absorb his words like one might read a book. When he finally finished, he waited, anxiously wondering what her reaction would be.

Time stretched on, and finally she gave a small sigh. "You creatures can be so strange. You know nothing of us, and yet you always seek us out, for good or ill. Although in your case, I wonder if the gods themselves had a plan for you. It has been a long time since I have heard a tale as unusual as yours."

Flexing her claws, the stone seemed like soft dirt beneath her toes, barely resisting as she left gashes in the floor. "I have much to explain to you, it seems, before you can even be of use to me. Very well. Follow me." She rose and began walking towards a huge tunnel at one end of the cave.

For the first time, Dannan really absorbed his surroundings as he began to follow her, and what he saw was almost as amazing as the dragoness was. Hundreds of feet of glowing golden moss covered every inch of wall and ceiling, spreading a soft yellow glow throughout the cavern. He was so stunned by the sight, he almost forgot to follow her, until he heard a harsh grumble, which he assumed was the sound of her clearing her throat.

Rushing to catch up, he followed her along the tunnel that seemed to stretch for several miles. Every so often a slightly smaller tunnel would branch off from the one they were in, but finally, a bright white opening stood before them.

Stepping through a curtain of snow that occasionally spilled into the tunnel entrance, the dragoness walked out into what could only be described as a blizzard. Dannan hesitated momentarily, then moved to follow when she stopped a short ways out.

As he stepped out into the whipping wind, he was struck by the sudden blast of snow that the tunnel had protected him from. He instinctively wrapped his arms around himself for protection, when suddenly he realized he felt no chill. Staring around from the enormous ledge, he found that he could see quite clearly, despite how bad the conditions were.

Walking up until he stood directly beside her, he gasped, the mountains spreading out before him. "This is what cannot be explained easily to you mortals. The Bond that we invoked gives you a portion of my deific essence, and ties you to me forever. What I asked of you was the truth; you are bound to me permanently, and at my will, I can force you to commit any atrocity, or give any kindness."

Swiveling her head to look at him, her eyes seemed somewhat sad. "The benefits you gain as one of the Bound are manifold. You are as inured to the elements as I am, and many of the characteristics of dragons, such as a vision sharper than any eagles, and a hearing that would shame a pack of wolves, are also yours. Those things, combined with the adoration you feel, are the reasons in the past that many felt pulled to our service. You will also live for as long as I do, your apparent age only changing as I decide. Whether you appear as a child of your race or an elder is within my power to change. There are many benefits to this arrangement, for both of us."

Turning to gaze out over the mountains, she stared off beyond the horizon. "Unfortunately, you will have to live with the knowledge that as those around you that you love slowly die of old age, you will not change. Time will not have any more hold on you than it does me. And when even the nations that you know crumble into dust, you will still be there, standing loyally by my side, even if you should come to hate me."

Dannan was suddenly struck by her words, and his eyes widened as he finally understood the implications. "So I imagine my training as a Swordmaster is over, then? Since living inside a town with your size, mistress, would pose a slight problem."

He tried to say this as jokingly as he could, but felt that it may have fallen a bit short. As she looked down at him, she snorted, a sound that came across as both derisive and amused. "It seems you have even less of an understanding of how the world of magic functions than I thought. Since you seem to have understood my point about being one of the Bound, then let us return to the main cavern."

Walking back towards the cavern entrance, her tail dragged a wide swathe through the snow, leaving a ditch almost as wide as he was tall. Falling in behind her quickly, he didn't say another word as they moved back inside.

When they arrived back in the main cavern, she curled up leisurely, her arms folded under her jaws in a very human-like pose. "I must start from the beginning, I suppose. It is so very easy to confuse mortals sometimes. Especially until you learn to think like an immortal."

Sitting cross-legged a short distance away, Dannan gave a small nod, concentrating on just following what she was saying.

"This world is one of many. And once, I was one of many dragons. Our race was created before any of the mortal races recorded time, and in fact before the mortal races were. I know of this because I have the privilege, or misfortune depending on how you see it, of being what my race calls a 'Record-Keeper'. You may think of us as a living history book for the dragon race. When Chaos and Order, the two 'siblings' created the universe, they made a pact. The concept of happiness as you know it would apply to them, and they maintained a very stable structure. Order gave structure to the nothingness, and Chaos created from it."

Dannan's eyes glazed over slightly as she spoke, and she snorted in very clear derision, before letting out a small chuckle. "Do not try to imagine the scale. You won't be able to grasp it yet." He shook himself back to reality and nodded, meeting her eyes once more.

"Chaos and Order were in alignment on almost everything. Eventually, they decided they wanted to create independent beings, and from them, the gods were born. And yes, before you ask, the gods do exist. And yes, they are more powerful than any being, even myself, than you could ever imagine." Her lips twisted in what he thought might be a wry expression, though he was having a hard time reading her face.

"The gods were their children, and Chaos and Order were once again happy for a time. Though, 'a time' in your race's history would most likely be millions of years. The gods themselves were given the ability to create their own children from the essence of themselves, and they did so. They created the dragons."

She let that sink in for a moment, waiting to see his reaction, and continued when it seemed like he understood. "As I said, dragons are not bound by time. We are... minor deities, if you must understand it in a sense of power. We live forever, growing in size and power as we absorb the magic found naturally throughout the universe. If the universe itself should end, then likely, dragons will be there as well."

Sighing, she closed her eyes. "But I digress. After dragons were created, the gods began to form the worlds that you and I live on. While I could live in the void between worlds theoretically at one point in time, I no longer know if that is possible. The reason for this is because of the Other, or Others. I do not know if it is even a sentient entity, or simply a desire. Chaos and Order eventually found the borders of this universe, and when they found that border, something found them as well. Again, whether it was a being, or an impulse, I do not believe even they know. But when it found them, it broke the border between this plane of existence and the next. It began to create crude likenesses of the gods, and these corrupt copies began to try and kill each other and everything that lived in our universe."

Opening her eyes, she stopped for a few moments, as if waiting for questions from him. Seeing that he had none, she resumed once more. "Chaos and Order did not create war here. They did not create conflict, or even hostility. I do not know if you could call it utopian, but it was peaceful. And when they were forced to wield their divine power to destroy the corruption, it was like smashing your fist into a puddle. It spread further, and though they could remove the main body's influence and eventually hold the Other outside, it came at a cost. Some of the gods themselves had been infected by this corrupting influence during the war, and they became... this would be the first instance of what mortals call 'Evil'. Unable to bring themselves to destroy their children, Chaos and Order gave the gods the ability to create mortals from their own domains, in hopes of something pure coming forth once more. Unfortunately, the corruption spread to the mortal races, and even dragons. This is, quite literally, where you come from."

She stared at Dannan intently as he gaped at her, his mind desperately trying to process everything she was telling him. "But what does that have to do with those hunters?"

She let out what could only be a disappointed sigh, and shook her head at him. "Mortals have the capability for magic. Until dragons taught them how to unlock it though, you were no more of a threat to us than ants were to you." Staring up at the ceiling, she snarled slightly.

"We made a mistake, in some ways, not recognizing the potential of mortals. But those of us who believed in your capability to think for yourselves assumed, I imagine, that you would always venerate us. Once there were hundreds like yourself, Bound, servants to us for eternity. As the understanding of magic spread further from those we had made it's stewards, those who would abuse it rose up. It is one such... wizard, as humans call them, who has set his sights on me."

She met his gaze for a few moments, then looked down at the scale he was wearing. "An evil dragon once created a ritual that allowed him to paralyze dragons whom he had a physical piece of. He tied this into a magical artifact, and used it to slaughter many of his kin. This wizard seems to have rediscovered the ritual, and, likely with the help of one of the remaining evil dragons, recreated the artifact. It is this item that the hunters have with them that allows them to challenge me."

Dannan nodded, suddenly remembering how Calkon had checked something when he was running from the clearing. "It's small, isn't it?"

She looked at him, the bone ridges over her eyes rising slightly. "You have seen it, then?"

"I didn't see it directly. But the leader of the hunters who are after you, I saw him looking at something, I think to see which way you went. So I just thought he might have it." Her eyes seemed to pierce through him, and for a moment, he was worried he had said something wrong.

"Do you remember what he looked like?"

Dannan didn't hesitate in describing the man, and she gave a small nod of approval. "If you can remove that item from his presence, then I have next to nothing to fear from them. Even if all of them are wielding magically imbued weaponry, they will not stand for long against my full fury."

Gnashing her teeth, she rose, her tail lashing the air behind her. "You see, the original ritual piece only allowed the wielder to halt his target's movements. Against any other dragon than the intended, it is useless, but once it has been tied to a new target, it is a death sentence to face it. It seems this new ritual also allows the wielder to unravel spells woven by their target. My mate could have fallen no other way"

Stopping, she glanced down at him sideways. "It seems you have provided me with a chance. You don't understand how magic works, but you have the will to use that power."

Settling down in front of him again, she met his eyes. "The principles of magic function on the basis that the wielder has the will to gather and draw out the energy I told you of that exists in the world around them. Those creatures, such as dragons and fey, absorb it naturally. The stronger the connection, the less need for any real maintenance of the physical form. For example, I have no need to eat. You, being one of the Bound, will not either. Lesser fey, elves, and many of the common creatures considered 'magical' by human cultures would need sustenance in one form or another."

Raising one of her clawed feet, an orb of frost began to slowly swirl into being over her palm. "By my will, I can weave countless things into being. There are limits, but some of them are massive in scope. The blizzard outside is my doing. By altering the moisture levels and wind patterns slightly, I have created a barrier that prevents the hunters from ascending quickly. This is how I have managed to remain hiding so long in these mountains." As the last sentence left her mouth, her voice took on a guttural tone.

"Hiding. Me." Letting the orb dissipate, she turned her focus back to him. "Your abilities will not be hindered by their artifact. We will set a trap for them, and you will kill this man named Calkon. With their leader dead and their only means of disabling me gone, they will be easy pickings. And without another piece of my physical body to tie it to, recreating the artifact will be useless to him." An angry smile crept onto her face.

"I look forward to their end a great deal."

Chapter 46

Dannan resisted the urge to shiver as he stood on the mountain path. At ten feet, it was comfortably wide. Standing in the frigid air, with the mountain winds swirling around him, he was forced again to face the fact he no longer felt the chill. The snow had stopped swirling several hours ago after Aofe had altered the weather again, to give the hunters a chance to ascend.

"You remember what I told you? There is an avalanche ready to fall, as long as you are able to upset the stones near the top of the mountain. If you are able to do that, the leader should be swept down into the valley below. Even if the fall does not kill him, it will separate him from the others. That will be more than enough."

He kept going over those words in his mind as he stood there, staring down the path, and he closed his eyes. Although he thought he understood what she had said, he kept trying to picture what she had told him to do.

"Concentrate on the stones themselves. Feel them like you would with your hand. Feel the movement as force is applied beneath them. Let the sensation of their descent along the mountain instill itself in your bones. Then, open your eyes, and let your will strike at them. If you are able to do that, we will have won."

Grinning to himself wryly, he unsheathed his sword, marveling at how different things had become over the course of only a single day. Idly swinging it, he began to fall into his practice routine, letting his focus fade into his blade.

"You may be live forever on your own, but a sword can end you as surely as it would before. Anything less than a fatal wound will heal with relative ease, but a blade through your heart can still be your undoing."

Dannan chuckled as he began to move faster, his own blade whispering through the air like a soft wind. "And yet, nothing changes in many ways." He muttered to himself.

It wasn't long before he heard the sounds of movement from

further down the mountain. Moving to the edge of the path, he glanced over, seeing that she had been correct. The hunters emerged onto the beginning of the path he was on about a quarter mile down. He quickly ducked back as they began to look around, and he cursed, wishing he had more time to practice his skills.

The hunters were even faster than she had estimated, and soon they were rounding one of the large boulders she had purposefully set up near the cliff edge to hide the approach. They looked even rougher than the last time he saw them, and he grimaced.

Covered by large, bear skin cloaks, each man had a bow strung across his back and a sword at his waist. Their unkempt hair and beards made them look like they had been living in the mountains for years, and Dannan felt a little afraid of their tenacity. Taking a deep breath, he sheathed his sword, and watched as the last of them were funneled around the corner. Finally, he saw the man he was looking for.

Calkon was as clean shaven as he had been the last time Dannan saw him, and his features seemed like they had only grown harder with age. One glance at his gray eyes told Dannan that this was definitely the man to be feared here.

"Why is a human boy on this mountain?" Calkon called in a tone that sounded like hammer striking an anvil.

Dannan stood there, motionless, and waited as they approached slowly, the other hunters parting for their leader. Stopping about thirty feet away, Calkon glared at him, a look that would have made lesser men quake. "I'm asking you a question. Are you here to delay us, perhaps? You don't seem lost."

"I am not here to delay you. Nor am I lost." Dannan replied, his voice as neutral as he could keep it.

Calkon looked him up and down, as if he could assess Dannan's potential like a horse at auction. "No, you have too much steel in your spine to just try and delay us. How is it that an assassin has come to be waiting here? Has the great Illinor decided to betray us, then? He found the last dragon he needed elsewhere, and we were a loose end?"

When Dannan didn't react at the name, Calkon grimaced. "Not that bastard wizard, then. Another wizard, perhaps? Doesn't like the power my employer is gathering? You certainly didn't stumble here by accident." As Dannan continued to stare at him stolidly, Calkon shrugged.

"Doesn't matter, if you're in my way, you'll have to die. You can still step aside. My prey is up there, and nothing will stop me from getting my reward." Letting the statement hang for a few seconds, Calkon watched to see if there was any hesitation. As Dannan continued to stare at him, he sighed, before motioning for the hunters to draw their bows.

The moment they began to unsling their bows, Dannan gripped his sword hilt. Closing his eyes, he focused on his blade, trying to remember everything the dragoness had told him earlier.

As the first arrowed whizzed narrowly past his head, he whipped his sword free, concentrating on extending his will through the blade, letting it spill forth like he could cut the wind itself. A sharp crack echoed through the air, and the hunters jumped slightly in alarm. Exchanging quizzical glances, they finally turned back towards him. It was only a moment longer before the rumbling started, and everyone looked upwards at the slope.

A sharp cleft had formed near the cliff above, and small rocks began raining down as even larger ones broke loose, some of them cut as cleanly as any piece of cloth. The hunters with the least experience began to scream, and Dannan turned back to see Calkon and another hunter leap forward just as the first large rocks struck the men on the path.

Several of the hunters were flung over the cliff side like rag dolls, even as the others tried to retreat out of the way. More boulders began to fall, sending screaming bodies over the edge one after the other. Eventually, all that was left on the path was a huge pile of rubble, Dannan, Calkon, and the other hunter.

Staring at the rubble where his team had just stood, Calkon slowly turned towards Dannan, a look of smoldering anger on his face. "You cur!" He screamed, his rage bubbling to the surface. "Do you know how long it took to collect fodder who wouldn't die before being useful to me?! How dare you!"

Rushing forward to one side, Calkon whipped his own sword up, a slightly curved blade with cruel little hooks that almost looked more like a saw blade than a sword blade.

Parrying quickly, Dannan was suddenly forced back by the strength of the man's blow. He slowly began to retreat, even as he saw the other hunter unsheathe his blade slowly and move towards Dannan's other side.

Backing up further, Dannan continued parrying desperately, trying to find a spot where he could force them to fight him side by side. The wide area he had chosen for maneuverability was working against him now, and he continued to back up, until he was almost at the corner that led back onto the ledge.

Cursing, he launched a desperate assault on Calkon, attacking as fast as he could before the other hunter could get within reach.

It was to no avail, as Calkon managed to block each blow, the hooks preventing Dannan's blade from sliding past with each deflection. Noticing the other hunter out of the corner of his eye, Dannan made a sudden decision, and hoped the dragoness had been telling the truth.

As the hunter stepped in with a sudden stab at Dannan's stomach, Dannan lurched back slightly, not trying to fully evade the blow. He felt the cold steel slide past, and hissed as he felt warmth blossom along his midsection. Grabbing the man's arm with his left hand, Dannan pulled the other hunter between himself and Calkon, just in time to prevent a downward slice from Calkon.

Grunting in anger, Calkon brought his elbow down on the hunters back hard, knocking him to the ground, and resumed slashing at Dannan, a manic glint now filling his eyes.

With the hunter on the ground between them, Dannan took a moment to step back, hugging closer to the wall as he backed up onto the ledge. Calkon followed close behind, pausing only momentarily to kick the other hunter in the side as he passed by.

Grunting, the man stumbled to his feet, muttering curses at Calkon even as he followed after him.

Dannan backed towards the tunnel, hoping that the dim light would help him with his improved vision. As he neared the entrance, Calkon and the hunter began to intertwine their attacks better, forcing Dannan to retreat with even more haste. As he stepped into the tunnel, he heard a roar of unimaginable volume boil forth, catching his opponents off guard.

Calkon recovered first, but the hunter was much slower. Diving in with his shoulder, Dannan hit the man in his midsection even as he struck the man's blade aside. Grunting, he fought back as Dannan tried to push him towards the edge. Dannan could feel the skin around his belly start to tighten, and he could practically feel the wound closing as he fought the hunter.

Suddenly, Dannan felt a boot on the small of his back, and a huge push from behind sent both he and the hunter surging towards the edge of the ledge. Falling to his knees, he dropped his sword even as the hunter slipped on one of the patches of snow Dannan had failed to clear in preparation of the fight.

A shrill scream was the last thing Dannan heard from the man as he went spiraling off the edge, but Dannan barely had time to register it. He threw himself to the side, avoiding Calkon's sword by a hairs breadth. Dannan scrambled towards his sword, but was unable to reach it before Calkon kicked it further away.

His opponent's cruel chuckling followed him as he tried to get towards it, only to be blocked by Calkon's legs. Standing up slowly, Dannan backed away, trying to look for any way around as Calkon slowly weaved his sword back and forth between them. "You are one tenacious bastard, I'll give you that. But now, you've got nothing. A pity you weren't more well prepared. Even a knife could save you now."

Grinning, Calkon slowly forced him back towards the cliff edge, his gloating chuckles echoing across the ledge. "I have to say, after how much you set me back, I'm going to enjoy seeing you fall to your death. I've found the challenges of hunting a dragon always did make the kill that much sweeter, even if they couldn't fight back."

Dannan's glare of hatred set the man back on his heels for a moment, then Calkon's grin returned, wider than ever. "So that's what it is. You have some connection to this dragon. Ahh, but that's so sweet. You've taken my team, and I'll take your life and your reason for living. It's times like these that I'm happy to be alive."

Grabbing the chain around his neck, Dannan slowly pulled out the dragoness's scale, gripping it between his fingers as he pulled it over his head. Watching him warily, Calkon moved to step forward, swinging a light blow towards Dannan's head.

A sharp ringing sound split the air as Dannan blocked the blow with the scale, the sword sliding off and almost taking one of his fingers with it. Cursing in surprise, Calkon drew back for a harder swing, and Dannan punched forward with his fist, the scale catching his foe square in the chest.

Grunting as he stepped back, Calkon swung at Dannan again,

unable to get much power behind the blow as he tried to regain his balance. Catching the blade with his upper arm, Dannan let out a hiss of pain as it bit in, and held in the urge to scream.

Taking hold of the blade even as it was imbedded in his arm, Dannan stepped forward, moving them both away from the edge. Grinning at him, Calkon reached for a dagger at his waist. "I told you a knife would've saved you." He said with a cruel smirk.

Pulling his head back, Dannan slammed his forehead into the taller man's chest, drawing another grunt from Calkon as he was knocked backwards by the blow. Using the man's fall to his advantage, Dannan wrenched the sword free from Calkon's hand with a twist of his shoulder.

Stepping to the side, Dannan pulled the blade free, shuddering and letting a small cry out as it made a sickening squelch. Gripping the blade with his free hand, he slid the dragon scale back into his pocket, and looked down at the furious Calkon.

His advantage only lasted for a moment though, as Calkon whipped the knife free, sending it flying towards Dannan's face. Batting it away with his injured arm, Dannan fell forward, driving the sword straight through Calkon's chest with his full weight behind it.

Looking down at the sword, Calkon's fury turned to dismay, then his eyes went blank, the glint leaving them as the life left his body.

Chapter 47

Dannan fell backwards off his enemy's corpse, gasping for breath as his body reacted to the pain of his wounds. Turning towards the body, Dannan began to search it slowly, hindered by the damage to his left arm. Finally, he found what he was looking for. A small glass orb that seemed to contain a miniature version of his scale was hidden in a pouch around Calkon's waist.

Taking it in his hands, he struck it against the ground repeatedly, letting out a desperate grunt with each blow.

After striking it for many minutes he let it roll free from his grasp, grimacing as he felt more energy moving through his body to heal his wounds. A sudden surge of power towards his arm made him scream in agony, and he gripped the wound, feeling the flesh knit underneath his fingers.

He heard the sound of claws on stone, and he looked up to see the dragoness several hundred feet away, at the edge of where he assumed the artifacts effect was.

"You will need to weave a spell to destroy it. Although it appears as glass, the magic contained inside prevents it from such a quick end."

Grinning and grimacing at the same time, Dannan crawled towards it on his knees, kneeling upright with the orb held high. "What do I do?"

"Concentrate on the feeling of the glass crumbling to dust in your fingers. Once you have destroyed the enclosure, the scale inside will be destroyed as well. Then just channel what energy you have left. That should hopefully be enough."

Dannan nodded haltingly, focusing his vision on the orb. The scale in the center seemed to draw his eyes towards it, and he felt the power slowly drawn through his fingertips as he concentrated.

Slowly at first, then with gathering speed, he felt his energy leave him. The orb began to glow, a tiny amount at first, but growing brighter with each passing second. Putting aside all thoughts of his pain, of his exhaustion, of his confusion, Dannan concentrated. He thought of his feelings for the dragoness, the feelings toward the wizard who would dare to endanger her, and brought them down on the orb.

With a sudden explosion of light and a wave of air, he felt the orb shatter into dust, even that fading as he was thrown backwards to the ground.

Walking over towards him, Aofe stood over him, wearing what was unmistakably a smile. "Congratulations. You saved me, my hero." She said with a slight chuckle.

Dannan closed his eyes, finally feeling the exhaustion from using all that power steal over him.

"Now, rest. It will be some time before we can go after the wizard. You have earned that."

And in his sleep, he smiled.

ABOUT THE AUTHOR

R.F. Keenan lives in Massachusetts. This is the first book in the Chronicles of Danaan trilogy.

Made in the USA
Middletown, DE
10 September 2017